THE LORDS OF FOLLY

THE LORDS OF FOLLY

GENE LOGSDON

Wicker Park Press
Academy Chicago Publishers

A Wicker Park Press Book

Published in 2007 by
Academy Chicago Publishers
363 West Erie Street
Chicago, Illinois 60610
www.academychicago.com

Cover and interior design by Sarah Olson

Printed in the U.S.A.

Library of Congress Cataloging-in-Publication Data on file with the publisher.

To the SBDC Boys, with affection

CHAPTER 1

The mail train rumbled slowly out of St. Paul, announcing its road crossings up the Minnesota River Valley as if each were some terribly momentous event. The steam whistle was a soothing nightly occasion for, well, who knows how many people within hearing range, people whose lives were quiet and solitary enough to appreciate the plaintive wail or who had an ear for lonely sounds contrasting with the social clatter that usually circumscribed their lives: for Marge Puckett surely, trying to study in her apartment near the University of Minnesota campus, but counting the days until classes were over and she could return to her parent's farm outside Grass Prairie thirty miles away; for professional escort Kadie Crockin, floating naked in her canoe on Fish Lake, counting stars, wondering what the hell life was supposed to be all about; for Ed Hasse, on his farm near Flying Cloud, milking his cows, counting the seconds between train whistles, a thousand one, a thousand two, a thousand three, knowing the distances between the crossings, and allotting for time between whistles, determining how fast the train was rolling, not that he gave a damn; for Axel Barnt, counting his jars of moonshine in the vault ruins of the long abandoned brewery along the Minnesota River upstream from Shakopee; for Nash Patroux, in his Western Range restaurant near Savage, checking the

Colt revolvers his waiters wore as part of the decor, making sure none of them were loaded—a waiter had once shot a man; for Red Blake, sitting in the now quiet dugout of the town baseball diamond at Chaska, counting up his strikeouts after a game, glorying in the fact that he had beaten every team in Carver and Scott counties; for Fr. Abelard Broge, of the Oblates of St. Joseph, counting the minutes as he waited at the Shakopee station to pick up the new class of oblates coming to Ascension Seminary. None of these people could know that on this particular night, June 15, 1953, the high, thin scream of the train did announce something momentous for them, a human cargo that would touch their lives in strange and traumatic ways.

No one listened to the train whistle more closely than did Jesse James waiting near the Savage station, a dusty old black Stetson askew on his head, a pistol stuck in a silver-buckled belt under a worn, white-embroidered, black cowboy shirt, his jeans so tight that he could barely walk without discomfort. His eyes blinked queerly as he listened for the approaching train, his head swaying back and forth as if he were slightly addled, which indeed he was.

Jesse James had dreamed of this night for many years, perhaps as long ago as the day, growing up, when he realized that he had been cursed with the name of a famous outlaw. Carrying a moniker like Jesse James could affect one's mind. Jesse James the First had tried to rob the bank at Northfield, not so far away, and Jesse James the Second's aged father, Donald James Brown, claimed that he could remember the event from childhood. That is why he named his son Jesse, he said. But Minnesotans in general did not take robbing their banks kindly, and although Jesse James the First might have been a culture hero in Missouri, Minnesotans were extremely proud that Northfield had been his downfall. To counteract the hundreds of thoughtless jibes that Jesse the Second had to endure, he had convinced himself that he was a descendant of the outlaw. He had in fact assembled in a cardboard box a jumble of random newspaper clippings to prove it. The clippings proved nothing except the probability that he was "not quite right in the head," as local judgment had long ago concluded.

But he would have the last say. He had planned his revenge for days while drinking cream sodas at the Western Range, where he was allowed to hitch his old horse, Blaze, out front, as other equestrians were encouraged to do to add western ambience to the restaurant. His horse was an aged trotter given to him by the town jokesters in Savage as another way to tease him about his name. But as they well realized, the horse served a useful purpose. Jesse could not drive and in fact possessed an almost irrational fear of automobiles and other motored vehicles. The horse enabled him to get where he wanted to go which was mostly to the Western Range and back to his father's farm. He was allowed to wear his pistol openly, as the waiters in the restaurant did, because the firing pin was missing and the trigger mechanism broken. Patroux seldom allowed him to drink beer because alcohol contrarily seemed to make him dully normal and not nearly as amusing as when he was cold sober.

Jesse James the Second had endured the taunts and made his plans. He had waited three nights now for the train to actually have passengers on it. He was going to resurrect the honor and glory of all the downtrodden Jesse Jameses of the world. He was going to rob the train.

Riding on the train, priesthood seminarian Blaise Rell was trying without success to see into the darkness outside the windows. He was sure that great adventures lay in wait for him in this new stomping ground of Minnesota. To his overworked imagination, Minnesota was "the west," or at least as far west as he thought he would ever get from his birthplace in Ohio. To him "west" was a magical word, part of the fantasy world that he constantly lived in, where roamed cowboys and outlaws and gunfighters. Perhaps here in the "west" he would find the little valley of his dreams, where he would raise cattle and where no one else could enter without his say-so because he owned the whole damn thing. As another indication of what his priestly superiors called "Peter Pan syndrome," he preferred to spell his first name, Blaise, given to him when he took vows, as "Blaze." Sounded more dashing that way, like Flash as in Flash Gordon. Of course there was some risk involved. His classmate, Gabriel Roodman, seated next to him, liked to point out that horses were often called Blaze and that it was a good name for a horse's ass too. Oh well. Better than a klutzy name like Gabriel.

Aside from his name, Blaze, at 21, was not sure just who the hell he was. He fantasized about becoming a cowboy, or sometimes a farmer as his father had been before he went broke at it. Other times he wondered if he might not find a way to play shortstop in the Major Leagues. So why, he constantly asked himself, was he becoming a priest? He wished he could answer that question sanely. He had once possessed an inordinate desire to help people. That was it, as far as he could figure out, but he was no longer sure if he could help anyone or if anyone deserved help. Or if help could actually be given. Other than that, the whole idea of being a priest was crazy in his case. Could a priest take Lou Boudreau's place on the Cleveland Indians? Could a priest herd cattle? On the other hand, a priest had a better chance than a layperson of taking over the Catholic Church, striking the superstitious beliefs from its theology and moving its headquarters out of Rome, another of his favorite fantasies. He smiled inwardly, stared out the train window and shook his head. Black impenetrable night. Black impenetrable future. Black like the mournful suit he wore, which, with the little blue insignia of a cross on the lapel above the initials OSJ, announced to all the world that he was a member of the Oblates of St. Joseph, a Catholic religious community of seminarians, priests and lay brothers bound by vows of poverty, chastity and obedience forever and ever amen.

Beyond the insignia, what was an Oblate of St. Joseph after all, he mused as he listened to the clackety-clack of iron wheels on iron track. He was not even sure what "oblate" meant literally, even after four years of seminary high school, a fifth gruelling year in St. Joseph's Novitiate in Indiana, the Josephians' equivalent of the Marines' Paris Island, and two years of seminary college in Detroit. Religious training and education had only succeeded in turning him into a heretic, a fact that he had managed not to reveal to anyone so far and could just barely admit to himself.

"Just what the hell is an oblate?" he asked out of the corner of his mouth, evidently a question aimed at the equally black-suited Roodman beside him.

His companion did not bother to turn his head either. Gabe Roodman had been sitting next to Blaze Rell now for seven years, and like blood brothers they were friends except when they were fighting. They were in fact always next to each other in the seminary because in any alphabetical listing of the names of their class, Rell and Roodman came back to back. Seminary tradition believed that chaos could be avoided by keeping everything in alphabetical order.

"An oblate is a species of reindeer found only in the Congo where it is the staple food of pigmies," Roodman replied solemnly. "Colloquially it also refers to the animal's dung. When in the Congo, if someone tells you that you are full of oblate, don't take it as a compliment."

Blaze laughed, always quick to laugh, always laughing at something. The two were a study in contrasts, Blaze with hair the color of ripe wheat, eyes pale blue, skin fair but tanned to a near bronze color, character outgoing, unable to keep from speaking his mind even when he knew it would only get him in trouble; Gabe, swarthy, brooding, reserved, eyes as bituminous black as his hair, as black as the suit he wore. However different they were, Blaze did not mind being chained to Gabe by the alphabet because he could never predict what was going to come out of his colleague's mouth. It would almost always be something funny, and if it were something serious, it would be even funnier. It was for such sentimental reasons that Blaze stayed in the seminary, he told himself. Where else could life be so drolly amusing while also secure from the financial fangs of the real world?

A black suit in the seat behind them leaned forward and spoke. "Take a gander straight ahead up the aisle." Neither Blaze nor Gabe turned to look at the speaker because they knew it was Fen, their only classmate who would ever say "take a gander." "If that's not a coal oil lamp, I'm full of oblate."

Blaze laughed louder then, for in truth, the swinging light was a lantern and to an incurable romantic, a delightful omen of the occasion. They really were travelling west, back in time, as he fantasized, in a coal-burning, lamplit rocket ship. He said as much. The fact that Fen was cradling a western-style guitar which he was idly strumming accentuated the feeling of time warp.

Gabe rolled his eyes. He endured having Blaze tied to him by the alphabet, even if his comrade did talk too much, because of Blaze's uncommon ability to see something enjoyable or exciting in their lives no matter how depressing or dull the situation. Most of the oblates were complaining about the coal dust and sulfurous fumes blowing through the coach windows, which had to be kept open because the temperature on the hot June night was only slowly coming down from daytime nineties. Not Blaze. He would have found life in a dungeon somehow enchanting and opportune, Gabe believed. Take the way the idiot had provided tobacco in the Novitiate year when there seemed no possible way to get tobacco. One of the quirks of Josephian religious life allowed seminarians to smoke pipes but not cigarettes. However, their pipe tobacco was severely rationed. Without money they could not buy tobacco, even on the sly, and so they were constantly suffering from nicotine withdrawal. Far from persuading them to quit smoking, which had been the intent of their superiors, all of whom smoked, the shortage only made Blaze more contrary and creative. He had looked out upon the real world and saw in it an unlimited supply of free tobacco in the form of cigarette butts strewn along sidewalks and streets, in public parks, even out of the ashtrays in the priests' rooms, which the seminarians had to clean. The butts he carefully straightened, unrolled, removed the filters, if any, and the ashy ends, and mixed the nicotine-soaked remains with their usual ration of Prince Albert. The tobacco supply in the Prince Albert can rarely diminished because Blaze kept adding to it. Gabe referred to it as the miracle of the loaves and fishes.

"This isn't 1953 after all. It's 1853!" Blaze now blurted, beaming with pleasure at the thought. Fen smiled too, as much at his friend's delight, which he had expected, as at the unexpected lamp. Fen was short for "Fenderbender" because of his skill at crashing seminary cars without injuring anyone. Some of his classmates thought this could be explained because Fen's real name was Christopher, as in St. Christopher, the patron saint and protector of travellers.

Now the whole crew of black suits began to point and laugh at the lamp: Banana Banahan, Clutch Pedali, Very Reverend Lukey, Danny Danauau, rhymes with bowwow, Little Eddie Sacher, Martin Luvore, and Melonhead Mullaney, who with Blaze, Gabe and Fen, made up the OSJ high school class of '49, the most troublesome class ever to have graduated from St. Joseph's Prep Seminary, according to their schoolmaster, Fr. Hildebrand. Not that Hildebrand minded. Never before in the history of the Oblates of St. Joseph had there been gathered together in one class so much sheer intelligence, at least by I.Q. standards. The Provincial, who was the equivalent of a Chief Executive Officer over the Josephians, and his Advisory Council, believed in I.Q. testing as much as they believed that the Virgin Mary had been physically carried by angels beyond the clouds and into heaven. They also believed that in brains lay the future of their Community, apparently seeing no possible oxymoron between intelligence and religious beliefs like Mary's "Assumption" up, up and away in the general direction of the pearly gates. Brilliant priests would bring honor and money to the Josephians by occupying high, well-paid posts in universities and writing bestselling books. The fact that the Class of '49 had an average I.Q. of 132 and highs of 145 and 150 in the despicably insolent Rell and Roodman, was viewed as a special blessing from God, a treasure trove to be coddled the way a farmer coddled his highest producing milk cows, even if they kicked too much during milking. One had to put up with a certain amount of travail when dealing with geniuses.

Gabe choked on the smoke in the train car, but it was Fen's incessant and mindless guitar strumming that was getting on his nerves. Even Blaze, who occasionally joined Fen in singing, began to hope that they would soon reach Shakopee and their destination, Ascension Seminary. There were only four coaches making up the train, two for mail and sundry other deliveries, one empty and one occupied by the oblates. Only a few years earlier, the train had stopped at little creameries all along its way up the valley to pick up milk or to bring back the empty milk cans from the previous pickup. It was a train soon to become obsolete—fit transportation, Blaze thought, for oblates who were also a throwback to the past.

The train slowed even more. From the rear of the car, the conductor announced the next stop, Savage, halfheartedly, knowing that his only passengers, in their strange black suits, were getting off at Shakopee. But if he did not call out the stations, it might occur to the railroad officials that conductors weren't really needed on trains like this anymore. He then went back to the mail car to toss off the bags of mail. The sleepy station master, standing by on the dock, had already indicated there would be no boarders, so there was hardly reason for the train to come to a full stop. As the mail bags plopped down on the dock and the train lumbered on, neither the conductor nor the station master noticed the figure that slipped out of the shadows behind the station and jumped onto the passenger car ahead.

The train picked up speed again, or rather increased from slower to merely slow. Blaze's eyes turned from the window to behold, with a start, a most unusual sight. In the Brigadoonish light of the coal oil lamp ahead a figure so strange was advancing toward him that for a moment he thought he was delirious from breathing the sulfurous smoke. He punched Gabe in the ribs with his elbow, and Gabe, in the act of punching him back, noticed the transfixed stare on his comrade's face and followed it with his eyes up the aisle. It was rare for Gabe to show total surprise about anything but now he did. Apparently the ghost of a long-ago train robber was swaying and weaving toward them, brandishing a pistol. Ratty gray hair dangled from under a dusty old black Stetson. A red bandana covered the lower portion of the face, above which a set of eyes showing mostly white, peered wildly from one side of the coach to the other.

The cocksure attitude of the seminarians dissolved and their faces paled. They remained totally motionless, Fen with his strumming hand poised above the guitar, as if some sudden cataclysmic weather change had brought on an instantaneous ice age and frozen them solid. Jesse James spoke his well-rehearsed lines.

"Pilgrims, git your hands up where I can see 'em. This here's a holdup. Put your money and jewelery into this here hat of mine or I'll blow your heads off."

Not a seminarian moved. Not a seminarian was capable of movement. Jesse James saw their fear and felt already vindicated. For once he was somebody. He stole a glance at his watch but it had apparently stopped again. Oh well, no need for it. Soon the train would slow again as it peaked the grade near Murphy's Landing where he had hidden his horse in the woods. He had to have the robbery completed before the train started downhill again, so he could leap safely to the ground. Then he would unpeel the once-fancy cowboy shirt which he had fetched out of the trash at the town dump, in favor of the blue chambray shirt underneath, his usual attire. He would stuff the shirt, bandana, and the old black Stetson in his saddlebag, don his usual white cowboy hat hanging from the saddle horn, ride off to the Western Range hardly a mile away, swagger into the bar, quaff a cream soda or two, establish an alibi. No one would raise an eyebrow because this was what he did every night. That asshole Nash Petroux behind the bar liked to make fun of him because he dressed western and wore a pistol like the waiters did, but ole' Jesse knew what he was doing.

"You deef, boy? Put your money and jewels in this here hat 'fore I cave your pukey little face in." He shoved the pistol into The Reverend Lukey's forehead and The Reverend Lukey promptly fainted.

Jesse James was not prepared for this, and for a second slipped from his role.

"You okay, bub?" Then he remembered his mission, stepped back and brandished the gun in the air again. "Don't none of you undertakers try to pull anything on me or I'll blast you all to hell."

Bypassing Lukey who had slumped over in his seat, the train robber thrust his hat in front of each seminarian in turn, very much like an usher in church taking up the Sunday collection, Gabe would later relate. Each in turn dropped his wallet into the hat.

Fen, possibly in the same spirit with which he wrecked seminary cars without injuring anyone, decided to object. "Sir, we don't have any money or jewels."

Jesse leered at the speaker. He had never before been addressed as "sir" and that was nice, but he was not buying this no money crap from a bunch of undertakers. Undertakers were rich.

"You triflin' me, boy? You can't breathe without money in this here goddam world, much less ride around in trains. Fork it over and be damn quick about it or I'll bust that geetar over your head." Fen thought he could discern a lack of resolve creeping into the robber's voice. Blaze thought he could discern the end of Fen's life approaching.

"Honest, we don't," Fen pleaded. "Look in those billfolds. We're religious seminarians."

"What the hell's that?" Jesse growled, trying to keep his eyes on the speaker while peering into one of the billfolds. By God there wasn't but two dollars in the first one.

Lukey came out of his swoon and began to pray aloud: "Our Father who art in heaven, hallowed . . ." Jesse looked at him with consummate pity. And people thought *he* was crazy.

Little Eddie took up the prayer; ". . . hallowed be thy name. Thy kingdom come, thy . . ."

"This is your last chance," Jesse James thundered, waving the pistol like a baton. "Your money or your life."

Now Little Eddie fainted. The Very Reverend Lukey prayed on. "Hail Mary, full of grace . . ."

The train was starting up the grade at Murphy's Landing. Jesse James knew he had to make his getaway soon.

"You won't find ten dollars altogether in those wallets," Fen continued, growing bolder, but still holding on to the guitar as if he were about to begin a concert. "We don't carry much money."

Blaze knew that Fen was going to get them all killed. There were two twenty-dollar bills rolled up to the size of cigarettes and flattened to hide in the deepest folds of his billfold. Vow of poverty or no vow of poverty, he had kept a little security beyond what the lilies of the field required, just in case. If this maniac found the money, he'd think that Fen was lying and kill them all.

Jesse James was having a difficult time keeping the pistol levelled with one hand while unfolding the wallets with the other and wedging his collection hat between his body and his elbow. Son of a bitch, there wasn't but a dollar in the next one he examined. None at all in the one after that. Son of a bitch. Time was running out.

"Okay, stand up, you dudes," he ordered. "Turn your pockets inside out."

Everyone did as ordered except Little Eddie who was still swooning away. For a swift second, Gabe was tempted to fake a faint, but he feared that one more swoon would convince the thief to shoot.

Jesse James peered closely from one pocket to another and collected another few dollars in change and a couple of necklace-like strings of beads with little crosses attached to them. Didn't look like jewelry but who knew about undertakers. There was no more time for a more thorough frisk. The train had reached the top of the grade. It was time to deliver his speech.

"I am Frank James, back to avenge my brother and all the poor Jesse Jameses of the world. Northfield ain't heard the end of us. I have risen on the third day, for you have seen me, and tell all them Bob Fords of the world to watch their backs because I am back." He thought his play on the word "back" was particularly clever. He stepped to the front of the coach, paused, and suddenly changing his mind before he leaped into the darkness, threw the wallets, petty cash, rosaries and watches back into the aisle.

"And you're the sorriest bunch of broke bastards I ever did see."

CHAPTER 2

After due consideration, Prior Robert, at Ascension Seminary, decided to do nothing about the harrowing experience that had befallen the newly-arrived class of oblates. Doing nothing, he had found, was often a wise policy. Most problems resolved themselves, given a little time. No one had witnessed the attempted robbery except the seminarians. Nothing had been stolen. Morever, investigation of the robbery attempt, if pursued, could only bring untoward publicity to the Josephian Order. In fact, Prior Robert, studying the records of Oblate Blaise and Oblate Gabriel, would not have been at all surprised if the two young men had made up the whole affair and talked the others into going along with it.

While their classmates lost interest in the event within a month, Blaze, Fen and Gabe continued to view the experience as a signal event in their lives. Their version of the "robbery" grew more harrowing with every telling and eventually the older seminarians at Ascension, not unfamiliar with the pranks of Oblates Blaise and Gabriel from previous years in college and high school with them, became more and more suspicious. Most of them decided, like their Prior, that the story was made up.

"Can you believe that?" Blaze protested to Fen. "They think we're lying."

"Maybe it was all hallucination," Very Reverend Lukey suggested, wishing fervently that it were true in order to cast doubt also upon whether he had actually fainted. Blaze stared pityingly at him. No wonder religious myth took such a hold on people. They actually wanted to ignore what really happened in life. Easier that way. He resolved on the spot to start keeping a journal. He would call it "The Story of My Weird Life," by Other Blaze. The world had to know what was going on here.

"We've got to find a way to get back to Savage and find that guy," Blaze said. "I gotta know what that was all about. I think he was crying out for help."

"I think you're afraid we saw a vision," The Very Reverend Lukey said primly. "You could never handle that."

Since the seminarians were rarely allowed to leave the seminary grounds and even more rarely were assigned duties that required car travel, Blaze's chances for documentation of the train robbery were slim. But not impossible. Life at Ascension was proving to be something quite different from the life they had experienced in other seminaries. This one had previously been a health sanitarium called Mudpura. It had fallen on hard times during the Depression and closed, after which the buildings began to suffer from neglect. So in addition to their studies, the oblates were expected, at least until the proper lay brothers could be enlisted, to help restore the deteriorating buildings, operate the dairy farm, and do the cooking for the whole community. Prior Robert thought doing work like this was good for students, despite the fact that it upset the younger priest professors who perceived the Josephian future to be in higher education. Seminarians should be studying scriptural theology and Thomistic philosophy even in their spare time, they grumpily complained, not learning how to make hay and lay bricks. But because the Josephians were poor in earthly goods, befitting their vow of poverty, fixing up the property, which had been given to them, made a certain amount of economic sense if not examined too closely. For the time, some of the traditional seminary schedule was suspended temporarily. Instead of rising at the crack of dawn to chant the breviary psalms and meditate on the Scriptures and attend Mass, followed by a long day of study and more breviary chanting in the evening, those oblates who showed aptitude or willingness for manual labor rose at the crack of dawn to milk cows or cook, or work at construction jobs.

For most of the Class of '49, anything was preferable to chanting the breviary. For Blaze, exemption from chapel exercises also might mean opportunity to find Frank James. From upper classmen, Blaze had learned that the farm crew was most often excused from chapel exercises. Pointing out that he was the only oblate who knew how to milk cows by hand except Walt, the lay brother in charge of the farm, he promptly got himself assigned to barn duty. That was Step One.

In principle, Brother Walt was not in favor of seminarians working on the farm. His experience with the three who had been sent to help him previously led him to remark often that "if someone gave all three of them each a wit, they would not altogether amount to a half wit." But this Blaze fellow actually could milk cows by hand, so he might be tolerable. Blaze said that Gabe had farm experience too, which was a lie, but Blaze knew his alphabetical partner was a fast learner. Gabe soon joined him in the barn. That was Step Two.

Surely there was a feed mill or farm supply store in Savage or Shakopee that could be used as an excuse to hunt for leads to the erstwhile train robber. That was Step Three.

Little Eddie and Very Reverend Lukey who, as Very Reverend Lukey wanted everyone to know, were not frustrated cowboys like their classmates, volunteered for the cooking crew because after farm work, cooking was the job most frequently exempted from chapel. Very Reverend Lukey denied that this was his intent. He said he actually liked chanting the breviary, learning the rubrics of Mass and bowing and genuflecting and lighting candles and burning incense. That's how he got his nickname, remember. But if he spent all the customary time in chapel that seminarians were supposed to spend, he might miss out on the adventures he was sure that that damned Blaze would be getting into.

All of the new class of oblates at Ascension were thus able to lead lives hitherto unknown in Catholic seminaries. Melonhead Mullaney, who secretly wanted to be a doctor, had himself put in charge of the infirmary and worked on the paint crew when not employed in dispensing aspirins and enemas. Danny Danauau and Banana Banahan became bricklayers, figuring that lifting bricks all day would strengthen their wrists and forearms, enabling them to swing a baseball bat faster. Mart Luvore and Fen, the latter irritated because Blaze could not get him on the farm crew, took up carpentry. Clutch Pedali landed the best assignment of all. He befriended the engineer hired to take care of the steam furnaces that heated the water and kept the buildings warm through sub-zero Minnesota winters. Being a clever lad, he soon mastered the workings of the furnaces and talked Prior Robert into letting him take over the job and dispensing with the engineer, thus saving that salary. Clutch, feigning infinite concern for the boilers, hardly ever had to go to chapel and could leave any time he felt that the temperature of the buildings demanded it, which was, well, most of the time.

"Who would ever have thought that the ability to read a gauge on a boiler might mean freedom someday," Fen remarked drolly.

Strangely enough, while others grumbled, "the most troublesome class in the history of the seminary" actually liked the more or less medieval Benedictine lifestyle in which they found themselves, although they put quite a bit more emphasis on labora than on ora, and managed to work in a considerable amount of sporta too.

Blaze decided that next to the phantom train robber, Brother Walt was the most fascinating person he had met yet in Minnesota. In his journal, Other Blaze wrote: "Brother Walt was a bartender before he came into the Josephians, can you believe that? He knows a lot about the world. He has all sorts of quaint expressions. When he's feeling good, he stands up on the tractor seat, flaps his arms, crows like a rooster, and hollers 'I'm the best in the west.' He says that oysters, especially raw, are an amazing aphrodisiac. (That's probably why they are never on our menu.) He says that he had oysters for dinner on the train coming to Ascension and that afterwards he 'creamed his jeans.' I'm not sure I know what that means, but I think I do."

"Do you guys like beer?" Brother Walt asked one day after he had become acquainted enough with his two new barn assistants to know that the answer would probably be affirmative. All three were busy forking manure out of the gutters behind the cow stanchions and into the manure spreader. Blaze and Gabe were once more re-hashing the mysterious train robber.

Blaze pondered the question of beer, not yet quite sure how well Walt could be trusted. Although lay brothers and priests were both allowed free access to beer, it was forbidden to seminarians without special permission, which was given only on festive occasions. This was a sore point with the seminarians.

"Well, I don't know as how I really like the stuff," Blaze said tentatively, "but I've been known to drink it."

"Oh yeah," Gabe said. "In seminary college, he stole a beer out of the priest's rec room refrigerator ten days in a row. Just to beat my record."

Walt hooted. He pointed with his fork at a milk can sitting in the corner of the barn. "Take a look."

A few bottles of beer bobbed in ice water in the can. The beer was Royal Bohemian. "If you notice, the label doesn't give the alcoholic content," Walt said. "Just says 'STRONG'." They all laughed, sat down, and had some STRONG.

The liquid emboldened Gabe. "Walt, you've got to help us. We have to find that guy who tried to rob us. Honest to God, it really happened. Somewhere between Savage and Shakopee."

Walt smiled. After years of standing behind a bar listening to all sorts of fantasies, he knew that it was best just to nod sympathetically.

"We hafta try to find that guy," Blaze repeated. "The train was going up a grade so we ought to be able to locate about where he jumped off. He had to know about the grade. He probably is a local. Surely someone saw something. Isn't there a feed mill over that way, or a cattle auction, or a tractor supply store that you might need to go to sometime? Something that would need our help loading on the truck or whatever."

"Don't know of any farm supply over that way, though that doesn't mean there ain't none," Walt said, mulling the possibility for adventure. "Tell you what is over there though. The damnedest saloon you've ever seen. I mean really. There are guns all over the walls. The waiters wear pistols. There's sometimes horses tied to the hitchin' rail out front. You'd swear you were walking onto a western movie set."

"You're bullshittin'," Blaze said.

"No, really."

"Wow. Hey, maybe that's a good place to start the search for a guy who thinks he's Frank James."

The three were silent as they considered the risks involved in going to a saloon. Bars were not places that even old softie Prior Robert would give them permission to enter. But unlike the seminarians, Brother Walt was allowed to carry money and go wherever he needed to conduct the farm's business. No reason why his helpers couldn't tag along, he thought. Once they were on the road, well, they'd need to eat lunch someplace. He'd speak to the Prior. He remembered that he needed protein supplement for the hogs.

///

Jesse James was half-way through his fourth cream soda when Nash Patroux, winking at another patron, asked him the question.

"Robbed any trains lately, Jesse?" Although Jesse was accustomed to jibes like that, and in truth it was that jibe that started him thinking about doing just that, but he could no longer just grin like an idiot, even though grinning like an idiot and thereby entertaining Patroux and his regular customers was how he earned free meals at the Western Range. The people of Savage took care of him because he gave even the stupidest among them somebody to look down on. But after the ill-fated robbery, Patroux's taunt might be more than a taunt. Did that fox know something?

Jesse had been living in torment ever since he had tried to rob the undertakers on the train. He could not imagine how he had actually worked up the courage to endure the stress of his escapade. Nor could he imagine why the undertakers had not reported the affair. Every day he expected the sheriff to stomp into the saloon and arrest him. No more cream sodas. Who would feed his trusty old horse, Blaze? Jail would at least relieve his father of the burden of caring for him. Hardly a day went by that Pap didn't look at him and mutter something about what would happen to Jesse when he was gone. Jesse could not bring himself to assure Pap that he would do just fine, that he was not as retarded as everyone thought he was. Exaggerating his mental quirks had been an effective way to avoid working for a living. But now his little game might be coming to an end. When the sheriff came to arrest him, he thought of using his fast draw and then the sheriff would have to shoot him, like in the movies. But of course, the sheriff knew Jesse's pistol didn't work and would just laugh.

Even while he tried to figure out if Patroux was only joking like usual, Jesse spied three strangers walk into the restaurant. They were not regular customers because they gazed around at the walls full of guns and stared at the pistol-holstered waiters with open mouths. Maybe they were Pinkertons looking for him. Jesse slouched over his cream soda, trying to pull his head down between his shoulders like a turtle, eyeing the strangers in the mirror behind the bar. He was sure he had seen two of them someplace before but could not place them. Maybe they'd been shadowing him and he had seen them but not consciously.

Walt had to lead the gaping Gabe by the arm to steer him to a table. Gabe was not sure he had ever been in a bar of any kind before, much less one like this. Blaze was so transfixed that he would not budge. He thought he had entered his fanstasy world again, or one of them anyway. Here was the old west, alive. There had been a horse at the hitching rail outside. Inside, the walls were full of firearms along with paintings of almost naked ladies over the bar. Oh wow. The chairs were framed in cattle horns instead of wood. Waiters really did wear holstered pistols. Tables were bedecked in red-checkered tablecloths. A shelf of books on the far wall caught his eye and he proceeded to it, ignoring his comrades. "Oh wow," he said out loud, reading one of the titles. "They got a copy of *Cole Younger, By Himself*."

Nash Patroux, behind the bar, perked up his ears. "You know that book?" he asked, surprised.

"Yeah. It's kind of rare."

Patroux nodded. "You collect books?"

"No, not really. I'm just a westerns fan. I read all the historical stuff I can get hold of. Younger wrote that book while he was in the Minnesota State Prison, right? After the Northfield raid."

"That's absolutely right," Patroux said. It was rare that anyone coming into the saloon knew anything about his passion, western outlaws. "Who might you be and can I getcha a beer?"

Blaze was not about to reveal who he might be. "Yeah. I want a Royal Bohemian and so do those two guys at the table. We farm across the river up Chanhassen way." He tried to put the accent on the second syllable the way the locals said it—ChinASSen, but it didn't ring true. "Name's Jack."

Soon the two were deep into a discussion of the Earps and Doc Holliday and the Youngers and whatever really happened to Frank James. Gabe, back at the table, kept shaking his head. All their years together, and he didn't know that Blaze could carry on a conversation about outlaws. In fact his sidekick seemed to know more about Wyatt Earp than he did about Thomas Aquinas. Eventually a waiter brought over the beer, but Blaze stayed at the bar in animated conversation. Actually, he was not thinking so much about what he was saying as about how to steer the conversation towards possible recent train robberies without sounding like an idiot. It was only now that he realized there was no convincing way to ask a perfect stranger about a train robbery in which nothing was stolen and about which no one but the almost-victims and the almost-robber knew. Who would believe a weird story like that?

"Yep, them were the days," he said, lapsing into a kind of slangy drawl that made Gabe, nursing his beer at the table, roll his eyes and shake his head again. "You hafta wonder why nobody robs banks and trains anymore. World's tamed some. I bet it's been years since there was a train robbery around here, right?"

"You gotta talk to Jesse James down there at the end of the bar about that," Patroux said, keeping up his perennial joke but remaining poker-faced. "He's our resident outlaw." He had raised his voice so Jesse would hear him and now winked broadly at Blaze, since the young man's face had unaccountably paled as if something terrifying had just occurred. He felt he better explain, too low for Jesse to hear. "Jesse is our village idiot. But be careful, he isn't always as crazy as he really is."

"J-Jesse James?"

"C'mere Jesse, man here wants to talk to you."

Blaze had thought the man at the end of the bar was one of the waiters taking a break, since he wore a pistol. But the would-be waiter made no move to come closer or even to turn his head to acknowledge the boss's order. Blaze stared at him. That there could be two people alive in the same locality within the same time frame, one named

Jesse James and one named Frank James with a hankering for robbing trains, was fantasy beyond anything even Blaze could imagine. The face of the man on the train had been hidden by the bandanna and so there was no accurate way to determine if he were the same as the fellow at the end of the bar. This guy did have greying hair, but it was combed somewhat neatly, and tied in a ponytail, not stringy like the train robber's.

Jesse's heart thumped so loudly that he was sure the Pinkerton and that goddam Patroux could hear it. For a moment he wished there were bullets in his pistol so he could whizz one past Patroux and scare the hell out of him. The son of a bitch didn't know that his goddamn joking was no joke and that he was getting Jesse into a pile of trouble. He tried to put on his ape grin but he could tell from the mirror that it only made him look guiltier. The strange man was walking toward him now, smiling, his hand out in a gesture of friendship. A Pinkerton for sure. Just exactly the way they did in the Jesse James movies.

"My name's Jack and pleased to meetcha," Blaze opened, trying to sound friendly.

"Sorry, I gotta see about Blaze. He's getting mighty curious about where I been," Jesse said, and scooted out the back door.

Blaze, mouth open and eyes wide, watched him leave. Oh my God. He could not see that Jesse circled the restaurant to the front hitching rail, climbed onto his horse and rode hastily away. What the hell was going on? How did the village idiot know his name? He looked at Patroux who remained as solemn as a deacon at a gospel reading.

Blaze walked to the table in a daze and swigged on his Royal Bohemian. Gabe for once was no help. He too was astonished. Walt of course could not appreciate what was happening and he only wondered, once more, if seminarians might all be as weird as barn owls. Blaze kept repeating Jesse's two sentences in a near whisper, looking for hidden meaning. "I. gotta. see. about. Blaze. . . . He's. getting. mighty. curious. as. to. where. I. been.' How could the guy know that?"

Gabe by now was shaking his head, as if trying to become fully awake. Something really creepy was going on but he did not want to say out loud the theory that was suggesting itself to him. Blaze would only sneer and say the Royal Bohemian was taking hold. But he said it anyway. "What if the train robber, alias Frank James, alias the village idiot who is also alias Jesse James is really a kind of phantom? Maybe he is Christ, or the devil, or an angel, appearing in the guise of a man, to tell us something? A second coming?" He paused. "Well, don't look at me that way. Scripture and church history are full of examples. Or maybe God is simply acting through a mere mortal to give us a message." He paused. "Problem is, wouldn't God, even speaking through a village idiot, use grammatically correct English?" He decided it was time for his favorite word. "Pretty chthonic, ain't it?"

Blaze laughed. "You're the village idiot if there ever was one."

CHAPTER 3

In the weeks that followed, Blaze experienced a kind of happiness he had not known since taking vows as a Josephian. The long summer days of farm work hardened his muscles and cleared his mind of the spiritual fog that had often hung over him because of the worries that bedeviled him about religious life. He was no longer really leading much of a religious life, but escaping into the world of the local community, a world of farms and villages. Getting to know people beyond his hitherto cloistered life, he and Gabe reveled in the normality of normal people who faced only normal worries like adverse weather in hay time or the closing of a factory or a drunken husband, and who otherwise seemed to think not much beyond the next bit of entertainment that they could find. More important, these people accepted the two oblates. No more the curious and circumspect looks which had so often made Blaze feel as if he were a monkey in a cage when for whatever reason, he had gone forth from the seminary in religious garb. Now, just a farm worker in jeans, he could laugh, joke, even cuss with them. Moreover he had a mystery to ponder and pursue that was so much more earthy and interesting and real than the mysteries of religion for which he had no solution or even belief. The phantom train robber was far more absorbing a puzzle than three divine persons in one God, or the number of angels on the head of a pin. The mystery of

Jesse James and the village idiot truly was chthonic. With a life fully satisfied on both a physical and mental level, Blaze began, as in earlier years, to love life again.

On the mornings when he was not on barn duty and so had no excuse not to attend chapel, he actually seemed to remain deep in thought during the meditation period instead of dozing off as he had done formerly. But in trying to solve the mystery of the Second Coming of Frank James, his mind could only run in circles. He dismissed out of hand Gabe's theory about God sending them messages through unlikely mortals. If God wanted to send him a message, there were surely easier or plainer ways to do it. And Fen's notion that the whole affair was mere coincidence or happenstance just could not be true either. No one robbed trains anymore, not even a village idiot who thought he was Frank James. He'd rob banks instead. Logically he'd do his robbing over around Northfield, not Savage, if he wanted to keep alive the memory of the famous outlaws. But it seemed even more improbable that the village idiot, whose name actually was Jesse James Brown, as Blaze had learned, would rob a train and openly identify himself as the robber even if he was crazy. Unless of course he really was a phantom or a word-made-flesh and then all logic was out the window. Maybe that was why the idiot from the outlaw past didn't take their wallets. Maybe he was just trying to make a statement. Which would mean that he was not really an idiot. And how the hell did he know my name?

The human mind can ponder a mystery for only so long before it manufactures an explanation or flees to the firmer ground of proven fact. So Blaze, unable by nature to be content with manufactured explanations, put his thoughts about the mystery on hold, and turned his attention to the landscape around the seminary, which revealed its own haunting mysteries. The complex of buildings, barns and fields sat on a sort of low sandy ridge, surrounded by a peculiar mingling of marsh and weedy tussock that lay between the Minnesota River less than a mile to the south and the high bluffs of the river valley to the north. There seemed to be no apparent geological reason for the swamps, which paralleled the river much of the way to its conjunction with the Mississippi at Minneapolis. Blaze wandered through the mucky terrain, learning with deepening fascination that if he jumped up and down, the soil surface shook like a giant mattress. Soon Gabe and Fen were accompanying him into this quivering landscape interlaced with crystal clear streams full of trout and muskrat and overgrown with watercress, marsh marigolds and cattails. Eventually the whole class except Very Reverend Lukey and Little Eddie, took to disappearing into this wilderness whenever their schedule allowed.

"One of the time-honored beliefs of monastic and seminary life is that students can be better protected from the evils of the world if they are isolated in a natural rural environment far from the fleshpots of urban life," Other Blaze wrote in The Story of My Weird Life. "What a boner. For me, wild nature is a more seductive mistress than Marilyn Monroe could ever be."

With permission from Prior Robert, the "most troublesome class in seminary history" was able to arm itself with rifles and shotguns previously belonging to Josephian priests who had passed away and whose belongings had been shipped to the seminary for storage. The weapons were necessary, Blaze believed, to actualize his vision of their woodland, swamp and river haunts as a frontier. They rarely shot at anything and when they did they missed. Rather than Lou Boudreau, Blaze now imagined himself the resurrection of Daniel Boone or Kit Carson. As an excuse for their wildlife wandering, he and his comrades maintained, with considerable good intentions if not logic, that they were preparing themselves for missionary work in the African bush where the Josephians had mission churches.

But most of the faculty and the other students were offended by their unseminarian-like colleagues. When Fr. Abelard could not persuade Prior Robert to confiscate the guns, which he called "penis substitutes" (Prior Robert loved to go jackrabbit hunting), he angrily dubbed the class "The Sonuvabitchin' Davy Crockett Boys." The SBDC Boys liked their new name and flaunted it.

The community of oblates came to almost despise the SBDC Boys. They just seemed to be having too much fun. Maybe the Provincial should expel the lot of them instead of treating them as if they were superior because of their high IQs. But since they had taken vows after the Novitiate, becoming with this step bonafide members of the Josephians even though they were not yet ordained priests, there was little chance of getting them expelled unless they lapsed into something deemed really dreadful like homosexuality or wreaking physical violence on a priest. Blaze fantasized delivering a hefty blow to Fr. Abelard's chin, but harming a priest carried the punishment of automatic excommunication. Besides, Abelard was built like a middle linebacker which is why he was called "Abs" for short. Blaze feared that if he were dumb enough to hit Abs, the priest would crush him. There was no excommunication involved in annihilating a lowly seminarian.

So for a time the swamps distracted Blaze, Fen, and Gabe from their fixation on the train robbery. One of the streams flowing from the swamps had been captured to provide a never-failing supply of water for the former sanitarium and it was still in use. Gabe galvanized his confreres into building a second one. He found these reservoirs most interesting to his long-range purposes. The water was pure and did not freeze, even when temperatures sank below zero. Gabe also figured that the watercress and the trout might be turned into low-cost, high-profit market crops. But whether or not that ever happened, these foods, along with cattail roots which he learned were quite tasty and nutritional, were always available no matter how cold the winter weather. The community could never starve or die of thirst. How marvelous. With the seminary restored to its former Mudpura glory, it could be self-sustaining in food and water and perhaps, medicine.

What if, mused Melonhead Mullaney, the would-be doctor, the peat in the swamps, if not the water itself, really did possess curative powers, as the old Mudpura doctors believed? That idea had brought the sanitarium to the site in the first place, Melonhead pointed out to the others. Naturopathic doctors in the 1920s believed that the peat, steamed hot and wrapped around the human body, could cure rich people of whatever they thought ailed them. If that didn't work, sulfur water flowing out of one of the springs might offer a cleansing so invasive that the peat treatment would appear to be effective anyway. Blaze, in a state of excited agitation, related some Mudpura history from an old book he had found in the attic. "Those goofballs actually dug that peat up, hauled it to the building on horse-drawn carts, warmed it up with steam, and wrapped those poor rich people in it."

"I wonder if it worked?" Melonhead asked, more than once.

"If it does, we'll get into the business as Mudpura Retreat House," Gabe remarked, more than once. "I can see it now. Come to Ascension to heal thy body as well as thy soul."

Very Reverend Lukey sniffed disapproval at these musings which he blamed on Blaze's propensity for fantasy and his ability to sell it to the more gullible of his classmates. He was tired of being associated with the SBDC Boys. He had not joined religious life to dig septic tanks, or lay bricks, or to start a sanitarium, but to study for the priesthood. "I'm here to learn how to think," he told Blaze earnestly.

Blaze replied with his familiar grating laugh. "Learn how to think? How the hell can you NOT think?"

"I mean to think properly," Lukey said, giving Blaze a pitying look.

"You mean you haven't been thinking properly up till now?" Blaze asked. "You weren't for instance thinking properly when you decided to join the Josephians? How about when you fainted on the train. Would proper thinking cure you of fainting under duress?"

"You are so arrogant," Lukey said, turning away.

"Since you haven't completed Thinking Properly 101, how do you know you're correct when you say I'm arrogant?"

Lukey whirled so fast that he caught the big rosary hanging from his wide, black Josephian belt around his pleated black Josephian tunic, on the door knob and jerked it loose from the two metal hooks that held it in place on his belt. The rosary clattered across the floor.

"I don't know why you're here at all," he blazed at Blaze while gathering up his rosary and fumbling it back in place. "You really are a Sonuvabitchin' Davy Crockett Boy."

Blaze hurried off to find Gabe and Fen to inform them that they didn't know how to think yet. He promised himself that when he took over the Josephians or became Pope, his first official act would be to put Lukey to work operating a soup kitchen in a ghetto. That would help his thinking considerably.

///

As summer passed into fall, the new lifestyle that Ascension Seminary seemed to provide for the SBDC Boys began to fade away. With the school year once more starting, the age-old rhythms of seminary and monastery began to reassert themselves. Classroom time dominated the daylight hours: Aristotle, Plato, Thomas Aquinas, Canon Law, Ethics, Cosmology, Metaphysics, courses in Greek and even Hebrew. "I learned today in Ethics that married people can have sex as often as they want to, even every day," Other Blaze wrote in his diary. "My God, I don't think I'd even like to play baseball every day. I also learned that if a fly crawls across a page of Hebrew text and leaves a speck, it might change the meaning of the whole sentence."

Blaze and his cohorts were still able to avoid some of the chapel sessions because of their mundane duties in kitchen, barn and boiler room, but more and more they were pulled back into the ancient schedule of the chanted hours of the breviary, Matins and Lauds at four o'clock in the afternoon, (better than at two in morning as the Trappists did, Blaze reminded himself), Prime, Terce, Sext and Nones in the morning along with Mass and meditation, and Vespers and Compline in the evening. Blaze found himself feeling again what he called "the miseries" that had often afflicted him in the seminary days before coming to Ascension. In chapel, he studied the other seminarians and priests as they chanted away or stared with such piety at the altar in front of the pews. They seemed at peace. Some of them anyway. Fen was asleep as usual and so was really at peace until Prior Robert made him kneel in the aisle as punishment. Gabe was looking out the window as if planning an escape, which is precisely what he was doing. But for the most part the others seemed content to be chanting psalms, oblivious of how much they resembled a flock of sheep, bleating back and forth at each other across a meadow.

Yet he understood that there really was something peaceful and tranquil about their life of prayer and study. Occasionally he felt it himself. But for him the peace was shattered almost constantly by his conviction that they were all insane to live this way. And when he quashed that line of thinking, he was battered by naggings of sexual desire. Sometimes desire was so intense that he thought his penis was about to explode. Sex every day? What about every hour? At least when engaged with farm work, he was not so besieged. Were the others similarly disturbed? Only rarely did anyone speak of it. Once, Melonhead remarked jokingly that upon waking up in the morning he found himself glued to the sheet by dried semen. Blaze was appalled. Although it had happened to him too, he would never dream of saying so out loud. He tried to pretend, out loud, that sex did not exist. But he started referring to them all as semenarians.

Classroom hours were only a little more tolerable than the chapel hours. Blaze could not understand the logic of cosmology. Two objects could not occupy the same space at the same time, Professor Rowan said, his face beaming as if divine truth were issuing from his mind.

Wasn't that too obvious to take note of? "Three," Professor Rowan gushed in ecstasy, trying to impress upon them the beauty of a statement that could not be contradicted, "is one plus one plus one." Blaze looked at Fen. Both rolled their eyes. What poetry did the priest see here that so totally escaped them?

Gabe could see that his fellow SBDC Boys, losing the freedom they had enjoyed in the summer, were sinking into a fit of the blues, as he called it. He considered himself above that weakness, but he had been noticing with a little trepidation, that the petals of the artistic floral design on the front of the altar curtain looked remarkably like a swirl of very feminine bare legs emanating from a central crotch. Some sort of distraction was in order, and he thought he had come up with one. It was time to help improve Lukey's thinking process in case the regular classroom courses in Philosophy didn't get the job done. Gabe's scheme was actually just a minor part of a grander plan he wanted to pursue to make Ascension the first financially profitable seminary in the world. "Scientific data demonstrates that the mud out there in the swamp will make one healthy," he said to Blaze. "Maybe it will help one to think better too."

"And just what do you have in mind?" Blaze asked with a delicious smile.

News of near miraculous cures began to filter out of the slaughterhouse next to the barn where the farm crew and other SBDC Boys gathered after the evening meal to smoke. Nothing definite. Just continuous and provocative rumors. When asked about the rumors, the farm crew members dismissed them as totally wishful theorizing on the part of people who hadn't learned how to think yet.

"Well, sure, Gabe had a bad cold, but it went away like colds always do. Had nothing to do with the hot peat fomentation and compote he tried," Blaze explained.

"Yeah, it's true that Blaze had a bad cut on his leg where the dumb butthole jabbed himself with a hay fork," Gabe admitted, "but it healed up okay on its own. You surely don't believe a poultice of that swamp mud did it, do you?"

"Of course there's instances in folk medicine where poultices of one kind or another have healed sores and cuts," added Fen, who had finally wangled his way onto the farm crew. "But come on, there's instances of Lourdes water healing sickness too, and surely you don't believe that, do you?"

In a week or so, strange stories drifted back to their starting point in the slaughterhouse. "Did you know that Oblate Gabriel had a temperature of 106 and he soaked himself in hot peat and got well almost immediately?"

"Did you know that Oblate Blaise healed a festering infected dog bite on his leg with a poultice of peat from the swamp?"

"You're not going to believe this, but Brother Walt put a wad of swamp peat and cobwebs on a cow bleeding from being dehorned, and the flow of blood stopped almost immediately." This story Blaze considered the best of all, because it was actually true.

The idea of soaking in hot peat seemed almost practical because in the slaughterhouse was a huge tank with a firebox under it and a rope and pulley affair over it. The tank was used to scald the hair off hogs in the process of butchering, the hog carcass hoisted aloft by the rope and lowered into the big tank. Conceivably a person might sit in the tank, as in a bathtub, and soak away his miseries if he didn't make too much of a fire underneath.

Digging the peat proved so troublesome that the SBDC Boys almost abandoned their plan. The stuff would not dig with shovels and only barely with forks. To get enough of a supply on hand in the slaughterhouse, Blaze used an antique hay saw he found in the barn. Sawing straight down the walls of a pit that they had dug initially, he could shear off slabs of peat about six inches thick. But he did not have to strain himself because Melonhead, with a vision of a life in medicine, soon took over and sheared away at the peat deposit with an awesome energy no one would have thought he could draw upon. His yen for doctoring had found an outlet. He immersed himself in hydrotherapy studies and by the time he had finished all 600 pages of Jethro Kloss's *Back To Eden* he had convinced himself that hot peat treatments were truly healthful and that what the SBDC Boys were contemplating as trickery was actually noble experimental medicine. "God works in wondrous ways," he said piously.

"God wills it too," Gabe answered.

"What do you mean?"

"The Very Reverend Lukey is sick with the flu or something."

"You mean it's time to teach him how to think?" Blaze responded.

"No time better."

A committee of SBDC Boys was formed to visit the sick Lukey in his room. Although he was miserable with fever, cough and throbbing head, Lukey was not so far gone as not to be suspicious of SBDC solicitude. But because Melonhead seemed to be the leader of the group and appeared totally convinced of what he was proposing, Lukey listened. Melonhead deserved trust. He was very good at giving enemas.

Melonhead thrust a thermometer in Lukey's mouth and at the same time took his pulse, all in a manner so swift and sure as to make one wonder if he were not at least a registered nurse.

"A hundred and five. Wow. You're really sick," he said, studying the thermometer which actually registered 103. "If we don't get that temperature down, you could have brain spasms."

"Brain spasms," Blaze echoed with a shudder.

"Could lose your hair from prolonged high temperature, I've heard," Fen offered. Lukey was especially vain about his curly brown hair.

"Brain spasms," Blaze said again. "Might deter one from learning how to think."

Lukey glared at him, but Blaze's countenance displayed only disarming, innocent concern.

"This is going to sound a little crazy," Melonhead intoned, and then proceeded to explain to Lukey how Mudpura began and why, and the numerous claims of renewed health and vigor that people with a lot of money gained from being wrapped in hot peat for a few hours. He, Melonhead, had gathered a sufficient amount of high quality peat in the slaughterhouse, and proposed to cure Lukey in the old Mudpura manner, which apparently had helped Gabe and Blaze. Melonhead's faith in his cure being somewhat genuine, he sounded convincing and Lukey was inclined to give The Cure a try. "Don't be hasty now," Melonhead counselled, playing reverse psychology not out of trickery but earnestness. He gave Lukey a book on Naturopathic Medicine, and the entourage left the sick man to think awhile.

Lukey's flu worsened. Wracked with aches and pains, he staggered to Melonhead's room the next evening after chapel. "I'm ready for The Cure," he gasped. "I'm ready for anything."

"We'll have to wait until tomorrow during recreation period," Melonhead replied, still inadvertently playing hard-to-get. "You understand we have to do this with some secrecy. I doubt the Prior would look favorably upon homeopathic medicine."

"Gotta do it now. Tonight," rasped Lukey. "I won't live till tomorrow."

"But it's against the rules to be out and about after lights out."

"I don't care. I'm gonna die."

"Well, okay," said Melonhead. "We'll get the scalding tank, er, the steam bath, fired up and after everyone goes to bed we'll come for you."

Exiting the building after "lights out" required considerable stealth. There was no lockdown in the seminary, of course, but Prior Robert was given to walking the halls at night, alert for mischief, or, horrors, homosexual dalliance. This night, all seemed as quiet and peaceful as an oyster in a cloister. Robert retired. When the light in his bedroom went out, a flashlight in the hands of Danny Danauau on the roof of the building wing across from Robert's quarters, blinked twice. Melonhead, from his room on the top floor of Robert's wing, flicked his flashlight on and off in reply, then slipped out of his room and tiptoed to Lukey's room. The fever-wracked oblate was waiting. Together they made their way silently to the fire escape and to the ground. Once free of the building, they could relax somewhat, but still dared not turn on flashlights for fear of attracting the attention of Fr. Abelard whose self-appointed job was, when not teaching theology, to oversee everything that went on at the seminary. This responsibility was fairly easy for him to accomplish since he had commandeered the top third floor of the priest professors' residence for his room. Nearer my God to Thee. From its windows, he could observe, especially with the marine telescope he had found among the possessions of Josephians who had gone to their eternal reward, everything that went on at the main building in one direction, to the barn across the road in the other direction, as well as all the fields and most of the swampland surrounding the compound. As theologian and overseer of Ascension, there was very little that went on there, in the heavens above or on earth below, that Fr. Abelard did not take great pride in knowing about.

Because the seminarians were well aware of Abelard's constant surveillance, the other SBDC Boys in the slaughterhouse had not dared to turn on the lights in the slaughterhouse, as they filled the scalding tank with water and started the fire below it. Nevertheless, under Gabe and Melonhead's direction and Blaze's constant running off at the mouth, they eventually had a tank of warm peat steaming away. As their contribution to the effort, Banana and Mart merely giggled nervously. Fen paced around in what little light escaped the door of the firebox. He did not like chancy escapades like this, but wouldn't think of not being there. Gabe appointed Clutch, the community's boilerman, to keep the firebox under the tank properly filled with wood, but continued to give orders on tending the fire. This irritated Clutch. Every time Gabe cautioned him about not getting the fire too hot, Clutch threw on another chunk of wood.

"Here they come," Fen whispered, and the assorted giggles lapsed to silence. By the light of the firebox, they saw Melonhead and Danny troop through the door followed by the feverish Lukey. Danny and his flashlight went back to the barn to keep watch from the hayloft in case anyone approached from the main buildings. In that case, he was to signal the others in the slaughterhouse.

Even in the semi-darkness, the apprehension on Lukey's face showed clearly. Only fever and aching pain drove him onward. Melonhead explained the process. "There's a nice layer of peat already in the tub," he explained. "We'll lower you gently into the tank and then we'll cover you with another layer of peat. Should take about an hour to soak out the poisons that are causing your flu. It's sort of like a sauna but the peat increases the lavatation."

Blaze looked at him, startled. What the hell did lavatation mean, he wondered. Melonhead did not know either. The word had just come to him and it sounded terribly impressive.

Lukey removed his bathrobe. "You might as well take off your pajamas too," Melonhead said. "You'll want something dry to put on afterwards."

Lukey hesitated only a second. In the semi-darkness, his nudity did not seem embarassing and by now the warm steam rising from the tank promised comfort beyond caring about modesty.

"H-H-How do I get in there. It's too high off the ground to step in," Lukey muttered in resigned misery.

"Reach up and get hold of that hoist rope," Gabe instructed. "We'll pull you up and lower you down."

Done.

Lukey groaned with relief as he settled into the warm peat and water. All his aches and pains seemed to vanish. A miracle. The SBDC Boys piled on more peat until only Lukey's head stuck above what now appeared to be a little pool of steaming algae. Or perhaps, spinach. Meanwhile, Clutch threw another log chunk into the firebox. Lukey groaned again in pleasure. "This is great." And a little later, "I haven't felt like coughing once since I got in here. I guess you guys are okay after all."

A seemingly long spell of silence followed. The only sound was the crackling of the fire. The more or less wet, uncured wood that Clutch had used for the fire was now drying out. The drier it got, the hotter it burned, which in turn made it dry even faster. And so forth unfortunately.

Meanwhile, Fr. Abelard, making a last sweep of the property with his telescope before going to bed, thought he saw strange shimmers of light coming from the slaughterhouse. He decided to investigate.

Back at the slaughterhouse, Gabe said: "Do you think he's done yet?" That was too much even for serious Mart. Everyone laughed. Except Lukey.

A human body in hot water tends to adapt to the situation remarkably well. It can stand surprisingly high temperatures if the increase comes very slowly, as it was now doing in the tank. Moreover the layer of peat under Lukey somewhat insulated his naked body above it, at least for awhile. But slow increments of heat can be accommodated only so long and then the resulting need for relief is sudden. Very sudden.

"God, I'm getting hot," said Lukey, suddenly. "Oh, God." He reached for the top rim of the tank only to find that it was too hot to grab so that he might vault out of the tank. He yelled.

Events started happening very fast right about then. Fen at the slaughterhouse door saw the warning blinks of Danny's flashlight from the barn loft. "Someone's coming," he said in a hoarse whisper. Most of the SBDC Boys broke for the door and disappeared into the night. Melonhead, after an agonizing second, decided, like a good doctor, to stand by his patient. Blaze, allowing his natural instinct for helping people to overcome his instinct for personal survival, decided to stay too and help Lukey out of the tank.

At about that time Lukey started snarling. "Get me outta here! I'm burning, BURNING!" Melonhead swung the rope hoist down to where Lukey could grab it and he and Blaze prepared to pull him from the soup. Lukey was by now standing in the big tank, hopping from one foot to the other, holding on to the hoist, trying to pull himself free of the scalding water. Melonhead and Blaze gave one more mighty heave, just as the slaughterhouse door swung open and a flashlight flicked on. There stood Fr. Abelard, his eyes bulging, realizing that his beam of light was revealing a naked body floating in the air above a steaming cauldron. The body was screaming in what might have been pain or some sadistic pleasure. About that time, Melonhead and Blaze, on the other side of Lukey and so shielded partially from Abelard's beam of light, grabbed the swinging body by the legs and pulled it away from the tank. All three fell to the floor in a tangle. What Abelard thought he saw was two or maybe three masochistic sadists involved in some sort of heinous sexual orgy.

"Holy Mother of God," he gasped, crossing himself several times. Then wrapping the rosary hanging from his belt around his neck as if to ward off vampires, he bolted out the door and did not stop running until he was in his protective aerie on the third floor of the priests' residence. Nearer my God to Thee. He went to his closet, withdrew a bottle of Old Fitzgerald and took a long pull on it. Nothing in his theology books covered the situation. The worst part was that the apparition had been so sudden, so ghastly, so shocking, that he, the Overseer of All Things In This World Or Out of It, did not know for the life of him which seminarians he had actually seen. Maybe they were not seminarians at all, but devil worshipers using the seminary property, where they would likely never be discovered, for their fiendish covens. The naked one had its back to him but he realized with chagrin, he probably would not have recognized him if it were someone he knew, because he had no clothes on. The suspended body had blocked the view of one or more other figures so he could not identify them either. Perhaps they were satyrs, not devils. Then an even more horrible thought came to his reeling mind as the whiskey took hold. Perhaps they were only the result of his own loathsome sexual fantasies. Oh, my God. He took yet another swig. Had he imagined the whole thing? Or dreamed it? Had he noticed furtive lights at the barn or only imagined that he had? Had he, in fact, ever left his room really? He looked out the window toward the barn. Only darkness. Oh, God. He would not dare tell anyone what he had seen because maybe he had not seen it. He tipped the bottle again.

Gabe swore later that Lukey ran naked through the barnyard, across the highway and all the way back to the main building before he had the presence of mind to put on the pajamas, bathrobe and slippers that he had grabbed up in his mad dash from the slaughterhouse. "Had he run any faster, he might have overtaken Abelard and that could have been very interesting indeed," Gabe said. Melonhead spent the night deciding which medical college he would attend after he was defrocked and expelled.

About four in the morning, gleeful chuckling suddenly emanated from Lukey's room. He burst out into the hallway, threw open the door to Blaze's room, and kicked the bed. He was by now laughing loud enough to awaken the Prior, but he didn't care. His days in the seminary were ended anyhow, he figured, so what did it matter.

"Blaze, guess what, you smartass." He waited for Blaze to come to full wakefulness. "It worked, damn you, it worked. I'M WELL!" Then he ran, still giggling loudly, back to his room, and fell into the restful sleep of those who have had the last laugh.

CHAPTER 4

There was urgency in Kluntz's voice as he sat on an overturned bucket in Ed Hasse's barn, scratching at his unshaven chin with one hand and continually yanking at the right strap of his bib overalls with the other.

"I don't like it. I don't like it a-tall," he said, referring once more to the sudden, distressing interest in religion around the neighborhood.

"What's it to you?" Hasse snorted, bent over, only half-paying attention to Kluntz as he checked the teat cup that was sucking air on Old Blackie's front left quarter. Because he was a dairy farmer and therefore always in the barn at milking time, morning and evening, Hasse, like the blacksmith of yesteryear, had to suffer a steady flow of visitors whether he wanted to or not.

"It ain't proper to get folks stirred up about religion," answered Kluntz, who had no cows and who therefore milked the neighborhood for gossip. "It'll just cause trouble. Why, it's just like, like, well, like talking about that damn blue clay gumbo you try to farm on the flats. You can't tell nobody how to farm it. About all you can say is that if you step in the goddam stuff when it's wet, it'll stick to your boots so hard you have to shake your leg five times before it'll come off." Then he added, as if to add credence to his observation, if not to a connection with theology, "Four's not enough and six is too many."

Hasse bent under another cow to hide his smile. Kluntz had made an art out of not exerting himself any more than absolutely necessary and that probably was theology to him. "How many times you suppose you'd have to shake a boot if you stepped into a pile of religion?" he asked.

"See what I mean? You get talkin' like that, it'll just cause trouble. Look. I'm not sayin' the Christians are right. I doubt it. But, by God, I mean to go along with them because if I'm wrong, there'll be hell to pay."

Hasse considered Kluntz's remarks with as sober a mien as he could muster. After all, he had his reputation as a barnyard theologian to maintain. Fathered by a Methodist, mothered by a Lutheran, and wedded to a Catholic, he considered himself something of an authority on religion. The subject was, indeed, of much interest to him—not as much as the subject of money, but he nevertheless studied the fervor for religion around him with the same perspicacity that he applied in studying the fervor for money. But his interest in religion had not borne fruit in the logical way that his interest in money had: religion only turned him into a closet atheist who secretly sneered at the versions of Christianity that had impinged upon his life. He kept his heresy to himself, however, because alienating Christians was not good for business. Since he led a moral life by Carver County standards, which is to say he drank little and confined his amorous intentions to his wife on those rare occasions when she would allow him, the neighbors hardly suspected. Who ever heard of a moral atheist?

Even Kluntz was not exactly sure where Hasse stood on religion because he knew his neighbor to be a master of disguise. Although Hasse was as genuine a farmer as Minnesota could produce, his farming was also or mainly, a front for the small loan business that he ran out of the breast pocket of his bib overalls. Hasse had long ago made the simple deduction that if bankers, most of whom, he observed, were not very bright, could lend his money out and get rich off it, so could he. Yet he affected an old-country accent and dressed, even at bank board meetings, in his weatherbeaten felt hat and faded, sometimes manure-specked, bibs to keep everyone guessing (including the IRS, Kluntz suspected) about his financial situation. The Hasse name was respected in banking circles in the Twin Cities, but locally he was just a middle-aged farmer who was liable to speak of other men's religious beliefs in the same tone of voice he used to point out their crooked corn rows and skinny steers.

That religion should be discussed at all in Hasse's barn, or anywhere else around Chaska and Shakopee for that matter, was because of the arrival there of the Oblates of St. Joseph. To have a group of monkish beatniks descend upon a rural populace that thought Henry Wallace should have ascended to the Presidency, was itself a subject of considerable moment. But for the Oblates of St. Joseph to take possession of a farm in an area where competition for farmland was savage, made them about as welcome as the Klu Klux Klan. Moreover, the farm that the monks had taken over bordered both Hasse and Kluntz, land which the two blunt-knuckled, grizzled farmers had been trying to snare for years but which Harriet Snod, the pious old widow in Chaska who owned it, wouldn't sell. To spite both farmers, people said, she gave it to the Josephians.

"They don't have to pay taxes," Kluntz reminded Hasse, referring to the exemption that religious groups enjoyed. That was the neighborhood's major objection to the Oblates of St. Joseph and Kluntz was chewing it for all the juice he could get out of it.

"Well, they don't believe in government subsidies either, so we may come out ahead on that score," Hasse replied. "Harriet had that land enrolled in so many government programs that she was making more money by not farming it than farming it."

"Well, monks shouldn't be competing with regular farmers," Kluntz grumbled. "We've got surpluses enough the way it is."

Hasse snorted. "I don't think you need to worry on that score either. The way they farm ain't about to contribute to the surpluses."

It was not that he viewed the Josephian farming effort any more favorably than Kluntz did, but Hasse had already thought of a way to turn this seeming setback to his expansion plans into an asset. His method of farming, which Kluntz sometimes referred to as "early Amish" was built on a precept Hasse expressed as: "Never spend more in a month than you make in a week and you'll come out okay." But his secret could be expressed even more succinctly: "Never borrow money and be careful who you lend it to." His first cows were "three-titters" bought dirt cheap at auctions because no one else wanted them. Hasse knew that three-titters almost always were heavy producers. That's why they went bad from mastitis in one quarter in the first place. And in any event, the ones his practiced eye selected for purchase gave just as much milk from three teats as most cows gave from four, and seemed to have built up an immunity to further attacks of mastitis too. And they threw calves that were heavy producers. If they did prove to be poor milkers, he butchered them and ground the meat into hamburger that he peddled privately for twice the money he had paid for the cow—the meat wrapped in packages stamped "Not For Sale" as government regulations required.

Hasse still used horses in his farming. Horses always started in the morning no matter how cold the weather, and they produced more horses with no pain to his bank accounts and no contribution to John Deere, as he put it. The tractors he did own were so old that they had not only ceased to depreciate but were growing in value as antiques.

To avoid borrowing money, Hasse always resorted to cheap labor, whether horse or human, rather than expensive machinery. And this was where the Josephians fit into his plan. Cheap help was not easy to come by since farm offspring were all going to town to work for the government or the banks. Hasse was tempted to say, sarcastically of course, that God had sent the Josephians along just in time to solve this dilemma for him. As he stood on his high hill where he could look down into the Minnesota River valley on the oblates at work, he felt almost sorry for them. Much of the land was either swampy, kept wet by springs, or lowlands flooded regularly by runoff from the hills on one side and the river on the other, or the sandy stuff in between that wouldn't raise a bushel of corn on a sack of fertilizer. The blue clay gumbo adjacent to the swamps that might raise a good crop needed drainage, something the Josephians apparently did not appreciate. They did not seem to appreciate anything about practical farming in fact, and spend much of their working day scurrying back and forth from the fields to the old sanitarium livery stable that they had retrofitted for a chapel, as if, Hasse remarked to Kluntz, they had to hurry back to church every hour or so to get instruction from on high. The Josephians represented to him a ready supply of cheap manpower waiting to be harnessed. And he meant to do the harnessing.

As Kluntz took his leave, dispirited by Hasse's lack of righteous anger over the Snod land slipping through their fingers into the hands of God, Hasse smiled mysteriously and reverted to the old-world vernacular of his father and which he himself tried to mimic when he wanted to appear stupid or ignorant, or, in front of Kluntz who knew better, to sound droll. Now he echoed his father, in sentiment as well as pronounciation: "Let da udder guy t'ink he's smarter dan you and den you got 'im." Then he added: "Dis vill all verk out chust fine. Chust you vait and see."

As he watched and waited for an opportunity with the Josephians, Hasse noticed from his lookout on the bluffs that a few new men had appeared on the scene below, after which the monks' farming operations took a more purposeful, if not professional, turn. The new look had begun the preceding summer and was now quite apparent. Instead of the meek, head-bowed manner with which the others went about their weedy gardens and forlorn fields, these new fellows seemed always in haste, heads held high, occasionally raving and ranting and even shaking fists when a tractor quit running. Their corn rows seemed to get planted straighter, fences seemed to sag less, and the oat crop became a bit more visible above the weeds.

One day as Hasse drove by the Josephians at work (slowly, to take in all he could), he spied the Josephian tractor mired at the swampy edge of a pasture field. That the tractor had bogged down was not a surprise to Hasse since he knew most of the Snod farm laid too wet. One reason he had not been very upset when Harriet refused to sell him the place was that he figured some fool would eventually buy it, go broke and then he could move in and pick up the farm for the value of the unpaid mortgage. Now the canny old farmer saw a chance to insinuate himself into the Josephian community. He sped away to his barn, hitched up his horses and drove them back to the scene of Josephian agony as if he were just casually passing by.

"Heaven sends us help," the one who liked to shake his fist cried jubilantly as Hasse approached. He stuck out his hand and with a bold, unmonkish briskness said: "I am Oblate Gabriel, just call me Gabe. And this here's Oblate Blaise spelled B-l-a-z-e as in horse, and this here string bean is Fen. We've got a log chain and careful those horses don't go down in this quagmire too. You must be Ed Hasse."

Hasse nodded, a little taken aback by the forthrightness of what he assumed was a monk. He brought the horses around in front of the tractor which was hub deep in the ooze and still sinking. He started to say something, but Oblate Gabriel didn't give him time.

"Mr. Hasse, you know we ought to drain this swamp. Most of the water comes down from your side. You could reclaim, right here, six or seven more acres and so could we."

"Many people haf tried und failed to drain dis swamp," Hasse said thickly, slipping the log chain through the iron ring of the doubletree.

Gabe, standing behind him, slapped at a deer fly. "I can drain it," he said, drily.

Hasse looked around sharply. "Vel now. Too much cost. For chust six acres, dat is for me not verth it. I can use dose acres for late pasture in drout' time widdout draining it." To himself he decided that he was perhaps spreading the accent on a bit too heavily. He never was consistent about which 'th' should be pronounced 'd', as his father had rendered it. And 'chust' might be too much to fool even a monk.

"Well, eventually we intend to revert almost entirely to a drylot feeding program and pasture the cows only rarely, so we won't need pasture," Gabe said primly. He confided, in a tone that sounded as if he had read it somewhere, that grazing livestock wasted grass. "I suppose you've observed," he said, "that cows crossing to and fro across pastures tend to make paths."

This declaration astonished even Blaze, who stared at his comrade and only with great effort refrained from bursting into laughter. Hasse's face remained as fixed as a boulder. Harnessing all this puffery to his benefit was going to be easy.

Blaze started up the tractor and Hasse clucked to his horses. Three tons of horseflesh strained against the harness, and the tractor, its wheels churning, wormed its way up out of the mud to firm ground. The oblates were grateful. Perhaps they could repay the favor.

Indeed they could. Hasse, assuming the look he supposed would properly mimic a poor sharecropper in Alabama, launched into a pitiful refrain about the hardships of farming, the scarcity of good help, milk prices so low that he had to keep on farming with horses instead of buying a new tractor. Haymaking was just about to start and he could sure use some help.

Blaze, born and raised on a farm, stared at the horizon, a wee smile on his face. But Gabe was sympathetic. He would talk to the Prior. Surely the Josephians could spare a couple of oblates to bring in the hay. "Then perhaps we can talk about draining this swamp again," he concluded pointedly. "I suppose six acres out of eleven hundred and twenty does not mean much to you, but we can use all the land we can bring into production."

Though elated, Hasse went home feeling a little uneasy. This Gabriel fellow would bear watching. There were people who lived in the county all their lives who did not know Hasse owned 1120 acres and who evidently did not know that all they had to do was look at a county plat map to find out. He farmed only a fraction of it himself, which is why few knew the extent of his holdings. He had found it more profitable to cash rent his land out at the highest possible price to other farmers and let them work it for what amounted to slave wages, or worse, in bad years, while he pocketed almost pure profit without doing anything. "No one ever made any real money farming," he liked to say, "but only from investing in land."

As he passed Kluntz's farm, Kluntz was working along the road cutting weeds out of the fence row. It was obvious that he was merely waiting for Hasse to return from the Josephians, since he had never cleaned out a fence row in his life. He put a fresh wad of Copenhagen under his lip as Hasse approached and prepared to enjoy the gossip. But Hasse paused only long enough for one sober question.

"Kluntz, did you know that cows crossing to and fro across the pasture tend to make paths?" And then he drove on, whistling, leaving Kluntz with his lower lip protruding with snuff, his eyes protruding with bewilderment.

CHAPTER 5

With the coming of another season of farming, Gabe and Blaze were full of joyful anticipation. The school year had been cut short so that the oblates could continue to renovate the buildings and develop the farm land. With the coming of Hasse, Gabe had found a sympathetic ear for his schemes of making monastic life profitable. Although he may not have used the same words, Ed Hasse understood what Gabe considered the "metaphysical nature" of making money. If one were blessed by God and intelligence, one could make money despite the vow of poverty, not for financial profit, not out of love of filthy lucre or even out of need for it, but simply for the sheer spiritual enrichment that greedy people would attain when separated from some of their cash. In this way, the Lord's chosen could teach weak human beings how to suffer a little and thereby build their characters. It was no different from exercising one's ability at playing baseball in order to teach other players how to accept defeat graciously and thereby learn humility. Gabe assured Blaze that Hasse agreed with that kind of logic even if he did not express it with those words. Together they could pursue money as a holy grail, a way to inculcate virtue in the greedy and make the world a better place.

"In other words, since rich men have a harder time getting to heaven than a camel through the eye of a needle, the way to save them is to take their money away from them," Blaze said, delighted with that kind of logic.

"Wellll, yes."

"Did it ever occur to you that always thinking about making money might be a mental disorder?"

Gabe sniffed. He had to live in a world of do-gooders like Blaze who were blind to reality. It was up to a few saintly entrepreneurs to ignore the accusations of greed heaped upon them and save mankind in spite of itself.

Presented with an opportunity to exercise his money-making missionary zeal to do good in the world, Gabe spent his hours of meditation in chapel (when he could not escape it) trying to figure out how to turn the Josephian farm into a profit center. He would drain that part of the swamp that was underlain with super-rich soil and grow high value truck crops on it. He would turn the undrainable part into a trout and watercress farm. If he could lure rich old Hasse into helping fund the project while keeping all the profit for the Josephians, so much the better. Here was a challenge far more interesting than the mystifications of Thomas Aquinas. Here was religion made practical. Why alienate and confuse people with all that crap about hylomorphism. Turn them to God by practical lessons, like how to make farming profitable.

His first move was to talk Prior Robert into allowing the seminarians, especially himself, Blaze and Fen of course, to help Hasse through the rest of the haying season. It appeared that Prior Robert could be talked into just about anything that might promise a pious result. In this case, Gabe spoke glowingly about how the oblates needed to mind their public relations. If the Josephians helped out their neighbors in need, farmers would be less inclined to view them as one more competitor producing too much grain and meat and so driving down farm prices. Helping neighbors in need might even soften the hearts of the rich landowners and incline them to contribute money to the future of the Josephians.

Gabe did not mention his whole plot to Prior Robert. The real reason he wanted to spend as much time around Hasse as possible, was to learn a lot about farming in a hurry. He didn't trust what Blaze told him. Blaze did not know a damn thing about making money. His father had gone broke at farming. Hasse was the man to listen to. To prepare himself to become an apt student, Gabe read studiously from the *Yearbooks of Agriculture* that had somehow found their way into the seminary library, as well as the *University of Minnesota Agronomy Guide*, and a complete run of *Farm Journal* magazines from 1925 to 1951 that he had reclaimed from the local junkyard. He and Blaze had gone there with Brother Walt to sell as wastepaper half a truck load of old *Sacred Heart Messengers*, *Catholicism Todays*, and *Our Lady of Fatima Newsletters* which Fr. Rowan, the librarian, wanted to get rid of because they were taking up space in the library he needed for books about theology and philosophy. Trading them for the farm magazines amused Blaze. "When historians look back," he joked to Gabe, "this seemingly trivial little trade will be remembered as the first symbolic sign of our takeover of the Church." Gabe did not ask him what that was supposed to mean. To live with Blaze, a person had to understand that it was not possible to understand him.

Hasse, being informed of the trade of magazines, told Gabe that *Farm Journal* was, in terms of belief in myths, in the same general category with *The Sacred Heart Messenger*, only on different subjects. "You can't believe all that agribusiness bullshit that farm magazines print," he said. Gabe, taken aback by this first showing of the real Hasse, let that remark slide by unchallenged for the moment, making a mental note to teach Hasse a little practical theology, if not agriculture, at an opportune time. The second thing Hasse told him was how to stack bales on a wagon so that they would not slide off when negotiating steep hillsides. As might be expected from a man of his nature, Gabe no sooner learned the skill involved than he discovered what he thought was a better way to do it and thereby lost a whole load when it slid off the wagon and tumbled down a hill. Brother Walt, who had been drawn into Gabe's schemes whether he wanted to or not, watched the bales go end over end down a slope that should never have been cultivated in the first place. "Mighty lucky they ain't them new round bales or they'd roll right off the edge of this farm and end up in the river."

At the very first chance, Gabe attempted a studious discussion of agriculture with Hasse.

"My plan is to build a herd of purebred Holsteins using Rag Apple Curtiss bulls for artificial breeding," he said, spooning huge helpings of food from Mrs. Hasse's steaming bowls that she pressed unctiously on him, pleased to have a man of God in her house for a change.

"Be better off to buy cheap three-titters that give a lot of milk," Hasse grunted, "and run a bull with them so they all get bred before next Christmas. Artificial insemination ain't what it's cracked up to be."

Loretta Hasse glared at her husband. Three-titters and breeding bulls were subjects she would prefer not be discussed at her table.

A second attempt at agricultural education ended as abruptly when Hasse allowed that he would not pay out good money to have his soil tested for trace elements because he grew all the corn, oats and hay he needed and he did not much care if the manganese content was where the university thought it should be or not. "All dat advice is ladled out chust to make a farmer spend money," he said.

Hasse looked forward to having the Josephians around because he wanted to argue religion. To prepare himself, he read at his wife's Bible when she wasn't watching and dipped into a tome called *A Book of Christian Homiles For Everyday Meditation* that Loretta had brought into the house. Conversations with Gabe about religion took on a certain strange similarity to their conversations about farming.

"Vel, if Lucifer was da first devil, who tempted him?" Hasse said to start their third day working together.

"Lucifer was tempted by his own pride. You don't need to have a devil around to blame for everything that goes wrong," Gabe replied.

He cared little about the fine points of religion, but he felt obliged to defend his calling in life.

"Den vhy do you haf devils at all? Dere is more dan enough pride and lust and greed around to explain all the bad t'ings that happen. Why inwent devils?"

"Satan is right there in the Bible. Nobody inwented him."

"Well, maybe da feller who wrote the Bible inwented him like all dat nonsense about Noah's Ark."

"The Bible is not always to be taken literally," Gabe said with righteous exasperation. "Sometimes it has an allegorical meaning."

"Heh? What's that?"

"The words sometimes should be taken in a figurative sense."

"Hah!" Hasse crowed triumphantly, socking his hay hook into a bale. "How can you say what is alleygoretical and what ain't?"

Realization flooded Gabe's mind. The wily old bastard had set him up. He glared. The gauntlet was thrown. If Hasse wanted to argue religion, then by God, he'd oblige.

Blaze tried at first not to laugh at the two adversaries, but by the end of the first week, his restraint in that regard abandoned him completely, and tears would come into his eyes as he giggled wildly at them. So perfect did the debate between the wily farmer and the wily Gabe mirror Blaze's own doubts about most theories, theological and agricultural, that for once he was not tempted to inject his own thoughts into the fray. Every evening, back at the seminary, he would regale the other SBDC Boys with the day's conversations, and then put it all down in his diary. Never had farming been so much fun.

Hasse, after being sandbagged by Gabe's habit of quoting various Church authorities to support his contentions, went to the library to look for appropriate authoritive support for his arguments too. After all, he knew his way around books, at least a little. In his younger years, when he believed logic ruled the way people thought, he had wanted to understand how his wife could accept her religious doctrines so unquestioningly. He had spent considerable time among the tomes of philosophy and theology. So now he dipped briefly into Kirkegaard, Tillich and Aquinas, looking for quotes that would turn Gabe's arguments on end. Thereafter, debate took the form of even stranger repartee.

"Oblate, even your own Thomas Aquinas says you can't prove that the world had a beginning. You have to accept it on faith. You know dat?"

Gabe didn't know that, but he did not let on. He did not want to go in that direction either. After a short pause, he replied, "Hasse, if you'd have your soil tested, so you could maintain better nutrient balance, you could raise better crops at less cost."

"And dat Tillich feller, he really agrees with me. He says God exists in your head, not out dere in the clouds someplace."

"And if you used herbicides, you'd save a lot of time and not open the soil to erosion with all that row cultivation."

"Yeah? If your experts know so much, how come they ain't farmin'?"

"And just because your fancy philosophers write books, doesn't mean they're saving their souls either."

Haymaking gave way to wheat and oat harvests. Gabe and Blaze joined the neighborhood farmers, following the thresher from farm to farm, growing daily more dark-skinned from the sun and more muscular from the work. They went to great pains pointing out to the Prior that becoming part of the communal harvest was the cheapest way for the seminary to get its own oat crop harvested. Whether Gabe continued to work in order to learn more about farming, or simply to argue with Hasse, even he was not sure. Blaze stayed on because he thought the two debaters, with Kluntz occasionally joining in, provided a show funnier than the Marx Brothers. But more than that, he was for once content with his life, going forth by day to meaningful work, able to retreat at night to the security of the seminary. But what made that experience singularly precious to him was his realization that the farming he was partaking in was passing out of history, just as was the kind of monastic life he was almost living. Communal threshing had ended in Ohio when he was a boy, except in the Amish communities, and it would end here in Minnesota, soon as more and more farmers bought their own grain harvesters. Monastic life was also declining everywhere. How many young people of the future would be daft enough to accept a life of poverty, chastity and obedience? Blaze realized that he was standing at an important juncture between past and future time. That realization tinged his peace with sadness, but it was the kind of bittersweet sadness that appealed to him. He thought that he ought to write something some day about how by an accident of history he was the only person in the world to be both farmer and monk at the precise time when farmer and monk were passing away before his very eyes. It was like being lucky or unlucky enough to watch the last dinosaur roll over and die, knowing it was the last dinosaur.

Blaze could see the signs. The Josephian leaders were talking about sending their oblates out from the enclaves of religious community to become educated at, and to teach in, more worldly universities. This change would keep the Order from becoming irrelevant and obsolete in modern times, so the younger Josephians argued. The same kind of thinking affected rural life. Farmers were becoming irrelevant and obsolete, like monks, forced off the land by financial competition. Their only hope, stated the high priests of economics, was to "go to town and get a job" so that the land could be consolidated into large, profitable "units" of production. As Kluntz complained, "Pretty soon the farmers left won't have any neighbors."

Blaze's father had been one who went to town and got a job. He sold the farm to pay off the debts he had incurred on it, and was thought to be better off for the move, although he never once said so himself. Now, when he, by force of habit, launched into a conversation about farming, he would suddenly stop, remembering that he was no longer involved, and stare silently into the distance. Away in the seminary,

Blaze was left without a home to come home to. That was the real reason he was loathe to leave the seminary. Whatever its drawbacks for him, the Order provided a secure haven, a home.

But for how long, he asked himself desperately. If the oblates were going off to universities, that would be the end of the secure haven. Then they would be truly homeless, like those salesmen who travelled endlessly in search of money; bums with briefcases. Blaze suddenly wished he had joined the Benedictines, the ones who took a vow of stability, a vow to stay home.

He listened with keen enjoyment but with no support for either side, while Gabe and Hasse argued devils and eternal hellfire, which Gabe acknowledged, and whether chemical fertilizers were better than manure, which Hasse denied. Over the grain thresher's hum, they shouted purgatory and limbo, which Hasse ridiculed, with occasional digressions like whether oats, if used in proper proportion with corn, was just as valuable a feed as corn, which Gabe doubted exceedingly. They wrangled predestination and divine grace as they filled siloes with corn. While hauling the manure out of Hasse's barn, they dissected the theological proofs for the existence of God as well as the claimed nutrient value of high-moisture corn. Whether Gabe stood high on his tractor and hurled verbal thunderbolts with the sublimity of Zeus, or whether Hasse, hunched against the barn wall, spoke in his thickest old-country accent, neither gave an inch to the other's tenets. Old-time religion was good enough for Gabe and old-time farming was good enough for Hasse.

Kluntz, who found excuses to show up at Hasse's barn almost as often as he showed up at his own, grew more and more distraught. By August he had all but forsaken his own farm to follow as a disciple of both God and mammon. Alone with Hasse, he could cleverly disclose what he thought were gaping inconsistencies in Christian thought; cornered by Gabe, he would not only renounce Hasse and the devil but even the issues of the new *Playboy* magazine he kept hidden on a beam in his barn beside his bottle of Old Grandad. When all three were together, he delivered his oration on gumbo and religion. It became an obsession with him. One rainy day, he even scurried down into the flats, scooped up a handful of wet gumbo, brought it back and plastered it on Gabe's boot.

"There, by God!" he roared. "Just try to get it off in less than five kicks!" Gabe stared at him in astonishment. He kicked. Sure enough, the glob did not let go until the fifth try. That mystified Gabe into silence for a whole afternoon, and Kluntz felt he had done theology a noble service.

CHAPTER 6

Melonhead's enthusiasm for do-it-yourself medicine, sparked by The Cure, flowered through the summer days. He set up a makeshift laboratory in the old building that had once been the milkhouse next to the barn and began investigating, among other home remedies, the springs of sulfur and iron water that in Mudpura days had been captured in picturesque round stone wells along the edge of the swampland behind the main building. He mixed the two waters in varying combinations, hoping to retain the bowel-cleansing attributes of the sulfur water while masking its rotten-egg taste with the pure-tasting iron water. Gabe figured that they could call the stuff Ascension Mineral Water and sell it for three dollars a bottle. Fen suggested that on the label after the name, a phrase should be added: "Ascend to the highest heavens of good health."

"This place looks like a medieval alchemist's study," Blaze observed, staring in wonder at the bottles and carboys and jugs and test tubes and hotplates that Melonhead had collected. "What's this pill bottle of white shit?"

"You are looking at the cure for cancer that will make me as famous as Mendel," Melonhead replied without taking his eyes off a pan of jewel-weed stems he was boiling. "He was a monk, you know. That white shit, as you call it, is milkweed juice. My theory is that it will cure skin cancers. All I hafta do is figure out a way to squeeze the stuff out of the plants in quantity. Took me all afternoon to get that much."

"Why will milkweed juice cure cancer?"

"Folk medicine says it will take off warts. I tried it and it worked. If warts, why not cancer?"

Shaking his head, Blaze walked next door into the main barn to start the evening milking. Everyone was crazy, he said to himself once again, but some, like Melonhead, were crazier than most.

But Blaze was working on an idea that would have struck Melonhead as crazier than the milkweed juice cure. Blaze's idea had begun to take shape when Walt purchased a used tractor that had the name, "Farm Zephyr," painted in silver on its red hood. Blaze, who had been around farm tractors all of his growing-up years, had never heard of a Farm Zephyr before. Walt had bought it because it was cheap. He soon discovered why. Though it reputedly had the horsepower to pull a three-bottom plow, it could barely manage a two-bottom one in the lowest gear. It was a curious affair, with, so the dealer had said, a Buick motor and an Oldsmobile transmission. Nobody seemed to know what company had actually produced it, but Walt joked that it must have been an auto theft ring, using parts from stolen General Motors trucks. Its strong point was that it could maintain a speed of 40 mph on the open road. With the front wheels together, tricycle style, it was extremely dangerous at that speed. Turning the front wheels sharply might flip the tractor end over end or simply snap the front axle post from the frame.

But Blaze and Walt loved the Farm Zephyr. They would take it out on the highway and wait for an old car or pickup to sputter by at 30 mph. Then they'd yank the gas lever on the Zephyr wide open and pass the slower vehicle with a blare of the Farm Zephyr's horn. This stunt never failed to jerk the other vehicle's driver bolt upright in fright and amazement and send Blaze and Walt into whoops of laughter.

And the Zephyr gave Blaze his grand idea. No seminarian was allowed to use the truck or the community cars without permission, and even Prior Robert was not going to allow him to go driving off without some very good reason. Going to the Western Range would hardly do it. And Blaze did not yet have a Minnesota driver's license. He complained that both Church and State were working against him. But now he saw a way to outwit both God and Mammon. He could drive the tractor without either the State's or the Church's permission. Aha! Since the Zephyr could cruise along at 40 mph, he could get all the way over to the Western Range in half an hour, to continue his theological research into the Second Coming of Frank James. If he pulled the farm trailer behind the tractor, he could say, if that creep, Abelard, spied him on the road, that he was going to the farm supply store after protein supplement for the livestock. He waited now only for a proper time to make his first foray into Frank James territory. He had to bide his time. All things come to him who waits.

Ed Hasse stuck his head in the barn door with a cheery greeting, but then turned around and entered Melonhead's lab. He, of all people, did not think that Melonhead was crazy. Or if he did, he also thought that there might be some opportunity in this craziness that had not as yet made itself evident. Even if not, there was little in his life by way of diversion, tied as he was to milking morning and evening no matter what. Compared to the languidness of his cows, not to mention his wife, the antics of the Josephians were marvelously entertaining. It was like living next to a circus. In fact, he had purchased most of Melonhead's lab equipment so that he had an excuse to drop by whenever he felt like it.

"Do you really think dat mineral water is good for you?" he asked Melonhead.

"If you don't think so, kind sir, drink a bottle of it sometime," Gabe said before Melonhead could reply. "I guarantee you that you will stick pretty close to the bathroom for a day or so."

Melonhead explained. "I can tone down the sulfur taste with the iron water and control just about how far from the bathroom you dare to wander after you've taken a good dose. And the iron is good for you too. Food from today's chemically enriched farm fields lacks minerals like iron, Louis Bromfield says."

Hasse did not know who Louis Bromfield was or if that claim were true, but he more or less supported Melonhead's belief in what was being called "organic" farming. He had leafed through *Organic Gardening and Farming* magazine and had a notion that those feverish people were commies, but he would take any opportunity to stand against the arrogant know-it-alls of the university who, in his mind, really were commies.

"Do you t'ink dat milkweed juice would squeeze out if we ran da plants through a roller mill?"

"Would you quit talking as if you just came over from the old country?" Gabe replied drily. "Why don't you try it?"

Hasse did not answer, but he knew where there was a mighty stand of milkweeds that he wanted to get rid of without spending money on herbicides.

Meanwhile, on the outskirts of Shakopee across the river from the seminary, a solitary figure hiding out in a crumbling vault of a long-abandoned brewery was about to collide with Melonhead's alchemy in ways no one, even the worldly wise Hasse, could have predicted. Axel Barnt sat on a makeshift chair he had assembled out of bricks from the crumbling vault wall and watched the fire under his moonshine still. The floor was strewn with hundreds of old beer bottles stamped "Rolling River," indicating that the vault must have been used for commercial beer storage sometime in the dim past. Axel's mind was not on his distilling, however, or even on the beer bottles which he thought might someday make him rich at five bucks each from bottle collectors. As had almost always been the case for months now, he was thinking about the man he had seen in his headlights running nekkid across the highway in front of the monastery last year. Up until that incident, Axel Barnt had led an amazingly humdrum life, considering his career as a moonshiner. Since his old cattle truck had a top speed of barely 35 mph, he had plenty of time to observe the strange sight of the nekkid man, and there was absolutely no doubt in his mind of what he had seen until the figure had disappeared into the darkness. Then he began to wonder. “By God, I’ve been drinking too much moonshine,” he had said out loud, used to talking to himself.

From that night on, he had brooded over the incident, going out of his way to drive past Ascension Seminary whenever he could think of an excuse to go that way and even when he couldn’t. First, he drove in daylight to look the place over, but observed nothing strange except two lunatics on an old tractor passing him at a tremendous speed. He eventually decided that he was hardly going to see a nekkid monk in broad daylight, if, indeed, that was what he had seen. So for a month, he made a nightly trip past the place. Nothing.

Now, as he watched the mercury rise in the thermometer on the still, he once more ran mentally through the possibilities. Perhaps he had seen not a monk, but a vampire. What if he had encountered an alien from a UFO? He had seen UFOs land down by the river more than once. What if he had seen a streaker who just happened to be in the vicinity of the seminary? What if the nekkid man were fleeing an angry husband who came home early? What if the phantom he had seen was a wild creature, like a Big Foot? What if, and this was the most troubling “what if” of all, he had only imagined the sight, and if so, why had he not imagined a nekkid woman which would have been more to his liking? Maybe the creature was a woman. He could not really tell, although whatever it was, it ran like a man. Women ran like Holstein cows, with their knees turned in and their feet splaying out.

The still demanded his attention. The first drippings were coming out of the cooling coils and he jumped up to make sure they did not go into the savings jug sitting under the coil spout. He once knew a man who had gone blind drinking the first stuff out of the coils. He did not test the purity of the liquor, however, mostly because he did not have a hydrometer and did not even know there was such a thing. He let the spout drip for the length of time that, from long experience, he knew was sufficient. Then he replaced the jug under the spout. He would watch the temperature gauge now. When the distilled alcohol rising from the corn and sugar mash reached about 195 degrees F., and the level of liquor in the jug reached the height he wanted, he would quit saving the clear white liquid and throw the rest away. He did not intend to do a third run through the still to get really good whiskey. His customers were not that choosy.

Then he went back to his ponderings. Since it appeared that two other figures with clothes on had been chasing the nekkid one, perhaps one of the monks had simply gone crazy and gotten loose from wherever he was kept and the others were trying to catch him. But if so, did they catch him? If not, where had he gone? If there had been a nekkid man hiding in the swamps, dead or alive, Axel Barnt would have known it. Nothing escaped his notice in the swamps on either side of the river, five miles up or down the river from Shakopee. He made a show of running trap lines throughout this area, but was really checking his moonshine aging in various stashes he cleverly placed inside old muskrat lodges in the swamps. He had enough hooch hidden there to keep him in cash for a year or two in case his still ever got raided.

Axel Barnt never did anything fast, except make whiskey, so now after weeks of turning over the question of the nekkid man in his mind, he knew that he would have to visit the monastery, which he pronounced moNASStry, and find out, if he could, what was going on there. He would stop at the barn where he had seen the monks at work although they did not look much like monks to him. He could pretend he wanted to buy or sell livestock. That's what he did anyway, as a front for his moonshine business.

Melonhead and Gabe were busy in their laboratory, studying a mat of swamp peat that they had dried. The matted peat appeared to be cohesive enough to use as a poultice. A dozen little squares, cut four by four inches, ought to sell for a dollar a box anyway, Gabe thought. Concentrating on their latest brainstorm, they did not notice the figure standing in the doorway until it cleared its throat. It hardly looked human, but must have been because animals do not go in for throat-clearing.

"Howdy," the figure said. "I'm Axel Barnt. I'm a cattle buyer. I live across the river, over by Shakopee."

The man was wearing a leather apron, the kind favored by horseshoers of an earlier age, strange garb to all those who did not know how protective it could be when working around a hot still. The apron was open at the back, revealing a worn pair of corduroy pants. A brown wad of what looked liked dead leaves stuck out the rear pocket. Above the apron, the creature wore a dirty flannel shirt, the pocket of which held a pen and notepad, which seemed equally incongruous to anyone who did not know that a livestock and moonshine trader needed to keep track of the numerous transactions in which he was involved. His face was so bearded as to completely hide it from inspection and his head was covered by a crumpled felt hat. He wore glasses with round and oversized lenses, which had the effect, along with the bristly, bedraggled facial hair, of making him look like an owl.

Gabe and Melonhead recovered enough to nod a greeting while wondering how they could get around him and out the door, should he attack.

"Yep. I buy cattle," Axel said again, stretching the words out to make them last longer, not knowing what else to say.

"We don't have anything for sale at the moment," Gabe said, hastily. Axel, having expended all the bravado he could sum up, nodded and started to leave.

"But why don't you wait a sec until the farm manager gets here," Gabe continued, suddenly realizing that he might be overlooking a very interesting opportunity. Axel turned back and stared queerly around the room. The shelves and tables filled with Melonhead's various incantations reminded him of making liquor. He looked questioningly at the seminarians.

"We're, ah, trying to learn something about herbal medicine," Melonhead explained.

"So," Barnt said. He examined a bottle of greenish liquid. "Smells like jimson weed."

"That's exactly right," Melonhead blurted, surprised.

"So. Jewelweed's better for pizzen ivy," Barnt said.

"Is that so?" Melonhead said, warming up to the bony old man.

"So. Actually, first drippin's of new moonshine is better'n either." Axel bit his lip. He had not intended to let that slip out.

"How do you know that?" Gabe asked, his intellectual antennae rising almost visibly from his head.

"My ole man knew all kinda things," Axel said, shrugging off the question. "So. You sure you don't have no cattle to sell? Lookin' for a good cow?" He fished what looked like a dead leaf out of his back pocket and from somewhere under the apron drew out a tobacco pipe. As the two seminarians gazed in awe, he crumpled the brown leaf into the bowl, struck a match and puffed away.

Gabe stuck his head out the door and yelled toward the barn. "Blaze, come here." This was going to be another Precious Moment, he was sure. "I take it that's tobacco you're smoking?" he asked, turning back to Barnt.

"So. Don't think it's maryjane, do ya?" Axel said, a little huffily.

"Where do you get your tobacco?" Gabe continued, giving Blaze, who had just entered, the look that meant something important was going on.

"Well, I growed it. Where do ya think I got it." These monks were nosy bastards.

"Grow tobacco in Minnesota?" Blaze chimed in, doubt in his voice. He thought of his days of gathering cigarette butts.

"So. They grow lots of it over in Wisconsin. It grows here too. Not so good but good enough for me."

"This man's a cattle buyer," Gabe said to Blaze, but never taking his fascinated gaze off Barnt. "He knows all kinds of herbal stuff. And he lives across the river outta Shakopee."

Blaze wasted no time. "You know the Western Range?"

"So," nodded Axel readily. He was about to add that he frequented the place but thought better of it, since it was one of his moonshine drop offs. "But I don't go in there much."

"Know a guy they call Jesse James?"

"So." Axel grinned for the first time, revealing almost perfect teeth, exactly the opposite of what Dr. Melonhead would have guessed. "Jesse's not wrapped too tight."

"Has he ever been known to do anything, like, illegal, like stealing anything?"

Barnt went on guard. Who were these guys anyway, ATF agents? They asked too goddam many questions. "Naw, Jesse's harmless. If he drinks alcohol he gets so sober he's boring. Why you ask?"

"Oh, just wondering. Say, I think we can do some cattle business with you," Blaze said, glancing at Gabe with the look that meant he was to go along with whatever Blaze said. "We need another cow. Let's talk about it when the farm manager gets here."

Axel pulled his notepad officiously from his pocket and pretended to study it intently. Some of it was in code. He never dealt in goats which he thought despicable animals because he had seen bucks suck their own peezils, for God's sake, so every reference to goats or kids in his notepad meant quarts or pints of whiskey. "Ah, yes, it so happens I do know where I can get you a mighty fine cow," he said, although no such notation appeared on the page he was staring at.

So began a relationship that neither the seminarians nor Barnt wanted to end. Axel found a cow for the Josephians and took their old bull in trade. He lost a little on the swap, but it gave him an excuse to return to the seminary. Sooner or later, evidence of the nekkid man would surface. The Josephians now needed another bull, and Axel knew just where to get one. After that, Blaze and Gabe talked Brother Walt into believing that they needed to be fattening a few more feeder pigs and Axel knew just where to get them too. Then they decided that Axel should find them a heifer calf, because the dairy herd wasn't increasing in numbers fast enough on its own to suit Gabe. Little by little, Axel became enchanted with the SBDC Boys and became a fixture at the barn, like Hasse and Kluntz. One morning Walt found him in the lab, sleeping off a bout with his moonshine. Walt knew because the snoring Barnt still clutched a bottle containing fluid as clear as water and heavy with the smell of alcohol.

"Axel, where are you getting that whiskey?" Walt asked when he had roused him. "That ain't bought stuff, and we both know it."

"It's none of your damn business," Axel said. "You guys is the nosiest things I ever seen. I bought it from an old river rat up by Minneapolis."

"You're lying, Axel Barnt," Gabe said, bearing down on the poor man. "A guy who'll make his own smokes is surely making his own drinks too."

"So, you got secrets. I got secrets," Axel retorted, more or less awake now. "How about that man I seen running nekkid up the highway outside this barn one night?"

Blaze's mouth gaped. "W-What are you talking about." But his face betrayed his pretense of ignorance. Barnt pressed his advantage.

"So. Here you guys are askin' me questions all the time and I axed you one, and you don't have no answer. So. What do you know about that nekkid man. He one of yourn?"

Blaze broke into laughter, and the others joined in. They summoned Melonhead because it was really his story, and hunkering down on milk stools and straw bales behind the cows, they hooted and giggled while he told the whole story again. At first Barnt listened in pure amazement, but by story's end, he too was laughing.

"I 'member when those doctor types was runnin' Mudpura. There'd be Packards pull in there half a mile long. This was one fancy place when those rich folks let themselves be wrapped in that goddam swamp mud. And people say *I'm* crazy."

"Thing is, the treatment cured Lukey when he was sick—you haven't met him yet."

"So. I bet some of my moonshine woulda cured him quicker."

And with that admission, Axel told his story. Never know, he was thinking. These guys might become customers. Or go-betweeners. A monastery would be a perfect place for a moonshine distribution center.

"Can I have a taste?" Blaze asked.

"Naw. Let me bring you some good stuff. You need to get started right in moonshine. This here'll rake the skin off your throat."

CHAPTER 7

The theological and agricultural debate between Hasse and Gabe came to a head in early September, when the third cutting of alfafa on all the farms roundabout lay mown, windrowed and ready for baling. With rain threatening, Hasse had his ancient baler in the field early, even though the hay was not quite dry enough for ideal baling. Time was crucial. The hay he was taking in happened to be in a field across the fence from the Josephians' mown hay. To his surprise, Hasse saw that the oblates were not also at work but instead, dressed in their long, flowing black robes, were marching in procession to the fields and singing hymns while the Prior sprinkled holy water generously over the cropland through which he was walking. Hasse, married to a devout Catholic, knew what the monks were doing—observing the ancient ceremony of Ember Days that marked the beginning of each season. One purpose of the Autumn Ember Days in September was to thank God for a good harvest. Amused, he stopped to watch, letting the tractor run at half throttle so that the plunger in the empty bale chamber clanged loudly and irritatingly. Gabe, who was itching to get started on the baling, could not contain himself and left the procession to speak to his godless associate.

"You are belittling the pious practices of worthy men, aren't you, you reprobate," he began by way of greeting.

"You don't need to t'row water on dat hay," the old farmer replied, glancing at the clouds. "It's soon going to get plenty wet straight from God."

"God protects those who trust in Him," Gabe countered before he could think better of his words.

"You saying God's not going to let it rain on your windrows?" Hasse shot back in a tone heavy with dark intent.

Damn him, Gabe thought. He's got me again. Out loud he replied righteously: "You ought to read a little. Meditate sometime on something besides money. 'Observe the lilies of the field, neither do they spin nor weave . . .'" he let the quotation hang in mid-air, unable suddenly to recall the rest of it, and stalked haughtily back to the procession.

The rain held off until Hasse had finished baling and the Josephians, their ceremony of blessing the fields ended, had just filled their first wagonload of hay. Then the skies opened and a downpour quickly rendered the hay still in windrows into a sodden mess unfit for anything except bedding when or if it dried out again. Hasse, his last load safely in the barn, drove his pickup back down the road to where he could watch the fun.

The sight of Hasse infuriated Gabe. His fellow Josephians huddled under the hay wagon gloomily staring at the rain. Blaze was the exception. He was smiling in anticipation of what Hasse would surely say. Gabe stood alone and defiant in the field, in the pouring rain, kicking at a wet bale and railing against his lot in life. Not only did he have to put up with the weather, poor machinery, and inexperienced help, but a flea-brained Prior who held religious ceremonies when there was hay to make. "Laugh," he thundered at Hasse, grinning in his truck cab. "Laugh a hole in your heathen head. But you haven't heard the last of this, I promise."

What he would do, Gabe decided, in the middle of a night in which holy wrath would not let him sleep, was drain the swamp or at least some of it. Hasse said it couldn't be done, so he would do it and shut the stiff-necked heathen up forever.

To that end, Gabe, with the canny power of persuasion he could work so well on Prior Robert, bent the energies of the whole religious community to swamp drainage. Through the swamp between Hasse's land and that of the Josephians, he had a deep ditch dynamited. Then he put twenty seminarians to work with shovels, digging lateral ditches on the Josephian side every fifty feet to drain into the main ditch. The soil dug from the laterals was scattered evenly over the plots between the ditches, raising the level of the land there high and dry with a rich black peaty soil that, freed of water, crumbled into a soft, loamy seed bed.

"Vhat you going to plant dere," Hasse said, trying not to notice the superiority in Gabe's smile.

"Whatever. Have you ever seen such wonderful soil for a swamp that some folks used to say was useless?" Gabe replied. "The ways of the Lord are indeed mysterious. And if you have any decency about you, you'll help pay for the dynamiting since you'll benefit too."

Hasse stomped back to his truck and drove off in a huff. But he still had to put up with Kluntz, who was rapidly losing faith in faithlessness. "I guess he's got you this time," Kluntz spouted at him over a full lip of snuff.

Melonhead had, in the meantime, stumbled upon an interesting concept in his need to justify to the community, especially Prior Robert, the work he was doing. He had come across a book about monastic life that delved in considerable detail into how monks had been pioneers in the fermentation and distillation of alcoholic spirits in the early Middle Ages. To his surprise, the perfection of various liquors, not to mention all kinds of herbal remedies, had been the work of monks seeking medical cures. In fact, monasteries had been the research farms, so to speak, of the Middle Ages, the safe repositories of knowledge during the upheavals of war and plague. It was fitting for Ascension Seminary to continue that great tradition, Melonhead pointed out.

"Think of that, Gabe," Melonhead said, knowing which of the SBDC Boys would respond with the greatest enthusiasm. "With this barn and this lab, we are carrying on the traditional work of the Church. Far from being chastised by pricks like Abs, we should be honored and encouraged. We are really engaged in saving rural culture and safeguarding traditional skills that are being forgotten by modern man. Making medicines, like making food, should be the divine right of the people, not just drug companies."

Gabe stared at him, the full implication of what Melonhead was saying coming only slowly. "Man," he said. "You are a genius." Melonhead's logic not only struck him as being undeniable but gave him the almost perfect way to make the Josephian Order over into something profitable.

"Melonhead, you are a genius," he repeated. "You don't know just how much of a genius." Then he paused. "Is it difficult to make liquor?"

"Axel says that it's easy. Alcohol boils at a lower temperature than water does and that's the whole secret of it."

"But it's against the law."

"Smoking isn't." Blaze was now getting into the discussion.

"Quit changing the subject. What's smoking got to do with it?"

"Well, if we can't sell liquor, we can sell tobacco. And homemade corncob pipes. I've been thinking. Axel grows his own tobacco. I tried smoking some of it, and you know, it really isn't all that bad. Better than cigarette butts. As part of our monastic mission, why don't we experiment with tobacco? My great grandmother always said that nicotine and whiskey in moderation was good medicine and she lived to 97."

All three of them laughed, but it was that kind of laugh that had a dangerously serious undertone to it.

The idea of Ascension becoming a place for alternative agricultural and medicinal research gained momentum. Gabe called a grand meeting of all the SBDC Boys in the laboratory, which they now frequented more than the slaughterhouse. Axel and Hasse were there too, which meant that Kluntz also had tagged along. Blaze joked about making them honorary Josephian lay brothers. Melonhead had his speech prepared. He told the others how religious monks had been responsible for most of the advances in agriculture and medicine and that for the Josephians to do the same was only keeping alive the spirit of Church tradition.

"Did you guys know, for instance, that the liqueur, Benedictine, whatever that is, is a monastery product?" Melonhead continued, warming up now. "Beer may have been brewed scientifically first in monasteries. Monks brought wine-making to California. In improving the process of distilling alcohol, those old monks were seeking a medicine, an elixir, that would prolong life indefinitely. Chartreuse, whatever that is, was concocted in 1605 in a monastery and combines 130 different herbs infused in alcohol. The formula is still a secret kept by three Carthusian monks if you can believe that. Of course no monk has come close to living forever drinking any of their mixtures, but they often do live to a very old age. Isn't eternal life what we are seeking?" He thought that last remark might be carrying his sell a little far, but it came out of his mouth before he could stop it.

"Maybe they just didn't find the right combination yet."

The remark came from Clutch Pedali, to the surprise of everyone in the lab. The Engineer of Ascension rarely joined in the barn escapades of his friends. Madcap was not part of his modis operandi, he liked to say. He had his own agenda. While the faculty and most of the seminarians complained about the freewheeling barn crew, it was Clutch who lived the most independent life of them all. Because he was the one man in the community who understood the secrets of motors and electrical relay switches and thermostats and refrigeration units and light fixtures and television tubes and radiators and fuses, he sat right next to God. He was the man without whom the technological comforts of life at Ascension might fail, a danger to be avoided at all costs. Clutch could therefore live much as he pleased, could come and go from all community functions, even come and go to town, with hardly more than a wave of his hand in the Prior's general direction. He was the keeper of the technological gods and was not to be disturbed.

"So happens I once saw an alcohol still in action," he continued now. "With Axel's help, I think I can build a little stovetop model that would not even look like a still to most people."

"So. I'll be glad to help ya," Axel said, grinning broadly.

"Axel, I can't help noticing," Dr. Melonhead interrupted. "You have beautiful teeth. Could that come from moonshine?"

"Nope. I chew road tar."

"Whaaaat?"

"Try it. Cleans teeth better'n anything."

Gabe made a notation. He had taken to carrying a notepad, like Axel. There were just too many wonderful ideas afloat to keep them all in mind.

"But it's against the law to distill liquor," Fen said again. Fen was not a man to enjoy risk. Only a strong sense of loyalty, his great weakness, kept him attached to the escapades of the SBDC Boys. He lived in fear of what trouble he might incur because of them.

"I've thought about that," Melonhead said. "We're not going to make liquor. Just medicine. Remember Hadacol? That had alcohol in it."

"And it was very profitable," Gabe added.

"But how are we going to keep the priests from knowing what we're up to?"

"We'll just explain that we are steaming herbs for tinctures and teas, which will be true, sort of," Melonhead replied.

Clutch snorted. "The typical Josephian doesn't even know what a dead fuse looks like, let alone a still," he said derisively. "You can tell 'em anything and they'll believe it. Remember how for awhile Very Reverend Lukey believed that a manure spreader was a marshmallow picker?"

CHAPTER 8

With the summer over and building construction ahead of schedule, philosophy and theology classes resumed in greater earnest, much to the chagrin of most of the SBDC Boys. They had a full schedule already. With the feverish activity in the laboratory at full throttle, and the crops to bring in, Blaze was having a difficult time finding an afternoon when he could slip away to learn the truth about the train robber and how Jesse James had known his name. Gabe had lost interest in phantom outlaws as he pored over manuals about tobacco farming, homemade cigars, making herbal liqueurs, mixing sugar into his road tar toothpaste so it didn't taste so bad, and trying to figure out a fast way to bunch and tie watercress for market. To complicate matters further, Brother Walt had persuaded the Prior to rent another farm since the seminary land was proving woefully inadequate to produce all the food needed, or so Brother Walt had argued. The farm he rented just happened to belong to Hasse who, for reasons of his own need for cheap labor, had offered it to the Josephians at a fairly low rate. With the increase in farm work, Gabe prevailed upon Prior Robert to assign Melonhead to the farm crew. That made it easier to continue the herbal medicine explorations that would bring Ascension back to the future.

Clutch of course continued his work in the lab, despite the increasing demands of the classroom. He had only to speak with consternation to Prior Robert about how the barn needed electrical re-wiring and as a result he could spend all the time he wished working on the still, which he described to those outside the SBDC circle as a high output churn to make homemade butter.

But finally a Saturday came when Blaze could sneak away. The priests had all left for weekend duty in nearby parishes, except Fr. Damien, whose turn it was to stay at the seminary and keep an eye on the seminarians. This was the break Blaze had been waiting for. Damien, a teacher and student of languages, was translating into English a rare book written in Hebrew and did not care what the seminarians did, so long as they did not bother him. Blaze fired up the Zephyr and headed for the Western Range, singing "Ghost Riders In the Sky" at the top of his voice.

He sidled his trusty steel steed up beside an old dappled-grey horse in front of the restaurant. He wondered if he might not be the first person in the history of the west not only to play the dual roles of farmer and monk, but to park a tractor at a hitching rail, next to a horse. "This goes in the journal for sure," he said, even though there was no one around to hear him.

He stepped into the saloon and, looking neither to right nor left, went straight to the bar. He was worldly wise now, not the fledgling out on his first attempt at bar-hopping as he had been last summer. Nash Patroux, never forgetting a face or a name, nodded. "'lo, Jack. A Royal, I believe."

"Yep," Blaze said, eyeing himself in the mirror behind the bar, liking the jaunty young man he saw there with his cowboy hat pushed back on his head. Jesse James was seated at the end stool, as he had been on the first visit. Blaze would act cool this time. He merely nodded at Jesse and sipped his beer. Patroux, behind the bar and bored as usual, winked at Blaze and turned toward Jesse.

"How come you ran out on this young man last time, Jesse? That was a little rude you know."

"Pinkerton," Jesse said, not even looking up.

"Whaaaat?"

"He's a Pinkerton," Jesse repeated, grinning goofily now, enjoying the surprise he had evoked. It was usually difficult to surprise his pal Nash, goddam him.

"Naw, he's no Pinkerton," said Patroux. "You know how you can tell? He doesn't have a watch on a chain. All those Pinkertons got gold watches in their vest pockets. This guy hasn't even got a vest."

Jesse kept grinning. Damn, that's right. Out loud: "I jus' foolin' round."

"I didn't think there were any Pinkertons around anymore," Blaze said, trying to sound serious.

"Ho, they'd like for you to think that," Jesse said. "They're lurkin' around everywhere. They still think Frank is alive somewheres."

"Frank?"

"Yeah. Frank James."

"Ooooh."

"They may be right too. I gotta a letter from Frank. I'm related, you know."

"You're related to the real Frank and Jesse James? Oh, wow."

Patroux remained expressionless. Jesse decided he liked this Jack fellow.

"Sure. I got papers to prove it. You wanna see?"

"I wouldn't mind," Blaze said trying not to sound eager. Things were going better than he had expected.

Jesse finished his cream soda and made for the door, beckoning Blaze with his head. Blaze had to gulp his beer. Outside, Jesse stopped suddenly. There were no cars in the parking lot.

"You come on that tractor, Jack?" he said, staring strangely at Blaze.

"You came on that horse?" Blaze said, trying to mimic Jesse's expression.

"I never heard of comin' to a saloon on a tractor. You must be crazier'n I am."

Jesse forked his horse, wheeled and headed out onto the highway berm. He had to slow down for Blaze because the Zephyr did not start right away. Presently though, farmers and residents all along the country road that Jesse took, less than half a mile down the highway, saw a strange sight: a horse, mane and tail flying, ridden by a somber old man with ponytail flying, being chased by an old tractor travelling at an unusual rate of speed, its young, cowboy-hatted driver laughing hysterically.

After about a mile over the stony, dusty road, Jesse reined the horse and turned into the barnyard of a run-down farmstead. He stepped down out of the saddle and the horse disappeared into the barn on its own. Blaze turned the motor off on the Zephyr, climbed off the tractor and followed Jesse through the screen door into the house. He thought how funny it would be if he were in a movie and the Zephyr would go to the barn on its own too.

"Pap's around here somewhere," Jesse said. "Or maybe he's in town. He pointed at a kitchen chair. "Sit down. I'll be back pronto."

Blaze surveyed the room. It had not been cleaned for a long time. Dirty dishes littered every horizontal plane. The screen door had holes in it, and the ceiling was dotted with flies and flyspecks.

Jesse reappeared with a shoe box; he set it on the table and elaborately lifted the lid. Inside was a jumble of slips of paper and newspaper scraps of different sizes, some folded, all helter-skelter. Jesse looked at Blaze triumphantly, as if the contents of the box proved without any further inspection, that he was related to Jesse James, the outlaw.

Blaze picked out a scrap of paper. On it was written: "G. James, son of P. James, son of F. James. Columbia, Missouri, Feberairy 22, 1942." Another said: "Isaac James ran filling station in Memphis, Tenn. 1937.

And yet another: "Need chicken feed. And Jimmy has clover seed for us." Included in the mix were several newspaper articles about the James Boys, and pictures of Northfield with the main street lined with autos.

Fishing through the shoe box, Jesse finally unearthed a page torn from a spiral notebook and presented it proudly to Blaze. Blaze scanned the page. The handwriting was large, perhaps deliberately, so that a child would have no trouble reading it.

> May 1, 1925
>
> Dear Jesse,
>
> Happy 21st Birthday. Don't pay any attention to folks who make fun of you for saying I am still alive. This letter is proof. Just show it to those buttholes like Nash Patroux. I am well and hiding out in Tennesee. They will never take me alive. Someday I will come and see you.
>
> Until then, here is my old pistol that I used to rob the bank in Northfield. It doesn't work anymore, but will someday be of great value.
>
> Your cousin,
> Frank James

Blaze read the letter a second time. When he glanced up, Jesse's face was glowing with pleasure and importance. Looking into that face, Blaze knew that whoever had written the letter had not done so just to make fun but to give the man pleasure.

"Wow, Jesse, this is great."

"He never did come, though. He'd be too old now, wouldn't he?"

Jesse stared at Blaze, as if hoping that Blaze would disagree. Then his manner changed, swift as an eye-blink.

"Do you think that goddam Nash wrote this to tease me?"

Blaze's head jerked involutarily. God. This guy wasn't really retarded. "Gosh, I don't think so," he replied hastily. "The date is about right. I mean Frank James could easily have been alive in 1925. But today he'd have to be over a hundred. You know there are people who think that his brother Jesse, wasn't killed by Bob Ford, as history says, but died just a few years ago, in 1951. They think they have evidence to support that. He'd have been 104 in 1951 if the birth records are right."

"Mabel Tuggle is over a hunderd and she still grows her own garden. Maybe Frank's still alive."

"If he is, that would be something, wouldn't it." Blaze paused. "Think he could still rob trains?"

Jesse eyed Blaze critically. He had to be careful not to reveal anything that might connect to his attempted train robbery.

"Jesse James dead, Jack. Frank too old if he is alive."

And then he launched into his real problem. What would happen to him when Pap died. He would have no one to take care of him then. "I really don't need any care, but I afraid they'll put me in a home."

Before Blaze could think of anything to say, Jesse started talking about his problems, how some days he could think of just about everything he needed to think of and other days, his mind would not settle, would not concentrate, "will not work," he said with great emphasis. "But I know nearly everyone's license plate," he continued. "If the sheriff stops and wants to know who all passed our house today, I can tell him the numbers. I never forget a number. Ask me anybody's license on this side of Savage."

Blaze did not know anybody on this side of Savage. "I bet you don't know the plate on the truck we came here in the other time."

"34071 OM"

"Oh, wow!"

"The sheriff says that's the truck from that monastery over across the river. You from there, Jack?"

"Oh, my God." There was no use lying. "Yep. I'm from there."

"Maybe I come see you?"

"Sure. Anytime."

Blaze's natural instinct to help people rose within him. And maybe in this way he would eventually get to the truth about the train robber. He could not promise Jesse the kind of help he needed. That would take the cooperation of his Josephian superiors, and he doubted they would give it. He promised anyway. "I'll make sure you don't have to go to a home."

"That's what Nash says, but I dunno. He's a busy man."

"I'll speak to him. But say, do you remember the first time we met. You called me 'Blaze,' remember?"

Jesse stared dully at his new friend. "What you mean? I never called you Blaze."

"Well, you did. You said, 'I gotta see about Blaze. He'll be wonderin' about me.'"

Jesse hooted. "Blaze is my horse. You shoulda figured that out. Blaze is a horse's name."

CHAPTER 9

The school year rolled on, one studious, dutiful week after another. Fr. Damien, the professor who taught Hebrew, finally gave in to the blank, helpless faces staring at him and said that if the seminarians learned how to write the Our Father and Hail Mary in Hebrew correctly or even almost correctly, they would pass the course. Then he looked out the window with a tiny smile and said, as if to himself: "The biblical Hebrew we are studying has not been spoken or written since before the birth of Christ." No one laughed except Blaze.

Even The Very Reverend Lukey was getting bored. His mind turned to other matters for relief. Deep in meditation in chapel, his eyes piously gazing at the crucifix above the altar, he thought that he had figured out why Fr. Abelard had not reported what he had seen in the slaughterhouse on the night of The Cure. Lukey wanted Blaze to hear his theory. He didn't really want Blaze to hear his theory, but he wanted to show the smartass how well he could think.

"You know, Blaze, your mystery about Frank James has given me an idea." They were both sitting in the library, pretending to be studying metaphysics.

"You mean you are finally learning how to think?"

Lukey ignored him. "Why hasn't Abs turned us in for what he saw that night in the slaughterhouse? You know I was hanging there buck naked and that should have raised alarm in the soundest of minds, let alone someone as paranoid as he is."

"Yeah. I thought by now we'd be working out some terrible punishment, like being defrocked." Blaze meant that as a joke since he would have liked nothing better than to be defrocked.

"You hardly ever wear your 'frock' anyway, you heathen," Lukey said. "But here's what I think."

He allowed for a dramatic pause and then continued. "You know how you are beginning to wonder whether the attempted train robbery really did occur?"

"Not me, Lukey. That's you. I know it happened."

"Okay, okay, don't get hot. Let us say that certain types of people would begin to doubt what they had seen if they had seen what we saw. Okay? Now let us say that Abs is that type of doubter. You have to admit that what he saw in the slaughterhouse was bizarre enough to make him wonder whether he really did see what he thought he saw. Now what would make him doubt the sight so much that he would not dare repeat it?"

"I can hardly wait to hear."

"Obviously, my dear Watson, if he could not identify the figures he saw in the slaughterhouse, he would be without proof that he had seen anything, right? My back was to him and I blocked a clear view of you and Melonhead, along with the steam. And he fled almost as soon as he switched on his flashlight. It was just a blur. He doesn't know for sure what he saw."

"Whom he saw."

Lukey ignored that too. "Now go one step farther."

"Further."

"We, or at least some of us, may doubt what we saw on the train, but we still talk about it because, as goofy as it sounds, the sight of Frank James returned to earth does not of itself denigrate our reputations other than that we might be going crazy."

Blaze stared at the ceiling. "Maybe you shouldn't do any thinking after all."

"However, if Abs tells the Prior he thought he saw a naked man floating above him, that's a little more self-revealing than saying you thought you saw somebody robbing a train. Seeing a train robber who might not have been there could be simple hallucination. Seeing a naked man levitating in the air who might not have been there, suggests possible personal mental problems of a sexual nature, does it not? Abs would fear that the Prior would suspect him of something dreadful if Abs could not substantiate what he thought he saw. Now here's the critical point upon which this all turns. What could that dreadful sexual something be? Surely something connected to homosexuality, right? Priest. Thinks. He. Sees. Naked. Man. Floating. In. Air. That has to be homosexual, otherwise he would think he saw a naked woman floating in the air, right? Would it not be logical to reason that Abs himself might suspect that he was only stricken with fantasy, especially if he had indeed entertained such fantasies on other occasions." Lukey paused, puffing up with his own cleverness. "That's why he can't talk about it to anyone, don't you see? It would reveal his own sordid character. That's what's driving him crazy. That's why he's drinking so much."

"Wow, maybe you are learning how to think," Blaze said, almost admiringly. But then he wondered if maybe Lukey was able to construct such a marvelous piece of logic because he entertained homosexual fantasies himself. Hmmm.

"Why don't you test your theory?"

"Whaddaya mean?"

"Go to Abs and pretend you have a sudden provocative interest in him. See how he reacts."

"Oh, I couldn't do that." Lukey answered hastily.

Later, re-thinking the idea, he decided maybe he could, if the right opportunity came along.

CHAPTER 10

Clutch gazed proudly at his masterpiece. Only someone familiar with the distillation of alcohol would recognize the contraption as a still. He had used an old pressure cooker for the boiler. He had removed the top valve and replaced it with a short piece of two-inch copper pipe upon which perched a copper cylinder about four inches in diameter and two feet tall. The cylinder he had filled with porcelain insulators, the kind used to hold electric livestock fence wire in place. Axel said marbles worked better, but Brother Walt made extensive use of electric fence around the farm, so cracked insulators, no longer usable for fencing, were plentiful. From the top of the cannister, a one-inch copper pipe led into an innocent looking five-gallon bucket in the sink next to the table where the boiler sat. Inside the bucket, out of sight, the copper pipe turned into the telltale coil of a homemade condenser spiraling downward and emerging from a hole near the bottom of the bucket.

"You mean that's all there is to it?" Melonhead gasped in wonder.

"Yep. Have to do a bit more soldering. Gotta use silver solder. Lead might contaminate the alcohol, Axel says. Then all we do is put the fermenting grain or fruit into the pressure cooker along with any herbs you want to infuse into the alcohol, and turn on the hot plate. Alcohol boils sooner than water and rises as steam up through the cannister of insulators which is called a stripping column, according to Axel. The insulators act like a whole bunch of little condensation plates and the steam keeps vaporizing and condensing as it passes upwards. The low-quality alcohol keeps falling back into the still for redistillation and the more refined, drinkable stuff goes on out through the cannister and over to the coil in the bucket where the steam condenses back into alcohol and drips out the end. Gotta have cool water going into the bucket all the time. You can set up or dismantle this thing in a minute. But even in operation, it looks innocent enough. You can't see the coil. To the ignorant, distillation will look pretty much like we're canning peaches or something and need to pipe off the steam to keep moisture down in the lab." He paused. "Well, you could say that, anyway."

"You can go to jail for doing this," Fen pointed out once again.

"I think you can only go to jail if you try to sell your hooch," Melonhead said.

"So. No," Axel said when he was asked about that later. "You can't distill alcohol for drinking, whether you sell it or not. Uncle Sam can bust your ass even if you're just a bystander at the still. You can make beer and wine for yourself, but you can't distill liquor unless you pay a fortune for a permit. That's the kind of tyranny we live under in this free country."

"Well, we're just making medicine," Melonhead said, defensively.

"Canon Law does not say anything about distilling alcohol," Blaze observed. "We are merely carrying on monastic tradition. Rendering to God the things that are God's and Caesar can just mind his own damn business."

"The process is just so beeeyoutiful," Gabe kept saying, in rapt joy, ignoring all risks involved. "After you distill a batch, the leftover mash is very nutritious for animal feed, especially if you're doing corn liquor. Could make human food out of it in fact. Make money coming and going. God, it is just beeyoutiful."

Meanwhile the elderberry juice fermenting in a crock under the table that held the still was making the lab smell like a winery. Melonhead had read in an old herbal that elderberries were good for warding off colds. To his way of thinking, fermented elderberries would do the job even better and might make a dandy cough syrup if distilled.

"We gotta get this stuff bottled up before one of the priests comes in here and smells it," he said now.

"I don't think it's ready. It tastes like furniture polish to me," Fen said.

"That's because you're trying to drink it in a barn atmosphere saturated with the odor of cow piss. It's probably absorbing the smell," Brother Walt replied.

"Medicines aren't supposed to taste good," Melonhead added.

"If you hadn't crushed the berries and stems together in that dumb mop squeezer, it might taste better."

"Speed was of the essence," Blaze replied, looking nervously up the lane from the barn to the main building from which the Prior, their very own version of a revenue officer, might appear at any moment.

They racked off their first wine, corked the bottles, and hid them in the hayloft above the cows. "No one needs to catch colds in our community next winter," Melonhead observed proudly.

Four mornings later, when Gabe and Blaze entered the barn to do the milking, they gazed, aghast, at garish purple streaks coursing down the whitewashed walls in front of the cows.

"Oh, shit," Gabe said. "Some of the bottles must have exploded."

"Looks kind of pretty," Blaze said. "Smells kind of pretty too."

"Darn it, for once get serious. We gotta get this cleaned up before anyone sees it."

They raced up the loft stairs and pawed around in the hay for the bottles. Even as they searched, another cork blew out with a muffled firecracker pop down in the bowels of the hay. They finally recovered all ten bottles and poured the liquid remaining in them back into the crock in the lab. Then while Blaze did the milking, Gabe worked furiously to blot out with fresh whitewash the surreal purple paintings on the wall.

"We'll not clean out the gutters behind the cows for awhile," Gabe instructed solemnly. "Maybe the stench of fresh manure will mask the wine smell till it goes away."

"There's enough kerosene wine left for Melonhead to distill some elderberry brandy," Blaze said, and then he scared the cows with one of his patented hyena-like laughs. All was still right in his world.

Fr. Abelard, from his third floor conning tower of the faculty residence, was not so sure all was right in his world. He had overcome his drinking binge and was once again hard at work overseeing all activities at Ascension Seminary. There was entirely too much coming and going at the barn these days. Not just comings and goings of the SBDC Boys either. A man whom he had learned was Ed Hasse regularly stopped by. Another visitor, in an ancient cattle truck, visited even more often, always looking furtively about as if he expected to see something terribly shocking at any moment. A third man, sometimes with Hasse, sometimes alone, stopped regularly too. When a fourth person riding a bony grey horse started showing up, Fr. Abelard knew a closer investigation than he could do with his telescope was in order even if it meant discovering that his experiences in the slaughterhouse really were pure hallucination. When he noticed that Oblate Luke started frequenting the barn, he was particularly intrigued. Oblate Luke was not like the regular SBDC Boys. He even professed disdain for the barn and his classmates on the barn crew. The lad had lately reminded Fr. Abelard of someone whom he could not put into a proper time or place. Something familiar about him, something about the way his trim little butt curved away from his waist. Oh, God, was he gay to think such a thought? He put it out of his mind. But even if Oblate Luke were an occasion of sin, he decided to cozy up to him to see what he could find out.

Clutch Pedali, without realizing it, provided the nearly perfect such occasion. Since Lukey had believed for a few days that a manure spreader was a marshmallow picker, Clutch wondered just how gullible he might be. With a solemn face, the Engineer of Ascension carried a box of spent light bulbs into Lukey's room and asked him if he would take them over to Abs who, said Clutch, had the job of taking old lightbulbs and batteries to town to get them recharged. He did not bother to inform Abs of his little joke, wondering if the priest would go along with it, or even better, if he might be just as naive as Lukey.

Lukey pretended to believe that light bulbs could be recharged. He needed an excuse to talk one-on-one with Abs. When he presented the bulbs to the priest, the latter did not so much as blink. He needed a reason to talk to Lukey. If the kid was daft enough to think that light bulbs could be rejuvenated, he could certainly be tricked into revealing what nefarious schemes were going on in the barn.

Lukey concluded similarly. If Abs were dumb enough to believe light bulbs could be recharged, he would surely be dumb enough to reveal what he thought had happened on the night of The Cure. The two of them played it cool at this meeting, both fairly sure that they could milk the light-bulb maneuver indefinitely. A few days later Lukey stopped at Clutch's room.

"I'm going over to the priests' house with the mail," he said. "Got any more light bulbs to recharge? Abs took the whole bunch you gave me."

Something like perfect joy settled on Clutch's face. He had only four dead bulbs today, but Lukey might as well take them along. "Ask Abs when that last batch is due back."

Lukey knocked timidly on Fr. Abelard's door and the priest greeted him with a marvelously sober (in every way) expression on his face.

"C'mon in," he said warmly. "See you have some more light bulbs for recharging."

"Yes, Father," Lukey said. "Just four today. Last batch back from the recharger yet?"

"Ahhh, no. Haven't been into Shakopee to get them. You are to be commended for your devotion to the vow of poverty. Would that all the oblates were so frugal."

Lukey had intended to say that the bulbs were from Clutch, but if Abs thought the project praiseworthy, it would help his own cause to take full responsibility. He beamed and nodded.

"Sit down, Oblate. How about a beer?"

Lukey looked at him, stunned. For a priest to offer a seminarian a beer in private like this was almost unheard of. Oh, my God, he's going to proposition me, Lukey thought.

"Y-Yeah. Don't mind if I do."

Fr. Abelard opened two Royal Bohemians, gave one to Lukey and eased himself into a chair. He could see that Oblate Luke was extremely nervous about something, which gave Fr. Abelard cool confidence for a change. He would finally have the truth about what the SBDC Boys were up to and what had happened in the slaughterhouse that night if anything did happen. He'd lull this idiot who believed light bulbs could be recharged into a false sense of self-esteem and then draw the truth out of him.

"I notice that you do quite well in class, Oblate Luke. What would you like to do as a priest? Have you thought about that?"

He must be trying to soften me up for the big come-on, Lukey thought. He wanted to be a professor of Scriptural Theology at the Catholic University of America in Washington, but remembering his present purpose, he affected a softness of voice that he thought sounded slightly effeminate and replied, "Oh, I don't know. I'd actually like to be an artist. I like to paint pictures." That was true, but he mentioned it because somewhere he had read that artists are often gay.

"Well, ah, that's a noble goal. I've tried to do some painting myself. I'm not aware that we have any other artists in the Josephians. Do we? Just the two of us?" Lukey's heart was pounding now. If that wasn't a double entendre, what the hell was it? Was there such a thing as a single entendre?

"I'm glad at least that you seem to have chosen a higher road than just working on that farm," Abs continued, jerking his head at the window that looked out towards the barn. "What do you make of your classmates down there grovelling around in the manure. No future in that, is there?"

"Oh, you might be surprised," Lukey said, thinking of the lab. But he immediately regretted his remark. Might get Melonhead in trouble. The vows of poverty, chastity and obedience were as nothing compared to the seminarians' traditional, self-imposed vow of silence to superiors about what other seminarians were doing that might not be permissable. To steer the conversation away from the lab, he added lamely: "But they will probably regret not concentrating on their studies more." Then, almost in panic now, he went back to his original purpose. "I agree with you that the way they carry on with guns is a penis complex."

Abs stared hard at Lukey. Why had the kid brought that up? Freud wouldn't be covered in class until next semester. Abelard regretted having made that observation about firearms and penises. It had irked the Prior, who loved hunting and who did not think much of Freud. At any rate, in present circumstances, making references to penises was not something Fr. Abelard thought he dared to do, Freud or no Freud. Was this little prick trying to patronize him as a teacher? Or was it more than that? Was the little prick trying to seduce him? He'd always wondered if Oblate Luke might be gay. Well, he could play along if that's what it took. He could be super-friendly if it helped to find out what was going on at the barn. "There's something about you that seems familiar in a strange sort of way," he said. "Like in a dream or something. It's like I've seen you in another life or at least in highly unusual circumstances. Could I have seen you someplace before?"

"Before when?" Lukey was holding his breath almost as firmly as he held onto the beer bottle.

"I dunno. Maybe before you came to Ascension. I can't explain this feeling I have about you."

Oh, God, he must be coming on to me, Lukey thought. Or did he suspect that Lukey was the naked satyr hovering in the air of the slaughterhouse and was trying to trick him into admitting something? What the hell am I supposed to do now, he thought desperately. Damn Blaze.

"You seem to be so out of place associating with those boors at the barn," Abs continued.

Oh, God, he *is* coming on to me. Out loud: "Well, they're my classmates. I'm stuck with them whether I like it or not." And then he took the plunge. "I'm sure you like some of the seminarians more than others, just as I like some of the priests more than others. You are my favorite professor."

By God, he *is* coming on to me, the priest thought, aghast. His wide-eyed stare only persuaded Lukey to proceed.

"I just wonder sometimes, if you priests really like any of us seminarians. You all seem so distant, like we are outcasts, even though in just a few years we'll all be priests together. You guys preach love but you show very little of it to us."

Abelard sucked in his breath. What the hell was going on here? He decided he didn't trust this little conniver even if he did have a cute butt. He made a U-turn in the conversation. "Actually, I worry about some of your classmates becoming priests. That Oblate Blaise in particular. He is so irreverent."

"Oh, that's just a front," Lukey said. He did not really want to defend the smartass, but he was so nervous that he could not think of anything to say except the truth as he saw it. "Blaze really isn't all that bad when you get to know him. He's very serious about wanting to help people. He can be a sucker about it, like that—" He stopped short, realizing he was headed somewhere he shouldn't go.

"Like what, Oblate?"

It wouldn't hurt to reveal something innocent. Besides, the beer was soaking away his caution. "Do you know that guy who rides the horse?"

"Well, I see him down there, yes. It kind of makes me curious."

"He's actually mentally retarded. Lives with his father across the river. I don't know how he got started coming here on his horse, but Blaze pays him lots of attention. Really nice to him. So he likes Blaze. Calls him Jack for some reason. Blaze can hardly get him to go home in the evening. He wants to stay here."

"Stay here?"

"Yeah. Being mentally retarded, I suppose he's attracted by the security a seminary offers."

Abelard stared at him. Oblate Luke was too fuzz-brained to realize the full meaning of what he had just said. But it was important not to be critical at the moment.

"You've been going to the barn quite a lot yourself lately," he remarked.

"Oh, just curiosity. Melonhead, er, Oblate Mel, is experimenting with herbal remedies that he thinks will be useful for the missionaries in Africa. I, ah, have had some luck with some of his concoctions, healthwise. He has a salve that took off a wart, can you believe it? You ought to see his lab down there. Have you ever gone to the barn?"

"No, I don't think so. All those defecating animals give me the shivers."

"You don't think you've ever gone to the barn?" Lukey asked sharply. The beer empowered him. He thought maybe he should have become a lawyer.

"I may have a time or two. I forget." To himself: Why the hell did I say I think. What's this queer up to? I have a dreadful feeling that he must know something more than he's letting on. But I dare not proceed with this line of questions.

Lukey was on a roll now. "Remember our escapade with the train robber?" he asked.

Fr. Abelard snorted. The Royal Bohemian was affecting him too. "You can't con me with that story, Oblate. What I don't understand is what your classmates think to gain by spreading such a weird tale. Why are they always playing tricks?"

"The train robber is hard to believe, I agree." Lukey tipped the last swallow from the beer bottle. "But didn't you ever see something so unbelieveable that you didn't know for sure if you saw it or not?"

"Of course not," Abelard replied, too hastily. He jumped up and pulled another bottle of beer out of his refrigerator, but did not offer a second one to Lukey.

"Well, when the disciples witnessed Christ ascending into heaven, for example, don't you think they must have wondered whether they really saw what they thought they saw?" Lukey knew that he definitely should have been a lawyer. He hadn't even planned to say that. It just popped into his mind.

"Are you questioning Church dogma?" Fr. Abelard asked archly.

Lukey shrugged. "Maybe the disciples only imagined the Ascension and thought the rest of the faithful would be smart enough to understand that it was an allegory. I dunno. I'm just saying that sometimes you don't know if what you have seen is real or only something you think you have seen. Don't you agree?"

Abelard swigged his beer. Oblate Luke could not be as smart as he was proving to be or he would know that burned-out light bulbs couldn't be fixed. Why was it that nothing made sense where the SBDC Boys were involved? They were all looney. It was evident that he was not going to find out much from Oblate Luke without revealing his vision of a naked man suspended in thin air, which may not have been a vision at all. He glanced at his watch. "It's time for Matins. You better get moving."

He did not go to Matins himself, however, but drank another beer. By nightfall, he was back in the drunken stupor from which he had, with so much effort, freed himself for nearly a month. He kept staring at his beer bottles, asking himself over and over if the disciples actually saw Christ ascend into heaven anymore than he had actually seen a naked man ascending to the ceiling of the slaughterhouse.

CHAPTER 11

With four days off from classes over the Thanksgiving weekend, Melonhead and Clutch decided to give the alcohol still its maiden voyage. Prior Robert and the faculty would be fully occupied with the annual visit of the Minister General from Rome and the Provincial of the American province. The SBDC Boys would hardly have to worry about any of them barging in on their medical research at the barn. The elderberry wine had turned to vinegar or to kerosene, depending on the opinion of the researcher who was tasting it, but a batch of wild plum juice had fermented nicely with a generous addition of sugar spirited out of the kitchen. Melonhead intended to make wild plum liqueur from it and infuse it with a concoction of herbs that included angelica, wormwood, chokecherry bark, and walnut husks. If nothing else, it would be very effective against intestinal parasites, he figured. Only he, Gabe, and Fen knew the exact formula and Melonhead was not really sure that Gabe and Fen remembered it, but "if three Carthusians can keep a liqueur recipe secret, so can three Josephians," he said primly. After he had quaffed generously from a jug of the wild plum wine he added grandly: "We'll be able to supply the poor with medicine enough to free them from the tyranny of high-priced doctors."

Gabe intoned a passage from Matthew in the New Testament that he had been saving for such an occasion: "And they brought to Him all the sick suffering from various diseases and torments, those possessed, and lunatics and paralytics, and He cured them."

Blaze, getting into the mood, also with a little help from the wild plum wine, escalated the endeavor to even loftier heights. "Perhaps we shall, in this humble milkhouse, achieve eternal life, literally, and heaven will be now."

The hot plate was turned on, the pressure cooker full of herbs and wine set in place on it, the copper pipes all connected properly, and the New Religious Revolution began, as Other Blaze wrote that night in his The Story of My Weird Life.

In the meeting room of the priests' residence, Prior Robert was making an impassioned plea before the Minister General. He was sure that it would mean that he would eventually be demoted back to the pastorage in Broken Bow, Nebraska, but that was fine with him. For an hour, the younger professor priests, with much nodding of assent from Fr. Basil, the Provincial, had argued before the Minister General, Matix Suenarich, who was a Belgian by birth and of rather liberal leanings by Church standards, for a new approach to the education of seminarians and to religious life in general. It was time for the Church to rid itself of the last vestiges of medieval tradition and march resolutely into the 20th century. It was time to close down seminary schools like Ascension and send the seminarians into mainstream universities for their education. It was time to make celibacy voluntary, not obligatory, for priests. It was time to realize that seminary education was inbred, perpetuating a hopelessly outdated kind of religious life. Young Catholics were falling away from the Church in droves. There was an alarming decrease in the number of young people entering the religious life. Josephians with advanced degrees from universities would become educators out in the real world and bring prestige to the Order—look what it had done for the Jesuits. This prestige would attract new and highly talented candidates to the Josephians to keep the Order growing. What's more, these professors, through their fame in the classroom, in scientific and philosophical research, in their writings, would command good salaries and bring in much needed money to the Order. After all, taking care of old and dying Josephians was becoming a heavy burden and the number of faithful willing to subsidize religious Orders was decreasing each year. It was time for the Josephians to take a page from the book of capitalism.

"All these points are well taken," Prior Robert said, when his turn came to speak. "But may I plead for a little caution. Are we sure this is the true spirit of our religious life, as Josephians. We were founded as a mendicant Order to help ordinary laypeople, especially the poor. Will such a purpose endure once one Josephian after another starts making his own way among the educated and the wealthier levels of society, while our religious houses become merely places to sleep at night, if that? The Josephians are a community"—he repeated the word for emphasis, "a community of men living together. We have more in common with monasteries at a time when regretfully monasteries are in decline. We are men who are drawn to this life because we like living in a brotherly, secure haven, because, among other reasons, let's face it, we don't have to worry about the day-to-day burdens of making money and raising a family. Within our rules, we can follow our talents unencumbered by the commercial and social pressures of life out in the world. In such a community, we gain a rare kind of freedom in which to pursue ideas. Furthermore, as a community outside the mainstream world, we can supply something unique to the intellectual and moral makeup of society. If we send our people out into the universities, or wherever, we will inevitably lose the ability to think differently from the world's philosophies, unable to provide that choice, that alternative to the commercial and intellectual world beyond our communities. And the more secular we become the less reason for people to be financially generous to our work."

He wondered if he were talking in circles, but he continued. "If we decide to ape the present trends away from community life, which is also the trend out in family society, if we allow ourselves to be pressured by the same financial stresses that apply to the mainstream world, what will we have to offer intellectually that is any different from what the world offers? Where will truly different, new ideas come from, if everyone in society is forced to lead more or less the same modern lifestyle? Do not sell short the wisdom that has been accumulated by monasteries and religious Orders over the centuries. That wisdom may hold more useful and deeper relevance for true progress than the most advanced conventional science. I believe what you propose is a kind of slow move to secularization that will be suicide for our Order and a great loss to society."

Prior Robert did not think that he had ever spoken that long in one spurt before and evidently to no avail, judging from the reaction. Shaking heads. Murmurs of disagreement. Outright snarls of disgust. But having gone this far, he stumbled on. "Furthermore, who says that university life typifies something good and beneficial to society in any sense that involves us? I say it is one of the more artificial segments of society, an oligarchy, a trend to elitism. It cuts off the formal pursuit of knowledge from the way most people live. If we go in that direction, what is to keep us from ending up like a bunch of university dons in ivory towers intellectually emasculated from generating practical solutions to practical matters for the poor and lower middle class society that we have historically bound ourselves to minister to?"

Mumblings of disagreement now became louder groans of dissent. The word, "anti-intellectual" could be distinctly heard above the rumbling. It was obvious to Prior Robert that it was time for him to sit down and so he did, head bowed in shame. It was unfortunate that the SBDC Boys could not have been in attendance. They would have stood at this moment and applauded, much to the amazement of everyone, including Prior Robert.

The meeting shortly adjourned because the conferees were shocked at Prior Robert's words and were not interested in arguing with him even if they had thought of an effective answer to his views. Robert was obviously an anachronism; why waste time arguing with him? After the meeting, the Minister General came over to Prior Robert and patted him on the back magnanimously. "I understand your fears, Robert," he said in fluent English. Deep inside him, he had a troubling notion that the Prior was correct, but he had to be careful. The pressures toward modernization within the Order and without were very strong, especially in light of dwindling financial resources. Money always ruled, never more so than under what passed nowadays for the vow of poverty. "I found your remarks particularly interesting, Prior," he said loud enough for all to hear.

Robert's face brightened. Did the Minister General really understand what he had tried to say? "Would you like to see some of the things we have been doing here?" he asked, with almost boyish enthusiasm. "If I could show you around and enlarge on what I was trying to say here, perhaps you might see some merit in what I evidently am not able to articulate very well."

Robert took the Minister General through the buildings, pointing out the carpentry and stonemasonry that the oblates had done themselves to make the residences livable and attractive. "Is it not extremely helpful to be able to base intellectual decisions at least partly on experience gained from practical skills?" he asked. The Minister General said nothing. Prior Robert showed him the new stone-walled reservoir that the oblates had built to hold the spring flow from the swamps for their water supply, replacing the one dating back to Mudpura times. "Where will metaphysics lead a student not grounded in concrete experiences?" Again the Minister General said nothing. "Look at their carvings on the altar front. They exhibit amazing talent, don't you think? The seminarians didn't realize they could do this kind of art until they tried. Is that not a valuable kind of education? To realize that you can do more than you thought you could do? Might not it be more fruitful for oblates to develop in this way than from mere book knowledge?" The Minister General still remained silent but he began to look alarmed. "Look how the oblates jacked up this foundation and reinforced it. To do such work without collapsing the building required much intellectual thought as well as mechanical knowledge. Oblates gaining experience in work like this will be in a much more informed position when making decisions about church and school and hospital structures which they inevitably will have to oversee. In mission countries they will be able to build their own churches where there is no one else to do it. Or fix their own trucks when there is no one else to fix them. A can-do attitude." The Minister General was still not talking but some of the alarm in his countenance faded away. Prior Robert showed him the walk-in freezer. "Look at all this food. It was produced right here on our farm. The walk-in freezer itself is a product of our labor." The Minister General managed a nod. He did not have the heart to tell Robert that the young professors had mentioned the monastic farm concept as a particularly dinosauric practice.

Perhaps the Minister General would like to see the barn where the oblates were breeding up a nice herd of Jersey cows and also raising the seminary supply of pork, processing all the meat and milk themselves. The Minister General brightened. He had not been in a barn since he was a boy half a century ago, and he would indeed like to see one in America. He beckoned the Provincial to accompany him, and Fr. Abelard decided it was a good time for him to tag along and surreptitiously spy for signs of suspicious behavior without drawing attention to himself.

It was possible to get into the barn without going through the old milkhouse, but Prior Robert, now in a hopeful mood, believing he had impressed the Minister General, decided that Oblate Mel's research into herbal remedies was precisely the kind of work he had been arguing for during the meeting. Leading the way, he pushed open the door to the lab and found himself confronted by six of his seminarians who appeared to be frightened out of their wits. Or five, anyway. Who the old fellow was he had no idea. They had obviously been so absorbed in their work that they had not noticed the entourage walking towards the barn. Prior Robert decided that the presence of the Minister General and the Provincial must have awed them.

There were introductions and mumbled greetings and in accordance with tradition the seminarians each knelt in turn to kiss the Minister General's ring, one of the customs the Minister General wanted very badly to do away with as soon as he had enough support in Rome where the Pope still, well, did not mind people bowing and scraping in his presence.

"Oblate Mel has been working hard at learning which of the old herbal remedies might truly be effective," Prior Robert explained breezily. "He has discovered for example that milkweed juice does indeed seem to have healing properties. And the peat from the swamps that surround us makes a good poultice to stop bleeding."

While he was talking, Blaze, Gabe, Melonhead, Fen, Clutch and Axel, the latter still confused about kissing the fat fellow's ring and whether he should have done it, had shuffled themselves together into a sort of knot blocking the eminent visitors' view of whatever was bubbling away on the hot plate on the table. Fr. Abelard could have sworn he smelled something strangely like, but not quite like, whiskey, and realized, with a start, that his breath must still be heavy with Jack Daniels. Oh, God, had the Minister General detected it?

"And what have we here?" Prior Robert continued with fatherly pride, pushing the group aside so that all could have a better look at the pressure cooker on the hot plate. "Don't tell me you are canning peaches." He had hoped to make a joke to relieve the dread that appeared to grip his seminarians. He thought it strange that at that remark, Blaze clamped his hand over his mouth so hard that tears formed in his eyes.

It was Fen, good old reliable in situations of panic, who rose first to the occasion. "We are making an herbal tea from angelica, Gubanosa ferferalis," he said. "A big batch actually." Why he had felt compelled to add the fake Latin name he did not know. How many times had he gotten in trouble because he went too far?

"It is slightly toxic and must be used carefully," said Melonhead, having recovered his wits and deciding that Fen's idiotic answer could be made more legitimate with some actual information about angelica. "I'm interested in it because among other beneficial possibilities, it is supposed to create a revulsion against alcohol. Think of how beneficial that would be to the Jo—er, in today's society."

The Minister General and the Provincial were fortunately not quite listening and wanted to move along. They had more important things to think about than some idiot seminarian interested in herbal medicine, although it was impressive that at least one of them knew a little Latin. But proud father, Prior Robert, forged on where angels and devils both feared to tread.

"And what is this clear liquid coming out of this spigot over here?" he asked, beaming again, thinking that for once his most problematical seminarians might do him honor. He could not understand why their faces showed grave dread instead of pride.

But Clutch was now back to being the Engineer of Ascension. "It's an intriguing experiment," he explained. "I got to thinking about all the herbal teas and tinctures and such that Oblate Mel was boiling and how I might make the process more efficient. Why not, I thought, capture the steam from the boiling and make distilled water from it. For Oblate Mel's potions, yes, but also for the car, tractor and truck batteries."

The Minister General nodded gravely as if he understood what Clutch was saying. Then he indicated that he was ready to move on to the barn. It must be getting near the time of Matins and Lauds. Fr. Abelard fished a handkerchief from his pocket and, affecting a cough, covered his mouth and nose with it. Might block the odor of liquor on his breath as well as the smell of manure from the barn.

Brother Walt was putting the Jerseys in their stanchions. The Minister General remembered his own father's barn. Tears came to his eyes either from memories or the rank odor of urine in the gutters. Fr. Abelard was sure that now he could detect a more winey smell than what came from his breath, and he sniffed around for a source. He might have noticed some faded purple stains in cracks and crannies of the walls that the last coat of whitewash had missed, but just then a cow raised her tail and arched a stream in his general direction. He clamped his handkerchief tighter and backed out of the barn followed closely by the others.

CHAPTER 12

At four o'clock on Christmas Eve, Prior Robert learned that Fr. Abelard had "slipped" again. He was too inebriated to go to Grass Prairie to help out with the midnight Solemn High Mass as planned. Nor could the Prior rearrange assignments, because all the other priests had already left for duties at various parishes in the Twin Cities area. He was about to call Fr. Lardigan, the pastor at Grass Prairie, and tell him of his dilemma when another thought occurred to him. A Solemn High Mass required three ministers: a celebrant, a deacon and a subdeacon. Fully ordained priests almost always served in all three capacities, but technically, Canon Law allowed in an emergency, just about anyone familiar with the rubrics to serve as a subdeacon. The position required no exercise of powers strictly reserved to a fully ordained priest. He would send that smart aleck Oblate Blaise who was always finding some devious way to get out of chapel exercises. Time for Oblate Blaise to grow up and realize he was in the seminary to learn how to be a priest, not to grow corn.

Prior Robert knocked on the open door to Oblate Blaise's room, trying not to appear gleeful. Blaze looked up from his desk trying not to appear as if he had been dozing instead of studying.

"I need your help, Oblate Blaise," the Prior said, with all the earnestness he could muster. "Grass Prairie needs a subdeacon at Midnight

Mass tonight, and I have no priest available. Fr. Abelard was supposed to go but he is, uh, very sick. I've decided to send you. You can drive the farm truck. The snow's getting heavy, but after all your experience with that truck, you should have no problem. I have full confidence in you." He dropped a book of rubrics on the young man's desk, waiting only to enjoy the look of dismay that flooded Oblate Blaise's face before he retreated down the hall, smiling broadly.

Blaze stared stonily at the book of rubrics. The realization of what it meant came slowly. He'd been had. And in a way, it was his own fault. If he had not pushed The Cure so energetically, Abs might not have lost his way and dissolved into alcoholism. He opened the book and started to read. He ought, of course, to know all about the role of a subdeacon at a Solemn High Mass, having witnessed a hundred such Masses anyway and even serving as acolyte at more than a few. The truth was that he barely paid attention to the conduct of the ceremony even when he was up there in the sanctuary.

He tried to concentrate on the rubrical details before him. His mind went as stolidly blank as it did when he tried to study metaphysics, another subject whose logic totally escaped him. A Solemn High Mass was the rubrician's dream come true. The entire troupe of celebrant, deacon, subdeacon, master of ceremonies, and passel of altar boys occupied themselves for nearly two hours with ringing bells, swinging censors of smoking incense, carrying cruets of wine and water to and fro, sprinkling holy water hither and yon, all to the cadence of mumbled Latin prayers and hymns that hardly anyone knew the meaning of. Every single move of the actors on this stage was supposed to follow detailed directions that hailed back to the Middle Ages at least.

Why hadn't Robert picked The Very Reverend Lukey? Lukey revelled in rubrics, the pious, hypocritical bastard. Lukey knew every detail of the service. Why me?

He knew why. Robert was trying to remind him of what he was supposed to be doing at Ascension Seminary. But the idea of wriggling into those rich brocaded vestments was alone enough to make him feel queasy. Why the hell had he decided to become a priest?

He knew the answer to that, too. His mind drifted back to sixth grade. In memory, he watched again the grainy, sepia-toned silent film that Sister Monica was showing in the school auditorium. The only sound was the projector whirring along like a coffee grinder. The movie was about Francis of Assisi. Blaze remembered it well, first of all because a little boy in front of him became so engrossed that while Francis was talking to the birds, he evidently didn't realize that nature was talking to him, telling him to go to the bathroom. At the end of the show, when the poor little thing stood up, there were brown streaks down the back of both his pants legs. He apparently was not fully aware of what had happened to him. In fact, Blaze had himself been so fixated by the movie that he had at first thought the little boy's rank odor that had assailed him during the movie came from the tattered beggar that Francis had embraced in the last reel.

It was the first movie Blaze had ever seen, and Francis of Assisi so captivated his imagination that for weeks he wandered around his father's farm with a piece of hay rope tied around his waist, trying to get barn pigeons to perch on his arm. When that fantasy wore off, he had reached the part in his sixth-grade American History book where Isaac Jogues, the Jesuit missionary, was getting himself martyred while trying to convert the "Heathen Indians" to the "One True Religion." The book said that the savages pulled Isaac's fingernails out, one by one, before killing him. Even to a farm boy, inured to hog stickings and chicken beheadings, that was luridly gruesome. For about six months, Blaze became the fearless missionary in the wilderness of the farm woodlot, practicing the sacramental ritual of Baptism on stick Indians and praying that he would have the courage to lose his fingernails and his life when the time came. There were definite benefits to martyrdom. Martyrs went straight to heaven when they died, even if they had been masturbating just the day before.

Francis of Assisi and Isaac Jogues remained the moving forces in the make-believe world that propelled Blaze toward the priesthood until Lou Boudreau replaced them in 1948, but by then it was too late. He had already entered the seminary high school and become enmeshed in the life there, which was much more fun than he had imagined it could be. Undistracted by conditions "out in the world," he could dream of becoming a great missionary, hunting lions in Africa like Ernest Hemingway. In the meantime, he could play shortstop for the seminary team to prepare himself for becoming the Famous Shortstop Priest, the Lou Boudreau of Catholic Action. The alternative of leaving the seminary was not particularly attractive, even though it would bring girls into his life. He had no money. His family had no money. His family had moved to a town from the farm, the only home he knew. In the town, he knew no one. He had no training or degree for a good job. Owning and operating his own farm, the only work idea that attracted him, required more money than he could ever dream of acquiring. Besides he was farming pretty much on his own now, except for having to put up with that looney Gabe. Out in the world, he would get married and get stuck in some boring job for the rest of his life, making just enough money to keep on making just enough money.

But he hadn't foreseen until this moment that the comfortable life he had managed to create for himself in the seminary would soon end. In another three years he would be ordained and would have to go out and do all those priestly things he didn't like to do but had decided he could put up with on the chance that he would eventually be assigned to Africa. There he could disappear into the jungle and save souls while living as he damn well pleased. He had a fuzzy, developing notion that he would teach the natives not the hopelessly obscure metaphysical theology of Catholicism, but the potential for paradise available through their own native animism. The so-called African heathens had a lot going for them, he believed, a life of simplicity not unlike what Francis of Assisi preached, if they would just raise their cultural sights a little.

That's what Blaze, Great White Theologian Hunter, would teach them. Yes, yes. It was coming to him. A new garden of paradise in the African bush. His superiors would think everything was wonderful when they heard how the natives were flocking to get baptized, which they would, once they understood that they were more truly Christian in their native religion than those First World white heathen materialists. He would recruit and train a whole new cadre of hunting and gathering priests. Yes, yes. And Melonhead could build a hospital in the jungle like Albert Schweitzer and teach the people homeopathic medicine, using cures that came from the jungle itself. He would begin the new reformation of the Church. Eventually, his black African priests would come to the United States to convert heathen Americans to true Christianity.

His reverie was broken by a scoffing laugh at the door. The Very Reverend Lukey was staring at him, knowing that Blaze was daydreaming as usual.

"You better get your ass in gear and learn those rubrics," he said.

"You're just jealous because I get to go to an outside parish and serve as subdeacon and you don't."

"I just wish I could be in that church to watch you screw up good."

By ten o'clock the winds were whipping the snow into a real blizzard and Blaze was glad for the truck instead of a car. But it was slow going. He had piled several dozen bales of hay on the truck to give it more weight and hence more traction. He drove the old crate as fast as it would go, hoping that it would slide off the road and make it impossible for him to go on. But no such luck. He stumbled into the sacristy of the church with only seconds to spare. Old Fr. Lardigan, already in vestments, looked relieved. "Roads pretty bad, eh?" he acknowledged. Blaze nodded. The assistant pastor, who would act as deacon in the Mass, was also vested and waiting. He managed a wan, milquetoasty smile of understanding. While the altar boys stared at him, Blaze went to the table where the vestments he was to wear were laid out. The Very Reverend Lukey had shown him how to get into them and Blaze proceeded in as knowing a manner as he could fake. He had trouble getting the cincture tied properly around his waist. The assistant pastor mercifully helped him. The alb was too long, so Blaze tucked it up under and over the cincture. Then he looped the chasuble over his head in what he hoped was an expert manner. It effectively hid the bulging alb. Not to mention a multitude of sins.

Out of the sanctuary the entourage marched: celebrant, deacon, subdeacon, four altar boys. Blaze's last hope had faded. He had banked on a master of ceremonies to guide him through his ordeal of ignorance, but, due to the blizzard, the priest who was supposed to act as one couldn't make it. The choir was beginning a flat, nasal midwestern rendition of Gregorian Chant, making those sonorous Latin vowels sound as if they had been run over by a John Deere disk. Kyrie eleison, Christe eleison. Oh, indeed, Blaze thought. God have mercy.

Fr. Lardigan, as celebrant, proceeded exactly as he did for an ordinary High Mass, that is, as if neither a deacon nor a subdeacon were present. Gradually it became clear to Blaze that this was his salvation. The celebrant did not know, or had long ago forgotten, exactly what to expect from a subdeacon. Standing to the left of the celebrant, Blaze didn't even have to turn the pages of the big missal, as a subdeacon was supposed to do. Every time he reached, Lardigan beat him to it.

Two of the altar boys, one holding the smoking censor and the other the little brass incense boat, knew more than Blaze did about how to proceed. Whenever the incense from the boat needed sprinkling on the hot charcoal in the censor, which was the subdeacon's official duty, they approached him and looked up into his eyes like two puppies waiting to be taken for their daily walk. When Blaze could not remember if he was supposed to incense the celebrant only, or the deacon too, or the missal or the tabernacle, he incensed everything. A smoky haze moved out over the congregation, like fog rolling in off the ocean.

The Very Reverend Lukey had told Blaze that he'd be okay if he just stayed on the celebrant's left when he was in doubt, unless he saw the deacon headed his way. Then he was to switch sides, genuflecting on the step lower than the step the deacon was genuflecting on as they passed behind the celebrant. This Blaze remembered to do, faltering and bumping into the deacon only once.

He was beginning to feel some inkling of control over the situation as the time for the singing of the Gloria approached. Celebrant, deacon and subdeacon descended the altar steps and strode to the three great chairs along the side of the sanctuary where they would sit while the choir performed. Blaze darted a little ahead of Fr. Lardigan and scooped the celebrant's biretta from where it rested on his chair, as was the subdeacon's job. But he handed it to Fr. Laridan backwards so that when the old priest set it on his head, the tassel fell down over his nose. He had to adjust it himself while Blaze was busy grabbing the celebrant's chasuble and lifting it up over the chair back in the proper rubrical manner. So unnerved was Blaze because of the backward hat fiasco that he forgot about his own biretta and sat on it. Kyrie eleison. "If you make a mistake," Lukey had counseled, "pretend you did it on purpose." How does a subdeacon reach under his vestment-covered ass to pull out a crushed biretta while pretending, with great aplomb, that he had sat on it on purpose?

The time came to say the orations in Latin that were part of every Mass, called the "Ordinary." At a Solemn High Mass, the celebrant, deacon and subdeacon recited these prayers together. Although he had read them many times, Blaze could remember nothing. To save face, he babbled nonsensical sounds in rhythm with the Latin phrases the two priests were mumbling, his ear slyly cocked to pick up the last word or phrase they pronounced before a pause so that he could mutter it too, as if he were saying the prayers right along with the celebrant but a split second behind. Blaze could not believe he was capable of such duplicity. What in God's name am I doing up here, his mind screamed. What are any of us doing up here? Were his empty babblings any different, really, than the Latin syllables that no one in the church, including the old priest, could translate any better than he could? Blaze felt as if he were in a nightmare, the kind where suddenly he found himself walking naked down a street. For the first time in his life, his gift for fantasy vanished. In a terrible rush of clarity, he knew that he could never, ever, be a priest. Then with an even more terrible realization, more like a leap of clairvoyance because it did not follow logically from the first conclusion and passed into his subconscious immediately, he knew that he did not believe in the kind of God to whom they were presumably praying. Humans created that God, not vice versa.

If Fr. Lardigan were aware of his subdeacon's desperate situation, he gave no indication. He proceeded mechanically on. Communion time came. The end in sight. Blaze heaved a sigh of relief. Too soon. His overly long alb was coming untucked from the cincture. Now as the trio headed out to the communion rail to distribute the communion wafers to the communicants, he stepped on the sagging edge of his alb, pulling it farther down onto the floor. He could hardly move now without stepping on it and lurching. Lurching was particularly inappropriate because it was his job, as subdeacon, to hold the gold-plated paten under each communicant's chin so that neither the wafer, the body of Christ under the appearance of bread, nor even one crumb of it might ever inadvertently suffer the desecration of falling on the floor. Blaze found himself thinking, despite his own wretched situation, that communicants waiting to receive the Sacred Host with tilted heads, with eyes open or closed, with tongues protruding, not to mention male Adam's apples or female bosoms, looked comically obscene. Then lurching and slouching along on the dragging alb, he accidently bumped Lardigan's arm just enough to make the celebrant fumble on his way from picking a wafer out of the chalice and delivering it onto the waiting tongue of the next communicant. The Sacred Host slipped from his fingers, fluttered in the air, and landed across the cleavage of a particularly awesome set of matronly breasts bulging above a low cut dress. It teetered there precariously. Any slight movement and it might be swallowed up in the folds of flesh. Kyrie eleison.

The woman did not realize what had happened and remained motionless, like a statue, eyes closed and tongue waiting. The assistant pastor turned as white as his alb. A glow of crimson spread over Fr. Lardigan's face. He looked zombie-like at Blaze and Blaze looked back just as dumbfounded. A grave theological dilemma confronted them. No one other than an ordained priest dared handle a Sacred Host under pain of sacrilege, so it would not be proper for the woman to retrieve the wafer unless there was no other alternative. But for the celebrant to retrieve it required groping into that heaving bosom. Where are you, Thomas Aquinas, now that we really need you, Blaze thought, his rational mind completely forsaking him. At first he thought he was going to burst into wails of insane laughter. Then he thought he was going to faint. But just before either insanity or unconsciousness overtook him, he responded. He did not think about what he did, or will it. His hands just did it on their own. With the paten held at the ready, he deftly hooked the Sacred Host with the nail of his little finger and flicked it from its precarious perch onto the plate. He then lifted the paten to the chalice and dumped the wayward wafer back into it. No problem.

Lardigan, acting automatically out of years of habit, re-delivered the host. The woman was staring straight ahead now, tongue back in her mouth, puzzled at the delay, but Blaze, still acting automatically, snapped the edge of the paten against her throat. She jumped a little and her mouth flew open. Lardigan placed the host on her tongue with the speed and skill of a hundred thousand deliveries, and barged on to the next communicant. The whole problem and its solution had occurred so fast in real time that no one beyond the three ministers seemed aware of it.

When the celebrant strode back to the altar, he stepped right along like a referee marking off a fifteen-yard penalty. Blaze shuffled furiously to keep up. At the steps ascending the altar, he took hold of the alb with his free hand, like a lady in an evening gown, bunching it together in his fist so that he could lift it more or less demurely as the trio ascended to the altar. But on the top step, his shoe came down on the alb once more, and the last fold tucked under the cincture pulled loose. Only his innate athletic agility kept him from falling to the floor. He swayed awkwardly and landed on his knees, a type of genuflection never anticipated or called for by the rubrics. The celebrant showed no indication that he was willing to stop the service while his subdeacon made the necessary adjustments. He took the paten from Blaze without looking at him, not even wondering why the peculiar young man was on his knees instead of standing beside him as he should be. He was not sure he should dismiss his subdeacon as a clumsy idiot or, considering his actions just minutes previously, as a very dexterous genius.

Free of the paten, Blaze struggled erect and improvised a quick solution. Lifting first one side of the alb and pinning it under one elbow, and then doing the same on the other side, he could safely walk, so long as he kept his hands devoutly folded and his elbows clamped against his sides, holding the alb up.

And so he hung on for the rest of the Mass, out of his mind with embarrassment and self-revulsion, making no effort to move the missal from the gospel side of the altar to the epistle side or vice versa, as he was supposed to do, nor to prepare the empty chalice for the celebrant to carry from the altar, nor to hand him his biretta as they marched off into the sacristy.

Neither the pastor nor his assistant said anything about what had happened. All that mattered to Fr. Lardigan was that a grave theological crisis had been avoided. The idiot subdeacon had not actually picked up the wafer, had touched it in fact only with the tip of a fingernail which is not exactly a living part of the body and so, broadly speaking, had skirted sacrilege. More importantly, he had not actually touched the poor woman either. Would have served her right, though, he thought, for wearing a dress like that. Who did she think she was,

Marilyn Monroe? With that, he dismissed the whole event. It never happened. He pawed through the collection baskets, a pleased look on his face. "Looks like a five hundred dollar take," he said jovially to the assistant pastor, who looked away in embarrassment. Fr. Lardigan had planned to invite Blaze to the rectory for a bit of "schnapps" but thought better of it now. Blaze was relieved. He had suffered all the sacerdotal company he could handle for one night. But most of all he could hardly wait to get back to the seminary and tell the SBDC gang about what he was already in his mind calling "The Sacred Host Caught Between the Horns of Dilemma."

CHAPTER 13

Not until he was clear of the village did Blaze understand the full fury of the snowstorm. Out on the country roads where there were no clusters of houses to block the wind, snow flew horizontally across the sweep of the headlights, the drifts inching out from the ditch on the west side. With the temperature sliding towards zero, he slowly realized that he might be in some real danger. The road was normally wide enough for two cars to pass easily, but now there was only one lane and one set of tire tracks broken through the rising snow ahead of him. Even those tracks were quickly disappearing under new snow. It was easier to stay on the road by watching the telephone and electric poles on either side as they loomed into view in the headlights, and try to steer exactly between them.

Still he was not really worried. The old truck, which had come along with the purchase of the seminary property, had been used to haul cans of milk from farms to dairy plants in an earlier life, a mission that, even more than the mail, had to go through or farmers would run out of milk cans for the next milking. It had dual back wheels and with the load of milk cans (or hay bales), possessed enough traction to push through a foot of snow or more. He felt fairly sure that he could manage the fifteen miles back to the seminary, come what may. And if not, what the hell. With his fur cap, old lined Army surplus pea jacket, heavy boots, wool mittens and insulated coveralls, he was ready for anything. These were his vestments. Survival tactics were his rubrics. He had even thought to bring along a thermos of hot coffee and a box of sweet rolls he had swiped from the seminary kitchen. Let the blizzard roar. The threat of it cleansed his tortured mind. He was his old self again, and yet not his old self. His old self would have been chuckling, mentally turning the Solemn High Mass and the blizzard into a comedy of adventure to amuse the SBDC Boys later. Instead, he now found himself settling into a resolve unfamiliar to him. He felt calm and self-reliant, keenly alert to the situation. Purpose flooded his mind, bringing meaning to his existence for once. He needed to stay alive.

Suddenly a car shape loomed through the blinding snow ahead of him. Barrelling along as fast as the old truck could go under these circumstances, he knew he could not stop in time to avoid the car, so he gunned the truck and pulled into what would normally have been the other lane. For a few seconds he thought he would plow right on through the snowdrifts and regain the middle of the road. But the extra weight of the bales, good for traction, now acted as a drag, whipsawing the back of the truck further into the drifts as Blaze tried desperately to pull back into the center of the road. The more the back wheels spun, the more they dragged the truck sideways until they slipped from the pavement altogether and sank deep into the snow-filled ditch.

A few attempts to free the truck failed. Now what? He tried to collect his thoughts. There was, first of all, someone in that car. The door on his side of the truck was up against a wall of snow, so he had to crawl out of the cab on the other side. The wind was moaning high in the sky now with a sound he had never heard before. It sent shivers through him that were not from the cold. The air and wind sucked his breath away. This must be the granddaddy of all blizzards. The car's headlights had flashed on when he had lurched into the ditch, so he could find his way, wallowing in the snow, to the car door. When he approached, the overhead light inside turned on and the window lowered but only a little. The face wreathed in fur collar and hat looked at him with apprehension. Not easy to tell, but the face appeared to be female. She also appeared to be afraid of him, a notion so novel to Blaze that he had to smile despite the desperateness of the situation. The smile disarmed her. She peered closely at him and relief replaced fear.

"Oh it's you, Father," she said and then with apology in her voice, "I got you stuck, didn't I?"

He started to explain that he was not a priest, but decided that would take too long and accomplish nothing at the moment.

"Are you okay?" he shouted above the moaning wind.

"Sort of," she said, managing a rueful smile, "but I can't budge this car another inch."

"I'll push," he said.

He tried. Nowhere. The snow was so deep it was lifting the car off the road as the wheels spun. "How far have you got to go yet?" Blaze asked, shouting in the wind.

"About three miles I think."

"Well, I guess we can walk that far. Have you got boots?"

"You don't walk in blizzards like this, Father." She sounded almost patronizing.

"Well, we can just follow the power line."

"No, Father. You can get lost between poles. You can get lost and freeze to death thirty feet from your barn."

Blaze looked at her. He had read about blizzards like that, but he was surprised to find a woman, who looked and sounded quite young, with that kind of survival sense.

"I'm gonna stay put," she continued. "That's what Daddy always said to do. The snowplow will be along pretty soon. Get in here before you freeze to death. I got a good heater which I bet that old truck of yours doesn't have."

She was right. "Just a minute," he said and retreated to the truck to retrieve the coffee and rolls.

"Can't let the motor run," he said, settling himself in the car beside her and unscrewing the lid on the thermos. "Carbon monoxide."

"Can if you keep the window cracked a little," she countered, "and don't run the motor constantly."

He stared at her. Damn, she just knew everything, didn't she. "What if the snow plugs the exhaust and we get gassed anyway?"

"We won't let that happen," she said. She sipped the coffee he offered her.

"Actually hot in here now, isn't it," she said, pulling her hat off. Damn, she was not only infallible, she was pretty.

"My folks don't even know I'm on the road," she continued. "Probably a good thing, or Daddy would be having a fit. I live in Minneapolis, going to college, and I told them I wouldn't drive out here till tomorrow. Then I took a notion to surprise them and come home for Midnight Mass. But they weren't in church. They had more sense than to go out on a night like this, I guess."

Blaze stared at her in the dimness of the overhead light, then looked away quickly when their eyes met. "My name's Blaze," he said. "Actually, I'm not a priest."

She turned toward him again. Quickly. "Y-you're not?"

Blaze detected more relief than apprehension in her voice.

"Just a seminarian. I've got a few more years to go to ordination. Just about anybody can serve as a subdeacon."

"Oh really. How about a woman?" There was challenge in her voice. Blaze knew where she was coming from. He thought he might like her.

"But why would any woman in her right mind want to be a subdeacon, much less a priest?" he countered.

She continued to look at him, sharply. Then smiled. That was not the answer she had anticipated, but she liked it.

"My name's Marge. Marge Puckett. And yeah, you're right. I wouldn't be caught dead at the altar."

The radio crackled with more bad news. Snowplows could not get to secondary roads any time soon. They were having trouble handling the main roads. Stay home.

"Have you got a flashlight?" Blaze asked, angry at himself for not having brought one. With a flashlight, he could follow the electric line from pole to pole down the road.

"No, but you'd never make it anyway," she said, reading his mind. "You ever try walking in snow four, five feet deep?"

"Oh, well," Blaze replied. "Be getting light in another three hours. "Wind'll die down by then too. Maybe." Marge turned off the motor to save on gas.

"I've never heard a wind quite like that," she said.

"Me either." Blaze cranked the window down on his side, leeside to the wind. The cold flooded in. In a few minutes the car began to cool noticeably. "I've got an idea," he said. He rolled the window back up, pulled on his hat and mittens, and bundled up his jacket. "I've got a load of bales on that truck. I'm going to cover the car with them. You're going to have to start the car up again and turn on the lights."

He floundered to the truck, forced to use swimming motions to manage the mounting drifts. The wind was blowing away his breath and he could exert himself only in fits and starts and then stop to catch enough air to go on. Climbing on the truck bed, he flung off the bales. Then he dragged them and himself one at a time to the car and ranked them around and over it, literally boxing it in with hay. After he had broken a trail, the rest of the bales were not so difficult to move. On the lee side, he piled the bales a little away from the car so he could get the door open to let himself back in, and to allow air space next to the window, building a kind of chimney higher than the car to form a vent, should the snow pile deeper. He made a little tunnel of bales at the end of the exhaust pipe too, so the fumes could get away from the car.

"That was pretty smart," Marge said after he had crawled into the car. "How did you think of that? A hay bale igloo. What in the world possessed you to drive a truckload of hay out on a night like this in the first place?"

Blaze laughed again and explained the unusual circumstances.

"Actually, my whole life is a rather unusual circumstance," he added.

"Think we're going to stay warm enough?" she asked, a slight tremor in her voice now.

"Well, the more snow that covers those bales, the more insulation we'll have. We ought to be as snug as hibernating bears, if we run the motor occasionally. I've read about people surviving in snow drifts just fine so we ought to be okay."

She shivered and involuntarily snuggled up next to him. Oh, God. He realized he might be the only man in America his age who had never in his life sat next to a pretty girl in a car in the middle of the night. No problem with freezing. He was sweating. "How about some more coffee? And a sweet roll," he offered.

She squirmed erect, flicked on the overhead light, nibbled at a roll, sipped coffee. He watched her, relieved to note that he could discern nothing in her show of intimacy other than stark practicality. Suddenly she startled him by laughing.

"It figures. You not being a priest," she said.

"What do you mean?"

"I saw you sit on that biretta," she said, and giggled involuntarily.

Blaze was glad for the semi-darkness to hide his blush. All he could think to do was laugh with her. It was a way around the awkwardness he felt, sitting so close to her. "So you saw that. Then you have to know I really screwed up the whole thing."

She laughed again. "I think you redeemed yourself when you flicked that host off Mrs. Chechory." And then she erupted into a near gale of giggling.

"How did you know?" Blaze blurted.

"I was the next communicant." And then she added, wickedly. "I've got good sidewise vision."

Blaze could not remember her, but at that point in time, with the communion wafer incident still overwhelming him, he would not have remembered the next communicant if it had been the Pope. They both laughed, louder than the wayward wafer justified. That relieved the tension. He sensed in her an irreverent humor not unlike his own. Before he hardly realized it, he was relating the whole sad adventure with the sagging alb. That led to expressing deeper thoughts about his mental anguish. It was a profound relief to be able to talk about what lay heavily on his mind. At least it kept them both from dwelling on the closeness of their bodies and the deepening cold outside.

"You know when you said you wouldn't be caught dead at the altar? Well, that's me too. That's what I learned tonight. I'm not cut out for the priesthood. The thought of having to give sermons and parade around in vestments and all that almost paralyzes me."

"Why on earth are you in seminary then?"

"It's a long story. Actually, I don't really know. It just happened. It's all so dumb. My life, that is."

"So's mine," she said. "I don't want to go to college, but Daddy insists. He says I need to know what's across the fence before I make a decision about my life. But I like living on a farm and I'll never change that."

"I like farming too," Blaze answered. "That's part of my problem. Working on the seminary farm, I've learned that I like it more than studying to become a priest. Farming is so mentally clear and clean and straightforward. Theology only mystifies me. Instead of confirming God's existence, it makes me doubtful about the whole business." Having finally said it out loud to someone else, Blaze felt relieved.

"Try taking a course in anthropology if you want to have your faith rattled," Marge said. "One of my professors says that every thinking college student becomes an atheist, but later on most of them unfortunately get over it." She chuckled at that.

Blaze could hardly believe what he was hearing. She was saying without guilt the sort of sentiments he was afraid to say at all. But then she changed the subject. Religion was evidently not important to her. "I'm going to raise horses on my farm. Maybe I'll name one Blaze." And she laughed again, a laugh that to Blaze was beginning to sound like the loveliest music he had ever heard. She was amazing. Someone as witty as Gabe, but a girl. Impossible.

By now the snow had covered the bales so thickly that the two people in the car could not hear the moan in the wind. Maybe it was dying down. Marge turned on the motor again to warm up and listen for news on the radio. Elvis Presley was singing. Blaze rolled his eyes in the darkness because he couldn't stand rock and roll. He called it "rock and wet your pants music." But Elvis's moan was at least better than the wind's moan. And the noise filled the silence with something more than their breathing.

"You know what this reminds me of?" She did not wait for a response. "Bundling." Again the merry laugh. She had decided that banter might get them through the delicate situation. Go straight to the heart of danger, she recalled from a Graham Greene novel.

"Bundling?" Blaze wanted to be sure they were thinking the same thing.

"Yeah. You know. Used to be common in New England before central heating. And if truth be told, in Minnesota too. Lovers visited in bed with plenty of covers between them."

"If you believe the covers stayed between them, you've got more faith in mankind than I do," Blaze countered. He could banter too.

Again she laughed. Why did she feel no apprehension? She decided to argue. "Oh, I don't know. There were other family members around, probably in the same room. I bet that nothing much happened. Most of the time."

"What do you mean by 'nothing much'?" Blaze challenged mischeviously.

"Well there was probably a lot of furtive kissing." She would not be out-bantered.

"Not if it was as dark as it is in here," Blaze replied. "I never realized it before, but when you can't see your hand in front of your face, kissing someone you are talking to is not necessarily a natural sequence of events. Kissing someone implies that you look into the other's eyes first, doesn't it? If I were to try to kiss you now in the dark, it would be sort of like trying to kiss a peach."

If she had laughed before, it was nothing close to the heartiness with which she burst out now. None of the boys in college would ever have come up with such an observation. Certainly not her boyfriend. Encouraged, Blaze blundered on. Talking about sex seemed to be an effective stratagem for doing nothing about sex. "I wonder how the seminary authorities would react if they learned that I was bundling with a university coed?"

"Not nearly as angrily as my boyfriend would."

Now Blaze laughed. "There was a girl I liked a lot one summer when I was home on vacation from seminary high school. Guess what. She went to the convent." He had thought she would laugh at that, but when she remained silent, he started telling her stories about the madcap adventures of the SBDC Boys, although he referred to them simply as the Davy Crockett Boys, without the usual adjective. He related how, when Very Reverend Lukey decided to take up rock collecting as a hobby, they had moved a huge boulder that required four of them to lift into the center of his room while he was absent. He told her about the time they had dismantled the hay wagon and reassembled it in Prior Robert's room, the front wheels in his bedroom and the back wheels in his office and the connecting wooden frame running through the little aisle between the two rooms. He told her about the Cure, elaborating it into a long and complex story. When she did not laugh at what he considered to be the hysterical climax of Fr. Abelard staring at The Very Reverend Lukey swaying above the cauldron of the

Cure, he stopped talking abruptly. Her breathing came in long, steady measures. He whispered her name. No answer. Again. Her answer was something close to a snore. He grinned in the darkness. She was sound asleep.

CHAPTER 14

As a part-time snowplow driver for the county, Kluntz had seen his share of freakish blizzard events. But he was not prepared for what he found in the middle of Township Line Road. "It was weirder than blue gumbo, I tell you." he remarked, as he related the story in George and Clare Puckett's kitchen where he had delivered Oblate Blaise and Marge Puckett. "There was this absolute mountain of a drift in the middle of the road so I stopped and had me a look-see. Under the snow was, well, you are not going to believe this, a pile of hay bales, and under the hay bales was a car. And when I dug down through it all and brushed off the windshield, damn but what there weren't these two kids in there not atall froze but sleepin' snug as two kittens under the stove."

The Pucketts listened with rapt attention, their gazes shifting from Marge to Blaze in something close to adoration. As the story unfolded, they became convinced that Blaze had saved their daughter's life. Clare pushed a heaping platter of ham and eggs and breakfast rolls in front of him and begged for more details. Neither Blaze nor Marge had much to say, mostly because Kluntz would not stop talking, which worried Blaze. How soon would it take Kluntz to carry this tale to Ed Hasse, who would surely speculate keenly on what a seminarian and a coed did all night alone in a car. But at least Kluntz's babbling gave him a chance to study Marge in the flesh rather than as a barely discernible body in heavy clothes in a dark car. Blaze thought that her demeanor did not do justice to the voice he had heard through the night. He had expected piercing dark eyes, pert lips, and a certain saucy, sexual purposefulness in her manner. But her eyes were an unremarkable blue-grey, her face broad and innocent, her lips thin, and her manner circumspect and matter-of-fact.

Marge was not that impressed by Oblate Blaise's appearance either. He looked younger than he had looked at the altar in church regalia. His face was almost childishly innocent, reminding her of the barefoot boy of Whittier's poem. For all of his forthrightness in the car, he now acted hesitant and diffident. The main difference between them at the moment was that she stared straight at him as he described their adventure, as if she had not been in the car with him all night. As if she were curious to know what had happened. He, on the other hand, found it difficult to meet her eyes, as if more than just talk had occurred between them.

"Well, I never felt we were in any real danger," he said for the third time at least, making sure he acted in a manner befitting a seminarian who only hours earlier had been standing before the altar at Midnight Mass adorned in priestly robes. He was especially careful not to cuss which required a certain amount of concentration. "After Miss Puckett fell asleep," (he thought he saw a faint smile flash over her face when he called her Miss Puckett), "I started and stopped the motor once more, and then I fell asleep too. I don't think it ever did get down to freezing in the car."

How could the Pucketts ever repay him? Blaze tried to point out that it was Marge, not he, who had really saved them by insisting on staying with the car. Marge looked pleased. It was not like a man to admit that.

"But can't I pay you something?" George asked.

"More ham and eggs will do just fine," Blaze said. "And maybe help me get that truck back on the road with your tractor."

"That's all been taken care of," Kluntz announced rather grandly. He was fidgeting now, wanting to get away and spread the news of the rescue. For once he knew something that Hasse was still ignorant of and it would be interesting to hear how the dirty old bastard would speculate on Blaze and Marge in a car alone all night.

Talk among the kitchen full of people gradually shifted to other neighborhood matters: "the electric" still was not on "over to Waconia and Chanhassen"; folks with more cows than could be milked by hand were having a hard time; someone near Carver—didn't have a name yet—had tried to walk home from a stalled car and was found frozen to death. Blaze was hardly listening because Other Blaze was already writing the night's adventure in his head. "It is almost impossible to overstate the curiosity one feels upon actually confronting in the flesh a person one has only talked to all night out of the flesh. She seems much more serious in mien now than her disembodied voice had sounded then. In fact there is a calculatedness about her that I would not have expected from the playfulness in her voice in the dark. (Note: check if calculatedness is a word.)"

Back at the seminary, Prior Robert had panicked. He had presumed that Oblate Blaise would spend the night at the rectory in Grass Prairie since only an idiot would have tried to drive in the fierce blizzard. When he heard nothing by mid-morning, he began to worry. He called Fr. Lardigan. At least the phones were working. Lardigan told him that Oblate Blaise had indeed driven away after Midnight Mass. Having heard nothing, the pastor presumed the young man had made it back to the seminary.

Prior Robert, overcome with dread, put down the phone. The poor boy was out there on the road somewhere frozen to death like the man near Carver. Maybe the man near Carver was Oblate Blaise. The Prior sank weakly into his office chair. With fatalistic certainty he knew the poor boy's death was his own fault. He had sent Oblate Blaise out into the night more to indulge his disapproval of the seminarian than to train the young man in God's ways. Now God had punished him. A dead oblate on his hands. No Prior had ever managed that in the history of the Josephian Order. He trembled. He had never wanted to be a Prior. He loved just being a simple pastor of the little parish church in Broken Bow, Nebraska. Why had his superiors promoted him? He had tried to decline. He hated being in charge of a community peopled with enough eccentrics to provide behavioral psychologists with material for years of study. Hated the way he was too weak to stand up to their petty, pretentious little plots, acting as if he didn't know how they were manipulating him. Why, oh why, had God wanted him to accept leadership? No one listened to him anyway. What happened to a Prior who allowed a seminarian to freeze to death on the road? What was a seminarian doing out on the road anyway? Serving as subdeacon in a rural parish hardly seemed a legitimate excuse, since Oblate Blaise was not yet an ordained subdeacon. Would the Prior be stripped of office? That would be a blessing in disguise. Would he be excommunicated? Oh, God, help me, he prayed.

He rushed into the chapel and knelt in prayer. "Heavenly Father, ordain that Oblate Blaise still lives, that this whole terrible error of mine punish me and not this young man." And then, as good men often do, he went one prayer too far. "I promise you, Lord Jesus, that if you see fit to save this boy's life, I will never again exercise my power over him in any spiteful or mean way, neither in body nor in spirit."

He felt better now. He called the sheriff's office. The frozen man near Carver had been identified and was not an Oblate Blaise, which the sheriff thought a queer name indeed. The county road superintendent said the highways were open to one lane and that the snow plows and front end loaders were digging their way down the back roads. No, he had not heard yet of an Oblate Blaise or an old truck. The hospital reported a few cases of frostbite, but no Oblate Blaise.

Prior Robert summoned the community to chapel. He strode to the front, turned, and with grim face, told the assemblage that Oblate

Blaise had disappeared in the blizzard on his way home from Grass Prairie and there was every possibility, and here the Prior's voice quavered, that Oblate Blaise might have frozen to death like the man near Carver. A murmur went through the little congregation. Even the Very Reverend Lukey bowed his head and prayed fervently that Oblate Blaise was not dead but just frostbitten enough to hurt like hell when he thawed.

In the silence, the oblates, bent in supplication, suddenly heard the front door of the building bang open and slam shut. There was the sound of a familiar cheery whistle, of boots stamping off snow in the entrance way, and footfalls clomping down the hall towards the chapel door. The door swung open, and there stood Oblate Blaise, a Santa Claus smile wreathing his face. "What are you all doing in here," he asked, puzzled. "Isn't it lunch time?"

CHAPTER 15

In other circumstances, Blaze would have gloried in the story of how he had not only survived the blizzard but saved the life of a damsel in distress. He would also have pondered with great but mystified delight the unctuous solicitude that Prior Robert now heaped upon him. There was something going on here that he didn't entirely understand.

But he could not get out of his mind the awful realization that had flooded over him in the middle of the Midnight Mass: that he was sure that he no longer wanted to be a priest. He was not even sure that he still wanted to help people. Making matters worse, the face of Marge Puckett kept intruding itself into his mind's eye. He could not say that he had any romantic feelings about the person behind that face, but he could not say that he didn't either. But more unnerving than that, he often found other oblates staring at him when he turned suddenly their way.

"What's going on, anyway?" he asked Fen finally.

"You really don't know, do you?" Fen replied.

"What the hell is that supposed to mean."

Fen laughed and looked at his friend with amusement. "They think you were makin' out with that girl in the car."

Blaze stared at Fen. Did his fellow oblates consider him so reprehensible that he would do such a thing? Did they suspect such behaviour because that is what they would have been trying to do? Or wanting to do? He shook his head. For having the reputation of being the seminary's bad boy, maybe he wasn't so bad after all.

"Do you think I did that?" he asked Fen, turning to him quickly.

"I know you didn't."

"How do you know?"

"I just do. Not you."

Blaze stared at him, puzzled. He was as suspicious of Fen's assumption of innocence as of the others' assumption of guilt. And Fen seemed somehow uneasy in his support. Did Fen think he was gay or something, for Chrissake?

From then on, Blaze's enjoyment of Josephian community life began to wane. Where before he had found comfort and identity in the companionship of his brethren, the only world he really knew, he now sought solitude. Where he had judged the conduct of his fellow oblates to be droll and charming, even when petty or narrow-minded or stupid, he now viewed them as simply pathetic. Nor did it help that as the winter deepened and there was less work on the farm to occupy him, the schedule of classroom studies intensified to make up for the summer hiatus. He grew morose. The more dissatisfied he became, the more he felt like lashing out at others. The more he examined church dogma, the less he believed in it. The problem was where to draw the line. He had previously concluded that if people wanted to believe absurdities like angels carrying the mother of Jesus bodily into heaven, it was all right. No harm done. But once he questioned one doctrine, he found that it became easier, in fact logically necessary, to question another, and then another. Reading Luther, he was startled to find his mind telling him that no matter what his textbooks said to the contrary, the errant Dominican was correct—that there was no good reason for insisting that the bread and wine be changed literally into the body and blood of Christ when it could only symbolize the body and blood of Christ. So much more practical. Why invent a miracle when none was needed? But the doctrine of the Eucharist, asserting that the bread and wine actually became the body and blood of Christ, was the central dogma of Catholicism. He could reject it only by rejecting the whole Church.

And then one morning, still half asleep, something in his subconscious brain clicked, almost audibly. The flash of insight that had sprung on him during the Midnight Mass debacle, but which in his duress he had not paid much further attention to, now came back in full force. Humans created their gods, not vice versa. He sat up in bed, marvelling at how that idea solved for him, in one broad sweep of clarity, all the inconsistencies of institutional religion that so bedevilled him. If men created their gods, of course their religions would be at times absurd or self-serving or illogical and at other times noble and honorable. No omnipotent, infallible intelligence was involved because such intelligence would rule out all the absurdities of religion. He tried to reject this most sinful of all doubts against faith, but it would not be rejected. He might just as well have tried to convince himself that one plus one added up to something other than two. Now he was not just a heretic but an atheist and apostate. Oh, God.

One day he heard a loud argument going on in a classroom between classes. A contingent of oblates led by The Very Reverend Lukey had surrounded Fen and were shaking fingers and heads in pious outrage. Blaze leaned in the doorway to listen.

"I can't believe you would say that," Lukey was shouting at Fen. "Look, it's right here in our moral theology textbook." He waved an open book. "You can't get to heaven without Baptism. You can't be saved if you remain a pagan, stubbornly rejecting the true Faith."

"I say not so," Fen replied, unperturbed. "A heathen has just as much chance for eternal life as anyone."

"But you can't say that. That's heresy.

"I just said it. It's just common sense and justice. If it's heresy, change the law," Fen said.

Blaze smiled. So doubts about dogma were not his alone. But it had seemed unlikely to him that Fen would be the one to go public. Gabe seemed better suited for attacking dogma, except that the fine points of theology only bored him. He didn't care. He knew how to manipulate dogma to his own designs, and beyond that what difference did it make? Blaze eyed Fen admiringly. There was more courage in him than he had reckoned. It was no accident that he was the one who had stood up to the pistol-waving thief.

The Very Reverend Lukey appealed to Blaze in the doorway for help. "Fen's a heretic. He thinks heathens can get to heaven."

Blaze tried to look serious. "Heaven? What's that?"

He began experiencing another difficulty. Absorbing information and repeating it on test papers had always been easy for him. Now his mind rebelled. It seemed unable to focus itself on the belabored ethics and dogmatism of moral theology and Thomistic philosophy. Church dogma and Canon Law too often struck him as just plain silly. For example, as he tried to study the finely-spun minutiae of Church regulations about the administration of the Sacrament of Baptism, he could scarcely believe the words of Canon Law. Even the kind of water that should be used for Baptism was specified, and what other fluids might be used in an emergency if regular water was not available. Among the fluids that could not be used, even if the person to be baptized was dying, were "milk, blood, amniotic liquid, tears, saliva, foam, fruit juices, wine, beer, oil, thick broth, and ink." But, and here was where his mind closed down completely, possible but "doubtful" fluids for Baptism included "weak soup and weak beer." He laughed and shook his head. What kind of insane quibbling possessed theologians who would okay 3.2% beer but not Royal Bohemian? Why weren't they wondering, like Fen, about whether the whole idea of Baptism for salvation might not be absurd?

Things came to a head in a discussion of sexual sinfulness in Fr. Alexus's Moral Theology course. Alexus was reading a sentence from their 1951 edition of Jone and Adelman, the standard English translation of Canon Law used in all American seminaries: "Because of the varying degrees of influence they may have in exciting sexual pleasure, the parts of the human body are sometimes divided into decent (face, hands, feet), less decent (breast, back, arms and legs), and indecent (sex organs and adjacent parts). The breathless young seminarians leaned forward in their desk chairs, anticipating with both rapt curiosity and dreadful embarrassment what might come next.

What came next was a grating laugh.

"What's so funny, Oblate Blaise?" Fr. Alexus asked in a voice heavy with warning.

Blaze started to mumble an apology and to lie that he had seen something amusing out the window. But suddenly all of his intellectual frustration boiled over. "Oh, for heaven's sake. Is everyone going crazy? You can't divide the human body up into safe and unsafe zones like that. How can your back be less decent than your foot? Jeez, what if you're one of those idiots with a foot fetish." The more he talked, the bolder he became. "If body parts adjacent to sex organs are indecent, where do the adjacent parts end? This is insane. And moreover, if God made the human body, how can a penis be indecent? How can sexual pleasure ever be bad?"

His classmates stared at him in gaping wonder. The idiot was going to get himself defrocked, Gabe thought. The Very Reverend Lukey, sitting next to Blaze, could not resist coming to the defense of the Church. "No doubt if I spent a night in a car with a young woman, I might be tempted to question Canon Law too," he said primly, looking at Fr. Alexus for approval.

"You wouldn't have to worry, Lukey. No woman would spend a night in a car with you even if the alternative were freezing to death." A tittering as soft as the sound of mice feet scurrying across a linoleum floor filled the classroom. The seminarians all turned to the speaker, none as surprised as Blaze. It was not he who had spoken, but Fen the Fearless.

Fr. Alexus' face paled, then turned red. In the secret depth of his mind, he more or less agreed with Oblate Blaise, but he did not intend for the Second Reformation of the Church to start in his classroom. That could threaten his chances of becoming the next Provincial.

"Outbursts like this are totally out of line," he intoned gravely. "All three of you go to your rooms. And stay there until you hear otherwise from the Prior."

Each of the three reacted in his own more or less predictable way. Back in his room, The Very Reverend Lukey paced back and forth in self-righteous agitation. Why was he being punished for defending Canon Law? He had always suspected that Alexus was soft on Church dogma. Lukey would inform the Provincial of this incident.

Fen sat at his desk staring glumly at the wall. Why had he opened his big fat mouth again? How many times would he let that idiot Blaze lead him into trouble? He had enough problems as it was. Lately he had been feeling so horny that he could hardly think about anything except sex. He had decided he must be homosexual. That's why he liked that idiot Blaze so much. He really did wonder sometimes if Blaze were homosexual, which was why he doubted that anything had happened in the car that night with Marge Puckett. Now the idiot was championing penises. But if Fen were gay, why did he dream of endless lines of girls standing against a wall, himself moving from one to the other, methodically coupling with each in turn until he awoke, ejaculating semen all over the sheets. Could the celibate life somehow turn a heterosexual man into a homosexual one? Maybe he was both.

Back in his room, Blaze would have been stupified by Fen's suspicions that he, Blaze, might be gay, since his secret thoughts were almost exclusively focused on Marge Puckett these days. But at the moment, he had much more combative issues on his mind. He banged away furiously on his typewriter, adding another chapter to "The Story of My Weird Life." All the pent-up anger that he had tried to keep bottled inside him with his Peter Pan playfulness, his grating laughter and his absurd fantasy worlds, welled to the surface. He pounded on the keys: "I will join the Jains of India, wandering naked through the world, eating no meat, knowing no woman, owning nothing, not even clothing, teaching that sexual organs are the most decent parts of the body and indeed the glory of the human race. The brassiere and the codpiece are sure signs of human decadence."

He stopped short, his thoughts careening around his mind like corn popping in a hot, covered pan. He tried to focus on one puffed kernel at a time but could not. "The Jews have their Passover and now we shall have our Takeover." He pounded away on the hapless keys. "Time to move the Josephians into the New Age."

He paused, his hands hovering over the typewriter, thinking about how to write down his thoughts. A new idea had occurred to him. By God, he would become a priest after all, just out of sheer contrariness. He and the SBDC Boys would take over the Josephian Order and turn it into a moral force that had enough relevance to the real world that they could eventually overthrow the Vatican. A sort of new Knights Templar without temples. They would show people how to obtain food, clothing, shelter not with money but with joyous work. They would make and dispense medicines for free. By God, he would. By God he would if he had to become Pope to do it. He paused in his thinking. No. Let's not get carried away here, Other Blaze. I will then marry Marge Puckett. Let Gabe be Pope. Yeah. Much better. Gabe can handle shit like that. Our message to the world will be that life is supposed to be free of all oppression. Feeding, clothing and sheltering your family can be fun as well as work. The rest of the time, play games or strum guitars or rock babies. Hell, say prayers and go to church if that makes you feel better. Do not spend time and money writing asinine dogmatic, nit-picking moral laws. Do not try to control others. The whole world should take a vow of poverty. If you aren't rich, you can't get power. Get rid of all those big fancy church buildings that cost millions of dollars. Build baseball diamonds not cathedrals. We need a new Martin Luther to nail 94 new theses to the church door. He started typing again.

Thesis No. 1: Humans create their gods, not vice versa. The only God that exists outside the human mind is the continuing act of love that flows between people and between them and nature.

Thesis No. 2: The concept of an all-powerful God existing outside the human mind is just a scheme to gain power over the ignorant.

Thesis No. 3: Money is the root of all evil. Take a vow of poverty.

Thesis No. 4: When you're dead, you're dead. On the other hand, no one knows how long you can live.

Thesis No. 5: The only paradise attainable is here in the material universe.

Thesis No. 6: The material universe had no beginning and has no end.

Thesis No. 7: There is no need for a formal body of religious dogma or a religious hierarchy. The only purpose dogma serves is to support oligarchies of power.

Thesis No. 8: Cathedrals, mansions, bank and government buildings are a waste of money and energy good only for supporting armies. Raise chickens in them.

Thesis No. 9: Nudity promotes sexual morality better than clothes. If everyone went naked for three hours, no one would notice but to remark on how ugly human bodies are, Marge Puckett excepted.

Thesis No. 10: (Wow, only 84 more to go.) All the clergy should be required to support themselves by the work of their own hands, like Amish ministers do.

Thesis No. 11: (I'm never going to make it to 94. That Luther must have been a real blabbermouth.) Persons nailing religious reform measures on church doors should not be prosecuted.

Thesis No. 12 . . .

He paused. Gabe had appeared at his door. "You're in deep shit," Gabe said.

"Do you think I was diddling that girl?" Blaze asked angrily.

"No. You would have been having too much fun fantasying about diddling her to actually get around to doing it."

Blaze glared at him. "Don't disturb me," he said. "I'm laying the groundwork for the New Order after we take over the Church."

"Be sure to make provisions for moving Church headquarters out of Rome. Rural Minnesota would be ideal. Possibly Sleepy Eye. There's a town that would make a wonderful address for a religious headquarters."

"Won't be any headquarters in the new Church."

"That makes Sleepy Eye an even better choice."

Blaze could not keep from laughing. He glanced at his eleven theses. He decided not to nail them to the chapel door just yet.

But he had a serious matter to attend to while Prior Robert was being so gracious to him. Jesse's father had died, and Jesse would hardly leave the seminary barn for fear that social workers would take him away to an institution. Melonhead had installed in the lab an ancient woodburning stove that he had found in one of the farm sheds so that he could keep his potions from freezing. That gave Jesse a warm place to sleep at night. Blaze kept him well supplied with food filched from the kitchen. Jesse had learned the barn chore routines well enough so that some mornings he had started to milk the cows even before Brother Walt arrived. Jesse had to be supervised because he tended to overfeed and undermilk the cows. But he could rattle off the number of pounds of milk each cow gave at each milking without looking at the chart record. Blaze was amazed and baffled by Jesse's profound power of numbers memory. He started reading books on mental retardation which led him to books on autism. He learned that such ability was by no means rare among autistic people considered to be mentally deficient. Scientists seemed to have no explanation other than noting that they were not so much mentally deficient as unable to cope with life on their own. Perhaps, Blaze thought, they were so mentally brilliant that they realized how insecure and dangerous life really was. At any instant, calamity and death could come and the autistic knew that, with more clarity than other people.

Blaze had to talk to Prior Robert anyway, about his classroom misbehavior. He knocked on Robert's office door and the Prior welcomed him inside, although warily. There was always more to anything that Oblate Blaise had to tell him than was apparent—even to Oblate Blaise.

"I have a problem," Blaze said.

Well, yes, Robert knew about the classroom incident. "And how can I help," the Prior replied.

"You know how that Jesse James guy hangs around at the barn. We've all become fond of him. Even you, I think."

"Yes."

"His father died recently. Here's the problem. Jesse is frightened out of his wits that he'll be put in an institution. He's not really all that mentally retarded, you know. In fact he can be very smart, expecially with numbers. Anyway, I got myself boxed in. I really do kind of like him and I promised him I would not let anyone put him in a mental institution." He paused.

"Yes?"

"Jesse's actually been staying at the barn most of the time. Sleeping at night in the lab. You probably didn't know that. He actually helps out considerably with the farm work. He knows how to do all the chores."

The Prior nodded. Could this be going where it sounded like it was going?

"Could we . . . do you think . . . is it possible that we could sort of adopt him into the Josephians? At least on a trial basis. Temporary until Nash Patroux and I figure out what to do with him."

"Who is Nash Patroux?"

"Ahhh, he's been sort of looking out for Jesse for years. Lives over around Savage someplace. I believe he owns a restaurant. But you know, we could be doing something really good here, taking this man in for a while. He really is no problem." Blaze felt like a little boy trying to justify to his mother keeping a dog that had followed him home.

"Well, Oblate Blaise, this would be highly irregular, would it not?"

"Not really. You remember that in addition to the First Order of Josephian priests and a Second Order of Josephian nuns, we have a Third Order of St. Joseph for people who want to live as much like us as they can, but as laypeople out in the world. Jesse could live here as a member of the Third Order, couldn't he?"

"Has he expressed any desire for religious life?"

"Oh, he practically begs me to let him stay here. He could be a lay brother like Walt. Walt hasn't taken vows yet. We could instruct Jesse in the Josephian life, you know, while he lives here. See how it would work." Since Blaze thought all Josephians were mentally abnormal, he almost said that Jesse would fit right in but decided to save that delicious thought for his journal.

The Prior did not believe he could just receive Jesse into the community. There would have to be a guardianship established. Some legal papers to sign surely.

"Couldn't I become his guardian?" Blaze asked.

"That's quite a commitment, Oblate. And Canon Law doesn't allow you to do that as an individual Josephian. Only a proper authority in the Josephians could do that, speaking for the whole Order. We would have to commit as a community."

"Well, then you could do it."

"You really want to take care of him, don't you, Oblate Blaise?" Robert asked, an admiring tone slipping into his voice. He had forgotten that he was supposed to reprimand the oblate for his impertinence in Alexus's class.

"Yes, Father. It's not really a big deal. We're taking care of him now. I just want some legal backing if the social services people come noseying around. If you just stand behind me, they'll go away after an official inquiry and then, you know, we can play it by ear."

Why did Oblate Blaise's suggestions always seem so logical even though they always ended up being so troublesome?

"Well, there will have to be family signing off, allowing us to take him in," the Prior insisted.

"He doesn't have any relatives, far as Patroux can find. Unless it might be Frank James." Blaze could not keep from making the joke that might not be a joke.

"Frank James? The outlaw? But he's dead."

"Yes, probably. Our Jesse James has papers purporting to prove he's a long-lost relative. And apparently, he really was named after the outlaw Jesse James. And believe it or not, it is mathematically possible that Frank James is still alive."

Prior Robert stared at the seminarian in amazement. What world had this guy come from and in what world did he really live? The priest knew he should just say no and be done with it, but remembering his promise to God about Oblate Blaise, he only shrugged resignedly. Maybe this was some kind of sign from God increasing Oblate Blaise's chances of becoming a good priest. "Okay. We'll take him in for awhile under one condition. You must get Mr. Patroux to sign something legal as this Jesse James' guardian stating that he wants us to care for him temporarily."

And so it came to pass that on Groundhog's Day, 1955, Jesse James the Second emerged from his hole in the Western Range, did not see the shadow of his former self, and was duly ushered into Ascension Seminary as Brother Jesse James Brown of the Third Order of St. Joseph. He called all the oblates "Pal" and all the oblates loved him.

Other Blaze wrote in his journal: "Now I have absolute proof that you can't tell the sane from the insane in religious life."

CHAPTER 16

Spring hung its dainty green lace out to dry on the hills overlooking the Josephian acres, and Gabe and Blaze, with Brother Jesse following along like a faithful dog, paced their newly-drained swamp ground with unbridled optimism and enthusiasm. They were true farmers facing another spring: full of hope, blind to the obstinate machinations of the weather that invariably beat farmer ambitions into dust or mud before the year was over. They would grow potatoes on their new land and sell them at the Farmer's Market in Minneapolis. And of course, make a fortune. Blaze cared nothing about the economic possibilities. He just thought it would be fun to spend time at the market. It was Gabe who dreamed of the possibility of profit because he had free Josephian labor at his disposal. Each night he prayed for success—not, he reminded God, to glorify his own lowly efforts, but to show the Hasses of the world the power of the Lord. Just to make sure of the power of the Lord, he consulted scientists and agribusiness experts at the University of Minnesota and scrupulously followed their every whisper of advice.

Hasse spied something from his hilltop that made him bustle down to the newly drained part of the swamp. Oblate Gabriel was seated on the back of his truck at the edge of the reclaimed acres, cutting up seed potatoes while Oblate Blaise worked down the plots between the ditches with a rotary tiller.

"Vel, Oblate, planting all dat to spuds?" Hasse asked, a sly grin on his face.

Hasse was butchering consonants worse than usual, so Gabe knew enough to be on guard.

"The oblates must eat," he intoned, invoking his own kind of verbal disguise. "God willing, we shall have a bountiful harvest."

"Like da lilies of the field, neither do dey spin or . . ."

"Potatoes should do well here," Gabe interrupted Hasse's taunt with his own. "The land is new, virtually untouched, seeing as how folks hereabouts are kind of shiftless if not ignorant about drainage methods. Were I a lifetime farmer of this area, I'd probably be a millionaire by now."

"Hup!" snorted Hasse. "You'd go broke on spuds for sure."

"Says who? I know all about raising potatoes."

"It's the wrong time of the moon for planting, dumkopf."

Gabe stared at his adversary, a look of perfect joy spreading over his face. "The wrong time of the moon?" He repeated the sentence, savoring every syllable. And then repeated it again. The chuckle in his throat climaxed in an unrestrained hoot. "You really do believe that, don't you?" he finally said. "I can tell it on your face. All this time you've been hiding your fearful soul behind a façade of rationalism while believing in the basest superstitions. This time, Hasse, I've got you. You pretend to believe in neither God nor devil, but you worship a silly man in the moon!"

Hasse remained unmoved by the rhetoric. "Any damn fool knows you gotta better chance to get a good yield if you plant spuds in the dark of the moon. If you don't, they go to vine too much."

Gabe cackled in glee. "And chust how, my friend, are you going to prove dat!"

"Prove it? Prove it?" Hasse groped for words, realizing that he had been caught in a trap of his own setting.

"Tell you what," Gabe said, the glow of victory in his eyes. "Let's mark off two equal plots right here where the soil is identical. You plant an acre your way, and I'll plant an acre my way and we'll see who grows the best potatoes, your infernal moon goddess or the blessings of the Lord."

"You got yourself a deal," the old farmer shot back, a smile returning to his face. Neither moon nor God nor lack thereof could help a fool monk out-farm him.

Never before in Minnesota, even out in the Red River Valley where farmers had forgotten more about potatoes than the rest of the world knew, were such pains taken on a potato patch. Hasse used his own Kennebecs for seed, which over the years he had selected and saved annually from his highest producing hills. He planted the hills 18 inches apart in rows 42 inches wide so he could get a horse and cultivator down between them. He planted when the moon was between full and last quarter in April, that is, between the 13th and the 20th that year. The specific day he chose was the 20th when the sign was in Capricorn. According to zodiac tradition, he could have planted just as well on the 14th or 15th when the sign was in Scorpio or on the 19th when the sign was in Capricorn again. He settled on the 20th because that was the first day the soil was really dry enough to work.

Gabe wanted to plant on the 20th too, for the same reason, but deliberately waited until the moon was between the last quarter and the new moon when the almanac specifically warned not to plant anything. He picked the 25th in the sign of Aries, which the almanac said was unfavorable for root crops. He spaced his hills 18 inches apart too, but only 30 inches between rows to get more hills to the acre, using the latest improved potato variety from the university, so new it did not yet have a name but only a number.

Since the soil did not warm up sufficiently to sprout potatoes until the 28th, both crops appeared above ground on the same day: May 10.

Hasse fertilized his potatoes with the richest, most well-composted manure in his barn and twice as much as he normally would have used. Gabe consulted his scientific oracles again, and applied nitrogen, phosphorus and potash exactly as the university agronomists recommended, and then added a little more just to make sure. He also primed the soil with additions of boron, manganese, iron chelates, sulfur, magnesium and other strange trace elements he knew little about, just as the sellers of these micronutrients instructed him to do, even though they knew little about them either. Hasse weeded his rows with horse cultivator and hand hoe, and manually knocked potato beetles into a can of kerosene with a stick. Gabe cultivated with rototiller and sprayed the most advanced insecticides, herbicides and fungicides known to the high priests of Dow and Dupont. Over both plots, Blaze sprayed the merry sound of laughter.

Plants grew on both acres with a lush vigor that no one could remember ever seeing matched before, not even Harriet Snod, whose memory stretched over nearly two centuries because she kept alive her mother's and grandmother's memories. "Land sakes, 'taters never grew that good even before the beetle came in eighteen and fifty-seven," she marvelled.

As word got around, farmers, gardeners and university extension personnel started dropping by to see how the contest was going. Gabe put up two signs. The one in front of his plot read: "God's Potatoes." The one in front of Hasses's plot read: "Mammon's Potatoes." Prompted by Blaze, Hasse made two more signs. The one in front of his patch read: "Profitable, practical, traditional potatoes." And in front of Oblate Gabriel's plot, Hasse's sign read: "Bankrupting, suckerbait, agribusiness potatoes."

CHAPTER 17

Life within the walls of Ascension Seminary had become placid, in fact boring, after Fen and Blaze decided to cool their budding religious reformation. But the year was now shaping up into what the SBDC Boys figured would be the very nearly perfect life. In addition to the Great Potato Race, and Gabe's experimental tobacco patch, Melonhead's Ascension Mineral Water and Ascension Wart Remover, not to mention his Ascension Blood Cleanser, were attracting local attention as Axel spread the word among his moonshine clients. People were stopping at the barn as if it were a drug store, leaving behind, if they were so moved, an offering of a dollar a bottle for the medicines.

More exciting was the prospect of working on the newly rented farm on Lake Wassermensch which was far enough away from the seminary to offer Blaze the chance to avoid the prayerful life all summer long. Moreover the farm was a kind of vacation paradise since it all but surrounded the sixty acre lake. The lake was full of fish and wonderful for swimming. There was even a farmhouse and set of farm buildings on the place. Perhaps, Blaze daydreamed, he and Gabe and Fen could just stay there all summer, sleeping in the house and living mostly on fresh bullheads, crappies, snapping turtles and cattail roots from the lake, plus deer, rabbits and squirrels from the woods. He planted a little vegetable garden by the lake too. Might come in handy.

"But you know, it's kind of sad," he said, standing on the porch of the old farmhouse and looking out toward the lake.

"What's kind of sad?" Brother Walt asked.

"Not so long ago, a family lived and farmed here. Can you imagine how idyllic that must have been, on a lake like this? All to themselves?"

"Yeah. Why do you think they quit?" Walt asked.

Blaze snorted. He knew. "Just like my father, I'm sure. They couldn't make enough money to expand, and if they didn't expand they couldn't make enough money."

Half-way through the planting season, another electrifying event occurred, at least for the SBDC Boys.

"Fr. Hildebrand is coming here to teach," Danny excitedly announced in Melonhead's lab where the gang had gathered as usual for a smoke and a wee sip of Ascension Blood Cleanser. He was waving a letter. Banana grabbed it and read. Both of them beamed. Hildebrand's arrival would mean that there was a chance of playing baseball with outside teams as they had done in seminary high school.

Sports was the other reason why, after their high IQ scores, the Class of '49, alias The SBDC Boys, had led charmed lives through the high school preparatory seminary near Paoli, Indiana. The prep seminary was the traditional place where candidates who lacked the proper attitude for celibate and obedient life were usually weeded out. But weeding the Class of '49 presented certain difficulties. Except for Clutch, Melonhead and The Very Reverend Lukey, the members of this class were all good at sports, and some of them were exceptional. Danny and Banana had in fact attracted the attention of scouts from the Cincinnati Reds who came to watch them play when the boys were home during summer vacation. This attention had vexed Fr. Hildebrand when he found out. He had big plans. Seeing exceptional sports talent lying unmined in the Class of '49, he had persuaded the Provincial and the Advisory Board, some of whom were sports fans as rabid as he, to allow St. Joseph's prep-seminary to compete in baseball and basketball with regular southern Indiana high schools. The Cincinnati Reds could just stay the hell out of it. As a result, St. Joseph's, the smallest school in the district, never lost a baseball game from 1947 through 1949, and won their sectional basketball tournament in 1948 against much larger schools. As long as Hildebrand held the high hand, there was little chance that anyone on the championship team would have been "weeded out," even if caught off-property, in a bar, drinking beer with girls.

Now Danny and Banana, the two superstars, began plotting their return to baseball glory. First they had to discuss in minute detail who would play where, which was their favorite pastime. Danny would of course pitch, he said, and Banana would catch as they had all through high school and two-year college. Blaze would lead off and play short because of his speed and Gabe could play third and bat second, because of course Blaze and Gabe had to be back to back no matter what. Every time they got separated, things went bad for the SBDC Boys. Little Eddie would play second, Fen on first, and Mart left field. They would have to pick up two players from among the other seminarians.

"That'll be Summerfeld and Algood for sure," Banana said.

"And Nickles for a second pitcher," said Danny. "He's nearly as good as I am. What a dream team."

"Better put Mart in right field. Summerfeld and Algood will bitch if either has to play right," Banana suggested. "They think right field is beneath their dignity."

"Well, that's pretty stupid, because if any righthanders are lucky enough to hit my fast ball, it will be only to right field so that's where we need the best fielder," Danny said.

"Your humility is most admirable," Blaze replied, unable to resist getting into the planning process himself. "But that's not your best team. Let Gabe pitch and you play short and put Mart in left field and I'll play center and then you got yourself a real outfield."

"You out-humble me," Danny said. "But who's going to play third then?"

"Put Fen on third," Blaze said.

"But Fen can't throw to first."

Fen rolled his eyes but said nothing. He knew that what was transpiring was as much fun for his classmates as actually playing the game. It reminded him of when, as a kid, he and his brothers spent their entire play time pretending to be cowboys by arguing over who got to be Gene Autry.

"Well, then, put Fen on first, yeah, that's good and Algood on third. Nobody hits it to third much on Gabe's curve ball."

And so they went, on and on, until Gabe said if they didn't shut up he'd refuse to play at all. "Jeez, you haven't even found out if Hildy is in favor of the idea," he said.

"Oh, he'll be in favor unless he's had some out-of-life religious experience during the last three years," Danny said.

As a matter of fact, Fr. Hildebrand had had a sort of out-of-life experience ever since he had found out that the Provincial was appointing him to teach at Ascension Seminary. Never had he thought that knowing a little about scriptural theology would work towards his true interests. He would be back with the Class of '49, who by now would surely have matured into real ballplayers. He dreamed grand dreams. He would take his boys to the big time. He would pit them against the University of Minnesota and beat the asses off the Gophers. Oh, how good God was, to allow him a chance to further His honor and glory. Hildebrand could see the headlines in the paper: "Tiny Seminary Whips Big University."

All of Danny and Banana's plotting about who should play where on the team was therefore unnecessary. Hildy was way ahead of them. He had the lineup already set and there was no question but what Danny would pitch. He waited only for an opportune moment to win over Prior Robert. The Prior was not too swift, everyone said, or at least was easily manipulated. Robert should never have been appointed Prior, the other priests said, but they all supported the decision because under Robert they could get permission to do almost anything they pleased.

On a weekend in late April shortly after Hildy arrived at Ascension, he found himself accompanying the Prior to one of the large parishes in Minneapolis to hear confessions, say Mass and preach over the weekend. After confessions on Saturday night, the two relaxed in the priest's residence next to the church. Hildy mixed the two of them drinks—seven-year-old Jim Beam, Hildy's favorite. Only he slipped a third shot into Robert's glass. He tried to get a ballgame on television, but the screen remained snowy no matter how he jiggled and wiggled the antenna on top of the set.

"Damn television," he muttered. He turned it off and tuned in the radio to the Cleveland-Chicago game. Chicago was winning, which pleased Robert, an ex-Chicagoan.

"Did you ever stop to think how intellectual and uplifting the game of baseball is?" Hildebrand said, sipping.

Robert eyed him, slightly surprised. He had never before noticed any philosophical turn of mind in Hildy. "What do you mean? You just hit a ball with a stick and somebody else tries to catch it."

Hildy acted as if he had just heard rank heresy. "Swinging that stick properly is a great gift from God," he said soberly. "It is a high form of art, as much so as Da Vinci wielding a painter's brush." He sipped again, quite surprised at what had just issued from his mouth. He made a mental note to remember to use it in a sermon.

"I suppose so," Robert replied rather absently, trying to listen to the game.

Hildy waited for Robert to take a few more sips before he continued. "It has always seemed a shame to me that the gifts that these professional players possess could not be used more for the honor and glory of God," he intoned. "Sports stars are society's heroes. What if we could use their great physical gifts for more spiritual purposes?"

Robert frowned into his whiskey. He had no idea what Hildy was up to, but up to something he surely must be. "The way some of them chase women, I don't think that idea would bear much spiritual fruit," he remarked drily.

Hildy's left eyebrow arched. "Well, ahem, I suppose not. But you have to admit that if Babe Ruth had been a priest, think how many more Catholics there would be today."

That amused Prior Robert exceedingly, knowing something about Ruth's private life. But he only nodded. He thought he had figured out where Hildy was headed.

"As you know, Robert, when our prep-seminary team that I coached won the Paoli sectional basketball tournament in '48, it was a great public relations breakthrough for us. It opened lots of doors in that largely non-Catholic area of southern Indiana. It actually brought us priesthood candidates from all over the Louisville-New Albany area."

"So now that you are back together with your players, you're wondering if you can do that again here."

"Well, ah, well, as a matter of fact, yes," Hildy said, taken aback slightly. Whoever said Robert was a little slow?

Prior Robert was inclined to refuse the request, since he had grave concern about what mischief the SBDC Boys might get into while playing baseball with outside teams, but he remembered his promise to God not to be mean to Oblate Blaise whom, he knew, would be one of the most eager players. Also, it appeared that the number of seminarians seeking advice on sexual matters had increased lately—in fact ever since they had been focusing on the sixth and ninth commandments in moral theology. Perhaps sports would take their minds off darker subjects in this season when young men's fancies supposedly turned to thoughts of sex more than at other times—a stupid notion if there ever was one, he thought. Besides, Prior Robert loved baseball himself and wished that in his younger days, he had had the chance to play on a real team. "Okay, but all our games will be at the seminary, not off somewhere else."

Hildy nodded as if humbly. When the time came to play elsewhere, he'd figure out a way.

Blaze forgot about solving the great train robbery mystery, about nailing his theses to the chapel door, even about Marge Puckett. Gabe forgot about making a fortune with potatoes and watercress. Fen forgot about worrying over whether he was straight or gay. The SBDC Boys quit roaming the swamps. They laid out and landscaped a ball diamond, which Blaze insisted on calling "Real World." Danny's muscles had filled out and hardened in construction work and now he could smoke the ball so hard into Banana's mitt that the latter begged for mercy. Blaze and Gabe, perhaps from the exercise of milking cows by hand, swung the bat with a crisp quickness in their wrists that they had not exhibited in earlier years. Banana, also strong from construction work, regularly pounded the ball into the swamps over the right field fence, even occasionally against Danny's best pitches. Hildy squirmed with delight as he watched. By May 20, they were ready for their first game.

Nearly every town in the surrounding area had its own, village-sponsored team. Baseball was serious business in rural Minnesota and when Ascension beat Chanhassen by the score of 18 to 1, the news travelled swiftly. Every village team wanted a crack at the "monks." The monks systematically mowed down Carver, Victoria, Savage, Waconia, Pryor Lake, even Shakopee. Danny and Banana became household, or rather barnyard, names throughout Carver County. An increasing number of people came to the seminary to watch. Melonhead set up a table behind home plate where he dispensed bottles of his potions and collected donations in a cigar box. He explained to prospective customers that the mineral water from the "springs of Ascension" was good for "cleansing the bowels and general health benefits." Occasionally a customer from a preceding Sunday actually came back for more. Prior Robert worried exceedingly about Ascension Mineral Water, but knowing that it was dear to Oblate Blaise's heart, and remembering his promise to God, he allowed the seminarians to continue in business. He also had a premonition that allowing his oblates to play so many games with outside teams was going to get him in deep trouble, but he loved what was happening so much that he could not bring himself to stop it. Even among the oblates who thought baseball inappropriate for Josephians, the games aroused a certain pride. Who after all, can resist the ardors of rooting for the home team?

Blaze lived in utter euphoria, hardly able to believe he was batting so well. After he stole home to win the game against Shakopee, he abandoned his ideas of taking over the Catholic Church and began to plot how he might possibly get himself sent to the University of Minnesota to finish his priestly education. He would join the baseball team as a walk-on. Move over, Lou Boudreau, here I come.

Never before had life at Ascension proceeded so smoothly. There were no complaints about the food. Scores in class tests rose. No more arguments erupted over moral theology. No reports of possible homosexual activities whispered their gossipy way into Prior Robert's ear. The SBDC Boys quit playing dirty tricks on their fellow seminarians. Work on the building and in the gardens proceeded with much less complaining. Brother Walt claimed the farm was showing a profit. The only negative was that a whole case of beer had on several occasions disappeared from the priests' recreation room whereas previously only one or two at a time had been missed. But, all things considered, a little stolen beer might be good for team morale, opined the majority of the faculty, caught up in support of the home team.

Hildy was quick to point all this out to Prior Robert. "These guys are actually passing even Biblical Hebrew," he said. "Can you believe it?"

"Well," said Robert, unimpressed. "All they have to do is memorize the Our Father and Hail Mary in Arabic letters."

To which Hildebrand replied: "You can bet that not even the Pope can do that."

Fr. Abelard knew exactly where the beer had gone. The damned SBDC Boys had thrown a couple of victory parties in the slaughterhouse. But since he was himself under considerable scrutiny because of his drinking problem, he took great pains only to prove to the Prior that he had not taken the beer to his room. He was terrified that if he squealed on the SBDC Boys, somehow it would lead to the revelation that he had been in the slaughterhouse that fateful night. Or, if he hadn't been there, it might become evident that he had fantasized the episode, which to his alcohol-numbed mind, meant that his true awful self and his nagging sexual attraction to males would be found out. It might even unfold, horrors of horrors, that his former habit of standing naked in front of his mirror and masturbating might somehow become known. He became more convinced every day that it was his loathesome private habits that had led to his imagining the naked satyr floating around in the slaughterhouse. So guilt-driven had he become that he could no longer stand to look at himself in the mirror even fully clothed, nor feel drawn sexually to anyone, including himself. He decided that it was alcohol that had rid him of sexual desire, and so he drank even more to keep himself chaste. He was thankful that the focus was on the missing cases of beer and that no one realized that a case of whiskey had also disappeared from the liquor cabinet.

In Chaska, a few miles from the seminary, Red Blake sat in the dugout after a game, swigging on a beer too, and gloating over the scorebook. His team, the Chaska Wildcats, had just trimmed Mankato by a score of 3 to 1, largely on the strength of his pitching and his homerun. He was well aware that were it not for his tremendous ability, Chaska would have been too small a town to sport a triple A, semi-professional baseball team and play against towns the size of Mankato. He could be playing in the minor leagues, might possibly even in the majors if he wanted to. But Red Blake much preferred lording it over players well beneath his skill level. He had, in fact, played a season in the minor leagues where he was reminded every day that he was no more a hotshot than the other minor leaguers. Accustomed to the adoring awe of the baseball crowd in Carver County, he did not appreciate being just another player in the minors. So he came back home. He understood the joy of finding a puddle small enough so that he could make a big splash.

"Twelve strikeouts," he counted. "If that goddam ump wasn't blind, there'd be fifteen." The team's manager, sitting beside him, nodded. He put up with Blake's bragging because without him, the Wildcats couldn't have beaten every team in the surrounding tri-county region for six years running.

Another voice interrupted Blake's glowing reverie. It was the ubiquitous Kluntz, the bearer of all local gossip. Kluntz never missed a Wildcat game. He had helped buy the scoreboard, the only time anyone could remember that he donated to anything. He thought that gave him the right to sit in the dugout any time he wanted to, which was always.

"There's one team in the area you haven't beat," he said, and there was something in his attitude that suggested maybe Blake was a yellow-bellied bully, which is exactly what Kluntz thought.

"Forget it, Kluntz," Blake replied, knowing full well what team the weathered old farmer was referring to. "We're not wasting our time on a bunch of monks. That would be slaughter. The fans wouldn't like it."

"'Specially if you lost," Kluntz said.

"Oh, for Chrissake, Kluntz. I doubt we'd even be allowed to play a team so far beneath our division."

"Yep, you can," Kluntz said. "I checked it out. Besides those monks have beaten every other team around them. People already startin' to talk, you know. Sayin' you're scared of them."

"Well, goddam, Kluntz. Bring the lambs to slaughter." Blake did not even bother conferring with the manager. He ran the team and everyone knew it.

"You gotta play on their diamond. They ain't allowed to play elsewhere."

"We'll play 'em in your barnyard if you like."

Next day, Kluntz showed up at Hasse's barn, where Gabe, Fen and Blaze also waited for his report. The three seminarians had become almost like family on the Hasse farm, as he had on theirs. "It worked. It worked," Kluntz said gleefully, dancing his little jig around the stanchion barn. "They've got an opening in their schedule next Sunday. Hee hee hee hee hee." Then he paused, never sure of anything. "You really think you can beat them?"

"Of course," Blaze said. "Take more than Chaska to beat Danny's pitching."

"What Kluntz means," the glittery-eyed Hasse explained, "is can we bet on you and win? Think we can get ten to one odds?"

"Hasse, if they made you president, this country would be outta debt in three months," Gabe remarked.

"I can tell you one thing," Blaze said. "They won't get many runs. Nobody can hit Danny Danauau when he's on, except Banana. The whole thing'll rest on whether we can get a run or two out of this Red Blake you keep talking about."

"Red's getting a gut on him," Kluntz said. "He ain't what he was five years ago. He's thirty-five, his fast ball's slower than Danny's. Other night, that bunch from Hutchinson got him for eight runs but he turned around and hit three homers to beat 'em anyway."

"Seems to me if you can get ten to one odds, you ought to take it," Gabe said to Hasse, never letting really important aspects of a discussion languish. "You can split your winnings with us. Give us a little incentive."

Hasse chuckled. If the Josephians didn't make Gabe the head monk as soon as possible, they would prove they were just as dumb as he thought they were. "I just might do that," he said.

"Put it in writing."

CHAPTER 18

Blaze thought Sunday would never come. He and Danny spent most of the morning raking the ball diamond in preparation for the one o'clock game. Prior Robert dispensed the entire community from chanting breviary for the rest of the day so everyone could watch the game. The oblates lined the first base side of the playing field to cheer their comrades on. A relatively large group of visitors settled into lawn chairs along the third base line, some of them to root for Chaska, others out of disbelief that monks could play baseball well enough to attract the Wildcats. Melonhead got rid of every bottle of Ascension Water and Ascension Wart Remover he had displayed on the table. Gabe had tried to get Prior Robert to invest in a coin-operated portable toilet, seeing as how the sulfur water could sometimes act fairly fast, but the Prior did have his limits. The crowd could use the cornfield across the road as usual.

Red Blake arrived only minutes before the game, toting a large bag with his five expensive bats, his three special gloves, his two pairs of spikes, and a selection of sunglasses. Trailing him were three adoring females, two adoring teenage boys and the manager. He threw only a few warm-up pitches to show his utter disdain for monks.

On the diamond he glared at the first batter who was grinning toothily at him. What nerve! He'd just whiz a fastball straight down the middle so fast that the toothy grin wouldn't even see it. That would wipe that goddam smile off his face in a hurry. He reared back and fired.

It seemed that he had barely released the ball when wood cracked against leather and the ball went whizzing back past his ear. Blake had the sickening realization that he would not have gotten his glove up in time if the ball had been coming straight at his head, and he might be dead now. His reflexes must be slowing a little. To add to his humiliation, the batter laughed gratingly all the way to first base.

All the SBDC Boys knew what was going to happen next. No signals necessary. In games they were not sure of winning, they always proceeded the same way if Blaze got on base. On Blake's next pitch, Blaze stole second, laughing gratingly all the way. Gabe was taking the pitch all the way too. Standard procedure. The SBDC Boys had not yet met the catcher who could throw Blaze out. On the next pitch, Gabe bunted down the third base line, a skill he had mastered over many years. Blaze did not even pause with the pitch, knowing the bunt would be down on the ground, not popped up, knowing that the third baseman would never have time to field it, wheel and throw to the shortstop covering third to get him. Gabe was out at first, but Blaze was on third, and Danny at the plate. A sacrifice fly would bring Blaze in, and no one could remember if there had ever been a time when Danny could not hit a fly ball when he needed to. He lifted the first pitch to the center fielder and Blaze sauntered home. Blake had made four pitches and the monks already had a run.

That could be enough, Danny told everyone. He proceeded to retire the Wildcats for five innings. But then Blake finally caught up with one of his fastballs and sent it over the snowfence into the swamp behind the field. Score tied.

Tension mounted. Fen's lips felt to him like ancient parchment. Gabe's and Banana's bravado disappeared. Even Blaze turned grim. "Baseball is life and life is baseball and he who remains in baseball remains in life and life in him," he would write later in his journal. Only Danny remained unruffled. Blake, by now fully warmed up, methodically worked his way through the monk batters, allowing only two scattered hits by Danny and Banana. Top of the eighth. Blaze on short took his practice groundball from Fen at first and decided to toss it to Gabe at third instead of the usual routine back to Fen at first. In turning towards third base, his eye caught a face in the crowd that made him stop dead in his tracks. Oh, wow. It was Marge Puckett and she was looking straight at him. Oh, wow. He grinned at her. She smiled back. Oh, wow.

Blaze's rockets of emotion blasted off. He ascended into heaven. This was the first time in his life that he felt something really great was happening to him. Red Blake at the plate smashed a hot grounder over second, a sure single. But Blaze was after it with a speed that was now inspired by more than muscular quickness. He dove, the ball skipped up and slammed into his glove at the very last possible split second before it otherwise would have bounced on into centerfield. His momentum carried him head over heels behind second base but he came up on his feet firing to first to catch the slow-running Blake. One out. Everyone was screaming. Trotting back to his position, he stole a look. Sure enough she was clapping and smiling at him. Oh, wow.

That play seemed to break the Wildcats' spirit because it wasn't likely that Blake would get to bat again. They went down lamely in that inning and in the next, last, inning. Now it was the bottom of the ninth and Blaze was leading off again. He'd bounced weakly to short his last two times up and Red Blake figured he had him in the palm of his hand, almost literally. But now Marge Puckett was in the picture, and Red Blake's fastball was, whether Blake knew it or not, not quite as fast as in the middle innings. A less bullying pitcher might have tried some curve balls, but Blake wanted to crush this smiling smart-ass with fastball machismo. His first one brushed Blaze back from the plate. Prior Robert smiled. "Pride cometh before the fall, Mr. Pitcher," he mumbled under his breath from behind the backstop. "I think if you put that fastball over the plate, it's all over for you."

Blake reared back again and in the ball came, not quite so lightning fast as five years ago and fat across the plate. Again there was the sweet sound of ash meeting leather and the ball whizzed past Blake almost in exactly the same spot as in the first inning. When Blaze stopped on first with a single he was cackling his irritating cackle. "You cocky sonovabitch," Blake muttered, just loud enough for Blaze to hear. The remark of course delighted Blaze. "And I'm going to steal second and there's nothing you can do about it."

Blake winked at the catcher, their sign for a pitch out. He stretched and threw, taking a split second longer than he usually would have in delivering the ball to tempt Blaze even more into stealing. But even as he released the ball, Blake knew he had done wrong. Because of his slight hesitation, Blaze had gotten a jump that even a pitchout was hardly going to work. Furthermore, rarely ever having to throw a pitchout, Blake threw a little too far out, and the catcher had to glove the ball off balance. Blaze streaked down the basepath, dove out towards the right of second base, throwing up a little duststorm in the middle of which his left hand snaked out and caught the corner of the bag. Safe.

Now it was up to Gabe to dump down his patented bunt. But this time Blake was ready. He gave Gabe a good pitch but just a tad slow so that Blake could be moving toward the third base line before the ball even reached Gabe. Gabe dropped down the bunt. Blake pounced on it like a cat on a mouse, grinning now because he had the smart sonavabitch going to third dead to rights. Out of the corner of his eye, however, he saw the smart sonuvabitch had never hesitated to make sure the bunt was down, and was streaking toward third a step farther along than Blake thought possible. Blake whirled and threw, too fast, to the shortstop covering third. The throw was high and Blaze came plowing through the dirt on his belly like a mole gone berserk, only his hand showing above ground, caressing the base. Safe. The monks were now all cheering in a very unmonklike way, even Very Reverend Lukey. The Prior was jumping up and down. Jesse was drooling while he shouted, "Jack, Jack, oh, pal Jack!" Through the dust, Blaze was squinting at Marge Puckett. She was on her feet screaming. Oh, wow, he thought. This was better than orgasm.

Now Danny Danauau had to at least hit a sacrifice fly. If Danny didn't do it, surely Banana would. The monks were roaring now, remembering their old highschool cheer.

Oh wow, Oh wow
Danny Danauau.
Oh wow, O wow
Danny Danauau!

A double play would negate the chance of a sacrifice fly, Blake knew, but that sonuvabitch with jets in his heels on third would make it home. Only a couple infield pop-ups or a come-backer could get the Wildcats out of the jam. But that was not likely to happen, he knew. The next two players had been the only ones to get hits other than the smartass sonuvabitch standing on third, taunting him. He deliberately walked Danny to load the bases to make a force out on any base. Fr. Damien, beside Prior Robert behind the plate, lost his priestly cool and yelled ancient Hebrew curses at Blake that, had anybody known, translated roughly into "May you fry in hell, you fat-bellied, illegitimate son of Islam."

Banana stepped to the plate. He believed that but for the hand of God, he might be stepping up to the plate for the Cincinnati Reds somewhere. Just as he knew the hand of God had steered him to the Josephians, he knew with absolute trust that God had foreseen this moment in the summer of 1955 and had willed that he would drive Blaze home and win another victory for Christianity. He let one good pitch go by. No matter. It was all pre-ordained. He could have closed his eyes and still hit the ball. Banana's big rawboned body unwound on the next pitch, the bat blurred in the hot summer air, and the ball disappeared into the swamp over the right field fence.

Oh, the bittersweet tragedy of life and the blessedness of not knowing the future. Banana, dancing around the bases, shouting in joy, was living the last truly happy moment of his life. Blaze, skipping home from third, looking at Marge cheering for him, was living the first truly happy moment of his. It was a good thing he had to go on to home plate to make the score legitimate or he just might have run instead deliriously into her arms.

After the cheers died down, and the fans had gone home, and the crazy story settled into local history of how a bunch of monks had beaten a Class triple A, semi-pro baseball team, Hasse was methodically counting up his winnings. Even if God did not exist, it paid to be on His side, he was thinking, just as Kluntz always maintained. "Hunderd twenty, hunderd thirty, hunderd eighty, two hunderd," he counted, collecting the fruit of his ten-to-one bet from the hapless Blake. He then started rather suddenly for his car. But the way was shortly blocked.

"Pay up." It was Gabe, covered with ball diamond dust, extending his hand. "You really ought to give it all to us so that God has mercy on your impenitent soul." Then, to his surprise, Hasse did exactly that. Gabe smiled. And so did Hasse.

CHAPTER 19

The baseball game eventually faded into memory, and the realities of life, however unreal they might be in this case, returned. Blaze began to fantasize about Marge Puckett again. Had she come to the game to see him? Should he have talked to her? Was that her boyfriend with her? Maybe it was her brother.

Meanwhile, the rumors about seminarians going to universities to complete their priestly studies were heard more frequently in the halls of the seminary. Gabe began to worry seriously. One scuttlebutt had him going to Rome. If that summons came as a direct order, he didn't know how he was going to avoid it. He could not violate his vow of obedience. But he had no intention of abandoning his "projects." His tobacco patch and potatoes were growing wonderfully. He and Clutch had almost figured out how to automate the packaging of watercress for sales to grocery stores. Sales of Melonhead's herbal remedies at the barn had picked up since the ball game. Their new product, Road Tar Honey Toothpaste, was almost ready for distribution. There had to be a way out of this stupid Rome dilemma, a way to be disobedient without being disobedient.

An idea finally came to him. He would demonstrate that he was not intelligent enough for the brainy education his superiors had in store for him. Screw Rome.

Fen was being overwhelmed again by dreams of sexual behavior so lewd that even to recall them in the morning ran the risk of committing the sin of impure thoughts. His wayward subconscious had returned to its insidious attack on his chastity. At least now he knew he wasn't gay. Couldn't be. Girls had come to the games almost from the start, and, studying them out of the corner of his eye, he was fascinated. His world had been almost exclusively male even before he went into the seminary at age 14. Blaze had grown up with a house full of sisters, which, he liked to say, was the reason he had gone to the seminary. But the only female that Fen had known well was his mother and she died of cancer when he was in the eighth grade. The only women he had become familiar with since then were the misty and voluptuous nymphs of his dreams. The dreams convinced him that he was not meant to be a priest, but it was too late for that. He had already taken vows, which meant that God hath spoken, Amen. He was trapped. But if he didn't find a way out of the trap, he would go crazy.

What to do? After he had reached the age of so-called reason, seven years old, he had trained himself, as the Church taught he must, to reject any direct complicity with sexual pleasure outside of marriage. Because of his iron will, he had seemingly succeeded. So strong had been his resolve that for a while even in his sleep, he seldom did anything actively to reach orgasm. His conscious mind could almost always stab down into his subconscious and stop the completion of any action that might result in sexual release. But nature eventually caught up. The more resolutely he tried to stop orgasm, the more strongly his libido asserted itself. His nightly dream of coupling with an endless line of supplicant women took a new turn. The women no longer remained passive. They came after him. They kissed him. They wrapped their legs around him. They did awful, loathesome things to him. And until he awakened fully and clamped his iron will down hard against his dreams, he knew he loved every bit of it and could hardly wait to go to sleep again.

Nevertheless, he tried to resist this anticipation of dreams or the "noctural emission" that sometimes accompanied them, which is what the Moral Theology textbook said you had to do. Sometimes as he was waking up, but not fully awake, he realized that he was masturbating and then the floodtides of guilt overwhelmed him. He could not determine whether what he did was willful masturbation, a mortal sin that could send him straight to hell if he did not confess it or "involuntary nocturnal pollution," to use the term in the textbook. Article II of Chapter 1, section 228, subsection B said that the degree of sin depended on the degree of involuntariness. But how could one judge the degree? He began to see a glimmer of a solution to his scruples when he read in Jone and Adelman that it was lawful "to wash, go bathing, riding, etc. even though one foresees that due to ones's particular excitability in this regard, 'pollution' will follow, so long as one did not consent to the pleasure." Hmmmm. How could anyone, knowing that "pollution" would follow, not commit a sin by doing these seemingly innnocent actions? And what all did that "etc." encompass?

But it was in Section 229 that Fen finally found his salvation. "Nocturnal pollution which was willed neither directly or indirectly, is no sin," the book said. "This is true, even when in a dream one takes pleasure therein." Hmmmmm. "But if the pleasure is experienced while half-awake, there would be a venial sin." Aha. Venial sins he could handle. They did not require going to confession to save one's soul.

But how did one know when he was half awake rather than fully awake? How about three-fourths awake? He was plunged back into the depths of his dilemma.

Over time, Fen developed a solution that if it did not entirely convince him that he was not headed for hell, at least kept him from having a mental breakdown. As long as he was fully conscious, his steel-willed mind could keep him from doing anything outrightly sinful. If he masturbated in his sleep, or anywhere between sleep and full, out-of-bed wakefulness, he was not going to worry about it anymore.

He wondered if other celibates came to the same conclusion, but to ask would have been unthinkable for him. Not even the SBDC Boys discussed such matters, at least not until Very Reverend Lukey made a discovery.

Very Revervend Lukey had gotten permission to do research at the University of Minnesota library in the Twin Cities for a paper he was doing, at Fr. Alexus's suggestion, on the history of the Church's teachings on celibacy. Since future plans called for the seminarians to attend secular universities, Fr. Alexus thought a trial run might have merit. Prior Robert grudingly gave permission. At least it would keep Oblate Luke, who had been relieved of his kitchen duties, from bitching all the time about how the farm crew members were playing around at the barn when they should have been in chapel chanting the breviary with the other oblates.

One of the first books Very Reverend Lukey read at the university, because it was the one everyone at the university was talking about, was Alfred Charles Kinsey's report on human sexuality. Lukey read with shocked absorption. Kinsey, he was sure, was the devil incarnate, writing all those lewd lies, but Lukey read to the very end and then started telling the other oblates what he had learned. Soon the Kinsey Report was making its rounds through the seminary and causing a theological earthquake of perhaps 7 on the Ethics Richter Scale.

"Did you know that according to the Kinsey Report nearly everyone masturbates, including religious celibates," Lukey said to Fen. "Do you believe that?"

Fen, taken aback, stared at him. He was more surprised that Very Reverend Lukey would repeat such a notion than whether it was true or not. He wondered if Lukey understood that by the very act of asking the question, he was hinting very broadly that he masturbated.

"Ninety percent of them masturbate," Lukey continued triumphantly, trying to elicit a reply.

"No one asked me," Fen said and walked away.

He was nevertheless thunderstruck by this information. Could it possibly be that he was not any more wicked than the others? That they were all preoccupied with thoughts about sex?

When Prior Robert got wind of the Kinsey Report he tracked down the book that was circulating and read some of it himself. His face blanched as he read. He doubted little of it, of course. Anybody who had been hearing confessions as long as he had, could have written the Kinsey Report off the top of his head and spiced it with a great deal more anecdotal material than Kinsey had collected. But to let seminarians, already aching with sexual desire, see this misery all laid out in print, God help us. Their minds would be warped even before they started hearing confessions.

He now had another reason to oppose sending seminarians to universities. He took the Kinsey Report back to the library himself and told The Very Reverend Lukey that for the time being, the seminary's own library provided research material enough.

Sexual repression had another effect on Fen which he could not understand. Walking alone along the river, or among the springs in the swamp, or along Lake Wassermensch, he had tremendous urges to go swimming naked. He could find nothing in moral theology that expressly forbade that. In fact, Section 228, saying that it was okay to "go bathing, riding etc.," surely applied to swimming too. Even without any sexual pleasure, he found swimming naked somehow exhilarating. Sunbathing after a swim, he often fell asleep, and sometimes during sleep he would have delicious sexual dreams that ended in delicious sexual climax.

By August of that long hot summer, he had developed a habit, whenever time allotted, of walking to the lake at the rented farm, or actually, running the five miles through the swamplands, up the bluffs, through the corn and alfalfa fields to get there. Hot and tired, he would swim out to the little island at one end of the lake, and then fall asleep on a promontory where the breeze coming across the water blew the mosquitoes away. He felt, on the island, totally tranquil and secure in his own little Garden of Paradise where no prying eye could see him basking naked in the sun. If sexual climax occurred, with or without a little help in his state of semi-wakefulness, so much the better, because, he told himself with his newly-acquired education, he did not directly will it. Besides, everyone did it. He would then walk slowly back to the seminary, refreshed and calm, at peace with himself at least for a while. He was just one of millions of weak mortals, thank you Dr. Kinsey. He had, he thought, solved his dilemma.

CHAPTER 20

Most of the little lakes in Carver and the surrounding counties were completely surrounded by farmland, giving them a privacy that would have astonished people from more populated lakeshore areas nearer the Twin Cities. Cows rather than humans frequented the shore lines, and fences had to be built out into the water to about a depth of four feet, or the animals would amble in the shallow water to another farmer's property. The farm at Wassermensch that the seminary had rented encircled the 60-acre lake except for a short stretch on the far side, where a township road paralleled the shore. Public access to the lake at that point made it a favorite spot for fishermen. Hasse often said that some day, all the lakes would be surrounded by houses and cabins. That's why he had bought this farm. He owned almost all egress to the water. In his eye, the shoreline was paved with gold.

Kadie Crockin pulled off the road at the sign announcing Wassermensch Lake and with practiced eye, scrutinized the water from her pickup. What was it about water that so lured her, she wondered. Were the evolutionists correct in theorizing that all terrestrial life had its beginnings in the seas, that therefore, all humans felt within them some long forgotten yearning to go back to their real roots? She did not think so. To her the attraction of water was its aliveness, the almost infinite surface changes the wind could mark on it, the play of light on its surface, and most of all, its tactile delight against the skin. To be immersed in water was a delicious physical pleasure. But maybe it was deliciously pleasurable because animal life had begun in the sea. Who cared?

Her aim was to swim in every one of Minnesota's ten thousand or so lakes. She was up to 150, and at 25 years old, figured she had plenty of time to test the waters of the other 9,850. There was a nice breeze today, so out on the water the mosquitoes would not be bad. There were no rowboats, no fishermen in view, so she would be alone. Were that not the case, she would probably have driven on to another lake. Solitude was her prime requisite, which was why she had to journey this far away from Minneapolis where she lived. Lake Minnetonka, for example, was so crowded on weekends now that traffic jams of boats occurred occasionally.

She backed the truck as close to the water as practical, turned off the motor, and untied the ropes holding the canoe on the pickup's bed. She was wearing a bikini with a short, wrap-around skirt over it. From the standpoint of beauty and proportion, her body was as perfect as that of a catalog model. She had a dark complexion and dark hair rolled up and pinned in a French bun. She pulled the canoe down off the truck and to the water's edge. The truck keys, her billfold, sunglasses and watch went into a waterproof box secured under the front seat of the canoe, along with a fishing tackle box. Pushing the canoe expertly ahead of her, she eased it into the water, and at the precisely perfect split second, sprang like a tigress into it as it headed into deep water. Soon she was far enough out on the lake that no prying eyes from the road could discern her in any detail. She stowed the oar under her seat, removed her clothes and slipped over the side of the canoe. The water consumed her hot body and she sighed pleasurably, rolling over on her back and floating.

For about fifteen minutes she swam around the boat, then pulled herself alongside it and just as expertly as she had rolled out of the canoe, she now in one swift motion pulled and rolled herself back into it without capsizing. She fixed a fishing line, tied it to the canoe, baited the hook with worms she had brought along, and tossed the hook into the water. Then she stretched out on the bottom of the canoe, using a lifejacket as a pillow, and basked in the sun. A feeling of tranquillity overwhelmed her as the lake breezes dried her skin, a sensual pleasure not matched by any other sensory delight that she knew. Reaching the perfect balance of four part harmony in a good choir came close, both more pleasant than the pawing embraces of one of the male clients that she escorted around the nightspots of the Twin Cities during the week.

She lay there thinking about nothing in particular for a while, alone in the world of nature, which was the world she had long ago decided was her true habitat. As soon as she had a little more money laid away in the stock market, she and her mother would pool their cash and buy a cottage on one of the ten thousand lakes. The thought of money brought her mind back to full consciousness. She hated the stuff and yet she loved it, just as she loved and hated her career. She did not think of herself as a high-class prostitute, but as the owner and operator of Quality Companion Service, a one-woman business that she had inherited from her mother. She did not know her father, having been sired by one of her mother's clients. Her mother would not say which one. "All you need to know, honey, is that he was mighty high-class stock, as successful and intelligent a man as you will ever meet."

Her mother had made sure Kadie received a quality education and the kind of training in manners and habits that would attract the higher classes she catered to—as if she were grooming her daughter for the Miss World pageant, she often said. Raised entirely outside the society of Christian culture and traditional family values, Kadie Crockin had no sense of wrongdoing about her way of life. She would argue, and sometimes did, that she was performing a beneficial service. She could point to occasions when she had curbed or stopped altogether the predatory business greed of restless, powerful men, soothing them with a sexual fulfillment that they had for one reason or another never enjoyed. Lacking that satisfaction, they had tried to compensate by driving competitors wolfishly out of business. Kadie made pussycats out of them and made everyone involved happier.

Also, she could point to dozens of children who, if they had known, would have thanked her profusely for saving their parents' marriages and their familial security. She supplied their fathers with the kind of intimacy that their mothers would not or could not provide and so the marriages went on, a farce for sure, but a secure haven for the children.

A few clients did not even want sex from her. At the end of a busy day of high-powered meetings made extremely stressful and exhausting by the testosterone-afflicted male competition that so often fuels the drive for success, these men merely wanted someone gentle and unthreatening to talk to in the evening. Kadie often said that she made more money listening than screwing. But, as her mother taught her, listening wasn't enough. A Quality Companion must also respond with conversation of her own, conversation that was stimulating, even controversial to a point, but never with even a hint of argumentative competition. It was a fine line, something that could not be faked, which was why Kadie, and her mother before her, had all the high-priced business they could handle. To win a bet with her mother, she had even succeeded in being so playfully imaginative and intellectual with one client that he became absorbed in their conversation and decided that contrary to his original intention, he didn't want the evening to end in sex after all. He went back to his rectory instead, went to bed with his wife, and next day delivered a sermon on the evils of adultery.

But there was a wearisomeness to her career too, physically and mentally. When she had to escort more than three men a week, she found herself finding sex repugnant, something that in the beginning she did not think possible. Mentally, she was getting tired of men in general. They were so vain, so predictable, and so easily manipulated. Hardly any of her clients were happy. That's why they came to her. So many of them had convinced themselves, or been taught, that making a lot of money was simply a matter of pushing all the right buttons. As the money flowed in, so would the happiness, they thought. Learning how untrue that was, they became petulant, morose, easily offended, hungry for sympathy. She did not believe she could ever have one of them around her constantly.

She rolled over on her side. The boat was slowly drifting across the lake. Still no one in sight. She closed her eyes, irritated that she had let the thought of business thrust itself into her tranquillity. She started thinking about her home, after her work years were over. Lots of gardens. Lots of fishing. She would produce almost all the food she and her mother would eat. She would not wear clothes in summer. She would sew what she did need and save oodles of money. She would require only the money that her investments brought in. And no men. She drifted off to sleep.

A gentle thump, the canoe touching shore, awakened her. As was always the case when she slept naked outdoors, she now did not feel uneasy about her nakedness. After only a short amount of time, especially time that included sleep, being nude became natural and normal. But she was aware that she had floated to a shoreline which could mean people around. She raised her head above the gunwale and looked around. The canoe apparently had not reached the true shore, but had floated up against a little island offshore a couple hundred feet. She loved islands. She would explore this one. The bank inclined continually upward. Obviously the island was an isolated little hill, common to the area, submerged except for its top. Leaving her clothes in the canoe, she walked up the incline. Suddenly she heard a groan. Panic-stricken, she froze in her tracks, looking wildly about for the source of the noise. With a start, she saw below her, around the curve of the island hillock, a man apparently asleep on his back and very obviously naked. Her first impulse was to race back to the canoe and paddle away as fast as she could, but the unusual sight arrested her. The man kept groaning and thrashing around in his sleep. He would intermittently grab at his crotch, then jerk his hand away hastily, groan again, subside to stillness, and after a pause, claw at his groin again.

She edged closer, so entranced by the sleeping figure that she forgot her own nakedness and how embarrassed she would be if the man awoke. But lying there naked, he did not at all appear threatening. Nudity loves nudity. Slowly, step after soundless step, she approached him. He was absolutely beautiful, she thought with an objective detachment that could only come from a prostitute or a sculptress. She was used to seeing older and much more portly men. She had in fact never been intimate with someone her own age, and realized that she had gotten into the habit of thinking of sex as work. Now she understood what she had been missing: an abdomen hard and rippling like a scrub board, a waist trim, a butt tight and lean, shoulders square and strong, bulging leg and arm muscles, a wild shock of hair begging to be combed by eager, questing fingers. And, oh Lord, what a gorgeous cock blooming grandly in the sun. This guy could get a permanent job posing for art classes at the university. But there was no model's detachment in him. It was obvious that his body craved sexual satisfaction, and she waited, rather clinically, for him to achieve orgasm, perhaps from some novel form of auto-eroticism she didn't know about but which might come in handy in her business.

But soon her observations went from being professional to wantonly sexual. She could feel her own body preparing for copulation. She had to get the hell out of there, but her feet remained rooted. This was so different from her usual experience. A man totally vulnerable, totally passive, not a leering, heaving predator grabbing at her. She began to feel as she had at age 17 before she became a Quality Companion. She had at least to touch him before she fled. Breathing as heavily now as he was, she knelt beside him, full of carnal desire that took away from her all caution. She would help the poor guy out. Put her hand where he apparently would not allow his own. She could relieve him without waking him—prove to herself just how damned good she was at her work. But then a more powerful wave of desire swept over her and she suddenly straddled him, carefully eased herself down upon him, her mouth on his, her legs carefully cushioning his penis between them.

Fen's eyes came open. He pushed her away with a cry of fear and surprise, then paused and looked at her. Surely he was dreaming. She on her part looked down on a face so incredibly innocent that she could only smile and bend down to kiss it. With a great shudder, he wrapped his arms around her and screamed as his body convulsed and reached orgasm.

Kadie wrenched herself free, the spell broken as suddenly as it had cast itself upon her. She was on her feet and running for the canoe. Fen had risen to his knees and was shouting after her.

"Wait. Don't go. I didn't mean to hurt you. Come back."

Kadie had pushed off in the canoe now, and was paddling fiercely. Fen ran to the shore, dove in and swam after her. But he was no match for the speed of the canoe and knew he could not swim all the way across the lake. He yelled at her again to come back, which only caused her to paddle harder. "What in the hell is the matter with me," she was muttering as she tried to put her clothes on and paddle at the same time. "How could I be so goddamned dumb."

Fen, dog-paddling, watched her fade into the distance, could see her, but barely, beach the canoe across the lake, shove it on a pickup and go speeding away. He swam back to the island, retrieved his clothes and then swam to the farmhouse, holding his clothes up out of the water with one hand. Sobbing, he dressed and made his way back to the seminary. His life, he knew, was changed forever.

CHAPTER 21

Fen went directly to the barn on his return from the lake. Blaze and Gabe would be doing the evening milking. Fen knew he had to talk to someone, and who else could that possibly be in his dilemma.

"You sure timed that right," Blaze said, as Fen walked into the barn. "We're about finished." Then he looked more closely at his comrade. "What's the matter?"

"Something terrible has happened," Fen said. Turning away he added. "Or maybe not so terrible."

What do you mean?"

"I've been raped. Sort of."

Blaze looked at Gabe. Both sprouted wry grins.

"Dammit, it isn't funny," Fen said. "I think I've been raped."

Blaze just stared at him, waiting for some indication that Fen was joking. Gabe, more practical, asked: "Who by?"

"Something sort of like a mermaid."

Normally, Blaze and Gabe would have erupted into laughter at that statement, but Fen's manner suggested caution.

"Sit down," said Blaze. He physically propelled Fen to a straw bale behind the stanchioned cows. "What the hell is the matter?

"You'll think I've gone crazy," Fen said, pleading for understanding. However being found crazy would be, he thought, a blessing. "I keep thinking it might be a dream, but I know it's not. She was real."

"She? Get hold of yourself," Gabe said, finishing the cow he was milking and coming over to sit beside Fen.

Fen started sobbing. Neither of his friends had ever seen him cry. They had never heard him say "dammit" either. Something really serious must have happened.

"You'll just think I'm nuts," he said, hopelessly.

"So what's new," Blaze said. "Spit it out."

"I can't."

"Look, Fen, men don't get raped." Blaze said. Then he looked at Gabe. "Do they?"

Gabe, still suppressing a smile, shrugged. How would he know?

Slowly, haltingly, his eyes cast down, Fen started his story.

"I've been going over to the lake a lot, you know."

"Yeah, we know," said Blaze. "Been kind of wondering about that, actually."

"Well, I've been going over there to be alone. Just wanted to sit and think a lot." He could never tell them the darker reasons for his desire to be alone.

"I swim over to the island, maybe fish a little. Watch for wildlife. Sometimes . . . sometimes I fall asleep. So peaceful there."

He paused, shook his head, sighed. "Oh, what's the use. You aren't going to believe me."

"Look, if you don't quit stalling, I'm going to take the milk to the cooler," Gabe said, losing patience.

"Well, I fell asleep and suddenly I woke up and there was this thing kneeling over me, a woman I tell you, with nothing on."

"I thought you said it was a mermaid," Blaze said, his eyes wide with wonder. This was better than any of his fantasies.

"Well, she had legs. Oh, my, you shoulda seen those legs."

That was too much for Blaze. He could not stop his habitual outburst of laughter.

"So, you have this leggy mermaid attacking you," Gabe said, humoring him.

"Well, okay, not a mermaid literally," Fen said. "Like I said, she had legs. And she had breasts. Oh, man. Do mermaids have breasts?" Something that was not fearfulness had slipped into his voice.

"And she . . . raped you?" Blaze prodded. "She actually—"

"I don't know," Fen said. And he really didn't know. He was not sure if sexual penetration had occurred. All he knew was that the encounter had brought to him a pleasurable release beyond anything he could have imagined. His terror was not in that pleasure, nor in feeling guilt about it, but in knowing, having experienced it, that he could never continue his studies for the priesthood, could never again be the person he had been. "I don't know," he repeated. "I just know that I came. Boy, did I ever come!"

For all their usual irreverence, Blaze and Gabe were embarrassed. They never talked about sex this way. They would have thought that Fen, of all people, would be the last to break their code of pretending that actual, physical sex was not something to talk about explicitly. Fen must be a case of Too-Much-Kinsey-Report.

"You guys think I'm a terrible sinner? I'm telling you that's what is really scary about this. Whatever happened, I want it to happen again. I can't ever be my old self again. Celibacy is bullshit."

Blaze looked off, out the barn door. Fen was reminding him of the way his own mind had overturned with the notion that men created their gods, thereby changing forever the way he viewed life. So powerful had been that logic to him that it had catapulted him mentally into a strange world of disbelief from which there was no turning back. Fen seemed to have gotten there through sex.

"You understand this never really happened," Blaze told him, not believing any other conclusion was sane. "You just imagined it."

"Oh, I wish it were that easy," Fen said.

"You've got to see some kind of psychiatrist," Gabe said. He had been reading Freud and thought he understood the problem.

"A psychiatrist would just think I was dreaming, like you guys do."

"Succubus," Blaze said.

"What?"

"There's a whole body of literature going back to the Middle Ages about angels or devils in human form hovering over and copulating with monks and nuns and others while they slept," Blaze said. "The female ones were called succubi. Honest. Come on, I'll show you."

After stowing the milk in the cooler, the trio trooped to the library and pored over the book Blaze had pulled from a shelf and blown the dust from. There was a drawing even, of a winged, apparently naked body hovering in the air over a terrified nun on her back in bed. "This is all shit of course," Blaze said, "but obviously something easy enough to dream. That's what happened to you, Fen."

Fen grabbed the book and read, then snapped it shut. "Nope. What happened to me was real. She got into her canoe and paddled away. She was some canoeist. I couldn't keep up with her, swimming."

"Oh," Blaze said. "And then you woke up, right?"

"I swam after her. I saw her get into her pickup and drive away," Fen said.

"You were chasing her?" Gabe said, a hint of scolding coming into his voice. "You wanted her."

Fen nodded, and not guiltily. "With every step walking back from the lake, I lost a little more of what I had been," he said. "Sort of like a snake shedding a skin. I'm a new man. It's horrible to realize this. I'm going to find that girl if it takes me my whole life."

"You can't be that crazy," Gabe said. "You've got vows, you know. You've promised yourself to the service of God, you know. You don't have a cent of money, you know."

"I tell you, something has changed in my mind. It is clear to me that the whole of Church dogma is built on thin air. I don't give a damn about vows. That's all stuff made up to keep us in stanchions like cows, to produce for the Order, for the Church."

"But you gave your word," Gabe said. "You gotta stand by your word."

"I'm not the same person that made those promises. And I'm not really disobeying my vows. There is more real chastity in having sex than in trying to deny sex. And when you say I can't leave because I don't have any money, isn't that what the vow of poverty is supposed to be all about?"

Gabe shrugged. Fen had flipped, it was obvious. It was a wonder more of the oblates didn't. They all took the dogmatic part of religion way too seriously. Didn't they understand that practical men did not really believe all that institutional dogma stuff literally, for God's sake. One had to keep religious beliefs alive so that the faithful would not get confused.

Blaze listened to Gabe's footfalls down the hall. Neither he nor Fen spoke for some time. Fen had suffered some kind of nervous breakdown, Blaze figured, but other than believing that there really was a real woman involved, everything else made sense to him. He knew about masturbating in his sleep, too. Finally he stood up. "I've got something I want to show you, Fen. Might help you find your way out of this." He went to his room and returned with a copy of his "Eleven New Theses, From the Second Coming of Luther." "Here, tell me tomorrow what you think of this."

Fen was gone next morning. The only thing missing as far as Blaze could tell was Fen's guitar and some clothes. There was a note on his desk addressed to Blaze: "Your Theses are correct. Goodbye. I will be over at the farmhouse for awhile. You know I love you guys."

Prior Robert paced the building in great anxiety, demanding to know, if anyone knew, where Oblate Christopher had gone. Blaze and Gabe thought that for the time being they would just lay low. Fen would probably be back as soon as he got hungry.

Finally the Prior, at the insistence of the rest of the faculty, particularly Abelard and Alexus, called the oblates into the chapel. The Prior himself did not really think it wise to do what he was about to do, but, well, the faculty had spoken. "We have reason to believe that one or more of you know what happened to Oblate Christopher." He looked directly at Blaze. "I am putting you under your vow of obedience to come forth if you have information bearing on this case."

This was serious business. Not to obey when "put under the vow" was a grave sin and sacrilege. This was Blaze's first test of whether he really believed his Eleven New Theses. He stared right back at the Prior. The God of power and might and religious vows and sacrilege was a creation of human minds but not his mind. That forbidding God was not his God. Blaze felt again the freedom that his new concept had given him. To know, deep inside, that dogma was the product of poor dumb sonsabitches who didn't know any more than he did, oh wow. He merely stared at Robert, his face a blank mask. But for Gabe, being ordered to do something "under" the vow of obedience was an awesome command behind which stood the entire power of the Church to grant or withhold salvation. He stood up. All heads turned toward him. He looked down. He especially did not look at Blaze. He would comply with Robert's command, but perhaps he could do it in a way that revealed nothing much.

"I do not know where Fen, er, Oblate Christopher, is at the moment, but I do know that he has experienced a terrible dream. He thinks it really happened. He has hidden himself away until he can straighten out the confusion in his mind."

Murmurs filled the chapel. The Very Reverend Lukey whispered to Clutch Pedali, "I told you that the farm crew was headed for trouble."

"It's for sure you will never get confused. You can't think enough to get confused," Clutch whispered back.

"Do you have any idea where he has hidden himself, as you put it?" the Prior asked Gabe.

Gabe, who from the study of the ins and outs of Canon Law, now knew, like a clever lawyer, how to manipulate the interminable defining exceptions of the Codex and English grammar. He decided that telling where Fen was staying was an undocumented assumption since he did not absolutely know, at this very moment, if Fen really was where he knew he was. "No, Prior."

Prior Robert began to fear that Oblate Christopher had wandered off into the swamps and sunk in the muck. Or maybe drowned in the river. But he wanted to refrain as long as possible from reporting a missing person to the outside authorities. And to the Provincial. Why was God testing him so? First an oblate almost gets lost in a snowstorm, now maybe another one is lost in the swamp. The oblates were ordered to form a search party and walk the swamp and river banks. Blaze and Gabe drifted apart from the others as soon as possible and when alone, ran back to the barn and rode off for Lake Wassermensch on the Farm Zephyr.

They found Fen at the old farmhouse, sitting on the porch that commanded a clear view of the little island in the lake. If the mystery girl returned, he would spot her.

"When are you coming back to the sem?" Blaze asked. "Robert is sick with worry about you."

"I'm not coming back. This is my home for the time being."

"You can't stay here."

"Oh, yes I can. Hasse says I can stay here if I work at remodelling the house. He's even going to supply the building materials and tools."

"Hasse will do anything for free labor," Gabe said disgustedly. "Have you told him your story?"

"Yep. And he doesn't think I'm crazy."

"He doesn't?" Gabe looked at Blaze. Hasse would lie in his teeth for free labor.

"He said I was probably the only normal Josephian in the bunch," Fen said, triumphantly. He paused, enjoying their discomfort. "And he likes your Eleven New Theses too, Blaze." He nodded toward the farmhouse door where he had hung Blaze's oeuvre in a picture frame.

Gabe walked over to the door to read the Eleven New Theses.

"What are you going to do for food?" Blaze asked.

"I'm working on that," Fen said. "Fish in the lake, wild berries in the woods, and thousands of acres of corn roundabout. I will live on cornpone if I have to."

"What about when winter comes?"

"Mermaid will return before then," Fen answered confidently. He had already given her a name. "If not I will beg food if I can't get enough otherwise. That's what the vow of poverty really means. I will beg. It will give me an excuse to go door to door to look for her."

"Can we tell Robert where you're living?"

"Sure. Tell him anything you want."

"And you aren't coming back?"

"No way."

"What if they come to get you? What if they commit you to an asylum?"

Blaze could see that Fen hadn't thought of that. Fen paused a moment, considering that possibility. Then he smiled. "I think if they can prove I'm crazy they would have to commit the whole Josephian Order."

Gabe stepped back away from the Eleven Theses, hardly believing what he had read. "Don't you two understand that you are cutting yourself off from all chance of salvation?" he said sternly."You know, it's one thing to joke about our life, but this is serious shit."

"You just don't get it, do you?" Fen said, softly. "Don't you see that none of that salvation stuff is true. My salvation is Mermaid."

Gabe looked at Blaze. "What about you?"

Blaze shrugged. "It's all a game somebody invented to make fools out of us, but now that I know, I'm not in a hurry to do anything about it. I want to stick around and see how it all plays out. How can life get any more interesting than this?"

Gabe shook his head. Maybe it was that damned mineral water.

Back at the seminary, Gabe and Blaze and Prior Robert held a meeting in the Prior's office. Fr. Alexus tried to hear through the wall, and Fr. Abelard stopped several times at the doorway with lame questions about Oblate Christopher and what ought to be told to the other oblates. Finally the Prior closed the door. He had never had a serious discussion with Gabe and Blaze before and surprisingly, all three being, at least for the moment, in accord in their anxiety about Fen, he found their company surprisingly agreeable compared to the counsel he usually got from the faculty. After he had listened to the whole unbelievable tale, he asked the two oblates what they thought he should do.

"I think you should just do nothing and be patient," Blaze said. "Fen is, or was, more conscientious than, well, than some of us, and whatever his problem, I think he'll come around. You know, Fen really does try to do the right thing."

"We think that Fen is having sexual difficulties," said Gabe. "Unlike many of us, he is so honest and conscientious that he tries to follow the letter of the law in these things."

Prior Robert arched his left eyebrow at Gabe. In any other situation, he would have felt duty-bound to challenge the young man on what exactly he meant by that, but decided now was not the appropriate time.

"Are you sure he will not obey a summons to return here if I really put the pressure on?" he asked.

"I would not do that right now," Blaze answered hastily, before Gabe could voice his opinion. Blaze knew that Gabe would vote for putting Fen under the vow to come back because he could not fathom what Blaze knew to be true: that Fen had reached a state of mental conviction where threats of even excommunication would mean nothing. Excommunication would just make it more difficult for Fen to come back in case he had a change of mind.

The Prior tapped his fingers on his desk, trying to think through a course of action. Finally he spoke. "I want you to be sure that the poor boy has enough to eat, clothes to wear, and some kind of bed. Oblate Blaise, I put you in charge of this. Take what he needs over to him. But I don't want either of you telling the others, including the faculty, that you are taking care of him. I don't want it to look like I condone his action in any way. For now we'll just treat it as a mental problem for which Oblate Christopher can't be held accountable in the eyes of God."

CHAPTER 22

Blaze decided that maybe the institutional Christian God did exist after all, because the Prior's decision played right into his sub-rosa schemes. Not only would he be able to take care of his friend, and talk with him about his plot to overthrow the Church hierarchy with the promulgation of the Eleven New Theses, but he now had a perfect alibi for being out on the roads on the Farm Zephyr almost whenever he felt like it. This situation would allow him to visit Marge Puckett on his way to and from Fen. Blaze had reached the point where he could no longer think of not visiting her. The Puckett farm was only a few miles away from Lake Wassermensch. The fact that the Prior stipulated some secrecy in the care and nurturing of Fen helped also the secrecy necessary in the care and nurturing of Marge. Using the Zephyr, it would just appear to the other oblates that he was going over to the rented farm to do farm work. The fact that the Prior had not included Gabe in the care and feeding of Fen surprised him, but so much the better, since seeing Marge Puckett was something he did not want even Gabe to know about. At least not just yet.

He filled a grain sack with enough food from the kitchen storeroom to last Fen a week, loaded it on the trailer behind the Zephyr, together with a mattress and blankets and a laundry bag of clothes from Fen's room. Fr. Abelard, who had for the length of about a month, again foresworn liquor and was hard at work spying on the community from his third-floor room, noted Blaze's strange departure and duly reported it to Prior Robert. The Prior told him that he would take the information under advisement but said it so icily that Abelard knew there was something going on he didn't know. Maybe Robert had found out about the night at the slaughterhouse. He went back to his room and started drinking again.

Blaze had noted previously that at 30 miles per hour the Zephyr's front wheels went through a violent wobble that would have suggested slowing down to most drivers. But then as he increased the speed to 40 miles per hour, the wheels lost their wobble and rolled smoothly along. It was sort of like breaking the sound barrier. On country roads he encountered more vehicles going 35 miles per hour or less than on the highway, so he could amuse himself almost constantly by passing astonished drivers. He did it to Kluntz once, who, in trying to identify the tractor operator, drove right off into the ditch.

Fen was busy at work remodelling the kitchen, while he kept one eye on the island. Blaze told him about Kluntz and Fen laughed, seemingly as normal as ever. "That story will be all over the township before you get back to the seminary," he said. "Kluntz has been here already, having found out about me from Hasse. You'd never believe what he brought me. Copies of some new girlie magazine called *Playboy*. Man you should take a gander at the women in it. I think Kluntz understands me better than anyone."

Blaze looked and was embarrassed. So that's what a woman looked like. Oh, wow. He told Fen what Prior Robert had said. Fen seemed disinterested. He now lived in a world where Priors and oblates and seminarians meant nothing to him. But he was glad for the food, admitting that he was getting tired of eating crappies.

"No sign of Mermaid yet," he said, as if he expected her at any moment. He had found an old rowboat along the lake shore and patched it up so that when the weather got too chilly for swimming in the approaching autumn he could get around the lake, just in case.

"Fen, aren't you having any second thoughts about this?" Blaze asked. Fen had not shaved in days and his hair was growing long. He looked like one of those beatniks wandering the roads, especially when he played his guitar.

"Actually, this is a pretty good life," Fen said. "I'm rather enjoying it. Winter is going to be tough, but she'll be back by then. If not I'll cut wood and feed this old stove."

"Well, you know, when Mermaid comes back, you'll want to look like you did when she saw you, right?"

Fen stared at him, then nodded.

"Well, if I were you, I'd shave and keep myself clean. I can have Clutch come over and give you a haircut. She won't recognize you the way you look now."

Fen thought a moment. "Yeah, that's a good idea."

Blaze congratulated himself on his ability once again to help others. He climbed back on the Zephyr and zoomed out the long lane to the road again. Out of Fen's view, although Fen surely would not care, he turned in the opposite direction from the seminary, his heart pounding in anticipation of his next stop.

Marge Puckett, working in the garden, could hear the unearthly whine of the tractor before it came into view. She leaned on her hoe and watched with astonishment as it careened past her and wheeled into the barnyard. Blaze hopped off his steel steed, raked his cowboy hat off his head, and walked jauntily to the garden fence.

"It's you," Marge said, not able to keep a little squeal of pleasure out of her voice.

"Yep, it's me. I just happened to be over at our rented farm, and thought I'd come around this way on my way back to the sem. Saw you in the garden."

"I saw you at the ball game," she said, knowing that he was well aware of that. "That was some catch you made."

He grinned. God, life was good. But he didn't know what to say, a condition in which he rarely found himself.

"What kind of tractor is that?" she asked, wrinkling up her face to stare at it and then coming out of the garden to inspect it.

"The fastest tractor in the world. I'm going to enter it in one of those tractor rodeos and win a million bucks with it."

"You're crazy," she said, good-humoredly. "I thought you said you were going to leave the seminary?"

"Oh, yes. I am. Just not the right time now. Too much going on."

She looked at him in amusement. Having spent a night with him, however preternaturally, she felt somehow at ease in his presence, as if she had known him forever. "You're a strange case, you know. I don't think you'll ever leave the seminary."

"Well, there's things going on that I have to see the outcome of," he said. "And once I made the decision to leave, I found that I felt no compulsion to do it right away. There's no hurry. I am a man without a country, without a place, without any particular identity. My purpose for the moment is just to see what happens and maybe write about it. As Yogi Berra says, you can observe an awful lot, just by watching." In his mind, he wondered why it was so easy to run on talking to her.

She shook her head, amazed and still amused. Her mind was racing for a way to keep him from leaving too quickly. "You should observe this farm, then. It is kind of unusual. I'll show you why I would rather stay here than go back to college this fall."

"Oh? Back to college? I thought you said you were going to quit."

Touché. She laughed. "C'mon."

She led him up a lane behind the house and farmstead buildings, across a fairly extensive stretch of cropped fields that ended at the top of a low ridge. On the other side was a sight that would have compelled a George Inness to reach for his brushes. They were looking down on a small lake, perhaps no more than twenty acres in size, entirely hidden from the road. In fact it was entirely hidden from all directions by the surrounding hillsides, a bowl of water with the sloping sides above the water covered by pasture fields. Cows, horses and sheep grazed the hillsides. The ridge that formed the top lip of the bowl was forested all around, except on the side where they stood. Marge waited for Blaze to react, wondering if he would understand more than just the beauty of it.

"Oh, wow," Blaze said. He understood the beauty and that was enough for him.

"If you look between here and the house, there's about thirty acres of cultivated ground," she pointed out. "Then there's maybe eighty acres of grass around the lake, twenty acres of woodland above, and the water itself. Our property completely surrounds that lake. For all practical purposes it is our own private pond. See how the fences divide the pasture into seven fields, all with access to the water. Dad can rotate the animals from one to the other and they always have water. He's big into grassland farming, as they're calling it, and he's learned how to manage grass so the livestock live mostly on it and only a little from cultivated grains. We don't have to do much farming at all. The pasture more or less renews itself constantly and the animals do all the harvesting. No erosion. No fertilizer. No chemicals. Pretty neat, don't you think? Very low-cost farming."

Her long explanation gave Blaze the opportunity to stare intently at her without seeming to be staring intently at her. He only half heard what she was saying. Her face had lots of little smile wrinkles around the eyes and mouth, and was peppered with freckles he hadn't much noticed before. But then she said something that turned his attention away from her.

"We are totally self-sufficient. We don't even have electricity, did you notice?"

"What?" Blaze was all disbelief.

"I told you my father was an unusual man. Actually, we have a little electricity from a wind generator. For lights in the house.

"And the radio. Dad wouldn't be without his radio. He draws water for the house and barn from the lake with a hydraulic ram. Needs only gravity for power. We heat with our own wood. We farm with horses. Totally self-sufficient except for the two cars. Daddy lived near an Amish settlement when he was young and decided he would live like them if he could find the right place. He wandered through five states until he found this farm. He would kind of like to join the Amish." She laughed. By now Blaze was giving her words his undivided attention.

"You raise all your own food?"

"Well, almost. We have to buy salt and stuff like that."

"You milk your cows by hand?"

"Yes. We only have ten and usually a couple of them are dry. Mom helps and I do too when I'm home. And my boyfriend down the road helps milk in the evening when Dad needs him."

"Oh." A frown, like a catspaw on water, rippled over Blaze's face but he made it disappear so fast he thought she didn't notice. Then he added: "My Mom and I used to milk the cows at home by ourselves when Dad was in the fields. But we never had more than six."

"You do the milking at the seminary too, don't you?"

"Yes, but we have lots of manpower down there. We could milk twenty or thirty cows by hand without difficulty. But of course hardly anyone knows how to hand-milk and I doubt that they could ever learn. Just not fit for that kind of work. We're getting an electric milker soon. Do you make butter?"

"Mom does that. Cans and freezes a lot of food too. Long about this time of year it gets to be real work. But worth it. And all our own meat. You know, girls complain about this kind of work, but I've never minded it. I like good food too much."

"So you're going to college again?"

"Yes," she said, not happy about it. "I told Dad I just wanted to farm and have kids, but he says I have to go to college first to learn what's out in the world. If I don't do that, he says, I won't come back here with the proper conviction."

"Your father is a wise man," Blaze said. They had been walking back towards the house for some time now, ever since, in fact, the boyfriend had gotten into the conversation. Now Blaze said he had to be leaving and climbed on his tractor. "Tell your Dad if he ever needs help with the cows, to let me know."

And he was off then, excitement over Marge mixed with dismay over the boyfriend. What did he expect? There was always going to be a goddam boyfriend. But she did not speak of him with a whole lot of portent, he decided. More like referring to an old shoe. Maybe he still had a chance.

CHAPTER 23

In a rural area where even a car passing on a country road was a Social Event, the Great Potato Race had taken on the trappings of festival: a cross between a county fair and a prayer meeting. Various interested parties began to descend upon Gabe's and Hasse's two potato patches. Horticulturists and agronomists led discussions in the use of sulfur in potato culture and on the increasing immunity of potato bugs to insecticides. Young farmers argued about whether close plantings producing a greater number of smaller potatoes would outyield wider plantings producing fewer but larger potatoes. Old farmers wondered if it made any difference whether big or small potatoes were used for seed. Harriet Snod's Garden Club discussed whether Pisces, Scorpio or Capricorn was the better sign to plant under. Impromptu contests occurred to determine whether anyone could kick wet gumbo from a boot in less than five tries. Blaze arranged a special ceremony that involved the Prior walking up and down the rows of God's potatoes sprinkling holy water, being careful not to do so in his usual ample manner, lest some of the precious liquid fall accidentally on mammon's potatoes too. Blaze, with fiendish deviltry, had tried to persuade the Prior to include prayers of exorcism over Hasse's potatoes. The Prior smiled and rolled his eyes.

In case holy water was not enough, Gabe turned to irrigation during a summer dry spell. He showed farmers and agronomists how he could easily irrigate his potatoes by damming up the laterals of his drainage system so that the everflowing spring water filled the ditches to the desired level, allowing the water to run out into the potato patch.

Hasse gave no indication that he knew of this cagey maneuver, but he added more mulch around his plants and let everyone know that this practice was much cheaper and not only as effective at holding sufficient moisture in the soil without irrigation, but also at controlling weeds without herbicides.

The director of the local Farm Bureau chapter dropped by, making his usual point about how his organization was against farm subsidies except when farmers needed them, which was almost always. The local chapter of the Minnesota Organic Farmers set up a booth in front of Hasse's potatoes and passed out literature on the effectiveness and benefits of organic food production. Hasse was more than a little embarrassed by this turn of events because he still suspected organic farming might be a socialist plot.

The organic farmers inspired an equal but opposite reaction. A hastily formed coalition of local custom spray applicators and chemical fertilizer dealers set up their own booth in front of the Josephian potatoes and proclaimed to all vistors how pesticides fed the world. It was now Gabe's turn to be embarrassed. He secretly believed that chemical companies did not care a bit about feeding the world but only about how much money they could make.

To take advantage of the situation, Melonhead set up a booth from which he dispensed his herbal remedies, his "Ascension All Natural Poultice Bandages" and his new "Ascension Natural Wormer—For Livestock But Okay For People Too." Some days his voluntary offering box was stuffed with dollar bills. Prior Robert worried about the efficacy and legality of Melonhead's potions, especially the wormer. "Relax, Prior, this is an all-natural wormer," said Melonhead. "You'd get a really terrible case of the runs and have to stop drinking it long before it could really hurt you."

Before long both the organic and the chemical congregations were locked in a wordy contest to see which could appear to the public as the most environmentally-pure group. Hasse, standing beside Gabe, feeling for once more closely allied to his adversary than to any of the groups supporting him, remarked out of the side of his mouth: "They remind me of two ministers using the size of their collections to measure which is the most god-fearing."

As the organic-chemical debate reached fever pitch, a Wildlife Agent from the Soil Conservation Service showed up to spoil all the fun. He scolded Oblate Gabriel and Farmer Hasse for destroying a wetland and ruining wildlife habitat. Until the situation was remedied, the SCS official officiously told them, both were disqualified from government subsidies. He then waited for the anguished objections and lame excuses that he was so used to hearing from farmers when informed of their sinfulness: they had not known, etc.; there was plenty of swamp left for wildlife, etc.; drained acres weren't destroying anything really, but utilizing nature better and increasing the habitat for some wildlife including coonhunters, etc. etc. But neither Oblate Gabriel nor Farmer Hasse reacted at all, only staring at the official in amused silence. Finally Gabe said to him: "The Josephians aren't in any of the subsidy programs."

"Neider am I," said Hasse, who despised all forms of government interference, good or bad. The official turned away, his crest drooping.

Harvest day in October found the area around the potato patches looking, with the various tented booths, more like a Medieval country fair than a farm field. A big crowd had gathered, with parked cars backed up a quarter mile both ways along the road leading to it, as at a farm sale. The potato vines had all matured and died and there was no way to tell, save from the bulging plant hills, just how good the crop was. But everyone knew that both God's and mammon's plots had grown as equally perfect during the season as any potato patch in the memory of Carver County. All that was left to see was whether Oblate Gabriel's potatoes had gone to vine even a little, for ignoring the signs of the zodiac, or whether Hasse's manure was as potent as he claimed it was to make up for his wider plant spacings. Bets were placed both ways and the odds stayed even. Caution ruled all pronouncements, agricultural and theological. The Prior, who was gripped by a secret panic that Hasse would win and he would be blamed for exposing the Church to ridicule, gave an invocation, asking God's blessing upon all and hoping that out of the contest, love would flow between everyone in the community. That much could hardly get him in trouble with his Provincial who was already uneasy with the attention that the Great Potato Race had brought to the Josephians. The Farm Bureau president once more informed the crowd of the foolishness of government subsidies except when farmers needed them, which was almost always. The County Extension Agent pointed out that he was there to serve all the people, regardless of race, color, or agricultural philosophy. He had decided not to include creed in this particular instance because he feared that could be interpreted as violating the separation of church and state. Then the crowd pressed forward and the potato harvester began to make its way down the rows.

Cries of wonder erupted from the watchers as potatoes rolled out of the Josephian rows over the shaker rods at the rear of the digger and fell in a steady stream onto the ground. "My God," Kluntz swore, "there must be thirty spuds in every hill!" So as not to lean too much towards God in his expletives, he added: "Hell, that's going to be an eight hundred bushel per acre yield!"

But when the digger bit into Hasse's rows, the murmur from the crowd buzzed with even more electric charge. Though perhaps fewer in number, potatoes bigger than softballs tumbled steadily from the rear of the machine. "Godallmighty and great balls of fire," Kluntz said, playing it both ways again, "some of those spuds must weigh a pound apiece."

Volunteers swarmed over the potatoes and gathered them in the sacks Hasse had provided. Each crop was weighed in turn by the County Agent at the scales, closely watched by the supporters of God and mammon, organicists and chemicalists, moon signers and PhDs.

As the weighing of God's potatoes ended, a murmur went through the crowds. Sixty thousand, two hundred and forty pounds, the county agent cried excitedly. Over thirty tons per acre! Who had ever heard of such a yield? Surely a new record. God be praised, the oblates all whispered. Except Blaze.

The county agent then tallied up the list of figures from Hasse's patch. He glanced up nervously at the crowd, a queer look on his face. He added the figures together again. And again. He recalculated God's potato yield. And again. He shook his head. How could this be? The crowd edged forward, craning at his every blink. He sighed. "This is amazing, but I get the very same yield on Ed Hasse's acre. Sixty thousand, two hundred and forty pounds."

Stunned silence gripped the crowd. The awesomeness of the fact that both plots had made exactly the same yield slowly sank into the collective mind. What were the odds against that happening? Finally The Very Reverend Lukey spoke aloud what the others had dared not put into words: "It's a miracle."

The crowd buzzed. How else explain what had happened? Even Hasse shifted nervously from one foot to another, looking as discomforted as if he had tried to swallow one of his big spuds whole.

But if it's a miracle, the Prior thought, along with everyone else, who is it a miracle for? Was it miraculous that organic, zodiacal potatoes equalled scientific, chemical potatoes in yield or vice versa? Was it a miracle for God or for mammon? Was God trying to be politically correct? Was that what the Bible meant by instructing the faithful to make friends with the mammon of iniquity? Would he lose his position as Prior for exposing the Josephians to this thorny theological question? He turned to Oblate Gabriel for some assurance, but Oblate

Gabriel was loading sacks of potatoes on the Josephian truck as fast as he could.

Uneasy and disappointed, the crowd broke up and drifted toward the parked cars. The reps from the chemical companies could not snicker at the organic gardeners nor vice versa. The Extension Service could not maintain its usual unctious air of superiority over the moon signers or the organic farmers. All the Farm Bureau president could think to say was that government subsidies were bad except when farmers needed them, which was almost always. Blaze, delighted at the outcome, went to the barn to get the Zephyr so he could tell Fen and Marge the outcome.

Eventually, only Hasse and Gabe remained in the field, loading the last of the potatoes on their respective trucks. They would ponder the meaning of the even yields later. Right now, business. Both were trying to figure out in their heads how much 30 tons of potatoes came to at $1.59 per five-pound bag. The loading completed, Gabe delivered what he had planned as the final victory of the contest. He handed Hasse a bill for $80, rental charge for one acre of farmland. Hasse looked at the bill a long time, but in place of the cussing he could barely stifle, a grin broke through, widening to his ears to match Gabe's own gleeful visage, the two men recognizing the full depths of their commonality. Then they turned away and climbed into their respective trucks, each pretending great weariness, telling each other they were going home to get a good night's rest. But both of them were thinking the same thought: As soon as I'm out of sight of that conniving bastard, I'll beat him to the Farmer's Market in Minneapolis and get a better price.

CHAPTER 24

As the Josephian authorities were making their final decisions about which seminarians would be sent to Rome, Prior Robert and the faculty noticed a change in Oblate Gabriel. Their prize candidate was almost flunking his classes. At first they attributed the change to a troubled mind brought on by Oblate Christopher's shenanigans and perhaps by the excitement of the Great Potato Race. Oblate Gabriel would in time recover, they were sure.

Gabe secretly sneered. He was dumbing himself down on purpose and if the others had any brains they should have suspected. He didn't want to go to Rome or any other university to complete his studies for the priesthood. The agricultural, mechanical, and particularly the economic possibilities that he had found on the farm had opened a new world to him. He had been brought up in a city and gone directly into the seminary before he could gain experience of any kind of work at all. Now he realized that the business world was far more interesting to him than the academic life and required more intelligence. If the Josephian Order wanted to stanchion him and milk his talents, they should encourage his cunning to further their financial interests, he believed, not send him to decadent Rome. Since they didn't seem to understand that, it was up to him to educate them.

His scheme was to demonstrate that those stupid I.Q. tests indicating a high intelligence in him were wrong. If he could demonstrate that by his actions, his superiors would not require him to study for advanced degrees. Then he would not have to violate his vow of obedience by refusing to go to Rome to get degrees in Scripture Studies or Biblical Archeology or whatever the hell they were planning for him to become expert in. Such studies required learning ancient, difficult languages like Sanskrit. And although learning weird languages required only memorization and, therefore easier than figuring out how to make a profit from watercress, his superiors didn't know that. Playing stupid at bookish knowledge, he could pursue business.

As he tried to make his show of stupidity more believeable, chance, or as he would always say, God, came to his rescue. Replacing the fence around the barnyard, he was trying to loosen and pull an old, half-rotted oak post out of the ground. As he jerked violently on it, the post suddenly snapped off at the base and the upper end smacked him hard in the forehead. He slumped to the ground, blacking out for a brief moment. Regaining consciousness, he was aware that Blaze was bending over him, laughing as usual, but also concerned because blood from the blow was streaming down his face. Gabe continued to sit on the ground in a daze. "You really do see stars, you know," he finally said. "I think I saw the whole Milky Way."

"You okay?"

"Who are you?" he stared at Blaze, feigning, or at least thinking he was feigning, dull confusion.

"We better get you to the infirmary," Blaze said.

Gabe was seized with a marvelous idea. He would pretend he had been knocked witless, or at least half witless. "What infirmary? And who the hell are you?" He jerked away from Blaze, noting with immense satisfaction that Blaze was fooled. Serves the idiot right for always wanting to help people. But he consented to let his comrade lead him to the infirmary, taking steps in the wrong direction occasionally to underscore his pretended delirium. What an actor he might have made!

"Wow, that's pretty nasty," Dr. Melonhead said, pleased to have someone to practice medicine on. "How'd you do it?"

"He hit himself with a post," Blaze said, unable to suppress his usual chuckle.

"How do you feel?"

"Nosh so good," Gabe said, slurring his words. "An' jush who the hell are you?"

Melonhead stepped back, delighted. This might be serious. "How many fingers am I holding up?" He held up three.

Gabe stared a long time, frowning and breathing heavily. "Four, I guesh."

Melonhead duly reported Gabe's injury to the Prior, who after a short conversation with Gabe, in which the latter proved he really did have talent as an actor, drove him to a hospital in Minneapolis to have a few tests run. Melonhead begged to go along. The Prior sighed. Okay.

"It's a nasty blow, no doubt about it," the doctor said crisply, "but there seems to be no fracture. He'll be fine."

"A hairline fracture might not show up on the Xray," Dr. Melonhead said. Dr. Armbuster directed her gaze at the young man. "Well, if it's that hairline, it isn't serious," she said, archly.

"Would it help if I fixed him a willow twig tea for the head pain?" Dr. Melonhead continued, having gained her attention.

She stared at him good humoredly. That was exactly the kind of question that she might have imagined a monk would ask, even a monk that didn't look like a monk and who couldn't have been much older than she was. "Well, I suppose, but an aspirin is a whole lot easier. How did you know willow contains the same ingredient as aspirin?"

Dr. Melonhead beamed. Gabe, standing by, trying to look confused, decided that if he drank Melonhead's willow twig tea that would prove that he was mentally deranged. He wanted to say that out loud but that might indicate that he was okay.

"How about a mustard plaster," Dr. Melonhead suggested.

Dr. Armbuster smiled again at him and he noted with some awakening that she had a very lovely smile for a doctor. "He'll be just fine."

But as the days went by, Gabe did not get "fine." To be sure, he didn't get worse. He just seemed to recede into a solitary dullness, mumbling nervous non-sequiturs when asked questions in class or out of class. Meanwhile, he kept close track of his tobacco drying high in the loft at the barn at Lake Wassermensch. Occasionally he chewed a leaf or smoked it in a pipe while carrying on learned conversation with Axel. Axel had moved his moonshine business to the barn.

"Got a good bite to it," Axel said.

"Melonhead says he read that chewing tobacco is very good for settling bowel pains. Wish I had bowel pains so I could see if it's true. You get gut aches?"

"Naw. Or if I do, moonshine keeps me from knowing it."

Gabe made sure he passed key philosophy, theology and Canon Law tests, but just barely. He didn't want to cash out of the priesthood altogether, just out of advanced studies in Rome or anywhere else. Much to his surprise he received a fairly good grade in Hebrew which he had not studied at all. Fr. Damien had decided that he needed to upgrade his requirements for passing the course and so made up a set of simple true or false questions in Hebrew for the seminarians to answer. By amazing good luck, or bad according to his viewpoint, Gabe put down trues and falses that he thought were wrong but which turned out to be mostly correct. This was not good. A talent for Hebrew would be interpreted as an indication of talent for Scripture Studies or Biblical Archeology overseas. "I have discovered an amazing paradox," he said to Blaze. "To pass a test about which you know absolutely nothing, give answers that you think are wrong and 70% of the time they will be right." Blaze considered this strange observation and decided the blow of the post was perhaps more serious than he had suspected.

"Gabe, are you faking playing dumb?"

"Faking? You can't fake insanity because, as you have said, no one knows what sanity is," Gabe answered. "Most people can't think logically. They just emote. If they say something sane, it's by accident. On the other hand, those who can think logically do not have all the facts in hand because no one knows all the facts. So if they say something sane, it is also an accident."

Blaze scratched at the corner of his eye. It was obvious that Gabe had been giving sanity almost as much thought as he had. Was there something in that homegrown northern tobacco affecting Gabe? Had he found some wild hemp to mix into it?

Despite Gabe's creditable grade in Hebrew, the rumors began to change. Maybe it was The Very Reverend Lukey who would go to Rome. The Very Reverend Lukey was thrilled. Blaze snorted. "Gabe, half witless is still smarter than you are," he said.

In any event, Blaze knew he could not yet leave the seminary and join Fen. Things were working toward some kind of unknown climax that he had to stay and see. He mulled over the delicious possibilities of Gabe's insistence that sanity was beyond definition. On the subject of sanity, the seminary provided plenty of material to work with. Jesse, for example. Jesse was considered retarded, but had the memory of a genius. Or rather the memory that one would suppose a genius might possess although there was the possibility, which Jesse demonstrated, that good memory might be a sign of insanity.

It was also intriguing that Jesse was adapting remarkably well to religious life. It suited him. He did not have to deal with the kind of stresses in life that frightened him. The Josephians took care of him. He liked to attend chapel in the morning when the oblates chanted the Little Hours of the Breviary. Something about the ebb and flow of chanted vowel sounds was as comforting as music to him, as in truth the chants were to many of the oblates, especially the older priests who had been doing it for years. At first he only listened, but soon he joined in, warbling his own bizarre sounds in place of the Latin phrases, in rhythmic cadence with the others. When the oblates, for example, chanted,

Confitemini Domino, quoniam bonus
Quoniam in saeculum misericordia ejus.

it would come out of Jesse's mouth as,

Ohniaymeenee omeeo oheea ohnoos
Oheeah ayuoum ezayrioria ayous.

The oblates all smiled at Jesse's renditions, understanding that that was not much different from their own. Hardly any of them took the time to translate mentally the Latin they were mouthing. Most of them couldn't translate it if they tried.

But Jesse soon memorized the antiphons that were repeated almost daily in the chants, and sing-songed them out with everyone else in perfect Latin. Eventually, he memorized every chanted psalm, refrain, and response he heard often. It was truly miraculous, most of the oblates believed, even when occasionally Jesse hit a wrong word or failed to remember the proper pause and chanted a solo. Then some of the younger oblates lapsed into helpless giggling fits.

The problem of who was sane and who was not was unendingly delicious to contemplate, Blaze decided. Was the calming effect of chanting unintelligible syllables over and over again an activity more fitting for the "sane" or for the "retarded"? Should maybe the chanting of the Divine Office be introduced into mental institutions?

Gabe was a different problem, but maybe not so different. Obviously he was faking his mental disorder to avoid going to Rome. But maybe he only thought he was faking. Even in fakery, he was acting differently than he would have acted in fakery before the post hit him,

Blaze believed. What if there really was something wrong with Gabe, and Gabe didn't know it? That thought made Blaze chuckle right out loud during the breviary chanting when no one could hear him. After all, to try to act insane when you were sane was surely more insane than trying to act sane when you were insane. But neither pretense could be as insane as trying to act insane when you really were insane.

And what about Fen? Fen was not putting on an act. He believed that Mermaid was real and had hovered over him naked and had some sort of sexual experience with him. It was obvious that Mermaid was a fantasy, since Fen was confused over whether she had actually had sexual intercourse with him. How could anyone be confused about that? But what if Mermaid were real? That would mean that Fen was sane and all the rest of them were the idiots for not believing him.

Fen's case was eerily like their Frank James' case. Blaze knew that Frank James had tried to rob him, or someone who called himself Frank James. His classmates knew it, but were in denial because the notion was so absurd. In Mermaid's case, if Fen had started to doubt what he had experienced, Blaze would have considered him more sane than if he had believed that it really happened. But when Lukey, or Little Eddie, or Mart began to doubt that they had seen Frank James, Blaze considered them to be less sane than if they had believed that he was real. Sanity, like God, apparently meant whatever a particular mind wanted it to mean.

Or how about the strange case of Abs and Lukey. Everyone involved knew without a doubt what Abs had seen in the slaughterhouse, but Abs dared not admit it for fear he would be admitting something about himself that no one had seen, which according to Lukey's theory, was that Abs was gay and scared to death he would be found out. Lukey insisted that Abs really knew that the naked man hanging in the slaughterhouse was Lukey, but had blotted it out of his mind because he was physically attracted to Lukey even before that fateful night. To insist that he had seen Lukey hanging naked in the slaughterhouse would only prove how sexually depraved he was, especially if he only imagined it all. But might not such a preposterous theory be explained by arguing that Lukey fantasized it because he was himself suppressing a physical attraction to Abs?

Melonhead was another absorbing study. He had wrung permission out of Prior Robert to take a short course in herbal medicine at the University of Minnesota School of Medicine. After Lukey's adventures into the Kinsey Report, the Prior was not particularly keen on outside study, but he was proud of what Oblate Mel had accomplished. So when the Provincial gave strict orders to stop the distribution of home remedies at the barn because an embarrassing number of cars were stopping there, the Prior soothed Melonhead's disappointment by allowing him to attend the university short course. What he didn't know was that Melonhead and Gabe had moved their laboratory to the farm at Lake Wassermensch so that going to the university also allowed Melonhead to swing around to the farm and attend to matters there. In the meantime, Melonhead bored everyone within hearing distance with his enthusiastic admiration of some brilliant doctor-teacher by the name of Armbuster.

Banana and Danny were evidently not as sane and normal as Blaze had once thought either. They had become uncommonly secretive, rarely even coming to the barn in the evening to smoke. When they asked to take courses at the university as Melonhead was doing, Blaze figured something unusual was going on.

"What are you guys up to?" he asked while they were playing catch one afternoon. It was late fall, far beyond baseball season.

Danny gloved the ball, motioned Banana to follow him and walked over to Blaze, looking around as if afraid he might be overheard.

"Promise you won't say a word?"

"Sure."

"We think we can get on the university baseball team in the Spring."

"Robert will never let you do that," Blaze replied.

"Hildy has a plan."

"You're kidding." Blaze paused, finding the idea wonderful because it was so absurd.

"He thinks somehow if we try out for the team, even if we don't make it, it will help him finagle a game between the university and us."

So maybe everyone he liked was looney, Blaze told himself. But what of his own case? What could be crazier than suffering along in the regimented life of a seminary because he actually enjoyed it even though he actually hated it?

CHAPTER 25

In November, a new lay brother arrived at Ascension, relieving Blaze of his barn chore duties. It hardly mattered now, since he had another way to avoid much of the regimen of the seminary that he found odious. As Fen's official caretaker, he had reinforced his position by telling Prior Robert that he feared Fen would take his life when he realized that Mermaid was a figment of his imagination. Blaze did not really believe that, but Prior Robert did.

"He not do that, pal," Jesse said when he and Blaze were alone. "He not crazy."

"How do you know?" Blaze asked. Getting Jesse to talk about sanity was bound to be interesting.

"Jesse know, pal. You're the one I worry about."

Blaze looked sharply at him even as he laughed. Jesse never kidded. Jesse didn't know how to do that.

"You look faraway in the eyes," Jesse said. "You going to put me in institution."

"No I'm not.

"Promise, Jack?"

Blaze had promised numerous times before, but maybe here was a chance to get at the truth. "Under one condition. You must tell me if you've ever tried to rob a train."

This was the first time Blaze had directly confronted him with the charge. But Jesse was ready. If he admitted that he had tried to rob a train, he'd admit that he was crazy and have to go to an institution for sure. "Rob what train? You going crazy, Jack."

"Why does he call you Jack?" Melonhead asked one day.

"Because Blaze is his horse's name," Blaze said, as if that were a perfectly logical answer, which of course it was. Melonhead walked away, wondering if Blaze were sampling his herbal teas too often.

Jesse followed Blaze around now like a faithful dog, afraid that if he did not stick close to his pal, the Pinkertons would grab him and put him away. Blaze at first did not mind having Jesse as a constant companion, even when he stopped at the Pucketts. Having someone with him made his visits with Marge seem merely social and not personal, as if he had no special interest in her, although he was hoping, contrarily, that she would understand that he did have a special interest in her and he brought Jesse along to obscure that fact. But Jesse could be trying. Making small talk for ulterior purposes was impossible with him around. For example, to one of Blaze's sly attempts to compliment Marge, he butted in.

"No, Jack, Fen never said that Marge was the prettiest girl he's ever seen after Mermaid. You make that up."

This caused Marge to double up with laughter while Blaze glared helplessly at his shadow.

Blaze had figured that he could get away from Jesse by driving the Farm Zephyr. Jesse was grievously afraid of the Zephyr and would not ride on it. He would not willingly ride in any vehicle powered by a piston engine. He would grow nervous and tremble in a car, and the faster the car went the more afraid he became. "Car not have feet and legs," he said once when Blaze insisted that he explain his fear. "Car monster." Blaze thought about that for days. Jesse was of course correct. Accident statistics proved it. Once more he wondered: who really was sane?

But not wanting to ride on wheels did not deter Jesse in the least. He turned to his reliable old horse and galloped recklessly along behind the tractor. Often, Axel, on his way to the new location of his still at the lake, would follow them, the three forming a curious caravan: the flying Zephyr, the galloping horse, and the groaning old truck. Once Marge encountered them as she drove home from college and was surprised that the strange sight did not amuse her as it did everyone else in the neighborhood. Why did Blaze insist on making a fool of himself, she wondered. Why did she care?

If Kluntz spotted the caravan headed for the lake, he would pursue it in his pickup. Sometimes Hasse was with him and they would joke that apparently Axel would soon join the Josephians. "Birds of a feather," Kluntz said once, but didn't finish the saying because suddenly he realized that it included him. Hasse didn't mind being included. The greater the number of people gathering at his ramshackle farmhouse, the bigger the haying crew. He had in fact put out an extra field of alfalfa in anticipation of the free labor. Meanwhile, he was experimenting with milkweed stems in the roller mill he had installed in the barn on the floor above Axel's still. Milkweed juice was the stickiest stuff he'd ever encountered. If it wouldn't cure cancer, it might make a helluva glue.

Sometimes, Jesse could be talked into staying with Fen awhile, and then Blaze would roar off to the Puckett farm alone. If Marge was not there, he visited her parents and helped with chores. The Pucketts still believed that he had saved Marge's life and since Marge was planning to marry the young man on the neighboring farm when she finished school, they saw nothing particularly untoward about a seminarian hanging around. They thought, in fact, that his influence might be good for her. Al, her boyfriend, was a rather unimaginative soul.

In the presence of the Pucketts, Blaze surprised himself by acting pensive, even serious. He had no inclination to be the jokester or to rend the air with his harebrained laughter. He asked question after question about the farm and its lack of dependency on the outside world.

"You two could teach the Josephians how they should be living," he observed one day, much to George Puckett's amusement.

"I doubt that," he said. "What Mom and I do here is too tedious. It takes discipline and the experience of generations. I learned it mostly working on Amish farms when I was a kid."

"But from what I see, it is a fact that people can live like this quite satisfactorily," Blaze insisted. "Do you know that Marge wants to live and farm like you do?"

"Oh, she's just trying to be loyal to us. You can overdo loyalty, you know. The world is passing people like Mom and me by. The younger generations don't want to live a life based on husbandry. When you farm like this, you have to be here almost all the time to care for the animals. Young people today don't want to be tied down like that. Can you blame them? Not enough money in it anymore anyway. College will make her see that there's no future in farms like ours. Hell, if you'll excuse my language, the agricultural school actually teaches that."

"Well, I'm a young person and I find being tied down to a place to be quite exciting," Blaze replied. "Do you think someone like me could live this way?"

Puckett laughed. "I don't know if you're steady enough."

"But Marge said you travelled through five states before you found what you wanted. Couldn't that be true of me?"

"Well, I knew from the beginning what I wanted."

"Maybe the reason I didn't is that I wasn't lucky enough to experience what suited me until now."

George did not answer. This Blaze fellow was not easy to follow.

When Marge was home, she and Blaze took long walks across the meadows around the lake. They were seldom at a loss for words. Marge intended to take over the farm whether her father liked it or not, and with Al inheriting the farm next door, they would do okay. She had some new ideas about grassland farming and solar energy she wanted to try.

Blaze described again the ranch he wanted to own, in a valley where the sun came up at one end and set in the other, with comforting hills on either side.

"And I'm going to have a portable record player in my saddlebag that plays the 'Song of the Faraway Hills' over and over again," he said. She could not tell if he were joking. The oblates had recently been allowed to go to the movie *Shane* in which that song was used as a background theme. Blaze stayed to see it twice and after that he scratched "Blaze" out of all the textbooks he had written his name in, and replaced it with "Shane." But he was not totally romantic about cowboying. He wanted to raise sheep.

"Shane would not have approved," Marge said, smiling.

"Sheep provide meat and wool both, and I've been reading about flocks in Europe that are milked just like cows for dairy products," he explained. "And if a ewe gets muley I can pick her up and throw her where I want her to go. Can't do that with a cow."

Here was yet another Blaze, Marge thought. A Blaze completely, almost brutally, practical. He continued in that vein. He saw in her father's self-subsistent farm a way out of his dilemma as a man with no money who did not particularly care about making money either. A self-subsistent farm life would require only a little cash flow and he'd be freer than a rich man, he told her. "I can't stand the idea of sucking up to some boss all my life. That's why I like the seminary even though I hate it. I've figured out how to do just about whatever I please, even with the vow of obedience, not to mention the vow of poverty."

Marge laughed. No one else she knew could come up with such droll and contradictory observations. "You would never have to worry about becoming a nine-to-fiver," she said. "You'd get fired regularly."

More than once Blaze pointed out that they really wanted the same lifestyle. It would be about that time that Marge would grow uneasy and mention her boyfriend. Until Blaze came along, she had decided that since she was bent on farming, Al was prime material for a husband. Now after being with Blaze, she was starting to argue with herself about Al and she felt guilty about doubting him.

Blaze knew that he was falling in love, but he kept the conversations on a chatty, joking plane, afraid to speak of his desire for her, afraid that she did not share a kindred feeling for him. He feared that after one of those sudden silences that came between them, in which they stared fondly at each other, she would say that she just wanted to be friends. If that ever happened he knew that he would have to excuse himself, go someplace private and throw up. He was in denial. When she talked about getting married and where she and Al were planning to live, he did not hear her. He concentrated only on the fact that she and Al were not yet engaged.

Occasionally Al was at the Puckett home when Blaze arrived. He was a nice enough fellow, Blaze thought, but so terribly sure of himself or else so dull that he didn't recognize even the possibility that Blaze might be a rival. Blaze pretended to be pleased with Al's and Marge's plan to marry. That's the way a really cool guy should act, he figured. But he didn't mind fantasizing about what a hard right might do to that cocky jaw of Al's. When Al was at the farm, Blaze would soon leave. Marge would watch him go, a troubled look on her face.

CHAPTER 26

"Carpe diem," Blaze said to Gabe one day as he mused about when to implement his decision to leave the seminary. Gabe pretended not to know what the words meant, although, come to think of it, at the moment he really couldn't remember what they meant. He had pretended being slightly addled so long that he sometimes wondered if he really were slightly addled and only thought he was pretending. Blaze wondered too.

Alone with his shadow, Jesse, Blaze asked: "Do you think that Gabe is losing his mind?"

"Gabe lost his mind long time ago, Jack."

"How do you know that?"

"He thinks I'm crazy. He don't know I'm pretending."

"How do you know you're pretending?"

"If I really crazy I wouldn't know that I was pretending."

By Christmas time, Blaze could see that the part of the Josephian life he had loved even though he pretended not to, was disintegrating before his eyes. Fen was gone; Gabe might as well be. Melonhead, Danny and Banana were at the university much of the time. He rarely got to work with Brother Walt. Clutch, as usual, kept to himself, although, curiously, he was spending more time at Fen's house than Blaze was. Clutch told Prior Robert that he was repairing and installing household appliances which Hasse had brought from one of his other rental properties, so that Fen could live with a little more comfort.

But that was only a minor part of Clutch's agenda. He told Blaze that he was building something in the barn that was going to save the world. Obviously, he was going crazy too. Maybe he was nipping at Axel's moonshine.

Lukey, believing he was headed for Rome, became so pompous that Blaze could no longer irritate him by asking innocently whether Abs had made any advances toward him lately. Even suggesting that "gays can always tell other gays" failed to get any kind of response other than "You are so pitiful, Blaze." Little Eddie and Mart, without the full SBDC Gang to give them security in numbers during escapades they would otherwise never have dreamed of becoming involved in, allied themselves with other, safer oblates in other cliques. They had by now convinced themselves that the train robbery was a case of group hysteria induced by breathing too much sulfurous smoke on the train, compounded by the excitement of travelling to a new home in the company of idiots like Blaze and Fen.

Even Jesse started to draw away from Blaze in a startlingly unforeseen development. He was growing fond of Josephian life in inverse ratio to Blaze's disgust with it. He had mastered chanting and amazed the oblates by sing-songing whole psalms without reference to a breviary. Where he had previously sung "The Old Grey Mare" in the empty silo at the barn, he now blasted out psalm verses from memory. Jesse was happy. He loved sitting in the community rec room in the evening, listening to the oblates joke among themselves. He liked the kind attention they paid him. Working in the barn and the kitchen gave him a sense of worth. Most of all he loved the regular meals. Never before had so much good food been available to him and he stowed it away in massive portions. His gnarled skinny frame filled out and his stomach began to bulge. When Nash Patroux brought him a present at Christmas time, the bar owner laughed outright. "My God, Jesse, you're turning into Friar Tuck."

"You still a smartass, pal," Jesse said, grinning his old idiot grin. "You turning into Fire Fuck."

Little incidents like that struck Blaze as so hilarious that he wondered if he could ever quit the seminary. He decided that he had to set a deadline for himself. He would seek dispensation from his vows in the spring and go live with Fen. Since it did not matter one bit to him if he got dispensed or not—such legalities were just meaningless idiocies of papal power, he kept telling himself—he realized it was ridiculous to set a deadline. His conscience would allow him to walk away any time he felt like it, dispensation or no dispensation. The truth was that he put off the day of departure because he was afraid to go penniless into an unknown world. He loathed himself for his fear. But it was much shrewder to remain within the financial security of the Josephians while he courted Marge and took care of Fen.

Not that Fen needed his companionship any more. With the constant flow of visitors seeking various medical potions at the farmstead plus Hasse, Kluntz, Axel, Gabe, Clutch, and Melonhead dropping by routinely, Fen had more comforting company than Blaze did at the seminary. Blaze had in fact started calling the farmstead "Seminary Two."

Besides, Fen had begun to find his way. To preserve his sanity, he often spent most of the night playing his guitar and singing. He made up forlorn songs about Mermaid, his favorite being one he called "Succubia": "I'm in love with a mermaid/ and I cannot yet tell/ If she's an angel from heaven/ Or a devil from hell. But whether from hell or the heavens above/ Makes no difference to me/ She's my one true love." Nash Patroux, at the farmhouse to transact a little business with Axel, heard Fen singing one day and stayed to listen for a long time, transfixed by the sound.

"You're pretty good, Fen. Would you come and sing in my restaurant? I could pay you well. Fifty bucks a night. You are just one whole helluva lot better than a lot of the stuff on the juke box."

Now it was Fen's turn to be transfixed. He could not believe his ears. God, he could make a living with his guitar maybe. But he had no transportation.

"You could ride over on Blaze (the horse)," Jesse said. "People come all the way from Minneapolis to see that."

"Oh, wow," Blaze (the man) said. "You are a genius, Jesse, no doubt about it."

"Can I sing all the verses to 'Succubia'?" Fen asked, warming up to the idea. Mermaid might hear about him and come to the restaurant. "Some of the verses are a little, well, dirty."

Patroux did not often laugh out loud, but now he did. "That is one thing you will not have to worry about with my clientele."

Blaze watched Fen take on a new life, feeling slightly jealous. Who would ever have guessed that all that guitar-strumming might lead to a good job. Fen no longer needed him. Gabe no longer needed him. Nobody needed him. Marge was his last chance. Carpe diem.

As soon as an occasion presented itself, he went to Prior Robert's office. "I would like to volunteer to take classes at the university in Minneapolis," he announced, trying to look as earnest as a saintly nun on her deathbed.

"But Oblate Blaise, you have more than once begged me not to send you to the university," Robert replied with open astonishment.

"I changed my mind. It appears we're going to be sent away anyhow, so maybe I should get used to the idea."

"I don't suppose your decision has anything to do with the closing of Ascension?"

"Closing Ascension?" Blaze's eyes widened and his mouth dropped open. "What are you talking about?"

Prior Robert never swore, not even to himself, but now he almost did. This impossible young man always outmaneuvered him, even when he did not know he was doing it. The closing of Ascension was a closely guarded secret which usually meant that everyone knew it. Now the Prior, overwhelmed by Blaze's surprise request, had let it slip.

"You can't close this place," Blaze snapped, suddenly forgetting the respectful voice he was supposed to maintain when addressing his superiors. "This is my home." He seemed embarrassed then, realizing that he had said something totally honest for once.

Blaze's words cut like a knife into Robert's heart. The seminarian had said better in four words what he had tried to say in four thousand, in opposition to the closing.

"Look, Blaise," Robert said, "Can I trust you to keep this news to yourself? I am not supposed to say anything just yet. The announcement will be made soon, but if it becomes known now, I'll be in trouble." His voice actually became pleading. "I've kept you out of trouble on occasion, you know." Blaze stared at his boss with a new appreciation. He had noted that for the first time the Prior had addressed him by his name without the loathesome "Oblate" tag ahead of it. And he was asking Blaze for trust. Oh, wow.

"Sure. I can keep my mouth shut."

"What subjects do you wish to pursue at the university? I believe you have an interest in writing, do you not?"

Blaze was surprised again. Being a writer was another of his fantasies, but how did Robert know? He asked as much.

The Prior shrugged. "You strike me as someone who ought to be a writer, that's all. You write well on essay test questions. You might be good at it."

"Do you think so, really?" Blaze was exposing his real self now, vulnerable, serious, lacking confidence. Writing was the only way he had as yet thought of that might allow him to make a little money when he left the Josephians. He had no skills, no training, no degrees, no experience in anything except farming. But to actually make a living as a writer seemed as far out of his reach as to actually make a living as a farmer.

"Yes, I really think so, Blaise."

Oh, wow. "I wonder if I might take some courses in Psychology too," he said.

Robert looked pleased. "You really do want to help Jesse, don't you?"

"What I really want is to learn how to tell sanity from insanity," Blaze said. He was telling the truth even if he were also into an elaborate scheme to be with Marge Puckett.

Prior Robert understood that a gifted leader does not try to do much leading of the gifted. He had known Oblate Blaise for nearly three years now, during which time he had learned that he did not know anything about Oblate Blaise and neither did Oblate Blaise. The boy was either doomed or destined to make his own way and no spiritual persuasion that the Prior might muster was going to mean anything one way or the other. Furthermore, he had promised God not to stand in the way of Oblate Blaise.

"I think going to the university for some classes can be arranged. I'm not personally convinced that it is the right course for you or for any of the seminarians, but those in higher authority think otherwise. I believe they will be pleased with your request. God has given you the talents to be anything you want to be, you know. In the meantime, get some money from the Procurator and get yourself a decent suit for the university. You can ride in with Oblate Daniel."

Blaze interpreted "decent suit" as broadly as possible. Instead of the customary black that the seminarians usually wore in public, he bought a navy blue blazer (well, almost black), a pink Elvis shirt with white stitching, and black jeans cut western style. He wore a white shirt when leaving the seminary and changed into the pink one in the car.

CHAPTER 27

Blaze had felt remorseful as he left the Prior's office. He was taking advantage of the one Josephian who really seemed to care about him as an individual. He also felt guilty over the enthusiasm with which Danny and Banana greeted his decision to join them at the university. They thought that he was entering into their scheme to play baseball. Blaze let them continue in their thinking because scheming to play baseball was less despicable for a seminarian than scheming to win the hand of a coed.

His first impression of college life was one of numbing cultural shock. He had no idea that so many beautiful women could be gathered together in one place. He concluded immediately that if the Josephians carried out their plan to send their seminarians to public universities, they were signing the Order's death warrant unless they also planned to change the Church's mind about celibacy. He found it impossible not to stop and gawk at the girls. Girls on the sidewalk, girls in the halls, girls in the classroom, girls in the dining room, girls in the gym, girls in the dormitories, girls, oh God, in the swimming pool, girls, girls everywhere. Fen would not last ten minutes here before he would tear off all his clothes and chase after them. And from the way many of them acted, they would not be hard to catch.

But Blaze was not to be deterred. He stared at girls mostly to find Marge. The fact that she would certainly turn up very soon, coming down a sidewalk or emerging from a building, set his spine to tingling right down to the end of his tailbone. To meet her finally without fear of parents or priests or gossips or friends casting suspicious eyes at them, to meet her totally on his own terms in his new clothes, oh, wow, he could hardly contain himself. He imagined the look of surprise on her face, since he had not told her that he was coming to the university. She would stare at him, realization slowly dawning, and then she would smile that big open smile of hers and fly into his arms.

It happened almost like that, except for the last part. The embrace ended clumsily because when Blaze moved to kiss her, she pulled back. She did not seem to be against kissing, Blaze made himself believe, but only that the moment was inappropriate.

"That's some outfit," she marvelled, eyeing the pink shirt. She wondered if Blaze were color-blind. "So you finally left the seminary," she said, still holding his hands.

"Well, not officially," he said, noting that the remark caused a split second of disappointment to flutter across her face. "I'll be leaving after this semester. I'm going to live with Fen then until I figure out what to do. Fen and I just might farm that place for Hasse for awhile."

She continued to stare at him with an open fondness but with her head shaking from side to side ever so slightly. He was so totally naive about the world. "C'mon, let's go get a Coke," she said, leading the way.

It would probably have been impossible for Blaze to study his coursework anyway, what with a trillion girls dancing before his eyes, but seeing Marge regularly sealed his fate as a scholar. He could not concentrate on anything except her. The psychology textbooks turned out to be boring, concerned almost entirely with making up new words for various suspected mental abnormalities and then trying to justify their definitions for these new words. He turned to reading case histories of autism. He could not find a case that paralleled Jesse's exactly but it became evident to him that he, Blaze, had at least a touch of every mental illness that psychology had found a label for, and so did everyone he knew. Also, he learned that autistic individuals often had phenomenal memories. Jesse must be suffering from some form of autism but apparently not much was known about the problem. If Josephians were going to be helping people, why weren't they studying autism instead of an Arabic Hebrew dialect no one had spoken since the fourth century B.C.

Because Danny and Banana had drivers' licenses to get to and from the seminary, Blaze and Melonhead had to check schedules with them often to make sure they had a ride home. That meant the foursome often ate lunch together in the cafeteria and attracted the attention of the whole dining area with their loud, carefree laughter. Danny and Banana were doing indoor workouts with the ball team and wondered why Blaze hadn't joined them yet.

"Haven't had time," Blaze lied.

"Hildy showed up the first day, can you believe it, still conniving to get a game between us and the university," said Banana. "He made a really big deal over how we beat Chaska's triple A team. But I don't think he needed to brag us up. The coaches watched Danny pitch to me just five minutes and put us both on the roster. Can you believe it? Hildy said not to tell Robert just yet."

"You guys are fantasizing and so is Hildy," Blaze said, suddenly becoming the practical advisor that had been Gabe's role before the fence post hit him. "Robert'll never let you play, you know, I don't care what Hildy does."

"We're prepared for that eventuality," Danny said, suddenly serious. But he did not explain.

Melonhead would hardly let them talk sports, however, as he praised the brilliance of his professor, Dr. Armbuster.

"She's terrific," he said, more to himself than to them.

"Ooooh, sheeee's terrific," Blaze teased. "Now I get the picture."

"Nope, not that at all," Melonhead replied, blushing. "She's just very supportive. I told her that I wanted to start a center for herbal medicine at Ascension and she didn't think that was crazy. She said she would help raise some money for it, in fact." Blaze wanted to tell him that Ascension was doomed, but had given his word not to. Let Melonhead enjoy his dream as long as possible.

Mostly, Blaze spent what time he could find at the university talking to Marge. She was much freer in her attitude toward him now that they were away from home. They actually held hands. They came very close to kissing. Blaze was sure he was winning out over Al. They would get married, Blaze plotted to himself, and take over her father's farm. But Blaze did not say anything like that out loud, for fear it would force her to tell him that she was not really in love with him, even though he was sure that she really was and didn't know it. Instead he just talked about farming and how, if he could once get to buy some land, he would need only the barest smattering of money to live happily ever after. Often she would start to tell him that he should think more about writing or teaching. But she would stop, knowing how it angered her when her parents suggested similar occupations when she expressed a desire to farm.

"Why is it that no one thinks a woman can handle a farm?" Marge said.

"Why is it that no one thinks of farming as an occupation requiring just as much intellectual acumen as any professional career?" Blaze said.

He tried to write a story for his creative writing class about a young man who thought he had been raped by a succubus. He included some lines from Fen's song. He received a D on the paper and a tart note from the professor saying that shock value did not substitute for writing talent. Blaze showed the story to Marge. Like everyone else around Wassermensch Lake, she by now knew about poor Fen's fantasy, so she was not shocked. She thought the story definitely showed writing talent.

"But I don't see how you can write so intimately about sexual relationships if you are a virgin," she said, pretending to be merely bantering with him, but in reality keen to see how he would react.

"How would you know that I'm writing intimately about sex if you're a virgin?" he bantered right back. They both laughed, nervously.

"Did you ever wonder what virginity really means?" Blaze asked. Marge was embarrassed. She thought herself sophisticated after four years in college, but her virginity was not a subject open for discussion. Blaze was, however, honoring her intelligence again, something few men she knew did to women. In fact he always acted as if he thought she were smarter than he, a rarity for males. And she was overcome with curiosity about his virginity.

"As I understand it, your poor Fen thinks he lost his virginity," she said and then added, as if jokingly, "Does that mean he really did lose it even if he really didn't simply because he believes he did?"

"Oh, wow, Marge. That's the greatest question yet." She was surprised at how enthusiasticly he reacted. "Wait till Gabe hears that one. Well, the former Gabe anyway." And Blaze did his usual cackle. "Yes, if you think you're not a virgin, you must not be one. How does anyone know where subjective thought ends and objective reality begins? If you've been so close to losing your virginity, whatever that is, that you think you have lost it, what's the diff?"

"I've always thought virginity was kind of a meaningless concept," Marge replied, nodding in agreement. "And if one loses what is considered virginity, could she not in her mind, repudiate her mistake, if that's what it is, and become a born again virgin?"

Blaze erupted again. "Oh, wow, that's rich. A born again virgin. Oh wow. No doubt immaculately conceived. Why didn't I think of that."

"You men have historically demanded virginity—whatever it is—of the women you want to marry while you try desperately hard to de-virginize the entire female population before it has a chance to get married," Marge continued. "The only thing dumber than that is the way women go right along, pretending to honor the concept of virginity just to please men. Shows how crazy the human race is."

"Exactly," Blaze said, beaming. Then he paused just the right length of time. "But even understanding that, we both still want to know if the other is a virgin."

Marge blushed. Honoring a woman's intelligence could go too far perhaps. Then she suddenly realized something. This was the conversation she should be having with Al.

"Well, it's none of your business," she replied, laughing in spite of herself, "but I am a virgin. I think."

Blaze chuckled. "Me too. I think."

CHAPTER 28

That conversation should have relaxed the sexual tension between them, but it did not. Marge still refused his advances even while giving the impression that she did not want to refuse. But at least now Blaze was more hopeful. If she had not yet had sex with Al, whatever that meant, it could be that she had not yet made up her mind to marry him.

Blaze found out that Marge's birthday was in May, quickly approaching. He decided to buy her something with the two twenty dollar bills hidden in the seam of his billfold. Parting with that money turned out to be more difficult than he had imagined. Forty dollars was a pittance for most people, but it was all the financial security he had in the world. That he was willing to spend it surely showed how much he loved her, he thought. Seeing her at lunch on a Friday, he told her to be sure to come to their usual meeting place on campus on Monday afternoon. Then he skipped a class, went to a jewelry store and bought her a necklace.

Marge arrived at the campus bench where they often sat, displaying a nervousness so tense that Blaze knew before she spoke that something extraordinary was in the wind. He immediately deduced that she had decided to give up Al and collapse into his arms. But before he could wish her a happy birthday and draw the necklace from his pocket with great ceremonial flourish, as he had planned, she kissed him fiercely, then pushed him away. Her face had paled to the color of old ironstone. Losing her resolve momentarily, she wished that he were more aggressive. If he would just take her now like most men she knew would try to do, she could "surrender" with the excuse that he had overwhelmed her. But he did not. Never had tried. It was this characteristic that she most loved. He did not seem to have an ounce of aggression in him. The savage world of commercial competition would grind him to bits.

"Blaze, Al gave me a ring last night. I accepted it." She held out her hand so he could see it. He seemed to double over in pain. "I've tried every way to tell you what was going to happen. You must believe me, that I do love you, and that I've been having a terrible time in my head. I love you, but not in a marrying way. And because of how I've been raised, or perhaps my own innate caution, I don't do sex outside of marriage. Our relationship is not to be, Blaze. Even without Al in the picture I don't think I would marry you. At least not now."

"What do you mean, not now?" He seemed to be taking the news with more toughness than she had thought he would. For Blaze, the toughness emerged because at least he knew now that she really did love him.

"I don't know how to say this without hurting you. You are the most extraordinary person I've ever met. But Blaze, you do not know your own mind. The fact that you can't quite leave your present life shows that, don't you see? You are play-acting half a dozen different roles and you don't know which one is the real you."

"That's not true," he snapped, his hard practical voice now in charge. She was surprised. She had expected him to collapse emotionally. "I act silly and kid around a lot because in my predicament, if I didn't, I really would go crazy," he said, harshly. "Can't you see how mad the whole world is, especially mine? I got into this seminary business before I even reached puberty. If you would look at it in a fair way, you could see that the fact that I have stuck with it so long proves that I am steady. Too damn steady. Otherwise I would have just run off a long time ago. I don't even like this stupid jacket and shirt I'm wearing. It's just a way, I don't know how to say it, to act nuts to keep from going nuts."

"Everything you say tells me that you need to settle into a steady job awhile and learn your own mind."

"Oh, you can't mean that. Do you know your own mind? Are you willing to settle into a steady job working for someone else?"

She started to say that she did know her mind, but stopped. He was right. She wouldn't want to work for someone else either. That's the main reason she wanted to farm. "We're not talking about me right now. I'll try to say this a different way. You are the most exciting person I've ever met. But I'm so blasted practical, I won't risk my whole life on that. I'm incapable of that. If I weren't so damn practical, I'd marry you in an instant. But a woman going into marriage gets very cautious. At least this one does. I want a stable life. I think of marriage as forever, you know. Al is okay and he's safe."

"And you don't think I am? Don't you realize that you're the reason I'm playing out this seminary business? I've got no choice because I've got no money. Do you have any idea of the kind of bondage one lives in when you don't have any money at all and no way to make any except very very slowly at the most menial of jobs? Would you marry me quicker if I quit the seminary and fried hamburgers at a lunch stand?"

Tears came to her eyes. This was a different Blaze. A Blaze as calculating as she. If she listened to this one very long she'd change her mind. Again she kissed him and then ran, sobbing, down the sidewalk. He started after her but stopped. She had to come back on her own or not at all. He sat on the bench a long time, feeling as if he were falling into a dark hole that had no bottom.

CHAPTER 29

The warm spring winds that sent coeds to sun bathing naked on the roofs of their dormitories were working their wonders out around Wassermensch Lake too. Farm wives who swore they never did it, took to tractor driving stripped to the waist like their husbands. Every back yard, every private woodlot, every stretch of river bank or lake shore became lovers' trysts in those lovely few weeks before the mosquitoes arrived. Fen swam to the island daily, even though the water was still brutally cold, then lay in the sun, warming up, determined to doze and dream of Mermaid. Sometimes he did. Mostly he wandered restlessly around the island, stopping repeatedly to look longingly toward the landing on the far side of the lake, as if his looking would make her appear. As the weather warmed, he was sure she would come.

Hasse could not stand the young man's agony any longer. He stopped Kluntz on the road one day when both of them should have been plowing.

"Kluntz, we've got to do something for that poor Fen and I think you're the man for the job."

"What the hell you talkin' about. I'm no shrink. That kid's a loser any way you want to call it."

"Kluntz, there's something you need to know. I saw Mermaid too."

Kluntz choked. It took him a full minute to regain his composure. Then he tried to grin. "You saw the nekkid lady too? Haw, Hasse. You been hangin' around monks too long."

Hasse remained unmoved. "Yep, I really saw her. The day it all happened I was mowing the hayfield that looks right down on the lake. And there she was, stark naked, running down off the island and jumping into her canoe with that poor Fen, bare too, chasing after her. I don't carry binoculars in the tractor over at the lake just to watch birds, you know."

Kluntz looked bug-eyed. Hasse wasn't fracturing consonants, so he was probably telling the truth. "But why haven't you spoken up? I mean that poor boy might be sane after all, and you coulda said so."

"I did say so, more than once and none of you damn fools would listen. Fen knows he's sane. I know he's sane. I kinda think he's doing the right thing getting away from that looney seminary. But I'm tired of watching him waste away. How can anyone be that goddam loyal to a cunt?"

"What the hell you want me to do about it?"

"Kluntz, you know everything that goes on in this part of Minnesota. I think you can find a blue 1953 Ford pickup with a red Outfitter canoe in it, with one helluva beautiful, dark-haired girl, mid-twenties, driving. That combination ain't gonna be repeated too often in the whole Twin Cities area."

Kluntz drew himself up importantly. It was true. What he didn't know about his tramping grounds he could, by God, find out. And if Mermaid came from farther away, that was a challenge that a snoop of his caliber could rise to. A brunette with a red canoe and a blue pickup narrowed the field considerably. He'd find her.

"Now you keep your mouth shut about this," Hasse said dourly. "If Fen learns for absolute sure that he wasn't dreaming, and we never find her, he just might really go crazy and I'd be out a hired man."

///

Kadie Crockin opened her eyes one fine early May morning, feeling the breath of spring flowing softly through her window, and realized that her winter-long depression had all but left her. She went downstairs, fried three eggs and four strips of bacon, ate them and decided to fry three more. Her mother, hearing the activity in the kitchen, came to investigate, and a smile of immense relief spread across her face. "Honey, you're eating."

"I'm starved," Kadie replied.

Ann Crockin hugged her daughter's emaciated body. The poor child had hardly eaten since that day late last summer when she had come home and announced that she was through with the Escort Business. Nothing Ann had said could change her resolve. Nor would Kadie tell what had induced her change of heart. All she said, all winter, after long periods of silence, was a short sentence spoken with intense feeling: "He was a Greek god." Occasionally when her mother asked her what she was thinking about during her long periods of silence, she would answer, almost absentmindedly. "Greek God."

Attacking her fifth egg and sixth piece of bacon, Kadie spoke to her mother. "I figured it out last night. Really simple. I'm in love with Greek God and I've got to either do something about it or not. I screwed all those men but was never in love. Instead I've fallen in love with someone I hardly had sex with at all. Isn't that amazing?"

Her mother gazed at her in astonishment, almost afraid to speak lest she plunge the poor girl back into depression. "I wish I knew what you were talking about," she said. "Who the hell is this Greek God?"

Kadie told her the story, which was really a rather short story to tell. The strange experience of suddenly lying down on top of a man she did not know and had never spoken to, of his tortured effort to push her away and pull her towards him all at the same time, and then the way he shuddered in climax and looked up into her eyes in utter adoration—it had left her unstrung. Over and over in her sleep she heard him crying, begging her not to run away. The memory made it impossible for her to continue the escort business. She had tried to go back to it, had looked at the poor old potbellied man she was escorting, and suddenly the idea of sex had seemed to her as sickening as the idea of food to an anorexic. She had fled the room and vomited.

Suddenly snapping out of her depression did not mean that she resolved immediately to go back to that ill-fated lake. First she thought she might, and then, thinking of all the risks involved, she thought she might not. Some days she drove out towards Lake Wassermensch but lost courage and returned home. Each time, however, she got closer before she turned back. Back home, or fishing on another lake, she would absolutely convince herself that whatever had happened, was over and for the best if left that way. But a few days later she would find herself driving towards Lake Wassermensch again. Sometimes it seemed like the pickup was driving itself.

Then one Saturday, on her way from canoeing Rice Lake to canoeing Lake Bavaria, which was close to Lake Wassermensch, she noticed that the rusty pickup behind her was the same one that had been parked close to her truck at Rice Lake. The old man driving the truck had been eyeing her as she loaded up her canoe. He had seemed to be working up the courage to approach her and so she had scooted away as quickly as possible. Being ogled and trailed by men was a pain in the ass and she could hardly believe she had once been amused by it. She stomped the accelerator and sped off down the highway. To her surprise, the old truck stayed right behind her. Had she known that under the hood of that old wreck of a truck was a newly rebuilt engine, she might not have been surprised. Kluntz always pointed out, to anyone who was surprised at the performance of his truck, that a new pickup cost $4000 but a rebuilt engine cost only $400.

Kluntz was the master snooper. Soon he fell behind, deliberately, assured that after the last turn the girl in the blue pickup was headed for Lake Bavaria because there weren't any other lakes down that road. He knew another way to get there, a dirt road not marked on the maps.

Kadie was surprised, therefore, when as she was taking her canoe off the pickup, up pulled the old man in the rusty truck. This time he drove right up to her, his teeth almost falling out of his mouth in a friendly grin. Staying in his truck was another sign of just how clever he thought he was at professional snooping. He had noticed that girls, like wild animals, were less afraid of men approaching in trucks and on tractors than approaching on foot. Sure enough, when he asked from the window of the cab if she needed any help, Kadie only grinned. Even though he was leering at her, he was trying very hard not to look as if he were leering at her. She decided he was harmless enough and if not, she could just throw the dried-up, pukey little thing in the lake.

"If I needed any help I'da brought my own," she said, tartly. The old man laughed, not at all offended.

"'Spect you wouldn't have no trouble finding help either," he said. "Actually it's me that needs help. From you."

Kadie looked at him sharply. Kluntz did not give her a chance to speak.

"I'm meanin' no harm to you, Miss, believe me. I'm a family man, just an old coot of a farmer, lives not so far from here, and, now don't be alarmed, I've been lookin' for you. At least I think I've been lookin' for you. No harm now, nothin' bad, in fact something pretty good, I think." He still made no move to get out of the truck, a move that might alarm her.

"Why would you be looking for me? I don't know anyone around here."

"You ever canoe Lake Wassermensch?" Kluntz asked, trying, as he would later dramatize the exchange to Hasse, to look as innocent as the Angel Gabriel informing Mary that she was the mother of God.

Kadie was immediately wary. This guy must be connected somehow to Greek God. They were going to get her after all.

"Don't know that I have," she answered.

"Well, okay, but will you stand still long enough to hear a true story? I think I can promise you that you'll be glad you did."

And then Kluntz told Fen's story, turning it into a melodrama worthy of a B movie, but leaving out the grittier details. "I know this really wonderful young man," Kluntz began, "and he's suffering turrible. It started one day when he was dozing on an island in Lake Wassermensch. He wakes up, he says, to see the absolutely most beautiful woman that ever lived kneeling over him. He didn't know if he was awake or asleep until she bent down and kissed him, etc. etc."—Kluntz thought his etceteras extremely clever, given the circumstances—"and then he knew he was not dreaming. But she ran away and jumped into her red Outfitter canoe just like yourn and paddled away faster than he could follow to the other shore and shoved her canoe into a blue 1953 Ford pickup just like yourn and off she went. Now this young man, and I can vouch for him being a helluva lot nicer than most men, he's pined away all winter long for this girl he thinks he saw. He gave up his career, can you believe it, and lives now in an old farmhouse beside the lake, and every day the weather is warm, he rows or swims out on that island where he saw her. He calls her Mermaid. And the rest of the time, he watches from the house. He is absolutely sure she will come back and he's startin' to kind of waste away with sorrow. Don't that just about tear your heart up?" He paused to emphasize the tearing heart. "You know if he never sees that girl again, I think it just might kill him. He's that much in love with her. A girl'd be mighty lucky to find that kind of devotion in this crazy world."

Kadie's face remained immobile. She did not say anything, but continued to finger the boat rope in her hands. Kluntz knew he had found the right girl, because such a crazy story would have caused anyone else to walk away in disbelief.

"Well, I just wanted to pass that story on to you, and I'll be leavin' now," Kluntz said. He started to drive away, then stopped again. "Oh, yeah, this guy plays guitar and sings over at the Western Range out-sida Shakopee. Every Saturday night. A person interested could check him out over there." He chugged away. If this approach didn't work, he'd get more insistent, but she didn't need to know that now. He wrote down her license number on an old grain elevator weigh card stuck in the ashtray of his truck.

If the middle of May, before mosquitoes and deer flies and hot sultry weather, could remain all year, Minnesota could easily pass for paradise, Fen thought. All that would be necessary for earth to become heaven then would be to halve the human population and find an herbal medicine that would allow a person to live forever. Living forever and reducing population were contradictory goals, he understood, but nevertheless that would make Minnesota mighty heavenly. At his age, however, life still seemed forever, and his little corner of Minnesota was sparsely populated. He was so busy practicing a new song for his show at the Western Range that he almost decided not to go to the island today. But the warblers were moving through, tiny blobs of color as violently red, yellow, orange, and blue as any rainforest could boast. The air was so full of the warmth and vibrancy of fertile new growth that his body ached for release, for the outdoors, for the sounds of nature, for baring itself totally to the gentle sun. Maybe today she would come.

On the island, a Blackburnian warbler worked the catkins of an oak tree for insects. A redstart flitted in shrubs low to the water. There was only one boat out on the lake. Ahhhh, spring! Fen shed his cut-off jeans, settled back on the grass, closed his eyes and tried to concentrate on Mermaid. He had played at the Western Range until two o'clock that morning, so he soon fell into sleep so sound that even dreams of Mermaid were slow to come. When they did, he was surprised that she was not naked, as usual, but wearing shorts and a blouse.

Then with a start, he realized that he was not dreaming. She was standing over him, her face a battleground between joy and fear. Joy won. A great sigh escaped Fen as he realized it was really Mermaid.

But he made no move, not even to cover himself. Even to breathe might make her disappear. Neither of them spoke, each drinking in the sight of the other. Finally Kadie stooped down and touched his face, her finger moving slowing over his forehead, around his eyes, along his nose, circling his mouth as if she were painting him on a canvas. He still did not move nor speak. No words were necessary as the long-suffering loneliness drained from their faces and peace flowed in to replace it. Slowly, deliberately, Kadie removed her clothes and lay down beside him. He still did not, could not, move. Slowly and deliberately she turned toward him and slid one leg over between his. Slowly and deliberately she rolled over on top of him and pressed her lips against his. Only then did he move, his arms wrapping gently round her in simultaneous conquest and surrender.

Afterwards, they sat and stared at each other, wondering who would speak first, knowing it was not necessary to speak at all.

"I listened to you sing over at the Western Range last night." She smiled. "You didn't recognize me because I had clothes on."

Fen smiled.

"I had to watch you awhile to make sure. I guess I knew I was in love with you all winter but when you sang, I loved you even if I hadn't before. I was going to introduce myself to you, but then I thought it would be better this way."

Fen still could not speak, afraid of breaking the charm. But she understood the question in his expression.

"There's an old man lives around here someplace that you owe a lot to. Or rather we both do."

Fen smiled. "That would be Kluntz or Hasse, but how did they find you? Nobody believed my story."

"This guy knew I owned a red Outfitter canoe and a blue 1953 Ford pickup. Did you tell them?"

"No. Never thought to. That means someone else must have seen you that day. Musta been Hasse. That's why he's supported me. He knew. Son of a gun." And then he laughed. "Wait till you get to know these two old owls. You'll like 'em."

"Do you live around here?"

"Right over there in that old farmhouse. I'll show you."

CHAPTER 30

Perhaps because they were spending so much time at the university, Danny and Banana had started to think in very un-Josephian ways. Or perhaps what happened was just sheer logic that anyone with all the facts could have predicted. At any rate, when they asked Prior Robert if they could play baseball on the university team, he reacted predictably, that is with utter amazement. "No, you can't play baseball at the university," he replied sternly. "Whatever has gotten into you? Did Fr. Hildebrand put you up to this?"

"Oh, no," they assured him. "Hildy, er, Fr. Hildebrand, was just trying to pave the way for a game between us and the university. He never thought we'd make the team."

"Is Oblate Blaise in on this?"

"Oh, no. He said you would never allow it."

"Well then, what in the world are you thinking?"

Danny and Banana, having exhausted their courage for one day, left his office without saying anything more. But their plan was far from over. When the Provincial announced that Ascension Seminary would be closed within a year, sooner, if a buyer was found before that time, the two were the first to react because they had already made a grave decision. They knew that the SBDC Boys were to be broken up and some of them sent to Rome, Montreal, St. Louis or Catholic University in Washington to finish their studies. If Ascension closed, their last chance of playing college baseball was over.

"What it comes down to," Banana said, pointing the open end of his Royal Bohemian at Danny in the Western Range where they had stopped on their way back to the seminary from the university, "is that we've got a choice to make. We can either play baseball or we can become priests."

Silence. Swig. Swig.

"Maybe it's not either-or," Danny said, influenced greatly by the beer. "Maybe we can be priests and play professional baseball too."

"Are you outta your mind?"

"Think about it. If you can be a scripture scholar and a priest, or a writer and a priest, why the hell not a baseball player and a priest?"

Swig. Swig. Well, why the hell not? Actually, it was just as logical. Like Hildy said, if Babe Ruth had been a priest, look at the good he might have accomplished for the Church.

"We'll just go to Robert and say we want to start a travelling team of Josephians. We'll preach the good word before and after the games. Like—what are those guys who play basketball?—yeah, the House of David."

"And when Robert says no, then what?"

Swig. "We'll call his bluff. We'll say either we play ball or we're outta here."

"Oh, God, Danny, are you serious?"

"I always thought I was born to play ball and now that I've made Minnesota's roster, I know it. God's telling me something. I'll play ball in the Order or I'll play ball outside the Order."

"Oh, Danny, are you sure?"

"Do you know that Blaze is quitting? He didn't tell me in so many words, but I'm sure of it."

"And Fen's gone," Banana added, agreeing with the direction of Danny's remarks. "And what in the world is going to happen to

Gabe?" He paused. "Well, if the gang is splitting up, I guess I'm for splitting too."

///

Prior Robert thought, in a community full of preposterous people, that he had now heard a suggestion so preposterous that it could not be topped in the annals of preposterous thought. He just sat in his office chair for awhile, staring stupified out the window. But he had to answer.

"Oblate Daniel, am I hearing you correctly? Are you serious in thinking that the Order would allow the SBDC Boys to travel around the country and play baseball as their mission in life?"

"It would only be during the summertime. Not that big a deal. I think we could be as effective in spreading the word of God this way as any other. And bring in a lot of candidates for the Order."

"And we'd surely make more money than the priests do from saying Mass and hearing confessions in weekend parish work," Banana added. "People would pay a lot to see a team of monks beat the best of their local boys."

Prior Robert stared out the window again. "Why me, Lord," he finally said. Actually what alarmed him even more than the seminarians' naivete was the fact that he thought the most preposterous idea of all time was actually a fairly good idea.

"Look, Prior," Danny continued, "it is a rare thing when you have a dozen really good ballplayers together at one time in a seminary. Isn't that a sign from God that we are supposed to do something with that talent? Remember what the gospels say about not hiding one's talents under a bushel. Banana and I have gotten on the roster at the university. Doesn't that tell you something?

"Look what Mendel did and he was a monk," Banana interposed. "There's a priest somewhere I just read about who's trying to get elected to Congress. Is running the base paths any crazier than running for political office?"

Prior Robert broke into zany laughter. He was losing control. After all these years, he was losing control. Tears came to his eyes as he continued to laugh uncontrollably. Danny and Banana had never seen him this way. No one ever had.

"The thing of it is, boys, it's a damn good idea," Robert said, now laughing more shrilly than Oblate Blaise ever did. "It's one helluva great idea." He bowed his head into his arms on the desk, trying to calm himself. "That's the hell of it." The two seminarians glanced at each other fearfully. The Prior never used crude language. And they would never have dreamed that he would think their hairbrained idea was a good one.

Finally Robert straightened up. "You really do have a good idea, I want you to understand, but way, way, way ahead of our time. Surely, surely you realize that it is never going to happen. You want to give the Pope a case of irritable bowel syndrome?"

Danny and Banana giggled. Prior Robert was an okay guy after all. And they'd never suspected it. So the next part of their proposal became even more difficult.

"We kind of figured that the answer would be no," Danny said. He took a deep breath. "We want to seek dispensation from our vows. We want to quit the seminary."

"To play baseball?" The Prior could not believe his ears.

"It's as good a reason as any I've heard," Banana said. "You want us to say we want to get married? Or we want to go in business and make a lot of money? I mean what is a good excuse for leaving the Order?"

Prior Robert again buried his head in his hands. "By God, I told them this would happen," he muttered, again startling the two seminarians. Then his tone changed to one of pleading. "I think you need time, a lot of time, to think this over," he said.

"We've thought about it seriously for three months." Danny said. "When we made the university team, we decided that was as plain a sign from God as any we're likely to recieve. We aren't going to change our minds unless we can start a travelling Josephian team."

CHAPTER 31

The one person who did not laugh hysterically over Danny's and Banana's baseball folly was Melonhead, who did not care a fig about baseball. He did not laugh because a team of ballplaying priests was much more ridiculous, by comparison, than his own proposal. He asked Prior Robert for a meeting. Robert did not appear apprehensive, but it was not because he assumed Melonhead's proposal would be saner than playing baseball. It was just that, after Danny and Banana, he was beyond apprehension.

"Do we have to sell Ascension?" Melonhead began after he sat down in Prior Robert's office. "What do you think about turning it into a Center For Herbal Medicine and Homeopathy? That's kind of what it was before except for rich people and now it would be for poor people." No sense beating around the bush.

"Homeopathy? Isn't that stuff mostly discredited by now?"

"Not any more so than the belief in the Assumption of the Blessed Virgin or the Ascension of Christ. If you'd like, I can get Dr. Armbuster to give you a proper evaluation. Herbal medicine and homeopathy have been maligned without justification. The medical establishment is opposed because it fears that it would lose money if people turned to the cheaper cures herbalists can offer or concoct for themselves. Researching the possibility of low cost, do-it-yourself medicine is a perfect project for a mendicant order like us. It should be part of our mission. There's hardly anyone doing research in these areas because this kind of medicine doesn't show the profit potential to justify the cost of development. Working without pay, a cadre of priest-healers supported by the Order, by the donations that the laity gives to us, is right in line with mendicant philosophy."

Prior Robert rubbed the back of his neck. Lately it had started to hurt. It hurt now because he knew that Oblate Mel was perfectly correct but didn't have a chance.

"I know an herb that can soothe that pain in your neck," Melonhead said. "In fact I'll wager that if you soaked in a tub wrapped in heated Mudpura peat, you'd get rid of it for a while."

Prior Robert laughed. "I'm afraid the pain in my neck can't be cured," he said pointedly. "It's not really my pain."

"What do you mean?"

"I mean that the Provincial, let alone the Minister General, is not going to allow you to do this. Even if you wanted to start a regular hospital and staff it with Josephian doctor priests, you'd be turned down because, well, we've just made this enormous commitment to train priests to staff liberal arts colleges. Even if the Order wanted to do what you suggest, which it never would, it would involve resources we don't have."

"But alternative education is exactly where Josephians should be working, not in regular universities. There's plenty of people to do that work. We should be doing things outside the accepted intellectual sphere, out on the ramparts of human endeavor. This is where new discoveries come from. And it would not take a big commitment of money. Gabe and I are the only two who are really interested right now, and maybe Clutch, and that's enough for the time being. After ordination, we can still do priestly work in the parishes on weekends."

What Robert said next he had not known was in him to say. "Look, Mel, you surely know the Order is not going to go along with this.

We don't have any revolutionaries at the helm any more. That's what's wrong with the Church. It's still got its nose in the Divine Office, inhaling and exhaling psalms. What you want to do is noble and good, but you want the old tired Order to pick up the tab. That isn't going to happen. You have to go on your own. With your persuasiveness, you can raise the money from private sources. You don't need the Order, don't you see?"

Even as he finished his little exhortation, Robert realized that what he was saying could be interpreted as telling Oblate Mel to leave the Josephians. What he meant to say was that Mel should carry on his herbal research as a sort of spare time hobby away from more traditional priestly assignments. He started to clarify himself but stopped. What the hell. He had fought against closing Ascension to the point that he knew he was losing every chance of further administrative position within the Order, which was fine with him. Serves his superiors right. Let them kill the idea of religious communities in the world but not of the world.

Melonhead left the meeting in radiance. All this and maybe Dr. Armbuster too.

The Prior had hardly recovered from Melonhead's proposal when he was hit by another just as astounding, but this time one that the Provincial would welcome.

Blaze sat down heavily in the office and looked at the Prior a long time before saying anything. Robert thought that Oblate Blaise looked somehow old today.

"I kept my promise to you," Blaze said. "I did not tell anyone about the closing before it was announced."

Robert nodded gravely.

"Now I want to propose something that you have to promise me you will tell no one but the proper authorities until I'm gone."

"Gone?" Prior Robert's voice quavered.

"I want to go to Rome to complete my studies."

A hand grenade exploding on his desk would not have blown Robert's mind farther away. He gasped. The ways of God were wondrous indeed.

"What's gotten into you?" he said. "First the university and now Rome."

"It's a long story that you don't want to know about," Blaze said, his face flinching. "I've looked at all the options. I got handed my deck of cards when I was a kid barely out of grade school and I'm playin' 'em out. The sonsabitches are breaking up the Sonuvabitchin' Davy Crockett Boys, and my world with it and I don't see anything else interesting on my horizon." He could say "sonsabitches" now to the Prior or anyone else without fear. He no longer felt fear inside his little world, but only outside it. He was going to Rome under the pretext that he was still bound in conscience to the regulations and traditions of the Church. But his real objective was to go to Rome to overturn those regulations and traditions so that future SBDC Boys would have the kind of homelike community and security that was essential to the creative impulses that infuse all humans but which were in danger of being destroyed by the desire for money. Or so he rationalized. The future Josephians might turn out to be fighter pilots. Or whiskey distillers. Or homeopathists. Or any damn thing that promised to help poor people have what only rich people could pay for. And he might see how far he could push his Eleven Theses too. If he were a genius, as his superiors claimed, then by God he would now outwit the whole goddam college of cardinals and make Gabe the Pope. He was, in short, fantasizing again, but this time to keep his heart from breaking because of Marge Puckett.

Prior Robert's voice interrupted his thoughts. "Living in an Italian seminary is not going to be what I know you consider a happy life," he said. "What assurance do we have that you will persevere?"

"What assurance do you have that anyone will persevere doing anything, anywhere? And what about all the people with assured perseverence who up and croak or get killed or waylaid by wine, women and song. I can't give you an assurance other than my word and my word is probably not trustworthy past next Monday."

"Oblate Blaise, you are sounding rather bitter. Has something happened I should know about? Are you doing this because Danny and Banana and Melonhead have disturbed you deeply?"

Blaze laughed. "I wish it were that simple. We're all nuts, Robert." For the first time he did not say Prior Robert. This was the new Blaze who had nothing to lose. If they wanted him to go to Rome because he was their pet genius, then they by God could just humor him a little.

"It is true that we had hoped you would want to go Rome to complete your studies. But your present attitude is not promising. I will talk to the Provincial. In the meantime, I will not utter a word."

After Blaze left, Robert slipped a piece of stationery in his typewriter, and began typing:

> Dear Herb:
> Can you come here at the earliest date. I have a mutiny on my hands. But first, the good news. Oblate Blaise . . .

Fr. Abelard, stone sober for two months now, could not keep up with the pace of unexpected events that were crashing along toward some climax that he felt sure was to be momentous beyond anyone's imagination. He had to resort to pencil and paper and keep lists:

> 1. Ascension closing. Looks like Knights of Columbus interested in buying for a retirement home.
>
> 2. Oblates Daniel and Bartholomew quitting to play baseball. Doesn't make sense unless they fell for a couple of girls at the university.
>
> 3. Oblate Mel turned down on request to pursue herbal medicine. Rumor is that he is sweet on some doctor. Can't confirm.

4. Poor Oblate Luke is worried that he isn't going to Rome after all. Says he senses something in the air. Says that Robert not acting right about it. Says that Oblate Blaise is looking at him with even greater pity than usual if that's possible. I tried to assure him and he told me to screw myself with one of my rejuvenated light bulbs. This kind of audacity bears watching. Guess he wasn't fooled by those light bulbs after all. Just trying to seduce me.

5. Sneaked down to barn when no one was around and found that Oblate Mel's laboratory has disappeared. A mystery.

6. Oblate Blaise not going to see Oblate Christopher at the lake as much as previously. He is acting strange. He cut his classes short at the university. Something here I can't figure out.

7. Oblate Gabriel almost flunked my easiest test. Robert is going to send him to psychiatrist.

8. Late flashing news: Something amazing must have happened at Lake Wassermensch. Don't know what yet, but Oblate Gabe came back from lake with liveliest look on his face I have seen all winter and went straight to the prior's office. I tried to eavesdrop from Alexus's room but couldn't hear anything.

CHAPTER 32

Marge Puckett stared in astonishment at her father. Then slowly the disbelief turned to anger and the anger to rage.

"You have sold the farm? You have sold our land? And not said one word to me? Don't you understand this is my home?"

George Puckett fidgeted and tried to avoid her glare. "But hon, don't you see. You will inherit enough money to do whatever you please in life. You won't have to work so hard like mother and me have had to do."

"What I please to do in life is to work hard like you and Mother have. Don't you care about what you have established here? Don't you want to keep it going? I do." She rushed from the house, slamming the door behind her so hard the window cracked. She did not look back, running towards the fields, sobbing and berating herself in turn. The pastoral world that she had so carefully fashioned in her mind for her future was not to be. Money truly was the root of all evil, just like Blaze said. It made people go crazy, just like Blaze said. Halfway back to the lake, she changed directions. Wait till Al hears this, she thought. He will be even angrier.

Al was milking when she walked, breathless, into his barn. "Something terrible has happened," she said. "Daddy sold our farm."

To her surprise, Al only nodded. He knew.

"We sold ours too," he said. "Some big development coming in. Bought up a couple thousand acres. We're rich."

"Aren't you angry?" she asked, unwilling to see what was so plain to see.

"Jeez, Marge. I'll never have to milk another cow as long as I live."

Her mouth sagged. "You mean you don't like being a farmer?"

"Jeez, Marge. This is pretty much, you know, shit work."

Marge's hand flew to her mouth. She'd been an idiot. A naive, stupid jerk of an idiot. "But what are we going to do?" she demanded.

He looked away, shuffled his feet, took a long time to hang the milker cups on the next cow's udder. That way he didn't have to face her. "Well, I've been meanin' to talk to you. I was comin' over tonight in fact. This land sale changes everything, doesn't it? They bought the little rental house we were going to live in too, you know. We're all going to have to move. I'm hoping some day we'll maybe have a big grain farm, you know, just tractor farming. But now . . ." he paused, ". . . now everything is kind of up in the air. I'd like to take a year off and just travel around and see what the world's like."

"Are you saying you don't want to get married this summer?"

He pretended to study the cow. His silence told her plainly that the answer was no.

"You don't want to get married this summer?" she repeated, the rage rising in her voice again.

"Well, um, in view of, um, the turn of events, wouldn't it be better to wait awhile?" He still would not look at her.

Marge suddenly realized something about Al that she had not noticed before. He was a little shifty. And crafty in a way that was repugnant to her.

"Well, um," she replied, her anger now beyond control, "While you're, um, making up your mind, um, you can have this back." And she wrenched the ring savagely from her finger and threw it at him. As she turned at the barn door for one last look, he was down on his hands and knees, trying to find the ring.

For three days she hardly ate. She would not go back to college. She stated that she would not take final exams. She would not send out invitations to her graduation. "Now that we're going to be so rich, Mother," she said sarcastically, "Who needs a college degree?"

Some nights she did not come into the house at all but sat out on her favorite thinking spot above the lake and cried. Occasionally her father came looking for her, calling her name, but she would not answer. She would never speak to him again, she told herself. Her home was going to become a country club, a golf course, a "new town" enclave of suburban homes for rich people from the Twin Cities. She gagged at the thought. One of the most efficient food production systems in the world was destined for a rich society's playground while poor people starved. Blaze would appreciate that.

The longer she sat there contemplating her stupidity, the smarter Blaze appeared in her mind's eye. She had made a terrible mistake. But to go back to him, after breaking his heart, after telling him that he didn't measure up to her notion of a husband, that would be even shiftier behavior than Al's.

"You stupid, crazy bitch," she said out loud. Even that didn't help because it reminded her of Blaze again, saying that when you realized that you were crazy, then you were the sanest.

Meanwhile, at Seminary Two, Blaze, Gabe, Fen and their friends were throwing a party to end all parties—literally. No one would say the fateful words, but it was apparent to all that for the SBDC Boys, their life together was over. The passing needed to be marked on the calendar of memory. Also, the union of Fen and Kadie demanded special recognition. Kadie had brought her belongings to the farmhouse and announced that she would never leave unless Fen did.

"Fen is the most insane Davy Crockett Boy of us all and that's because he is the sanest," Blaze said, standing on a chair in the kitchen, trying to get his breath back after a sip of Axel's Best and a puff on one of Gabe's homemade cigars. "And Mermaid is the second sanest for having recognized that." All the SBDC Boys cheered except the Very Reverend Lukey who had only come to the party, he tried to tell himself, because he could not bear missing the insanities he was sure would transpire. He felt particularly smug anyway. He wondered if he should announce that he, not Gabe, was going to Rome.

Then came another celebration. Mermaid, Jesse, Hasse, Kluntz, Axel, and Patroux, who were all present, were officially entered into the society of the SBDC Boys and given special plaques of recognition: dried cow pats.

Wobbling dangerously on his chair, Blaze offered a toast: "From henceforth, let it go out to all the world that the SBDC Boys have passed into history. We are now officially 'The Lords of Folly.' We look out beyond the seminary and realize that we belong in the world as much as anyone because the whole human race is as insane as we are." Another throaty cheer. "And to prove it, let us toast particularly Danny and Banana, the only two people ever crazy enough to, first, enter the seminary and then, second, to leave it to play baseball."

Melonhead, brandishing a Royal Bohemian, stood up to speak, but was wise enough not to mount a chair. "There are other distinguished members of this august assemblage to be recognized. Let us toast Oblate Clutch, the Engineer of Ascension, who has completed what he calls a monument to the salvation of modern man." He paused, blinking unsteadily. "Oblate Clutch has built an alcohol still that converts corn to fuel. Never again will we have to depend on outside sources for gas. And—and—it is entirely legal. He got a special experimental license from good old Uncle Sam. Good old Uncle Hasse paid the fee. Of course Hasse made Clutch promise to provide him with free tractor gas." Everyone howled. Inspired by the laughter, Jesse showed that he could still do his old trick of standing on his head without the support of his hands. And Brother Walt hopped up on the table, flapped his arms as if they were wings, crowed like a rooster and shouted: "I'm the best in the West."

"And furthermore," Melonhead continued, "my friend Dr. Armbuster (snorts and chuckles filled the room) has promised to commit a thousand dollars as the first contribution to the Center For Herbal Medicine which Gabe and I want to establish if we can get the Order to go along with it."

"What if the Order won't?" Clutch asked. The room was suddenly quiet.

"Then we'll do it anyway."

Lusty cheers again. Jesse howled like a wolf and shouted what Walt had taught him: "I'm the beast from the East!"

Blaze waited for the party to wear down before he got back on his chair. He was now strangely solemn. "As you know, our good Prior gave permission for this party, something he would not normally do. Even gave permission for the beer. He's going to be here shortly. He says he has an announcement to make. Please refrain from Axel's Best while he's here."

A car pulled into the barnyard. The seminarians waited silently until Prior Robert entered the room and then saluted him with a cheer. He seemed surprised. He did not remember ever being applauded before by anyone and figured it would be the last time. "I've come here to say I'm sorry," he said, when the room quieted. "I'm sorry because the Church is not ready for you guys and I can't do anything about it. The ideas you have proposed strike me as exactly what the Josephian Order would do if its founders were starting out today instead of 400 years ago. I've come here to say I'm sorry because I don't have the power or the courage to support you more. I'm too old to go where you are going. But I want you to know that I don't think any of you,"—and here he looked directly at Fen—"have done wrong even if you may have violated the rules by which you promised to live as Josephians. You didn't make those rules and you promised yourself to them before you had any idea what they would entail. I'm fairly sure that if you were starting the Josephian Order today, you'd propose different vows to profess." Now he took another labored breath, almost panting in fact. "You would probably make rules more on the order of Oblate Blaise's Eleven Theses."

Even Blaze gasped at that remark. Gabe was thunderstruck. Robert was openly professing heresy. Lukey tried to appear deeply shocked but only succeeded in looking slightly drunk. The priest did not give any of them time to react. "You must appreciate that what I'm doing here is very difficult for me," he continued. "I am going against what I have always believed. I don't know what will happen to me in this world or in the next."

Then he walked over to Fen, who was holding Mermaid's hand. "I have judged you wrongly, Oblate Chris—er, Fen. I ask your forgiveness. I really thought that you had lost your mind. I am beginning to realize that I should start worrying about my own mind, not yours. But I would ask a favor of you. A sort of old fashioned favor, to please an old-fashioned man. Would you and your beloved companion allow me to bless your marriage?" He paused. "I do not do this out of concern that you are, in the old-fashioned cliché, living in sin. It would just be a comfort to me. I don't know who's living in sin and who isn't anymore. I suppose we're all living in sin by someone's standard."

Fen bowed his head in embarrassment. Mermaid squeezed his hand. "I think it's a great idea," she said to him, then turned to the priest. "But, Father, maybe you should know something first. I've been a whore for five years."

The SBDC Boys were as quiet and motionless as fossils in a museum.

Prior Robert, even to his own surprise, smiled. "We are all whores where money is concerned," he said. The Very Reverend Lukey, who could hardly wait to report what was happening to Alexus whom everyone said was destined to be the next Provincial, caught his breath and proceeded to have a coughing fit. "Are you sorry for what you consider to be wrong in your past?" the priest asked her. "Do you promise to remain faithful to Fen from now on?"

"Sure. I've been faithful to him for half a year without even knowing who he was, or even, for sure, if he existed. Lost me a helluva lot of money too."

Even Lukey had to chuckle.

"I'm sure Fen feels the same way about you," the priest said, frowning to hide a smile.

And so the two were joined in what Lukey would always refer to as "unholy matrimony." Blaze, looking on, felt his spirit sagging downward into even deeper despair. If only Marge and he could be as Fen and Mermaid were at that moment. If he had Fen's courage or craziness, whatever it was, perhaps Marge would be standing beside him right now. Now he was the one about to commit suicide. He was going to try to kill his true spirit by going to Rome.

"There's one more thing to celebrate, although I doubt that's the right word," Blaze said, after Fen and Mermaid had been properly toasted. "I've . . . I've volunteered to go to Rome to complete my studies." He kept staring at the floor. "I'll be leaving for Chicago day after tomorrow. And on to Rome shortly afterwards. Lukey is going too, to keep an eye on me." He paused for the titter he knew would follow. Then he looked at Gabe. "Tough luck, ole' buddy," he said. "I knew you wanted to go so bad and I just hated to take the opportunity away from you."

That brought on a few laughs too, but they dwindled away to silence. Lukey, who had not been told about Blaze, looked thunderstruck. Gabe appeared to have hit himself with a fence post.

CHAPTER 33

Gabe pondered his dilemma through the night, slicing all the facts and suppositions at his disposal into tiny fragments of possibility and studying them under the microscope of plausibility. Blaze would not volunteer to go to Rome under any circumstances that he could fathom. Although they were best friends and although Blaze had a ridiculous weakness for wanting to help people, he would not volunteer to take Gabe's place in Rome. Blaze had already admitted that he thought going to Rome would kill him, at least spiritually. Nor was Blaze so enamoured of his fantasies that he would volunteer to go to Rome to undermine present Church policy with his Eleven Theses crap. Blaze was way too smart to do anything as smart as that.

Gabe continued in anxious thought throughout much of the next day without coming to a conclusion. He tried to talk to Blaze, but Blaze would not answer his questions, would not in fact speak to him at all. He just kept jamming clothes and keepsakes into his suitcases, woodenly, as if he were preparing for his execution. Confronted with insanity, Gabe decided to speak to the resident expert.

"Jesse, do you have any idea why Blaze wants to go to Rome?"

"I know why he leaving."

"You do?" Gabe was stunned.

"Yep." Jesse made no attempt to continue. If he knew, surely it was plain to everyone.

"Well, hell, Jesse, spit it out."

"Blaze in love with Miss Puckett and she turn him down."

Gabe's hand flew to cover his open mouth. "How do you know that?"

"Little bird told me."

If Gabe looked stunned, his mind was not. It was crackling through every bit of information he possessed about Blaze with the speed of nerve impulses sparking across the neurons of his brain. "By God, that figures," he finally muttered. "Jesse, you're not witless; I am."

"Hee hee hee. I know that."

"I've got to stop him," Gabe said, not really talking to Jesse. "If he goes to Rome he really will go off the deep end." There was no time to lose. He turned back to Jesse. "I don't suppose you know the Puckett phone number?"

"Miss Puckett's car license is AM404T. Her papa's is 54TX77. His truck is . . ."

"That won't help, Jesse. But you are really, really, something."

Jesse beamed. Maybe Gabe not so crazy after all.

There was no formal farewell for the Rome-bound oblates. That had taken place at Seminary Two. But as soon as the Prior drove off to the train station with Blaze and Lukey, Gabe went into action. All the other priests were away for Saturday parish work as usual, so Gabe had easy access to the telephone in the Prior's office. There was only one Puckett listed in Grass Prairie in the phone book. He realized suddenly that he had rarely ever used a telephone. Phones were off limits. And before he entered the seminary he was too young to do much calling either. He could count on his fingers the number of times he remembered calling anyone in his whole life. He had to follow the directions in the phone book to call long distance. He listened to the phone ring at the other end of the line. Jesse was leaning over his shoulder, trembling with the nervous tension he dreaded.

"Hello. Puckett residence."

The voice sounded like an older woman. "This is Oblate Gabriel, calling from Ascension Seminary. I need to talk to Marge Puckett, please." His voice was strained. It seemed to him to come from somewhere other than his vocal chords.

A pause. "Just a minute."

This was going to be easy. He had expected that he would have to get a number for her apartment at the university.

"Hello. This is Marge Puckett."

She had a soft voice, full of curiosity. Gabe thought he could maybe fall in love with her too.

"Miss Puckett, this is Oblate Gabriel at Ascension Seminary. I don't think we've met formally. Perhaps Blaze has spoken of me. I'm his friend." He realized that he had never admitted that before.

"Is something the matter? Is he okay?"

"Well, maybe, maybe not. He is doing something he will regret, and I think it's because of you."

Silence. He could hear the phone line humming. Finally she replied: "Oh? How would you reach that conclusion?"

"A little bird told me."

"What's he doing?"

"He volunteered to go to Rome to finish his studies for the priesthood."

There was another long pause on the Puckett end of the phone. "That's hardly likely," she finally said. "Then again, I'm not too surprised."

"Believe me, Miss Puckett, he does not want to go. He's out of his mind. Because he loves you. I am going to try to stop him, but I think you could do it better. He is taking the train from Shakopee at 8:12 PM tonight and then changing trains in St. Paul for Chicago. There's time to get to the station before he leaves, or if not, to catch him at the Savage station or in St. Paul. Look, even if you don't love him, won't you help me stop him. He saved your life, you know."

Another long silence. Then Marge hung up.

So, Gabe thought. Just like a woman. Not to be trusted. It was going to be up to him. He knew how to do it. He would tell Blaze that Marge Puckett wanted him back.

With all the cars gone because the priests were all out on weekend parish work, he ran to the garage and tried to start the old farm truck. Battery dead again. That left only the Farm Zephyr. At forty miles per hour, he still had time to get to the Shakopee station. As he backed the tractor out of the barn, he saw Jesse, trembling with dread, watching him. "I'm going after Blaze," he yelled above the roaring motor. "Tell Fen."

Jesse was not trembling only because of the fear he felt for the Zephyr. The realization that Jack was actually leaving him was finally sinking in. His pal was abandoning him. He would be put in an institution without Jack to protect him. He had to stop that from happening. He thought he knew how to do that.

He waited until Gabe had pulled out on the road and disappeared into the twilight. Then he ran to his room, rooted around in the suitcase of treasures he kept under his bed, found his bedraggled Frank James costume and hastily donned it. He had to leave the waist unbuttoned because it no longer fit around his stomach. The zipper on the fly would not go all the way up either. He hitched the belt and holster over it, two holes down from its usual place. He hurried back to the barn, climbed astride his old horse, and galloped away. He was not headed for Lake Wassermensch to tell Fen however, but for the Western Range to borrow a pistol that worked. Rescuing Blaze was something not to be entrusted to a crazy nut like Gabe.

Marge had gone to her room after Gabe's phone call. She stood looking at herself in the mirror in great perturbation. "Damned if you do, damned if you don't," she spat at her reflection. "If he had the guts of a real man, he'd have run that damn Al away and taken you."

But she knew that was folly. She'd never let anyone "take" her, and Blaze knew that as well as she did. But if he truly loved her, he'd come back from his stupid flight to Rome on his own and she'd be waiting and then she'd know. And he'd know. But that was folly too. She had refused him and only a slobbering wimp would come crawling back after that. And why would she be waiting if he did come back? Only if she really did love him. Did she? Oh, hell yes, she did. She pulled off her barn clothes, threw them at the mirror, and put on the dress she had been wearing the day she had told Blaze of her engagement to Al. She'd have to hurry. "I'm going back to my apartment to study for finals," she told her mother as she flashed through the kitchen. Her mother smiled. The girl was finally coming to her senses.

Gabe had rarely driven the Farm Zephyr and never at high speeds on the highway. That was Blaze's department. Moreover, he lacked the experience of growing up driving tractors, as Blaze had. He did not understand the intricacies of handling tricycle-type models with the two small front wheels together. As he throttled up the Zephyr, those tires went into their usual worn-bearing wobble. The tractor shook as if it were about to fly apart. Terrified, Gabe slowed down. But he'd never get to the station in time this way. To hell with it. He jerked the throttle wide open again and clenched the steering wheel in mortal fear. The Zephyr worked up to top speed and the wobbling ceased. Gabe sighed with relief. A miracle, surely. God must be looking out for him.

But he had no appreciation of the danger he was in. At forty miles an hour, the tractor was an accident looking for a place to happen. If he had to turn quickly, it could easily flip over. A sharp bump could jolt the front wheels sidewise, wrench the steering wheel out of his grasp, and send the tractor careening out of control into the ditch or into an oncoming car. To make matters worse, the lights were dim, barely capable of warning other drivers of the tractor's presence on the road, let alone provide much visibility of the road surface.

Had Gabe stayed on the highway, he would have been safer, but fearing possible collision with cars, he moved over to the road shoulder whenever one approached. Even then, if he had slowed down during this maneuver, he might have been okay. But slowing down would not get him to the station on time. As he neared the bridge that led across the river and into Shakopee, where the ditch was deepest because the roadbed was built high over the marshland through which it traversed at that point, he moved onto the shoulder just a tiny six inches too far. In the dark, he could not discern the little dip in the roadside bank, perhaps carved by runoff water from the last flood, but more likely the track of a car tire made during spring thaw. Not enough of an indentation to be of any danger normally, the track was deep enough to catch the front tires of the Zephyr and pull it sharply toward the ditch. When Gabe over-reacted and tried to yank the front tires back toward the road, the speed of the tractor jammed the front wheels instantly perpendicular to the forward motion. The steering wheel spun out of Gabe's grasp. Before he could stamp on clutch and brakes, the tractor lurched down the steep ditch, the front wheels sliding sideways until they slammed into the soft mud at the bottom of the ditch. The tractor upended and when it landed upside down, Gabe, frozen in fear on the tractor seat, disappeared beneath it. He did not even have time to scream.

But someone did scream. Marge Puckett, approaching the tractor in her car, saw it catapult into the ditch. She knew it was the Zephyr even in the darkness and although the figure in the seat could hardly have been Blaze, she screamed first because Blaze was the only person she had ever seen driving the stupid thing. Maybe by some strange coincidence it was Blaze, playing out his madness by taking one last ride on his beloved tractor before the long journey to Rome. Two cars ahead of her pulled off the road, and she followed. Along with the other drivers she ran to the tractor which now tilted crazily upside down, the one free back wheel spinning eerily in the air. The motor was still running. She turned it off. She was still screaming. She could see a hat. Definitely the one Gabe always wore. The body must be pinned down in the muck of the marsh under the tractor. If Gabe had not been crushed to death, he would surely be drowning. She wedged herself down under the machine and began clawing in the mud and cattails, still screaming. One of the other witnesses to the accident had a flashlight and crawled down beside her, trying to help. What they uncovered first was hair, the back of a head, black hair. Even in her desperation, Marge felt a little twinge of guilty relief. It was not blond Blaze. The other rescuers had hold of arms now and were slowly inching the bloody body out of the ooze. By now a traffic policeman was in the mud with them, feeling for a pulse. None. Someone fished a billfold out of the trouser pocket. Someone read. "Oblate Gabriel Roodman." Marge was still screaming. The others helped her back up to the road. An ambulance had arrived. Nothing more for her to do when with every second, Blaze was getting farther away.

She answered the questions the traffic officer asked as quickly as possible, jumped into her car, and sped away.

Meanwhile, Jesse had reined up in the blackness beyond the accident and crept forward on foot, leading old Blaze. He dared not get close to the spotlight of the police cruiser playing down on the scene. He was Frank James now, train robber, black hat on his head, bandanna around his neck. The sheriff would hardly let such a strange figure pass unchallenged. Besides, in the stark, mathematical logic of his strange mind, Jesse felt no particular horror at the scene before him. He had always known that something terrible like this was going to happen to that tractor, especially if someone as crazy as Gabe drove it. His absolute conviction that every powered vehicle was a death trap, a coffin on wheels, sure to crash sooner or later, now kept him curiously aloof from the horror of the accident. Tragedy was as certain to follow in the tracks of motored vehicles as rain falling during a thunderstorm.

Besides, saving Gabe, if he were not already dead, was out of his hands. Stopping Jack from his mad flight to some place called Rome was his problem. Miss Puckett down there in the muck was not going to make it to the train station in time. Jesse led his horse in the ditch on the opposite side of the road until he had cleared the accident area. With all eyes on the crash, no one noticed him. He pulled himself astride old Blaze again and galloped on. As on the night he had robbed the train, some inner resolve had come to his aid, allowing him to overcome the debilitating dread of tension that normally would have rendered him helpless and incapable of action. For Jack he could do anything. Jack was the best friend he ever had. Jack would make sure they didn't put him away with lunatics. Once across the bridge and in Shakopee, he headed not to the train station but by back streets and then country roads toward the Western Range. He knew what he was going to do.

It was Blaze's idea to take the old milk train from Shakopee to the Twin Cities. Prior Robert had wanted to drive on into the terminal in St. Paul, and so did The Very Reverend Lukey. But Blaze would not acquiesce, just as he had insisted on wearing his pink Elvis shirt under his dark blue jacket against the wishes of both the Prior and Lukey. By heaven, he had volunteered for Rome with its church ceilings full of fat naked angels, so the Order could just humor his choice of clothes a little. I am a different Blaze now. I'm a dangerous fellow, he said to himself, even though he knew he wasn't. If the Church thought that Luther had given it a hard time, just wait. "Besides," he said out loud, "I think this strange old train is a time machine that brought me into my Brigadoon. The only way I can get out is to ride the train back to the real world."

Lukey rolled his eyes and said he would not sit in the same seat with him. Lukey wondered how he was ever going to put up with folly like this all the way to Rome. But he was in too good a mood to argue. Now they both shook hands with Prior Robert and boarded the rattling old coal burner. To Blaze's chagrin, the coal oil lamps were gone, but otherwise the coach was as decrepit as ever. The train was an every other day occasion now, going out from the Twin Cities one night and coming back the next. As had been the case three years ago, there were no other travellers.

"Rome, here we come!" Lukey said jubilantly as the train rumbled out of the station. Then, smirking at Blaze, whom he had decided to sit beside after all, he added: "Think we'll see Frank James this time?" Blaze pretended not to hear. If he had ever wanted to pray, it was now. He wanted to beseech God to make Frank James appear again and scare Lukey totally shitless.

A few minutes out of the station, the train reached its version of top speed in preparation for laboring up and over the hill at Murphy's Landing. As it slowed going up the grade, Blaze remembered the train robber and once more wondered what really had happened that fateful night and if he'd ever know. Seated next to the window, he stared out into the darkness. Had it been a dream? Were the entire last three years a dream? Was he about to wake up and find himself back in the staid seminary college in Michigan preparing to shove off for Minnesota?

As he stared out the window, suddenly a vision. He almost cried out but instead looked quickly away, trying to clear his brain of what he thought he had just seen. He looked again. The vision was still there. Again he looked away. His mind was playing tricks on him. But he had to look again. This time the vision was gone. He had sworn that he had seen a horse, a very familiar horse, galloping alongside the train with what sure as hell looked like Jesse, a bandanna over his face, astride it. He tried to get hold of himself. He had imagined it. No way did he dare to tell Lukey. That would be Lukey's final victory. He closed his eyes. He would not look out the window again. But then he looked again. Nothing. Relief. But he began to tremble. He had suspected that he would lose his mind if he went to Rome. Now he suspected that he was losing it before he even got out of Minnesota. Or perhaps he had always been crazy, as Lukey insisted. The imagination is a powerful thing. He so much wanted Frank James to board the train and scare Lukey shitless that his mind had conjured up the vision. Shades of Lourdes and Fatima. Is that what had happened three years ago? God almighty, that goddamn Lukey might be right.

The train was crawling to the top of the grade now and would soon begin picking up speed, going downhill. A presence, more felt than seen, caused both oblates to turn to look behind them. An involuntary yelp broke from Lukey's lips. He was staring directly into the business end of a Colt 45. The Frank James of three years ago pushed the pistol against Lukey's forehead and once again the hapless seminarian fainted.

Blaze was smiling. What was happening came to him in the rush of a split second. The God he no longer believed in had granted his request and scared Lukey shitless. Blaze knew who was standing behind him, knew now the whole mystery of the train robber. He started to smile. Jesse had fooled them all. And the reason why he had staged the first robbery was exactly what he had said it was: to take revenge on a society that treated him as if he were insane. That would be enough to drive anyone to doing something as crazy as trying to rob a train.

But then Blaze noticed that the revolver staring him in the face was not Jesse's old broken, rusted hulk, but a very well-oiled and sinister looking weapon. Jesse just might have gone over the edge of what constituted sanity in the insane world, and might for some crazed reason, actually be intending to shoot someone. He had better humor Jesse. It would keep Lukey scared shitless for awhile longer too.

Lukey revived in time to see the masked man turn his attention to Blaze.

"I am Frank James, come to avenge my brother's memory as I told you before. Git your hands up. You're comin' with me, or I'll blow yer head off." The voice was faked, high and whiney, like a sawwhet owl. The pistol poked and beckoned Blaze out of the seat, forcing him to step over the seemingly paralysed Lukey as he edged into the aisle. The outlaw pushed him roughly toward the head of the coach, for now the train was starting to gain speed. Soon it would be going too fast to jump from safely.

"Git, Jack, git out the door."

Blaze turned on the gunman, victory on his face. "You called me Jack, Jesse. You gave yourself away."

A pause. The arm holding the pistol sagged to the outlaw's side. "Hee hee hee. I sure fool ole' Lukey, didn't I. Jump."

"I'm not jumpin' out of this train and break a leg or something. You think I'm crazy?"

Jesse screamed in Blaze's ear. "Miss Puckett wants to talk to you!"

Blaze jumped.

Jesse came right behind him and as the two rolled and tumbled down the railroad embankment, they started giggling like children tumbling down a haystack. They came to a stop in a heap and finding no bones broken, continued to laugh and pound each other.

Then they just lay there, looking at the stars. Life was too, too unreal. Blaze, the horse, finally found them. "We gotta ride to Western Range, Jack. Gotta take gun back to smartass Nash. He don't know I borrowed it outta his drawer. If I use my old one, you not be fooled. Hee hee hee. I sure fool you good, Jack. Three year I fool you good. I not Frank James. Hee hee hee."

So full was he of his exciting second reincarnation as Frank James, Jesse did not even remember to tell Blaze about Gabe until they went into the Western Range and then he did not have to tell. Customers were talking about the monk who had gone crazy, run away from the monastery on a tractor, and was killed when the tractor overturned. News like that moved lightning fast in rural Minnesota. Probably the same monk reportedly seen a year or so ago, running naked away from the barn. Creepy place, that monastery was. Fen was trying to sing, but could only weep.

Blaze sat down at the bar, feeling life draining out of him. Had it not been for the thought that Marge wanted to talk to him, he might at that moment have sunk into a depression from which he would not have recovered. Gabe dead? After so many years side by side, Blaze could not even imagine a world without Gabe. Most of his identity sprang from Gabe. He might as well be dead too, be born again, start over as someone else. In fact that is exactly what Gabe's death meant. The end of his first life. He would have to start over. Who would he be in his next life?

Lukey got off the train at Savage. He was having difficulty breathing and could not think at all except to wonder if he were having a heart attack. He only knew that he had to get away from that devil-possessed time machine of a train. He had revived just in time to see Blaze jump out the coach door with the crazed outlaw right behind him. Now he had to find the idiot. But why? Blaze deserved getting kidnapped, robbed, killed, whatever. Lukey paused in his thinking. Blaze really had to be in danger. It was a hard thought to hang onto because the idiot never really seemed to be in danger. He was a case study in living beyond danger. But he, Lukey, had to help him if he could. Zombie-like, he stumbled into the darkness, headed back down the railroad tracks, leaving even his suitcases behind.

Meanwhile Marge had finally gotten back on the highway and was barrelling on toward the Twin Cities as fast as her car would go. She knew that the train had already left Shakopee and her only hope was to get to the terminal in St. Paul before Blaze's train left for Chicago. She opened the window, sure she was going to vomit. She could not get the vision of the mangled Gabe out of her mind. Her dress was splattered with mud; one stocking torn. Her hands were encrusted with dried mud, and her fingernails black with swamp muck. But she was heedless of her appearance. She had to stop Blaze or she feared she would never see him again.

Every traffic light through St. Paul seemed to take an eternity to turn green. But finally, the station. She rushed frantically inside, ignoring the strange looks cast her way, shouting his name, checking at ticket counters, running to the boarding areas. Too late. She sat down and began to cry uncontrollably. The tears would not stop, even when she got back into her car and headed for home. Her world had collapsed. She might as well be as dead as poor Gabe.

Passing the Western Range on her way home, she decided to stop and have a beer or two. Or three. Fen would probably be singing by now and she could tell him the terrible news about Gabe. She rarely participated in beer parties at college because she was always intent on getting home on weekends to help with the farm work. But that was all in some other world now. Maybe she would get drunk. See what that was like.

She took a table in a dark corner. She was such a mess that she wanted no one to see her. After a beer she would clean up a little in the ladies' room, she told herself. She noticed a woman staring raptly at Fen who sat on a tall stool, strumming his guitar and singing, ever so sadly. No doubt that was Mermaid. Next to her sat Melonhead, Danny and Banana, whom Marge had gotten to know at the university. They must have stopped on their way back from classes to the seminary. Next to them sat Jesse, dressed ludicrously like the fake-cowboy waiters. How had he gotten there? Next to him was an empty chair and a half glass of beer, as if someone had abruptly left the table to go to the bathroom.

"This one is for Gabe," Fen said, and then launched into "Streets of Laredo." So, Marge understood, they already knew. "Beat the drums slowly and play the pipes lowly, play the death march as they carry me along." Marge downed a glass of Royal Bohemian without stopping. "Sixteen gamblers come carry my coffin, sixteen young maidens come sing me a song." She downed a second glass, bowed her head and started crying again.

"Tears are always on the verge of falling, aren't they?" she heard a familiar voice say. Her head jerked up and her eyes popped open. She was staring directly at a silver-buckled belt holding up a pair of black jeans, cut western style. Her eyes rose slowly to a pink shirt with white stitching and above that the handsomest face in all the world was smiling through tears at her.

"Blaze!" She screamed the name so loud that Fen stopped playing. All eyes turned toward her. Marge barely had time to jump out of her chair before Blaze wrapped his arms around her.

Fen started playing "Yellow Rose of Texas," which he knew was one of Blaze's favorites. But Blaze did not hear. Marge was sobbing and shaking uncontrollably as he hugged her, trying to calm and comfort her even as he himself wept. Even when Nash Patroux shouted "Beer on the house!" they continued to sway in each other's arms. What finally brought them back to earth was Jesse, who had surveyed the crowd and satisfied himself that there were no Pinkertons present. "Hee hee hee," he said loud enough for everyone to hear at the now quiet bar. "I sure fooled that Jack. He think I Frank James."

"Sit down, Marge," Blaze said gently. "Jesse told me what happened. Told me you had come after me."

As if the clash of terrible tragedy and ecstatic happiness in the Western Range could possibly become more poignant, into the restaurant stumbled a man wearing a black suit with the letters OSJ stitched in blue on the lapel. His hair was uncharacteristicly disheveled and his face a ghostly white, appearing almost deathly in contrast with the black suit. He looked as if he had just seen the devil himself, an observation with which he would readily have agreed.

The Very Reverend Lukey, far from looking very reverend, had been walking around in the darkness for an hour, not quite able to make up his mind about what to do or even to gather his thoughts for any concerted action. He had walked all the way back up the hill at Murphy's Landing but found nothing. Was the train robber real? Was Plato right? Did real existance occur in the mind, and everthing the eyes saw only a reflection of the reality in the mind? Or was he going crazy because he really was gay and was trying to deny his true self? He did not know the answers to any of these questions. He did not think that he could go back to the seminary. He could not at the moment understand why he had been attracted to that life in the first place. Those few moments on that devil train had suspended his ability to think. He had developed a strange form of amnesia. He could remember the what of everything, but not the why of anything. He had been walking aimlessly down the highway when he spotted the lighted sign at the Western Range. He had never been in the restaurant, but he remembered that Fen sang there. Fen, whom he had always considered sexually depraved, was the very one he now realized might be able to help him separate fact from fancy.

But the first person Lukey saw when he walked into the saloon was Blaze. He came close to fainting again, especially since Blaze was in the arms of a girl. Surely, Lukey thought, I have stumbled into a hangout of devil-worshippers who must have kidnapped Blaze and bewitched him into joining them. Looking around, he noticed Frank Jameses all over the restaurant, pretending to be waiters. Vampires in western drag? One of them approached him, smiling, to usher him to a table. Oh, my God, they want to seduce me into their lair of witchery, he thought. He turned and fled out the door.

Blaze had been as surprised to see Lukey as Lukey to see him. But instead of relishing the obvious fact that Lukey was frightened out of his mind, Blaze suddenly felt pity for him.

"Marge, hold on a sec. I gotta settle something."

He ran out the door after Lukey. Lukey, over his shoulder, saw him coming and crying out again, ran faster. Surely he was being pursued by the devil in the disguise of another devil.

"Lukey, for heaven's sake, stop!"

Blaze had to tackle him half-way across the parking lot and wrestle him to the ground. Lukey began to pray out loud.

"Oh for crap's sake. Calm down, you idiot, "Blaze said. He was surprised at how kindly he sounded, talking to a man he had always thought he despised. "There's an explanation for all of this."

Lukey abruptly stopped his whimpering prayers. "Some kind of elaborate joke you've been playing on me, you sonuvabitch?"

Blaze had to laugh. Lukey would always be Lukey. "No, Lukey. No joke. Awful things have happened." Blaze's voice broke. "Gabe is dead, Lukey."

"Whaaaaat?"

"Gabe is dead. He turned that goddamned tractor over on himself." And suddenly Blaze was sobbing helplessly. He had not cried like this since he was a child.

Lukey did something he would never have predicted of himself, especially where Blaze was involved. They were both sitting on the parking lot. He reached over and put his arm around Blaze and pulled his weeping comrade close against him. And Blaze made no effort to stop him, did in fact surrender to him. They sat there, then, on the blacktop, bound to each other, crying. And they both knew something. It was okay to show love for another man. Didn't have to have a damn thing to do with sex.

"Come back inside and have a beer with us," Blaze finally said. "Melonhead's here too. There's more happened in the last few hours than you'd ever believe could happen in a lifetime."

Nash Patroux herded the Lords of Folly into the upstairs party room and shortly joined them. It was a very quiet party, considering the people present. Not a word of banter. Not one laugh, not even a quiet chuckle. The events of the last few hours had driven the merry playfulness of seminary life out of them. They were feeling real-world suffering. To help Lukey understand, Blaze made Jesse put his bandanna over his face and brandish a pistol and make noises like a saw-whet owl. At any other time, Blaze would have been pounding the table in glee at Lukey's total embarrassment, but because of Gabe, he could not. Gabe was gone; the Blaze of yesterday was gone too.

About that time Hasse and Kluntz walked into the room. They had come to tell Fen about the accident. Kluntz was a little nettled that everyone already knew.

Blaze and Fen stared at Hasse. They had never seen him so visibly in agony. Always the old farmer was the cool one, looking down on miserable stupid human beings in the way he figured God would observe them if he believed in God.

"He was like a son to me," Hasse said, seating himself heavily at the table. "A son. I never had a son." He looked at the others. It was obvious that he needed comfort, that he wanted someone to hug him, but who would ever hug a man like Hasse and live to tell about it. "The last three years have been better for me than all the rest before," he said, in a forlorn, lost tone of voice that Blaze had never heard before. Hasse was not murdering consonants. He was not being sarcastic. Blaze decided to risk it. He hugged Hasse. Hasse looked startled, then hugged back.

"Gabe lost his life to keep me from losing my mind," Blaze said. No one responded so he said it again.

"Gabe lost his life to keep me from losing my mind."

"You know something, Blaze," Fen replied. "Even when you speak a plain truth, you're still fantasizing."

Where sorrow is deepest, laughter is only a breath away. Funeral goers often start laughing inanely through their tears. So now, after that remark, there was no way to keep the Lords of Folly from laughing, relieving the crushing burden of their sorrow.

"That's exactly what Gabe would have said, you know," Blaze remarked.

Through the night, the Lords of Folly pretended to tell their antic seminary adventures to Marge and Mermaid, but they were really telling them to each other as soldiers do. "Remember when . . ." "You won't believe this but . . ." "How we managed to live through that . . ." Marge and Mermaid pretended to find the stories funny rather than boring. They understood. Men told their war stories over and over again because that was how they taught themselves to almost accept death.

Patroux listened with rapt attention. When he would withdraw to get more beer, he made notes. He had always wanted to write a western and the Lords of Folly had inspired him. He would write a novel called *The Second Coming of Frank James and His Apostles*. It would be a best seller, he just knew.

The eastern sky was beginning to pale by the time the Lords of Folly ran out of stories and tears. But no one wanted the gathering to end.

"What are you guys going to do?" Lukey asked because he had no idea what he was going to do.

Marge spoke up. "I know what Blaze is going to do."

Dry laughter. Almost like the SBDC Boys of yesterday.

"And we all know what Danny and Banana have decided," Melonhead said. "And Fen."

"What about you, Melonhead?" Fen asked.

"Well, Gabe had it all figured out, you know. How we were going to establish our herbal medicine center for poor people. He said he had a way to convince the Minister General to go along with the idea. He said he knew where we could get the money. He figured that the Josephian authorities would never turn down money, even if it were for a gambling casino. But Gabe never told me the source of that money."

"I know," Hasse said and all eyes swivelled to look at him in astonishment. He smiled, retreating back into his disguise. "Dat sonuvagun found out somehow dat I was rich."

Again laughter, but subdued.

"I've got an idea," Marge said. They all looked at her in surprise. She and Blaze had become so engrossed in each other that she did not seem to be listening to the conversation. Hasse's admission happened to jell with an idea she had been toying with ever since she had learned what her father had done. "There's something even Blaze doesn't know yet. My father sold our farm. There's a big development coming into our area. Neighbors sold out too. Big money." Kluntz, hearing such news, fidgeted like a rabbit in a pen surrounded by foxes. He hadn't heard. He must be slipping in his old age.

Blaze started to express his surprise and disappointment, but Marge put her finger over his lips and continued: "I'm going to have some money too, Mr. Hasse. I am going to buy a farm for Blaze and me. Here's what I'm thinking. Why don't you sell the farm at Lake Wassermensch to us at a ridiculously moderate price. That would mean that Fen and Mermaid could go on living there. And Melonhead could make his medical center there. And we could sort of adopt Jesse to live there too."

Once more, Blaze looked at Marge in awe. She had never seemed particularly interested in the visions of Gabe and Melonhead. But she was looking at Hasse. She knew the right button to push. "Then you could actually use your money to build and furnish the medical center."

"And Clutch could go on perfecting his gasahol plant," Melonhead said, his eyes as wide as full moons as he contemplated all the possibilities.

"And, just think, Hasse. You would have a built-in hay crew for as long as you live," Fen said.

Hasse trained gimlet eyes on each of the Lords of Folly in turn, taking a long time to answer. They could almost hear the calculator in his brain clicking away. Finally, he reached a conclusion. "That Gabe. He is something, isn't he. He's getting the best of me even when he's dead."

Then Kluntz, lips pouting and not with snuff this time, added: "Hey. What about me? I've got some money too, you know."

"Can I join you?" The voice came from Lukey, but did not sound like Lukey. It was a voice of surrender, of finally learning almost how to think.

Now it was time for Blaze to prove that he really was born to help others in his own weird way. "No, Lukey, you belong in the priesthood and you know it. And now that we have taught you how to think, finally, you'll make a good one."

Lukey frowned at Blaze, trying to figure out if his adversary were making fun of him again.

"No, I mean it," Blaze said. "You will make a good priest. When you thought I was in trouble being shanghied off that train, what did you do? As much as you despised me, as much as you wanted to keep on going, you came to look for me." Then winking at Fen, he added, "And besides we're going to need an inside man in Rome when we take over the Church."

The sun had risen now, and the bustle of the world had to go on, sleep or no sleep. Lukey, Danny, Banana and Melonhead went back to the seminary, Lukey to stay, the others to prepare to leave. Hasse went home to milk his cows. Kluntz went scouting for more gossip about the new development. Fen and Mermaid returned to Seminary Two. Marge and Blaze drove on to the Puckett farm to tell her parents that they were getting married. Blaze refused to go back to the seminary. They would stay with Fen and Mermaid until they had sorted out their lives. They then climbed up to the high pasture hill overlooking the Lake Wassermensch farm that would be theirs, and with many a contented sigh, began their life together.

EPILOGUE

A 1999 Ford Taurus stopped in front of a large, institutional brick building crumbling into ruins. Faded lettering over the entrance read "Ascension Seminary." The driver, a tottering old man in clerical garb and Roman collar, climbed painfully out of the car and stretched carefully. At 89 Fr. Robert probably should not have been driving anymore, but no one in the Josephian Order had the guts to try to make him quit. His superiors barely had the courage to demand that he retire as pastor of the church in Broken Bow, Nebraska, where he had happily ministered to the people for forty-four years. He had been largely left alone in Broken Bow after the "unfortunate incidents" that had occurred right at the place where he now stood. Forty-four years. He could hardly believe that this place had been so full of life such a short time ago and was now crumbling into ruins. A painful smile spread over his face as scenes of the past flooded into memory. He stared a long time at the pathetic field of drought-wilted corn right south of the crumbling building. Forty-four years ago that field had been a sandy ball diamond where a bunch of seminarians under him had beat the ass off a semi-professional baseball team. What mad mayhem! But was it any more madness to try to grow priests on ball diamonds than to try to grow surplus corn on soil so poor it would barely raise sand burrs? He looked through the sagging door of the building into the hallway, hearing in memory, the voices of a community of men happy to do God's work without pay, to sing, to cook, to paint, to build, to craft, ora et labora and as that imp of a Blaze used to say, plenty of sporta too.

He did not go inside. His heart was in bad enough shape. It had been broken forty-four years ago. For the same reason, he did not go across the road and into the barn with the words, "Ascension Seminary," still faintly visible, painted on its grey, faded siding. He just stood there while the tears rolled down his cheeks. Trees had already grown up along the barn foundation. How quickly the forest reclaims all signs of human activity if given a chance. How puny is the work of humankind.

Robert had not kept close track of the place after the Josephians had sold it. He had heard it changed hands several times, but he had not imagined that finally it would be allowed just to fall into ruin. Sad as that was, it seemed symbolic to him of what had happened to the traditional Church. It was gone, gone, gone, like the traditional farms, the traditional villages, the traditional people. Gone, gone, gone. All that an old man could do was weep. Weep and drive on. Drive on, drive on, drive on. That was history in two words: drive on.

But before he drove on, he had another stop to make. Over the years, he had exchanged letters several times with Blaze and Fen, who had caused him so much pain and grief. They had been the cause of the biggest furor ever raised within the 400-year-old Josephian Order. By some absolutely remarkable miracle, they still lived here, at what forty-four years ago was known as the Lake Wassermensch farm, or, to a few, Seminary Two. He meant to see what had become of them before he went on to Chicago to die.

The countryside through which he drove was hardly recognizable. Roads that forty-four years ago had been narrow, gravel, one-lane affairs, were now two cars wide and paved. Many of the bucolic farms he remembered were now suburban landscapes. The Hasse farm, the Kluntz farm, the Puckett farm were houses and golf courses and office buildings and expansive lawns. The little lakes that forty-four years ago were surrounded by fields and cows, were now choked by human residences. Country villages had disappeared into a cauldron of feverish growth: subdivisions, office buildings, strip malls, new highways. He was lost.

Eventually, backtracking several times, he found the road to Seminary Two and what he saw there made him smile. The farm was still intact, though its appearance changed somewhat from forty-four years ago. Over the entrance to the lane back to the house and barn was a big sign that read: Folly Farm. The fields were dotted with sheep, groves of trees and small fields of strange-looking crops. A windmill turned on the highest knoll of the farm. Several long, one-sided greenhouses full of exotic plants bordered the lane, facing the southern sun. Was this, after all, the fruition of the visions of those seemingly zany former students of his?

With a start, he thought the young man who waved at him from a field beside the lane was Blaze. Sure looked like him. Would have to be Blaze's son.

The old farmhouse had been remodelled. The barn looked about the same but restored somewhat. Chickens squawked and strutted everywhere. Ricks of firewood filled several sheds and nearly every roof was bedecked with solar panels. He noticed, curiously, that no electric power line ran back to the farmstead. A fairly new house stood on the hillside above the barn, but lower than the windmill. Evidently, in the old manner Robert remembered from his youth, water was being pumped by wind to the highest elevation from which it could flow by gravity to buildings below.

The lake shore was still wild and natural. No noose of housing development surrounded it as with the other lakes. Down the hill from the newer house an older couple was walking toward him. Despite the intervening years, they were unmistakably Blaze and Marge. And they knew their visitor was Robert. Aging had been kind to all of them.

For the longest time they just stood and stared at each other. Finally, Blaze spoke—bluntly as usual: "Can't believe you're still alive."

"I remember thinking the same thing about you, on several occasions," the old priest replied, smiling. And then they hugged each other. The years and the philosophies that separated them had only strenthened their mutual regard.

Yes, Marge explained, in answer to Robert's question, that was their son in the field. He and his family lived in the old house, and had largely taken over the farm work. Yes, they raised sheep and the herbs and food crops that Folly Farm sold. Actually, Folly Farm was rather well known locally for its herbal products, sheep cheese and woolen goods. Yes, Melonhead was still alive and still doing a good business in herbs. Herbal remedies had become popular, just as Gabe had known they would, and Folly Farm made enough money selling them and putting out books about them to get by. "It's kind of ironic," Blaze said, "but the residential development we despise for filling up the countryside with suburbs is actually the reason our farm thrives. People with money are crazy. They'll buy about anything we produce if we take it to them. I think they'd pay us to spoon it in their mouths if we offered." Blaze did his hyena-like laugh which had only grown louder with age. "Melonhead has just retired from teaching at the university," he added. "His wife—that Dr. Armbuster, remember her?—died a few years ago. She helped us too, even though it cost her loss of status, and probably money, within the medical establishment. The AMA is a lot like the Church. Both afraid they will lose business to mavericks like the Lords of Folly."

Yes, Clutch was still alive and lived on the farm too. He was away right now, working on a big alcohol plant that a private company was building. He had become a leading expert in ethanol fuel distillation. "We still use that first still he made for our own fuel," Blaze said. "Clutch fixed the tractor to run on it quite efficiently.

Yes, Fen and Mermaid still live close by, down the shoreline a bit, in a little cottage they built themselves. They help with the sheep and the herb farming. But before we go on down to their place, we'll have to ring the bell at the head of the path leading to it," Blaze said, grinning. "Fen and Mermaid still don't much like to wear clothes and on a nice day like this . . . well, we'll be sure to ring the bell."

To Robert's continued questioning about what had happened to the other SBDC Boys, Blaze beckoned. "Come. Let me show you the cemetery."

He drove the priest to a little knoll on the far end of the farm. Over the entrance to the cemetery was a wrought iron sign that read: Final Home of the Lords of Folly. It was a strange graveyard indeed. Dominating the plot was an ancient tractor permanently resting on a slab of concrete. A copper sign read: "The Farm Zephyr. In memory of the beginning."

Next to it was a real tombstone with the inscription: "All hail to Gabe Roodman, who died to make it all happen."

Nearby stood a huge rock quarried from one of the fields, into which was carved: "In memory of Ed Hasse, one of the founding fathers of Folly Farm."

An ancient copper still marked the spot where one Axel Barnt was buried. An old manure spreader, kept well painted like the tractor, recalled another founding father of Folly Farm, Ed Kluntz. A cowboy hat in bronze rested on a stone pillar with lettering that said: "In memory of Jesse James the Second, one of Carver County's sanest men." Two large crosses formed by aluminum ball bats fused together memorialized Danny and Banana.

"So they're both gone," The old priest said.

"Very tragic," Blaze said. "Danny made baseball his whole life and when age forced him to quit, he took up slow-pitch softball. He actually became much better known for that than for the years he played minor league baseball. He was still going strong at age sixty when he had a heart attack going around second base. He made it home anyway, crawling the last ten feet, and died right on home plate, so the story goes. They say he knew his heart was bad but kept on playing anyway." He paused. "I presume you know about Banana."

"No. Should I?"

Blaze showed surprise. "Wow. When the Josephians want to forget someone, they sure can do it. You don't really know?"

Robert shook his head.

"Didn't you ever wonder why the seminary buildings were allowed to fall into ruins?"

"As a matter of fact, I did wonder about that. I had not known till I saw it just today."

"Well, this is just a theory. Marge will tell you that I'm just fantasizing as usual. But after what happened, tell me what you think. All the stories that emmanated from the seminary when Gabe got killed had people wondering about the place exceedingly. You know that most people around here believe that he was trying to escape from the seminary when he wrecked the tractor. You can't get that notion of escaping the monastery out of peoples' heads even to this day. And there were long-held rumors that a naked man was once seen running out of the barn and across the road." Blaze paused, relishing that anecdote. Robert smiled too. He knew. "Well, anyway, the property changed hands twice but was never used for anything. Just sat there. Probably a tax write-off or something. Then about fifteen years ago Banana showed up here at Folly Farm one day. He was in bad shape. Admitted he was an alcoholic. Said he had not long to live anyway, but would not explain. He never made it as a ballplayer and the woman he married left him. He really didn't ask for help from us but I now think he wanted us to take him in. Sat up all night with him while he told all the old seminary stories again and got hopelessly drunk. He was gone in the morning and we didn't think much more about him."

Blaze paused. "But about a month later, here was this article in the paper. The body of a man was found in the old seminary slaughterhouse, hanging from a rope. There was a note pencilled on the wall:

'In memory of the Sonuvabitchin' Davy Crockett Boys who gave me the only truly happy years of my life.' The authorities were having a hard time identifying him but I knew right away of course. Since then I think there's an unspoken fear of the place in peoples' minds. Like it was haunted. And you know, it really is haunted. I still get chills every time I pass there."

Robert started to cry again.

"Look, Robert, it wasn't your fault what happened. A million times I've condemned myself for all that nonsense about going to Rome. If I had just faced the truth about myself, if we all had, Gabe would be here today. And when Banana stopped here, he was asking for help and I didn't want to admit it. He was, well, you know, our lives were established with family and all. What were we going to do with him? I wasn't generous enough and he didn't give me time enough to get generous. I've come to think we can't blame ourselves for misfortunes like that. Luck has a lot to do with what happens. You would say God, but God didn't make Banana hang himself or throw the Farm Zephyr into the swamp or force Danny to overemphasize sports. Sooner or later we would have all left the Order anyway. Not your fault. Surely you must know that. You couldn't have stopped us from blundering on our blundering ways. Why it turned out right for Fen and Melonhead and me, I don't know. Just plain luck, I tell you."

"You'd never admit that God had anything to do with it, would you?" The priest countered.

For answer, Blaze pointed to the large copper tablet at the very center of the cemetery. "There's the Eleven Theses, and that's still what I believe. I think you do too but won't admit it."

For answer Robert said: "Do you know what happened to Oblate Luke?"

Blaze shook his head.

"He went to Africa as a missionary and was killed by insurgent guerillas while he was trying to protect the women and children of his little parish. He was a martyr. A brave, fearless, and generous man in the end. Knowing Lukey like you did, won't you admit that the hand of God had to be at work there?"

Blaze was first amazed by that revelation. But then, as usual, he turned it to his own advantage. "For Lukey to become a brave, fearless and generous man would be a tall order for your God of power and might, but something that my God of human love could do without half trying."

The priest smiled, unwilling to counter Blaze's remark. He'd settle for that. They left the cemetery to visit Fen and Mermaid. They rang the bell at the entrance to their property. The couple, not quite nude, were weeding their garden. Robert, who had fancied himself quite a gardener in Broken Bow, was amazed at the lushness and variety of their plants.

"Yes, we raise all our own food. And drink, thanks to Axel's teachings," Fen explained. "No, I do not sing publicly anymore. What little money we need comes from Social Security and from wages that Blaze and Marge pay us for helping with the herbs, sheep and and chickens. Mermaid's woven wool rugs and dried flower arrangements are in great demand locally. We don't own a car. Why should we? We rarely go anywhere we can't walk to."

"A little money just drops out of the skies, seems like, every time we need it," Mermaid said. "We only had to spend a little over $9000 last year, on everything."

"We don't have health insurance," Fen explained. "That's a huge savings. We've had rather good luck with natural medicines. Don't know if we can make it all the way without hospitals and retirement homes, but we might. I hope to be like Scott Nearing. At age one hundred, he split one more cord of wood and laid down and died."

Robert prepared to leave. Blaze watched him climb painfully into his car. "You're too old to drive to Chicago," he said. "Why don't you just stay here? We'll take care of you."

Robert smiled. "I told you a long time ago I was too afraid to change." He paused. "But I've got a favor to ask. If I can work it out with the Provincial, can I be buried in your cemetery?"

"Hey, we'll put up a monument for you for sure even if they won't give up your bones," Blaze said. Then as usual his quicksilver mood went to playful teasing. "Who cares where the actual flesh and bones rot away? Doesn't matter. When you're dead, you're dead, you know. It's the memories that never die."